SO MANY CHILDREN

SO MANY CHILDREN

Anne Baker

LONDON NEW YORK SYDNEY TORONTO

This edition published 2002
by BCA
by arrangement with Headline Book Publishing
a division of Hodder Headline

CN 110015

Typeset in Times by Avon Dataset Ltd, Bidford-on-Avon, Warks

Printed and bound in Germany by
GGP Media, Pössneck

I wish to acknowledge my debt to Bill Holden, deceased, who lived in Dock Cottages between the years 1915 and 1938 and wrote his reminiscences of those days in a booklet called *Up Our Lobby* which was published by the Birkenhead Central Library.

Chapter One

The bus was crowded in the evening rush hour. Elizabeth Hubble swung on the strap as it jerked forward. Usually she walked the few stops to save the fare, but tonight she felt numb and drained of energy. She'd half expected it, but it had still come as a shock to see the diagnosis, stark and painful, written in the notes. It had scared her. Her mother had been feeling unwell for some time; the whole family had been worried about her.

Beth felt a shiver of guilt. If she hadn't been so engrossed in her own affairs, she might have done something for Mam sooner. Everything was coming right for her at work and, even better, she felt so happy about Andrew. They were getting to know each other well.

She'd tried to persuade her mother to see the doctor eighteen months ago, but Mam had been reluctant to pay his fee. In the end, she'd had to go. This afternoon Mam had come to see a consultant at the Borough Hospital where Beth worked as a staff nurse. During her tea break, she'd rushed over to the outpatients department, but her mother had been and gone. The clinic had finished and the files of those seen were piled neatly on the desk. She flicked open the top one and saw today's date and knew they'd been written up and were waiting to be filed away. The clinic nurse would be having her tea.

Quickly, feeling her heart race, she found the one with Violet Hubble's name on it. She had to know. It took only a moment. The words 'congestive cardiac failure' leapt out at her, confirming her worst fears. Poor Mam, she hadn't had much of a life, and this meant . . . But it hurt to think about that, she couldn't, not yet.

It was already dark; Beth caught sight of her frightened face reflected in the window of the bus. She mustn't go home looking like this. Her green eyes looked unnaturally big and bright. She shook her head and her bright flame-coloured hair tossed about her shoulders, freed at last from the starched confines of her nurse's cap.

Her colouring was muted in the glass, and tonight she looked too thin and all eyes and hair. Most children brought up where she had been were thin even as young adults, and she would be twenty-three in June. She forced a smile; it slid uneasily away.

The bus had stopped and passengers were forcing themselves past her. In the nick of time, Beth caught a glimpse of St James's church and jumped off too. The last thing she wanted was to be carried past her stop. What was the matter with her?

She followed the crowd down Stanley Road towards her childhood home. The gaunt, oppressive blocks of Dock Cottages towered threateningly over her. Built of smoke-blackened brick and set with small windows, many of which had panes filled with cardboard instead of glass, Dock Cottages looked like a prison or a barracks. These were tenements not cottages, and had been built by the Birkenhead Dock Company between the years 1844 and 1847 to house the workers they needed to build the docks on this side of the Mersey.

Dock Cottages were the first flats ever built in England. Three hundred and fifty of them; block after block, each five storeys high, with dark narrow alleyways separating them. They were said to have been built in the Scottish style to provide the greatest amount of comfort for the tenants, combined with a fair return on capital invested.

Nowadays the tenants were unanimous in thinking that the flats had been built too cheaply and their tiny rooms and steep stone stairs provided anything but comfort. Only extreme poverty kept anybody in this cramped and overcrowded place.

Once the name Dock Cottages became infamous as the home of every rogue and petty criminal in town, they'd been re-named the Queen's Buildings. To the occupants they were known simply as the Blocks. Everybody on Merseyside had heard of them, they were notorious as their worst slum. But they housed honest tenants too, who wanted only to live in peace; they formed a close-knit community.

Several people recognised her and asked, 'How's your mother, Beth?'

'Just going home to see her,' she returned, trying to look cheerful. She couldn't talk about it, couldn't tell anybody just how ill her mother was. Their neighbours were used to ill health, the damp conditions made sore throats, chestiness and joint pains rife among them. Overcrowding and a shortage of food, warm clothes and fuel for heating made matters worse.

The streets teemed with life. Children played under the gaslights,

2

street hawkers pushed handcarts piled high with goods. Constable Cummins, a familiar plump figure, walked his beat.

'Hello, Beth.'

She heard Ken Clover's voice before she saw him. A rag and bone man's cart passed slowly between them before he could cross the road to her side.

'Your mam's feeling a bit down.' Ken's mother was Mam's friend, Beth knew she'd accompanied her to the hospital today. Mam had not felt well enough to go alone. 'I'm afraid she might have had bad news.'

'She has.' Beth was sure of that.

His brown eyes were full of sympathy. 'She didn't want to talk about it.'

Feeling agonised, Beth shook her head.

'Like mother, like daughter,' he said gently.

That brought a brief smile. She'd known the Clover family all her life, they lived in the same block but on a different floor. Beth had spent much of her time in their company. Ken's sister Maggie had been in her class at school. They'd egged each other on, all determined to get out of Dock Cottages at the first possible moment.

'I came out to get something for our tea.' Ken was dark like all the Clovers, his curly hair fell all over his forehead.

He brought her to a halt alongside a handcart smelling of the sea itself. It was piled high with silvery herrings sparkling under the greenish gaslight.

'I'm glad I've seen you, I was wondering whether I should get some for your family too.'

Ken was kind, his family were the sort who thought of others. Once, Beth had been sure he'd get clear away from Dock Cottages. He'd gone to sea, tramping for months on end round the small ports of the Mediterranean, but early in the war his father had been killed in an accident at the munitions factory where he'd worked, and his mother had been left with two younger children to bring up. Ken had come home and found work on a small vessel plying up the Mersey to Runcorn and round to Fleetwood or down to Cardiff, which allowed him to spend more time with his family.

Beth said, 'Herrings? Just the thing. I told Mam I'd bring something for tea. Thanks for reminding me.'

'Eight for threepence,' the trader shouted. 'Good and fresh. This morning's catch.'

'I'll have three penn'orth,' Ken said.

3

'I need twelve fish,' Beth said. 'Fourpence ha'penny, is that right?'

Trying not to hold the newspaper parcel against her coat, she walked with Ken to the end lobby of Block E. She left him on the ground floor and raced up to the top of the building. No lights were provided on any of the four flights of stairs, but she didn't need them, she'd done it so often, every step was familiar.

She reached the cramped living room where the single gas mantle was already lit. Her mother was lying on the couch that at night served as a bed. It was from her that Beth had inherited her bright red hair, but Mam's was faded, there was grey in it now and grey in her cheeks too. Her lips were tinged faintly with blue; her blue eyes were restless and over-bright.

'Mam?' She looked exhausted and disheartened. Her arms were cradling Bobby, Beth's youngest brother, who had fallen asleep against her. 'How are you?'

'No better, nor likely to be,' Violet Hubble retorted with a touch of anger. She was forty-two but looked ten years older; the deep lines etched on her face contorted in distress.

Beth felt for the table with its worn oilcloth cover and sank down on a chair. Mam was upset, deeply troubled by what she'd been told. 'What did the doctor say?'

'Oh, it's heart trouble, like you said. You were right about that.'

'And he gave you medicine?' She knew exactly what he'd prescribed, she'd read the notes, but Beth was afraid it wouldn't alter the prognosis.

'Iron tablets. He said I was anaemic and if we could get that right, he'd do something else.'

'Venesection?'

'Yes. What's that?'

'He'd bleed you, take about a pint and a half away.'

Her mother looked frightened. 'Do they really do that?'

'It's said to lessen the strain on the heart. He's given you Digoxin, that'll help, as well as a diuretic to take the fluid out of your chest so you can breathe easier.'

'My ankles too. He said it would take the swelling down.'

'But what advice did he give?'

'He told me to take things easy.' Beth met her mother's gaze. She could see the aftermath of desperate tears staining her cheeks. 'But how can I take it easy? Washing and cooking and cleaning for seven of us here? A top flat with all these stairs to get up and down, carrying Bobby . . .'

4

Bobby was almost two years old, he'd been late learning to walk and it would be some time before he could climb the stairs. He was a lightweight and somewhat frail, but he was too heavy for Violet to manage.

'You mustn't carry Bobby upstairs, Mam. Mustn't even try.'

'The doctor told me I must rest more if I want to keep well, but he didn't tell me how to do it. It's all right for him sitting comfortably in a big office which somebody else cleans for him.' Violet was breathless after that outburst but was trying to get to her feet. Bobby whimpered at being woken up.

'Stay where you are, Mam, I'll get the kettle on and make a cup of tea.'

'I've had one at the Clovers'.'

'Don't you want another?' Tea was their balm for everything. 'I could do with one anyway.'

Beth felt through the darkness to the scullery and filled the kettle, then made up the fire in the living-room range and set it to boil.

Her mother hadn't got her breath back. 'And you know . . . what else that doctor said?'

'What?'

'Don't have any more babies, Mrs Hubble. Your heart . . . won't be able to stand . . . the strain. He didn't tell me how to avoid that either.'

Beth felt a cold shiver run down her spine. 'Did you ask?' This was a forbidden subject, she'd never heard anybody talk of it before.

'Of course I asked . . . I asked twice. He just smiled . . . at me and patted my arm and said I must know what made a baby.' Her mother was looking at her with large, frightened eyes. 'He must think . . . I had you ten from choice.'

Beth was turned to stone. She'd never seen her mother so frightened. Never heard her say such things. She'd always given the impression that she welcomed each baby.

'And two miscarriages. Not that I was sorry when they happened . . . I can tell you.' Her lips were a darker blue. 'Better than . . . them dying later . . . when you've . . . got attached.'

Epidemics raged through the Blocks from time to time, nobody living here was a stranger to death.

'Our Gerald,' Beth remembered.

'Yes, Gerry, he was a lovely little boy of seven . . .' He'd died of diphtheria. 'And a dear baby girl of three months, Louisa. She caught whooping cough from the rest of you. I'd have had fourteen . . . with them and the miscarriages.'

5

For a long moment, the silence hung heavily between them. Then Mam gasped, 'I wish I could look after the babies properly.'

Beth tried to comfort her. 'You looked after us very well.'

'You were only the second. I had only you and Peggy to care for then . . . and I was younger. I can't look after Bobby as I'd like to. I'm getting very stout and breathless and my varicose veins play me up. Can't feed them properly either . . . not any more . . . not on what your dad earns.'

Beth sat appalled while the blackened kettle filled the room with steam. The subject had always been taboo. Mam never spoke of having babies. Never told them she was about to have another. In recent years, she'd just waited until it became obvious and they'd all accepted the inevitable.

She ended with a sob. 'I'm so tired . . . so dreadfully tired.'

Beth saw a tear roll slowly down her cheek and felt wrung out with sympathy. She went over to kneel on the floor by the couch, took Mam's work-roughened hand between her own and put her head down on top.

She had great admiration for her mother. She'd always put her family's needs above her own. It was she who'd held the family together, made sure they all went to school. Juggled pennies to put food on the table, encouraged her children to leave home to better themselves when they were old enough.

'I can't do it any more.'

'You aren't feeling well,' Beth said gently.

'Too many babies.'

'You mustn't have any more, Mam.' Her mother stifled another sob. 'It's not just having the baby. It's the extra work looking after it, carrying it about, up and down stairs.' Mam could hardly get upstairs herself without help these days.

Beth had awakened Mam's anger again.

'I don't need you . . . to tell me that. Only how to go about . . . avoiding any more.' Violet was struggling to get her breath now. 'Do you know, Beth? How . . . to stop the babies coming? I mean you're a nurse. They taught you that, didn't they?'

Beth shook her head. 'No.'

They'd taught her the anatomy and physiology of those parts of the body, and all the problems and diseases women were prone to, but not how to stop babies. Nobody talked about such things to young girls, not even to nurses.

The living-room door crashed open and two children burst in.

6

Four-year-old Colin climbed up on the couch. His pullover had soup stains down the front and had shrunk in the wash. He looked in need of a bath.

'Is tea ready?' Seven-year-old Esther looked little better.

'You shouldn't go out without your coats,' Beth scolded. 'It's cold out there.'

'The doctors won't tell me though they all know, don't they?' Mam went on weakly. 'They have only . . . two or three in their families. Marie Stopes knows, there's bits in the papers about her all the time, but all they do is hint, nobody ever says exactly what it is.'

'We'd need to get her books.'

There was nobody in the country whose name was more familiar to the population at large. Marie Stopes had written books on family planning and achieved huge notoriety by doing so, but Beth had never seen any of them.

'We can't afford them, Beth.'

'Like everything else.'

'I could have coped with . . . two or three of you. You'd all be grown up now. And I wouldn't have . . . sweated my guts out trying to keep this place clean . . . and feed the five . . . thousand.'

'I'm hungry.' Colin tugged at his mother's arm.

'Right,' Beth said. 'We'll start cooking. It's herrings. Esther, help me peel the potatoes.'

Violet was trying to get to her feet again. 'Is that the time! Your dad'll be home any minute. He'll want his tea, we should have started cooking by now.'

'We'll do it, Mam. You stay there.' Already her mother was puffing again.

'He likes a meal ready for him . . . as soon as he comes in.'

'He'll have to get used to doing a bit more for himself,' Beth said.

She lit a candle to take to the scullery. It was a five-foot-square cubbyhole where a deep sandstone sink took up most of the space. A single cold water tap above it dripped constantly.

Beth cut the heads off the fish and rinsed them under the tap. Everything had to be washed here, themselves, the children, the dishes and their food. She wrapped the heads and entrails back in the newspaper and pushed it under the flap into the dust hole. This was one of their conveniences, they didn't have to carry their rubbish downstairs, it fell to a dust cellar below ground level.

Beth looked in the bread bin, there was only the heel of a loaf left. The front door slammed again and two more of her brothers came in.

Mam's seventh child had been named Wilfred on his birth certificate to please his father, though Mam had wanted to call him Septimus. She'd said, 'Two members of the family with the same name? I don't hold with that, we'll get mixed up,' so he'd always been known as Seppy. He'd taught himself to play his father's mouth organ when he was eight and now had two of his own. He was always pounding out tunes and loved ragtime and jazz. Beth was particularly fond of Seppy, he had red hair like her own. He was now almost fourteen and on the point of leaving school; they'd already started to ask around about a job for him.

Ivor had nut-brown hair and was twelve. He was passionate about horses and had made friends with the milkman, the coal man and everyone else who brought a horse near Dock Cottages. Once he'd dreamed of being a jockey, now he hoped to work in a riding stable when he grew up.

'Ivor, run and get a couple of loaves before the bakers close.' Beth went to her coat which she'd hung behind the bedroom door and felt in her pocket for some money.

She was cooking the first two herrings over the range when her father came home. Wilfred Hubble was a docker who loaded and unloaded cargo from ships. He was a big and brawny man, still handsome in maturity, even in the greasy flat cap and dirty coat he wore for work. He took his big steel hook with its wooden crossbar from his pocket and hung it on a nail by the grate. Dockers used these hooks to lift bales and packages.

He said to Violet, 'How d'you get on at the hospital then? Did they give you a tonic to pick you up?'

'A tonic won't help,' Beth retorted as she turned the sizzling herrings over.

Concerned, he went over to his wife. 'What's the trouble then? Is it bad?'

'It's bad,' Beth told him. She knew her father believed he worked harder than most for his family, and as the breadwinner expected to have his every whim catered for at home. She knew him to be quick-tempered and sometimes violent if he did not.

Violet said, 'Heart trouble . . . the doctor said. I've got . . . to take things easy.'

'She's been doing too much,' Beth confirmed. 'Looking after a big family like ours – all the cooking and washing for them, all those stairs.'

Wilf tipped Colin off one of the dining chairs and sank down.

'You must do what he says, you'll soon feel better.'

'It'll take time,' Violet said faintly. 'A long time.'

'How long?'

'For ever,' Beth said, turning the herrings out onto plates. 'Mam needs complete rest for a while.'

She could see that scared Dad too. He ran his dirty fingers along the cracks in the worn oilcloth. 'Is that my tea?'

'No, Dad, I've cooked the two smallest fish. These are for Bobby and Colin. I've taken most of the bones out, will you make sure there's none left in them?'

He said irritably, 'I'm hungry, I've been working all day loading a ship, humping bales of cloth about. A hundredweight in each.'

Seppy asked, 'Where was it going to? Was it—'

'I don't give a damn where it's going. I want my tea ready for me when I come in. I've been hard at it, with nowt but a butty for my dinner.'

'I'm afraid things might have to change, Dad. Mam can't wait on you the way she always has.'

'Wait on me?' He was indignant. 'Do you expect me to cook my own meals?'

Beth tried to cut off his anger. She was upsetting Mam as well as him. 'I'll do yours next. Why don't you take your coat off and have a wash?'

The two biggest fish now filled the frying pan. She tossed lard in another pan to fry the thick potato slices that she'd parboiled. She jerked back from the spluttering. There was no way Mam would ever be well enough to go through this every evening. Dad came back to the table and she put his plate in front of him.

'If you're saying Mam won't be able to manage, you'll have to give up that job and stay home to help, Betty.' He called her Betty to annoy her. He knew she didn't like it.

'Dad! I can't! I'd be another mouth to feed. What would we do for money?'

All the time she'd been growing up, Mam had impressed upon her that getting out of Dock Cottages was to be her first goal in life. And it wasn't just Mam, the Clovers discussed it all the time. 'We've all got to escape from this place,' Maggie, her best friend, had said. And Beth congratulated herself daily that she'd succeeded.

'You can't expect Peggy or Jenny to do it, they've got families of their own. But you haven't, you owe it to your mother.'

'No,' Violet protested weakly.

9

Beth felt suffused with guilt. Was she being selfish? 'You know I've got my holiday coming. Only another day to work and then I'll take over.'

'But you've just said this'll take a long time. What good is a week?'

'It'll give Mam a rest. Give us time to sort something out; get somebody else.'

'Damn and blast. Who else is there to get?'

Beth said, 'Mam, your fish is nearly ready. Can you come to the table while I dish it up?' She saw her mother slowly swing her feet to the floor and struggle to stand up. 'Dad, could you give her a hand?'

'Can't you see I'm trying to eat my tea?' He sounded angry, impatient, unreasonable. But Seppy was already helping Mam.

Beth said, 'There's Seppy. He does a lot about the house.'

'He's a boy,' her father scoffed. 'What good would he be?'

'He can light fires, carry up the coals and do the shopping. And he can cook well enough to get your tea.'

'Your mam needs someone to clean and wash and look after the baby. Someone to take the work off her shoulders.'

'Seppy can do all that.'

'Damn it, Betty, it's your duty. It isn't good for a boy to do woman's work.'

'I can't see why not.' Beth didn't turn round from the frying fish.

'What about our Lottie then?'

'Dad, no! Not Lottie. She's supporting herself and helping Mam out of her wages. The same as I am.'

Charlotte was seventeen and in service with the Wisharts in West Kirby. Beth had worked for them too when she'd first left school.

Her father shovelled a large piece of fried potato into his mouth. 'I don't see why you can't do it. I'd have thought you'd want to help your mother. You could easily take a few months off and go back to your job later.'

'No, no.' Violet's voice sounded strangled. 'Our Beth's doing . . . so well. Better than . . . any of the others. She could marry that boy . . . who works at the hospital and get right away from here. No, I don't want her brought back on my account.' That had sparked her mother's anger again. 'We mustn't . . . spoil her chances, drag her down.'

Mam called her children her blessings; she loved them all and supported them in every way she could. Beth thought she wasn't happy with Dad and took her side, as did her brothers and sisters. They all understood it was Mam who struggled to keep the family clean and adequately clothed and fed.

'Nothing would drag that one down,' her father grunted. 'She's very full of herself.'

Beth put a cup of tea in front of him. 'Seppy's the obvious choice. He's a good lad, very willing, and I'll be here all next week with him.'

'You don't want to do woman's work, do you, Seppy? You said you wanted to go to sea like our John.'

'I do want to go to sea,' Seppy sighed, 'but I want to help Mam too.'

'For a year or so,' Beth said. 'Until Ivor leaves school, then he can take over for a bit.'

'Seppy won't know whether he's a man or a woman when he grows up,' her father growled, 'and it'll be your fault.'

'For heaven's sake, Dad. There's no reason why he can't do a bit about the house. No reason why you can't do more yourself. You let Mam wait on you hand and foot. If she could get more rest and better food, then she could get over this bad patch and be all right for a long time yet.'

Beth hadn't finished. She knew what was worrying her mother. She felt very daring as she went on, 'And the doctor said she's to have no more babies, Dad. You could certainly see to that.'

He swung round to stare at Beth with savage intensity. His eyes of cold steel told her she'd overstepped the mark.

'Don't be disgusting,' he spat out. 'A slip of a girl like you talking of such things to me.'

'I'm just telling you Mam's heart isn't strong enough for another baby. You mustn't   '

'That's enough! Don't you tell me what I mustn't do.' His voice was ferocious. 'I won't have it from the likes of you. I don't know what the world's coming to.'

Beth was scared. He'd laid into her too often in the past not to know what she could expect from him. Dad kept a wide leather army belt with a heavy brass buckle hanging next to his docker's hook beside the fire. It was in full view and intended to act as a warning to his family that they must do as he told them without question.

'I'm sorry if it upsets you, but it's better if you know what the doctor said.'

His favourite saying was: children should be seen and not heard. At the first sign of any defiance he would unhook the belt and bring it crashing down on the table. The sound of it slashing through the air terrified them all. It could still make Beth shudder. It always had the desired effect, it scattered the children to cower behind the couch or hide in their bedroom. The living-room table was pockmarked with

11

small dents and scratches that the belt had made over the years. He would bellow as he thrashed the table. 'I'm the head of this household. While you live here you'll do what I tell you and like it.'

'Please don't, Wilf,' Mam would say with more firmness than she ever said anything else. 'Don't frighten the children.'

Beth was unable to look at her mother. The fear and anger that had made her so forthright and outspoken when Beth had first come home had evaporated; now she was quiet and withdrawn. Beth was afraid for her; Dad was too set in his ways, too domineering, too ready to demand his rights. He wouldn't be able to change any of his habits. To think of that made her shiver.

Chapter Two

Violet Hubble cringed into the stained cushion as she listened to her husband laying down the law to Beth. She was scared rigid. The trip to the hospital had drained her strength and made her realise how ill she was. For the first time she was facing her own mortality.

Her head ached and her varicose veins were throbbing tonight. It was some comfort that Beth understood and was daring to stand up to her father. Violet felt Wilf never listened to her, but Beth had spelled it out in words he couldn't misunderstand. She was glad of that and wanted to cling to Beth.

Ever since Jenny had been born she'd been trying to talk to Wilf about limiting their family. They couldn't afford to feed more, they had no room for more in these small rooms. It took energy and effort to care for them and bring them up properly as they deserved.

When John was born, it was lovely to have a son, and she thought Wilf should be satisfied with a family of four children. In fact, he was; he thought four quite enough. He told her they talked about Marie Stopes in the pub, and he'd heard there were things he could buy from the barber's shop that would prevent them having more, but there was always some reason why he didn't get them.

She'd pleaded with him not to make her pregnant again and he'd promised he would abstain altogether. Vi had done all she could to help him; sometimes pretending to be asleep when he came in from the pub, sometimes staying up until he was asleep himself. Nothing worked for long; he pleaded with her, promising to be careful and withdraw in time. He said that was the best method but it never worked for them. He was a passionate man, strong and virile, and with beer in his belly all his promises were forgotten. If she refused, he'd insist and be in a bad temper as well, taking it out on her and the children.

She'd never told anybody but Wilf that she went in monthly dread of finding herself pregnant yet again. Now she had ten children and she couldn't bear the thought of not being here to look after them and see the little ones grow up. Little Bobby was always ailing, always catching

13

coughs and colds. He'd had a bad dose of croup last month, he needed her. She had to get better for his sake. Get stronger so she could look after him. She mustn't start another, even Wilf must see that now.

She opened her eyes to see him reading in the armchair by the fire.

Violet hadn't been born in this slum, she'd grown up in more comfortable circumstances but she'd come here eagerly. She'd been so sure that she and Wilf were head over heels in love and it would last for ever. What a romantic fool she must have been.

Even now, she could accept Dock Cottages if Wilf hadn't proved to be such a disappointment. She hadn't realised he couldn't read or write until after they were married. Well, he could sign his name but not much more. He'd left school at twelve and got a full-time job by claiming to be fourteen, but he hadn't attended regularly even up to that age. He didn't attach much importance to schooling and she'd had to fight to keep her children there. He felt they should be helping to support themselves long before the age of fourteen and had wanted to find jobs for them on the market stalls or in the little shops around here.

She hadn't realised that she wasn't strong enough to survive in a place like this and she was afraid her children might not be either. By trying to bring them up here she'd given them problems that now seemed insurmountable.

Violet counted herself very lucky to have a daughter like Beth. She was proud of her. Wilf had wanted to name her Agatha Maud after his mother, Aggie for short, but she'd insisted on Elizabeth. A decent name was one luxury they could still bestow.

'Elizabeth? Much too highfalutin, but I suppose she could be called Betty.'

'No! This one's to be Elizabeth or Beth for short, much nicer. I have an Auntie Beth.'

In his pig-headed way, Wilf had insisted on calling her Betty throughout her childhood and sometimes still did. Beth said she thought of Betty as her Dock Cottages name and at times felt like two different people. She was a State Registered Nurse and Violet thought she was the one most able to help her.

She closed her eyes and tried to relax. Beth had fed them all and had the knack of getting the children to help with the work. She and Esther were washing up in the scullery. Ivor was bringing up coal for the fire. Seppy was giving Bobby some milky tea in his bottle.

Violet struggled to pull herself up on her arm. 'Beth?'

'What is it, Mam? I'll help you wash in a moment, and get you into bed before I go.'

'Bobby's cot, his sheet's wet. I didn't get round to changing it.'

'Don't worry, I'll see to it.'

Violet lay back; Beth would know where to find clean sheets. Within minutes, Ivor was being called in to help move the cot.

'So Mam can get her rest tonight,' Beth was telling him, 'I'd like to put Bobby in with you lot.' Both bedrooms opened directly off the living room.

'There's no room,' Ivor said. 'We've tried it.' Beth went to see for herself. 'Nothing's changed since you slept here yourself.'

The children's room had a double iron bedstead and, in addition, a local carpenter had fitted three narrow bunk beds one above the other to the outside wall. There wasn't much room for anything else in a nine-foot-square room, certainly not the cot.

She said to her mother, 'We'll leave Bobby in the living room. Seppy will see to him if he wakes up.'

'You're a good girl.' Violet lay back and drifted into a stupor that was neither sleep nor wakefulness.

Beth was the one most like herself, Violet mused. The one with a bit of go about her. When she said she was going to do something, she did it. From the age of ten she'd been determined to get out of Dock Cottages. When she'd left school at fourteen to work as a housemaid in the big house in West Kirby, she used to come home on her monthly day off with such tales of the place: the starched linen cloths she spread on the mahogany dining table and the silver and hand-cut glass she set out at every meal.

Beth had been happy there and her younger sister Charlotte had taken her place when she left, and was still working there. Lottie, too, was happy there. 'Better off away from Dock Cottages,' she said. 'But I miss you, Mam, and the rest of the family.'

Beth had been aiming higher than domestic service even though she'd had a good place. She'd always talked of being a nurse one day.

Violet was suddenly aware of great mounds of soiled clothes and sheets collecting on the living-room floor.

'Beth,' she said. 'Don't strip everything, it makes too much washing . . . can't do it all at once.'

'You can't do any of it, Mam. You're not to try getting up and down all those stairs.'

In each block there was a steam-filled communal washroom on the ground floor. Sinks were provided and a huge clothes boiler and a mangle.

'Then who?' she asked faintly.

Beth turned to her father. 'Dad, Mam needs some help. How about starting on this lot?'

He lowered the newspaper he was reading. 'The washing? I've been at work all day.' He sounded indignant.

'So have I.'

'I'm tired.' There was irritation in his voice.

Beth rounded on him. 'So am I.'

'Washing is woman's work. I can't go into that room with all those women. They'd make fun of me.'

'They wouldn't,' Seppy said. 'I do it. Anyway, there'll be nobody else there at this time of night.'

Wilf slapped his newspaper down and got to his feet. 'You know I always go down to the pub for a drink at this time.'

'That's not likely to help Mam,' Beth retorted.

Violet held her breath, she was afraid he was about to reach for his belt and give Beth a hiding.

The moment passed, he grabbed his greasy cap and went out, still struggling to get his arms into his grubby coat. The door slammed behind him.

The silence lengthened. Beth frowned. 'He usually gets changed before he goes out.'

Wilfred Hubble was choking with anger as he felt his way down the four flights of stone stairs in total darkness.

Beth had altogether too much lip. He didn't like the way she stood up to him, telling him he was wrong and she was right. She was so damn sure of herself and always trying to take him down a peg or two. He was head of the household but she thought nothing of challenging his authority. Tonight he felt diminished by her. To look at, she reminded him of Vi when she was young, but Vi had always gone along with what he wanted.

He hadn't really believed Beth when she'd first talked of Vi being ill. Violet had been complaining of being tired for a long time, but she had a lot to do with all the children. Yes, she was a bit breathless, and recently she'd been avoiding the stairs as much as she could. But she always put a brave face on things; she always smiled and said she'd be better in a few minutes when she'd had a little rest. He really hadn't thought she was as bad as Beth was making out.

Wilf set off at a good pace down Stanley Road to the pub. Beth had insisted on taking Vi to the shop on Corporation Road where old Dr Cane had been in general practice for the last thirty years. Wilf knew now he should never have argued against that visit on the grounds of cost. Beth had whirled on him like a tiger.

'Mam's ill, seriously ill, she needs help.' He had felt his cheeks flush with guilt. 'You should insist she sees the doctor, not let her put it off like this. Honest, Dad, I know what I'm talking about.'

She'd made him feel wanting, so had the fact that she had paid for that visit herself. She'd hardly been civil to him on the subject of Violet's illness since. He'd known Vi was finding the stairs a struggle to climb with babies and shopping. He'd known she was asking the neighbours to help her, but Beth never stopped nagging him about it.

'She can't manage four flights of stairs, Dad. She's a prisoner up here. And she needs some fresh air.'

'Fresh air? Where would she get that round Dock Cottages?'

'Couldn't you find a place to rent where the front door opens on to the street? I'd help you move.'

'Haven't you heard? There's a housing shortage, no houses at all were built during the war.'

'They're beginning to build more now.'

'But could we afford them? And how d'you think I'd find time to look? I've got to get down to the docks and wait on the stand in the hope of being taken on for work.' They all expected more from him than he could give. 'Your mam isn't the only one who gets tired.'

Beth had said shortly, 'If you're standing around half the day waiting to be taken on, it can't take too much out of you.'

Wilf felt very resentful about the system. Early every morning, dock labourers had to present themselves on the stand hoping they'd be picked out for work. For most, it depended on luck and how many ships were tied up wanting to load or unload. None of them were able to get work every day. The system wasn't fair and they were all fiercely militant about it, out on strike at the drop of a hat. The hope was that one day they'd be given a guaranteed wage.

Wilfred had made his own arrangements with one of the men who picked out the gang to work for him. If the bosses took a dislike to you, you didn't stand a chance of getting work, and the wages they paid in the end didn't keep a family. He'd had to make his own arrangements about that too.

He'd said to Beth, 'Why don't you find a nice house for us?'

'You could do a lot more to help, Dad,' she'd retorted.

'Your mam knows I do my best for her.' He was fond of Vi, he'd always seen his wife as quite a prize. There was more about her than the

17

rough women who'd grown up round here and knew nothing better. Violet could read and write properly. She kept the house clean and tidy and was fussy about such things. Her family put on such airs you'd think they were royalty and he was rubbish. When they were first married, she'd said she'd teach him to read and write as well as she could. He could write his name and read a little now but there had been more exciting things to do when his day's work was done.

He'd promised Vi they'd find somewhere better to live than Dock Cottages once they were on their feet. He'd tried hard but he'd never been able to manage it; the babies had come too fast, there'd been too many mouths to feed before he'd had time to look round. She'd accepted that as she accepted everything else.

Vi had been properly brought up. Her father had been head of the household and the family understood that he made decisions for them. The head of the household had authority over his family; he provided the money to feed and clothe them from what he earned. He protected his womenfolk.

As Vi saw it, it was a wife's duty to submit to her husband because he'd taken the place of her father, and power now rested in him. Wilf had found he could make her do anything he wanted. She could always be persuaded. It made him grow in his own eyes, particularly since he knew her to be socially his superior. He realised, in a way, that this power brought out the worst in him.

Vi was all duty and hard work and had no sense of fun. She was a bit of a doormat but that made him feel more of a man. He kept exercising this power, it made him feel better about himself. It made him keep her on what he thought of as a tight rein, short of money and stuck on the fourth floor in Dock Cottages.

If Vi had a fault, it was that she was inclined to nag. Mostly, it was because she thought he was laying into the kids too heavily or was using foul language in front of them, but it could be about money.

On pay day, he always tipped part of his wages on to the table for her. They all had to be fed, but a man had to have a few coins to rattle in his pocket to make life worth living. He liked a glass of beer at the pub, and he liked the company of other men, and of women too.

Outside the New Dock Hotel he paused. His anger with Beth had evaporated, he was shaking with cold. He could hear the buzz of men's voices inside the pub. As another customer went in, beery fumes wafted out. For once they sickened him; the bad news about Vi's illness had upset him, really upset him. Scared him.

* * *

18

Violet watched Seppy start to gather up as much of the washing as he could. 'I'll take this down and make a start, shall I?'

'You're a good boy,' she told him gently. 'You're sure you want to stay home and help with all this?'

'Yes, Mam.'

'Put the whites on to boil, Seppy,' Beth said. 'Go and give him a hand, Ivor. I'll come down later. Come on then, Mam. I'm going to give you a wash and get you into bed first.'

'I'm not really dirty,' Violet protested. 'I had a good wash after dinner to go to the hospital.' Beth was taking the pins out of her bun and running her fingers through her hair.

'Well, apart from my hair,' Violet sighed. Straggling bits of it reached halfway down her back but it was pitifully thin. It had been falling out since she'd been ill.

'It could do with a wash,' Beth said.

'Yes.' Violet couldn't remember when she'd last had the energy to do it.

'Shall I cut it first? It's a lot of trouble for you to put up in a bun every day. If I cut it short enough, you'd just have to run a comb through it.'

'Yes, cut it.' Vi didn't care, she wanted to be rid of the bother of it.

The next moment she was being helped up onto a straight chair and the scissors were crunching cold against her neck. Beth had had plenty of practice cutting the children's hair, she was proud of her expertise. Violet was turned round to the table then, and her head brought over the big enamel bowl of hot water.

'There's nothing but Sunlight soap to wash it in,' Beth sighed. 'I could have got you some soft soap if I'd thought.'

There was no stopping Beth once she got loose with soap and water. Years of working in hospitals made her believe cleanliness was next to godliness. But Violet felt refreshed by another wash and a clean nightdress. Esther was given a towel and told to rub her hair dry. To her it was a game.

It was only when Violet was escorted to her bed that she realised Beth had changed the sheets and pillow cases on that too. It was a long time since she'd felt so clean.

She tried to thank her, but Beth smiled and said, 'I'll go down and see how Seppy's getting on. It's a fine night, the washing will dry by morning if we put it out.'

Violet lay back feeling helpless. She wasn't used to being waited on like this. She could hear her younger children talking in hushed voices in the next room because Beth had told them not to disturb her. She called out to Esther, who pushed open her door and peeped round it.

'Are you feeling very sick, Mam?'

'I'm feeling a bit lonely,' she whispered.

Esther came and lay beside her on the bed. A moment later, Colin came in and lay down on the other side of her. Violet put an arm round each of them and received comforting hugs in return.

It was the best part of an hour later when Beth came back to her bedroom, buttoning up her coat.

'Right, a hot drink? Esther, will you warm some milk for Mam?'

Violet objected. 'If I drink it, there won't be enough for breakfast.'

'Then somebody else will go without,' Beth said. 'You don't look after yourself properly.'

'You're certainly looking . . . after me now. All that washing.'

'It's all hanging on the lines on the roof. Remind Seppy to bring it down in the morning. The kids are all washed and ready for bed. I'll drop in at Jenny's on the way back to the hospital and ask her to look after Bobby and Colin tomorrow.'

'I can manage, love.'

'If she takes them away it'll be quieter for you. It's Saturday so they'll all be home, but with Seppy to help, you should be all right.'

'I'll be fine.'

'And I'll be back tomorrow evening and here all next week to sort something out.'

'Some holiday for you.'

'It'll be a change. Anyway, I want to get you better. Here's Esther with your hot milk. Is there anything else you want?'

'No, love, thank you. I'll go to sleep when I've had this.'

Beth bent over her to kiss her. 'Dad'll be home soon.'

Violet sighed. If it was just Beth and the kids she'd be all right. She was still feeling overwhelmed with dread. It had been a constant fear all her life, but now she dared not start another baby. She wanted so much to see Esther and Colin grow up. Bobby too, and he was still a baby.

Beth set off briskly to see her younger sister Jennifer. She had recently moved with her husband and little daughter to a pleasant house in Newling Street which was quite close to the hospital. Jenny had been her companion and friend all the years they'd been growing up; she was sixteen months younger and Beth felt closer to her than to any of her other sisters.

20

Like many of the girls in Dock Cottages, Jenny had got a job in the tapestry works when she'd left school. At seventeen, she'd fallen in love with Tom Swales, who had also grown up in Dock Cottages, and within weeks she was asking Dad for permission to marry him.

Beth had been torn in two about Tom. She liked him and felt a twinge of envy that Jenny had found someone who could make her happy, but at the same time she was afraid Jenny was following in Mam's footsteps. Peggy's footsteps too if it came to that.

Tom had been a docker like their father. He and Jenny had started married life in a rented tenement in Morpeth Buildings in Wood Street, which had been built by Lord Morpeth to house the navvies who came to dig out Morpeth Dock in the last century. Their place was no better than Dock Cottages, some said the rooms were even smaller, but there were fewer tenements and Morpeth Buildings didn't have the notoriety of Dock Cottages.

Jenny had been expecting her first baby when in 1916 Tom had been conscripted into the army. She'd clung to Beth for help and support when he'd gone, and Beth had spent what little free time she had with her. The whole family had been on tenterhooks about Tom while he was serving in France. They'd hovered round Jenny doing what they could when her daughter Noreen was born.

Afterwards, she'd gone back to work part-time, leaving Noreen with her mother, or with Peggy.

'I enjoy my job,' she'd told Beth, 'and the other girls are company. It's too quiet at home, with just Noreen and me. I want to save up so we can afford to rent a nice house when Tom comes home.'

Beth had heard Jenny's plans for the future many times, they were as definite as her own, but with Tom away she'd been a ball of anxieties.

'Without him, I feel as though I'm marking time, waiting for real life to begin again.'

Every newspaper was full of news about the war. Jenny couldn't stop herself turning to read the lists of those killed and missing, printed inside black borders. She was scared stiff by the terrible death toll and by the stories of what life was like on the front line. She never hinted in any way that she was afraid Tom wouldn't come back, but Beth knew she was.

'I can't relax, can't be happy while Tom is in the trenches.'

'Of course you can't,' Beth told her. 'You're better off at the tapestry works with all those girls.'

'Too much of my own company drives me over the edge.'

Tom had been injured early in 1918 and had been sent home to have

21

several operations on his leg. Jenny had been so relieved to have him in England where no more harm could come to him. He'd recovered but it had taken a long time and he could no longer do heavy labouring on the docks. Beth knew Tom was as determined as Jenny that they would have a better life than their parents. During his long convalescence he'd studied accounting and three months ago had found a job as a clerk in the dock offices.

Jenny had been ecstatic when things started going right for them and up on cloud nine when she'd moved house. The whole family had been delighted for her. As Beth saw it, Jenny was at last having success. Not only had she got away from Dock Cottages, but Noreen would be three this April and had remained an only child.

Beth turned into Newling Street. She could see no light in Jenny's house, but their parlour was in the front and they lived in the room behind. The hall flooded with light as soon as she let the knocker fall and she heard Jenny's footsteps coming quickly to the door.

'Hello, Beth. I thought you'd forgotten about coming, it's getting late.'

Jenny was a happy girl, very contented with her lot. She had a wide smile and blue eyes, her hair was long and honey-coloured. She and Beth were not at all alike to look at.

'We're just making some cocoa, will you have a cup?'

Beth followed her into the kitchen, where Tom had the biscuit tin out.

'No, thanks, I'm tired, I need to get to bed.'

'I'm glad you came, I've been worried about Mam. How is she?'

'Really ill,' Beth told her. 'I'm afraid she won't be able to look after Noreen while you work, not any more.'

'Oh dear!'

Tom said, 'You'll have to find someone else, Jenny. Perhaps Paula next door would do it.' He was dark and looked more like an overgrown schoolboy than a war veteran.

'Are you going to work tomorrow?' Beth wanted to know.

'I was going to. I'll have to ask Paula . . .'

'I came to see if you'd have Bobby and Colin tomorrow, so Mam can have a bit of peace.' Beth was apologetic. 'Our Peg's too near her time to do anything now.'

'Of course. I'll go round to the works and tell them I can't stay. Then I'll call at Mam's on my way back and bring them down here.'

Chapter Three

As he approached the pub, Wilfred decided he couldn't face the crowd inside tonight. He was too upset. At teatime, Seppy had brought Vi to sit at the table facing him. She'd hardly eaten any of her fish, though Beth had cajoled her. It went through him now to think of her purple lips and exhausted face. He needed a bit of comfort. He'd go down to see Ethel instead.

Ethel was a jolly person, she'd cheer him up. He turned round and walked back to St James's Church to catch the bus into town. Dock Cottages were nearly two miles from Woodside where Ethel had her shop.

Once on the bus, he had second thoughts. He usually changed, put on a clean shirt and some better trousers when he went to see Ethel. He felt he had to when he was going to see his lady friend.

Ethel was quite likely to screw up her nose and say, 'You've come out in your dirt. You know I don't like you in your working clothes.'

Besides, Ethel never wanted to hear anything about Vi. But the bus was already slowing to stop outside Hamilton Square Station. He got out reluctantly and shivered again. He might as well go now he'd got this far. He turned along Bridge Street, sniffing the air. Ethel could make the whole district smell appetising with her steak pies and her roasting and baking, but she'd be getting ready to close at this time. Wilf felt hungry again, there was nothing in herrings to fill a working man. Ethel would give him something to eat.

It surprised him to find her shop already had the closed sign on the door, but the lights were on and he could see Clara, the fifteen-year-old maid she employed, scrubbing the floor.

Wilfred rapped on the glass and she got up off her knees to open the door. He stepped inside and was unbuttoning his coat.

'Mrs Byrne ain't in,' she told him. Ethel had never married. By rights she was Miss Byrne, but since she'd had Molly fifteen years ago, she made out she was a widow. 'Molly ain't here either, they've gone to the pictures.'

'Oh!' He was having a bad day all round. There was no comfort to be had here and none of his favourite roast pork either. He could see a tray of unsold pies on the counter. He crossed the wet floor, leaving dirty footprints, to help himself to one. 'Tell them I'll be round tomorrow,' he said.

He turned back the way he'd come, biting into the pie. It was steak and kidney and still slightly warm. Ethel could make top-class pies, he wished he'd taken two. He had to admit she'd done very well for herself in business. She'd started making pies and selling them from the front room in her father's house in the North End, near Dock Cottages. But nobody had enough money to buy her wares up there and she'd done better since she'd taken this shop. She had a woman who came in to help her now.

Wilf reached the bus stop; there was nobody else waiting. He should have gone in the other direction, down to the terminus at Woodside. The bad news about Vi had knocked him out of kilter, he couldn't think of anything else. He loved her, always had, and their kids – well, most of them. Beth could be a pain.

Things hadn't turned out as well for him and Vi as he'd hoped. When he'd first set eyes on her she'd really set him on fire. It had seemed almost too good to be true, a good-looking girl like Vi, the boss's daughter and showing such an interest in him. He'd really thought that if he could marry her, he'd have his fortune made. He hadn't believed any well-heeled father would want to see his daughter go short. Wilf had expected to get a foothold in the family business, a share. After all, there was no other way he could support Vi at the standard in which she'd been brought up. But it wasn't to be, her father had turned out to be a right bastard. First he'd sacked him and then he'd thrown her out.

It had been a setback to his plans to find Vi wasn't going to be his ticket to riches, but he'd done his best not to let her see that as the disaster it was, and being optimistic he'd expected to find something else sooner or later.

All the same, as Wilf saw it, he'd done his duty by Violet. He'd kept his promise and married her so she had nothing to complain about. He'd never breathed a word about the other girl he'd got into the same trouble before her. He'd been brought up in Ormskirk and had been working in a big market garden there when he'd had to flee from Liza Platt.

Wilf strolled through the crowded streets; there were plenty of shops still open. He looked in the windows, wanting to buy a present for Vi, to show her how much he loved her. He saw the bars of Cadbury's milk chocolate in the newsagent's window and went in to get her one, she was fond of chocolate.

He stopped at a pub in Corporation Road when he was nearly home. He needed a rest now and was desperate for a drink. He sank two pints but it was a miserable pub, he didn't know why he hadn't gone to his usual one in the first place.

When he reached home, the place was silent and they'd put out the gaslight. He tiptoed around, only Seppy was awake on the living-room couch. He put the chocolate on Vi's pillow so she'd see it when she woke up. That would please her.

Beth walked on to the nurses' home feeling exhausted, but pleased she had only one more day to work before her holiday. She needed to get back to look after her mother.

It wouldn't be a real holiday but it would be a change. To get right away for a real rest was a far-off dream, she would never have the money for that. Too much of the twenty-five pounds a year she earned, over and above her board and lodging, went to help her family. She loved her job, it lifted her right out of Dock Cottages, but she was earning as a staff nurse what the Wisharts paid for a maid. By now she'd have been getting more from them without the gruelling training or the responsibilities of the job. But being a nurse was her passport to a better life. She was no longer at the bottom of society. She was sure the decisions she'd made for herself had been the right ones.

When she'd reached the age of fourteen and left school, domestic service had been the first obvious step that many of the Dock Cottages' girls took to get away. She'd been lucky, she'd been taken on as a tweeny by the Wisharts in West Kirby. In the mornings she'd helped the parlourmaid clean up and light fires, and during the afternoons and evenings she'd helped the cook prepare meals. Both had been easy to get on with and she'd soon settled in.

Going straight from Dock Cottages, she'd found the standard of living almost unbelievable. Fires were lit in all the downstairs rooms every day. Sumptuous meals of many courses were cooked for the family, and the catering was on such a scale that luxury foods Beth had never heard of appeared on her plate. She was provided with meals of unaccustomed size and richness, and also a bedroom to herself that was larger than the one she'd shared with five brothers and sisters at home. Beth felt she had every comfort and it was a delight to work in such a place.

25

Mr Wishart had taken the train to Liverpool every morning to work in the Cotton Exchange. He had three daughters; the middle one was already married and had left home. The youngest was engaged and arrangements for her wedding were being discussed. Dorinda, the eldest, was then twenty-five and dissatisfied with her life.

'Looks like she's going to be left on the shelf,' the cook said as the staff sat round the kitchen table at their lunch. 'She's tired of waiting for Mr Right.'

Like many girls of her class, Miss Wishart had been brought up to expect her life to be that of wife and mother, but a suitor was slow to show himself.

When the war started, the Wishart family bought every daily newspaper they could, and read avidly every line of news about it. Beth, together with the rest of the staff, could hardly wait to get their hands on the papers to read them too. The progress of the war was discussed at every meal.

Dorinda was deeply affected by the wave of patriotism that swept through the country, and became passionate about doing her bit. They heard she was taking lessons in first aid from the St John's Ambulance people, though her parents would have preferred her to knit socks and blanket squares.

When Dorinda announced to her family that she wanted to become a nurse with the Voluntary Aid Detachment and go to France to help with the thousands being injured in the trenches, it caused a family crisis.

'I forbid it,' her father exclaimed loudly across the dinner table just as Beth was carrying in the cheese soufflé. 'No daughter of mine is going to France. You'll get yourself killed, it's much too dangerous.'

Beth had plans for her own future and she felt for Miss Wishart.

The upset and the arguments reverberated through the house for days. In the kitchen, the staff discussed it at length.

Cook said, 'Her father expects to be obeyed. It must be awful for her, compelled to stay home and knit when she wants to help the war effort.'

'It's not as though she's got anything else in her life. She's near enough an old maid already.' Ruby the parlourmaid was scornful. She was the same age but had a boyfriend and planned to marry soon.

A few days later, Miss Wishart upset her breakfast tray in her bedroom and while Beth was sweeping up the fragments of broken crockery she said to her, 'I've thought of being a nurse too. I'd love to be a VAD.'

'You?' Dorinda Wishart's rather horsy face broke into a gentle smile. 'Easier for you to do what you want.'

'It isn't. They wouldn't want someone like me in the VADs, and anyway, I couldn't afford to work for nothing as they do.'

'I meant you don't have to fight your family to leave home.'

Beth said, 'They thought it was the best thing for me. My home's crowded, one less means more room for the others. When we turn fourteen, we all have to find work.'

Miss Wishart's eyes stared at her apologetically, then she said, 'Don't you like working here?'

'Yes, I've been very happy here, but with the war . . . I'd like to do my bit too, and I've always fancied being a nurse.'

'I'd love to have a job. I've pleaded to be allowed . . . I'd hoped that with the war . . . It'll be over before I get a chance to do anything.'

'I've decided to start the training. I'm old enough now.' Beth had had her eighteenth birthday in June.

'You'd be a real nurse, even when the war was over.' There was a note of envy in Dorinda's voice.

'Aren't VADs real nurses?'

The Voluntary Aid Detachment had been set up by the Red Cross and the Order of St John because there were not enough trained nurses to cope with the casualties of war. Neither were there enough hospital beds. The upper classes threw open their houses as makeshift hospitals, and their wives and daughters became VADs to run them.

'They're wartime nurses,' Miss Wishart told her. 'They take short courses in first aid and bandaging and within a few weeks they're running these new emergency hospitals.'

'How can they deal with . . . well, you know, all the things we read about – the smashed limbs and foul-smelling wounds and gassed men struggling for breath?'

'I don't know, they must find it hard. They're spoken of as heroines.'

'They're brave, and of course they are ladies.' Beth smiled. 'And they wear very glamorous uniforms.' Each had a large red cross on her apron bib.

A few days later, Dorinda had a head cold. Beth was lighting a fire in her bedroom when Dorinda said, 'Father and I have reached a compromise. He agreed to allow me to be a VAD provided I promised to stay in this country. Mother has spoken to Lady Speechley of Brancote Hall about me going there. She said she'd be happy to have me.'

'I'm pleased for you, it's what you want, isn't it?'

27

'Well, I've been thinking about what you said the other day. I think I'd do better to train like Florence Nightingale did and become a real nurse. I've been looking into it.'

Beth was keen to do it herself because it would lift her up the social scale and take her away from Dock Cottages but she couldn't understand why Miss Wishart should want to leave her luxurious home. She said so.

'I'm bored, nothing ever happens here. I'm expected to help with the flowers and go visiting with Mother. All her friends are her age and rather dull. We knit and roll bandages.' Dorinda sighed. Then she went on, 'You must be careful to choose the very best training school when you apply.'

Beth had already written for an application form to the Borough Hospital which was less than a mile down the road from Dock Cottages. 'Which would that be?'

'Why, the Royal Infirmary in Liverpool. That's where I'm planning to go. It's a long-established voluntary hospital with a very good reputation. Their certificate of training will carry more weight than most.'

She went on to explain that each hospital did its own teaching and issued its own certificates. That was why it was important to train at the best.

'There's no national standard of training, and no national register of nurses, though it's been talked about for a long time.'

Beth hesitated. 'But would a hospital like that take someone like me?'

'Of course,' Miss Wishart said. 'You do know there are two kinds of nurses?'

Beth didn't.

'Well, what I mean is there's a two-tier system of training . . .'

Beth listened carefully to what Dorinda had to say. Young ladies like herself from the middle or upper classes who could pay one pound a week to be taught all they needed to know would be issued with a certificate of competence from the hospital after one year. Working-class girls like Beth were being taken on without payment and received their training in exchange for their labour. They would be given their uniform, board and lodgings and even a shilling or two pocket money each month, but for them the process would take anything from two to four years – whatever the hospital laid down. And after receiving their certificate of competency, they might be expected to stay on and serve as a staff nurse for another year.

Beth was beginning to think the Royal Infirmary might be a good place for her too and applied for a training place. The nurses would come from a much wider area, and with a bit of luck they might not have heard of Dock Cottages.

She discussed nursing with Miss Wishart on every possible occasion after that, and learned a great deal from her. She was the first in the Wishart house to hear that Dorinda's application had been accepted, and a few days later Beth helped her pack.

'Thank goodness for Florence Nightingale.' Dorinda smiled. 'She raised nursing from being a job for skivvies to a profession for gentlewomen.'

By the time Beth started, Miss Wishart was two months into her year's training. Beth found she hadn't told her everything.

She, together with the other working-class nurses, went on duty at seven thirty in the morning, whereas the lady pupils came on at nine, and could even attend morning service in the hospital chapel after that, should they choose to. They were kept apart; Beth's sort of nurse had inferior rooms and ate in a separate dining room, with cheap tableware. She saw less of Miss Wishart than she'd expected.

It seemed to Beth that the sisters and the doctors explained everything very carefully to the lady pupils, and demonstrated techniques to them, while the rest of them had to push themselves forward to listen and learn in between bouts of scrubbing and polishing and handing out meals.

They were told that nursing was a vocation. They were expected to have a nun-like attitude and put up with long working hours and very low pay. Their labour ran the big voluntary hospitals, while the lady nurses smoothed pillows, talked to the patients and doctors and arranged the flowers. Promotion to sister and above came quickly to them. The uniforms they wore designated their status for all to see and the lady pupils wanted to keep things that way.

Having worked as a maid in the Wishart house, Beth was very aware of the gulf between the social classes. In the hospital the resentment felt by her sort of nurse festered below a surface politeness. They wanted training and promotion to be equal for all. The Registration Bill had now been passed and all teaching hospitals had to run a training course that would lead to competence, and all nurses had to sit an examination to be eligible for registration.

Some of the nurses who had already undergone training were allowed to apply to have their names put on the register straight away. Beth's certificate from the Liverpool Royal Infirmary was considered acceptable.

She was grateful to Dorinda Wishart for guiding her towards that hospital and felt incredibly lucky to be on the same register of nurses as she was. Beth felt she'd taken a great social step upwards, even though her work had much in common with that of a domestic maid. For the patients and the public, the lady pupils had left some of their glamour on the profession.

Beth had started her job as a staff nurse at the Borough Hospital just before Christmas two years ago. All the ward staff had worked without off-duty on Christmas Day and not until 29 December could they enjoy any festivities.

The night staff came on duty an hour earlier at seven that day, to allow the maximum number of those on day duty to eat their turkey dinner and attend a dance in the outpatients department. Coloured Christmas streamers still crisscrossed the waiting hall, giving it a festive look though the holly leaves were now brown and beginning to curl. French chalk was put down to make it possible to dance on the stone floor and a six-piece band was hired to play until eleven o'clock.

At that time, Beth was still finding her feet and knew nobody apart from the probationers working on the same ward. They advised her to invite a partner if she could – to the dance not the dinner, that was only for nursing staff.

She'd asked Ken Clover if he'd come. He seemed pleased to be asked but the day before, he was unexpectedly summoned back to his ship which was sailing for Cardiff.

At the dance, all the girls seemed to know each other. They were all wearing their best evening finery and Beth found it hard to recognise any of them out of uniform. She felt very much on her own.

The members of the band were middle-aged to elderly but they played the popular tunes of the day to a strict tempo. Matron had invited the ancillary staff from the laboratories, X-ray department and office in order to provide some partners. Some of the hospital consultants had agreed to put in an appearance, and a few junior doctors were already there.

Most of the men wore dinner jackets with black ties. Beth knew Ken Clover didn't own clothes like that. The few men wearing lounge suits looked self-conscious and out of things. But Ken had his merchant navy uniform which would have been fine.

She couldn't believe her luck when a handsome man standing in the small group by the door came over and asked if she'd partner him in the military two-step. He was tall and slim and had straight dark hair brushed back from his forehead.

Beth said, 'I haven't seen you before but I've only been working here since the beginning of the month.' He looked well-groomed and very middle-class. His dinner jacket was new and smart. 'Are you one of the doctors?'

'No, I work in the laboratory.' She thought him rather stiff and formal. 'I should introduce myself, shouldn't I? My name's Andrew Langford.'

'Beth Hubble, staff nurse on Ward Three.'

'Are you enjoying it?'

'I'm sure I shall once I settle in.'

'I meant the dance.'

'Yes, that too.'

He held her well away from him and danced with precision. Matron would approve of him as a partner.

She asked, 'Have you worked here long?'

'Four years.'

'You must know a lot of the nurses.'

'No,' he said awkwardly. 'Matron does her best to keep her nurses away from us men.'

Beth sat the next two dances out. Many of the nurses were dancing together because they didn't have partners. She couldn't keep her eyes away from Andrew Langford as he danced with a girl in a scarlet dress.

When the band struck up a quick waltz she was pleased to see him coming back to her. As they whirled round the floor, he told her a new and much enlarged outpatients department would soon be built to replace this one. When the music came to an end, they were both breathless.

As he escorted her back to her seat, he said, 'I wonder if you would allow me yet another dance? Though I shouldn't ask, it's wrong to monopolise your dance programme.'

'I'd like another dance with you,' she said, 'and we don't have dance programmes here. Does anybody in this day and age?'

'Oh yes. At most of the dances I go to.'

'I hardly know anybody here,' Beth told him, 'so I'm very glad of your company.'

He danced every dance with her after that and their steps seemed to match, though he didn't have very much to say and his manner seemed stilted. She thought that perhaps he was shy.

31

When the band struck up the last waltz, he led her out on the floor and before it had finished he asked her if he could take her to the cinema on her next evening off. By then she was feeling quite smitten by his looks. She readily agreed. She'd never known anyone socially who had so much middle-class polish – clean hands with manicured nails, professionally cut hair, and not a trace of a Merseyside accent. He looked as though he'd been brought up with his every need met.

Matron, the only person still wearing her uniform, was at the door saying good night to the dance partners and making sure they left the hospital premises.

Beth really looked forward to her first outing with Andrew. She met him outside the hospital shortly after five when they'd both finished work for the day. Sitting beside him on the tram going into town, she thought him even more handsome than he'd seemed at the dance, and couldn't believe he'd think of his smart coat and bowler hat as working clothes.

He took her first to a cafe for what he called 'a bite of supper' though she'd just had her hospital tea of bread and jam and a biscuit. Then they went to the first house at the Argyle Theatre and he bought not only a programme but chocolates too. Beth loved every minute of the variety show and thought he enjoyed it as well.

He insisted on escorting her back to the hospital, though he'd have found it easier to get a train back from town to where he lived in West Kirby.

'I've had a lovely time,' she told him. 'Thank you very much. You've treated me royally.'

'Shall we do it again?'

Beth was delighted. She tried to say she wanted to pay her way – with friends from Dock Cottages that was essential – but he wouldn't hear of it. He shook her hand before saying good night.

When she recounted this to Mam, she said, 'That's how a gentleman should treat a lady friend.'

Andrew had continued to invite her out, mostly to the pictures, but only once or at the most twice a month. Beth would have liked to see more of him and get to know him better. He still seemed rather aloof. Mam said no lady would take it on herself to suggest they meet more often. He would think her fast. Anyway, she had to work on most evenings.

The nurses' home felt warm when Beth let herself in, and there was the clean scent of furniture polish in the air. The sitting-room door was ajar; Celia Collins, another staff nurse and a friend, was playing the piano, but Beth was tired and went straight past to her bedroom. She knew her fellow nurses considered the rooms to be fairly basic but Beth thought hers luxurious.

It was furnished with a comfortable bed, a dressing table and wardrobe, a green Lloyd Loom armchair and matching laundry basket that did duty as a bedside table. There was a small rug on the polished parquet floor, and it was all for her, she had privacy and warmth from a hot water radiator. All was cleanliness and order and very different to what she'd had at home. She felt she lived in two different worlds.

Beth went to the bathroom and started to run a bath. It was a luxury to lie back in hot water, to have it deep and scented with bath salts, a birthday present from Celia, particularly when she thought of how hard it was to keep clean at home.

She had her job and her hope for a rosy future with Andrew, but her mother's illness had destroyed her contentment.

She'd been going out with Andrew for months before he started giving her gentle kisses when they met and when they parted. That made her realise just how shy he was, especially of girls. She still knew very little about him; he was a very quiet and reserved person and said little about himself. Beth didn't think she was naturally reserved, but she was on her best behaviour with him and determined not to put a foot wrong. She was careful to say nothing about where she came from either, in case that should put him off. Mam was adamant that she shouldn't.

'Don't bombard him with questions' was another piece of advice from Mam, and since she didn't want to appear to be prying into his personal affairs, Beth curbed her curiosity. Mostly he wanted to take her to the cinema or the music hall so they didn't have much chance to talk anyway.

This holding back on both sides meant they'd each taken a long time to know how they felt about the other. When she managed to break through his barrier of reserve he could be an entertaining companion. He was passionate about birds, and would stop her when they were strolling in the park or along the promenade to point out plovers or terns or guillemots. He gave her a book on different species when she showed interest. He was also keen on golf, but she couldn't share that.

Beth began to want more from him and did her best to show him how much she appreciated him and enjoyed their outings. When he put a shy kiss on her cheek, she returned it with a hug and greater warmth. He responded, but very slowly. She began to think he saw her only as a

33

companion, and that their friendship would develop no further.

She began to fear that she never would have what she wanted. She thought of it as unrequited love and found it painful. While Andrew showed less affection than she hoped for, her love for him was growing stronger. Her friends and family kept asking if he'd given her a ring yet. She'd known him for more than a year before she accepted that her future would not be with him and began to think of other ways to fill it.

Seated across the table from Andrew in the cafe where they often had something to eat early in the evening, she said, 'I'm thinking of applying to the Liverpool Maternity Hospital to train as a midwife. Several girls I know will be going soon, it's easier if I go with a crowd I know.'

'Beth! Don't do that!'

'Why not?'

'Please don't leave Birkenhead. I wouldn't be able to see you.'

'It's not a million miles away. I could meet you here.'

'But not so often.'

'We don't meet all that often, Andrew.'

Beth had taken her present job to be nearer to her family, so she could see her mother when she had a few hours off in the morning or afternoon. Mam wasn't keen on her leaving either.

'Please stay here at the Borough,' Andrew had implored. 'We get on so well together. I'd miss you terribly.' She was surprised he felt so strongly. He must love her after all. She felt aglow with pleasure.

So Beth had stayed on and Andrew invited her out more often. It was her long hours of work that prevented her seeing more of him now. She had only one or two evenings off each week when she could go out with him. She had one day off a week, but Andrew was at work then, and once a month she had a half-day on a Sunday too.

On summer Sundays, he'd take her bird-watching along the Dee marshes, or for walks and to a cafe for afternoon tea. He had more money to spend on entertaining her than anyone else she knew and he was very generous.

And now she could feel passion behind his kisses; they excited her, lifted her away from everything else.

A few times in the summer, he'd come back to the hospital to meet her after eight o'clock when she came off duty for the night. There was little they could do at that hour because she was expected to be back inside the nurses' home by ten thirty, but the park was just across the road and they could walk across the grass and sit close together on the benches by the duck pond. The park gates were locked at ten so they had to take care to be out before then; he worried that they might be locked inside. Sometimes, he'd take her to a cafe near the station for a cup of tea and a bun. Before she let herself into the nurses' home, he'd pull her into the shadows and kiss her good night.

Recently Andrew had been speaking of the future as though they'd spend it together. Beth had been delighted with the change.

When she thought of him now, she was walking on air and began to hope that one day he might propose. If she did get her wish, her life would be very different from that of her mother and sisters.

Chapter Four

The following evening, Beth packed a suitcase and called at Jenny's house to collect Bobby and Colin before she went to Dock Cottages. Although her case had to be balanced across Bobby's pushchair, they walked the rest of the way. The night seemed dark and damp and the towering blocks malevolent and brooding as she walked through them.

She was afraid crime was bred in many of their neighbours because they could find no escape from poverty in legal employment. Rarely did she pick up the *Liverpool Echo* or the *Birkenhead News* without reading of some inhabitant of Dock Cottages who had appeared in court on charges of theft, burglary, fraud, rape or even murder. Though there were plenty of honest people trying to survive here too.

When the three hundred and fifty tenements had been built in about 1847 the Birkenhead Dock Company had meant them to be good homes for their workers. Churches had been built nearby, together with schools for five hundred children. Nowadays, they were home to porters, stevedores, coal heavers, watermen, carters, millers, and railway men of many kinds.

Many of their neighbours were Irish. Following the failure of the potato harvests in the 1840s, the Irish had come to Merseyside in great numbers seeking work. Many had been starving and ill when they got off the boats to seek lodgings in the already overcrowded courts and cellars of Liverpool where lavatories were shared by several families. Epidemics of cholera and typhoid had broken out regularly on both sides of the Mersey, killing not only the poor but the wealthy too.

Because of this, bylaws were passed making it illegal to build new dwellings without their own mains water supply and sewage system. In this part of town, the water mains and sewage systems were laid out below the streets before building commenced, in an effort to reduce the number of deaths by contagious fevers. In those far-off days, Birkenhead had been spoken of as the city of the future.

Beth sent Colin up the grim stone steps to the fourth floor of Block E to get help. Ivor came running down to help her lift the pram.

In the living room, her mother was sitting in the only armchair; she looked calmer and more rested. There was a good smell of bacon cooking in the range and the knives and forks were out on the table. Beth slid her case under the couch out of sight. The younger children were huddling together on top, playing some card game.

'How are you, Mam?'

'Much the same, love.'

'Where's Seppy? I thought he was going to stay with you.'

'He wants to carry on with his Saturday job at the butchers. They let him have meat a bit cheaper, so we've eaten better since he's been doing it.' Beth heard the pride in her mother's voice. 'He's a good boy.'

'I'd forgotten.'

'He brought sausage and bacon home in his dinner hour, enough for our tea tonight. He set it out ready in the pans and I got Ivor to put them in the oven at the right time. With you here as well, Seppy didn't think he'd be needed.'

'No, of course not.'

At the table, Ivor was cutting a whole loaf into slices. He'd already got the brown sauce on the table. Beth was surprised and pleased to find everything under control.

As soon as her father's step was heard on the landing, Ivor had the pans out of the oven and was breaking eggs into them. They were all sitting round the table and eating within a quarter of an hour. Everybody seemed in a good humour.

Beth took Bobby on her knee to feed him. He kept opening his mouth like a baby sparrow for the egg. They were all eating hungrily, no child refused food in Dock Cottages. Afterwards, the table was cleared and the washing-up done in the usual orderly fashion, without Mam having to lift a finger. Dad had already gone out to the pub when Seppy came home bringing a nice piece of brisket big enough for Sunday dinner for them all.

'How much d'you pay for this?' Mam wanted to know.

'Mr Donovan let me have it for two bob. It would have been half-a-crown to anyone else. I've been serving in the shop today. I liked doing it.'

Seppy was just sitting down to eat the meal they'd kept for him when his eldest sister Peggy arrived bringing her own four boisterous children with her. She collapsed on a chair by the table out of breath, but had to raise her voice to make herself heard above the squeals and shouts of the children. 'I thought I'd walk round and see how you are, Mam.'

Beth got up to fill the kettle while they talked. Everybody who called in was offered tea.

The corners of Peggy's mouth drooped with dissatisfaction. She said, 'It's a terrible pull up all those stairs. I'm out of practice.'

'Not surprising, in your present state,' her mother told her. Peggy was eight months pregnant.

Beth knew it bothered her mother to see Peggy looking so despondent. Beth felt she'd grown up in her sister's shadow; she'd had to accept that as the firstborn, Mam favoured Peggy. Peggy's hair had once been golden, and Beth had heard their mother say with much satisfaction that Peggy had the face of an angel.

Beth had always been acutely aware of the rivalry between them. Only at schoolwork had she managed to surpass Peggy, and though Mam had praised her for that and encouraged her to work harder, Dad had discounted it.

'Bookwork won't get you anywhere,' he'd said contemptuously. 'It's done nothing for your mother.'

Beth could remember when Peggy had been a keen ballroom dancer, going out to dance halls several times each week. She'd had to buy her dance dresses second-hand, but dresses of satin and taffeta didn't get a great deal of wear from their original owners. Mam had made them fit and Peggy had stitched sequins on to make them sparkle under the dance-hall lights and gone in for competition dancing. As far as anyone in the Blocks could be said to have the world at their feet, it had been Peggy.

They'd all believed she'd get clear away to a better life when she won the foxtrot competition at the Grafton Ballroom with Sidney O'Connell. Sidney was a sailor on the passenger ferries running between Liverpool and Dublin.

Beth lifted her eyes to the framed photographs which had stood on the mantelpiece for years, reminding them all of Peggy's triumphs. She'd won a beautiful baby competition when she was nine months old and the foxtrot competition when she was seventeen.

Peggy had been glamorous when she dolled herself up with powder and lipstick. As glamorous as anyone living in the Blocks could be. Both she and Sidney had been full of ambition.

They'd had such plans, Beth had listened to them with awe. Sidney was going to leave the sea and they were going to start a school of dance to teach ballroom dancing. The whole family had been excited at the prospect, Beth had been thrilled and had sounded out her friends, seeking prospective clients for Peggy.

But the school of dance had never been started. They'd saved up and were married when Peggy was eighteen; she'd become pregnant within weeks of their marriage and the war had started the following year. Sidney had sailed with a merchant freighter bringing food into Liverpool.

Beth studied her elder sister now. Peggy had had her twenty-fifth birthday in October; she had been married less than seven years and by next month she'd have five children. When the war ended, Sidney had wanted to stay at home with them and was glad to be offered a job as barman in the New Dock Hotel.

Peggy did not have the time, the money or the energy to go dancing these days. Her figure had gone from reed slim to stout, even when she wasn't pregnant. Beth could see her changing almost before her eyes. Her once bright blonde hair was dark with grease and her delicate complexion was showing faint lines. Marriage was wearing her down; she looked ill-kempt and shabby in her maternity pinafore. Her fingernails were grimy and her blouse torn, she was no longer taking care of herself.

Beth watched her stir two teaspoons of sugar into her tea. She had only to look at their own mother to see where Peggy was heading, but until she became ill, Mam had always managed to keep herself and her children clean and tidy.

Peggy said, 'I'll look after Colin for you tomorrow, if you like. Take him out so you get a bit of peace.' Four-year-old Colin was chasing Peggy's toddlers round in the very confined space.

Beth thought Colin was half wild, though he looked a tousle-haired cherub. She knew he spent much of his day playing outside and getting into mischief. He'd say he was going down to a play area in Stewart Street, where there were swings and seesaws and space to kick a ball about, but too often she saw him playing in the street or on the stairs or the roof, with a gang of like-minded pre-school tearaways.

Beth said, 'Peggy, you're in no fit state to look after him, he's a right handful. Anyway, Mam needs a more permanent arrangement. I was thinking of taking him down to the school on Monday to ask Miss Thompson if she'd take him in early.'

'What a relief that would be.' Peggy smiled. 'You want to go to school, don't you, Colin? Big boys go to school.'

He smiled up engagingly at his eldest sister. 'Yes, want to go to school. I'm a big boy now, aren't I?'

'I wish all mine could start school straight away.' Peggy had three under school age, the youngest only fourteen months. 'Quiet, you lot.

I'll send you all out to play if you don't shut up. Are they too much for you, Mam?'

Beth was afraid they were. In a room this size, there were too many boisterous children. After working all day, Seppy was playing soft tunes on his mouth organ, stretched out on a cushion in the corner. Esther was reading by the fire, she was always quiet.

'I'd better take them home,' Peggy said. 'It's time Eric was in bed.' But she sat on a bit longer, talking of this and that almost as though she hadn't the energy to move. When she finally went, Beth heard her mother sigh with relief.

'Poor Peggy,' she said. 'I was so proud of her when she was a little girl. She was so pretty I used to buy camomile to make her hair shine with gold lights.'

'You made her lots of clothes.'

'From remnants I bought in the market. I wanted her to look nice.'

'She did.'

'She stood out in the swarm of Dock Cottage children, didn't she? I instilled politeness and good manners into all you children. I wanted to bring you up so you could go anywhere once you were grown up.'

'You were specially ambitious for Peggy.'

'So was your dad. We wanted to give her the best chance of getting away from here and having a decent life. We wanted that for you all.'

'She managed to get away.'

Her mother sounded sad. 'But she's still plagued with the same problems. She hasn't found a better life.'

To Beth, Peggy seemed to be going downhill faster than Mam ever had. 'What's happened to her, Mam? She seems to be getting old before her time.'

Mam didn't seem to have heard. 'Poor Peggy. Your dad . . . took her to the Argyle Music Hall for her twelfth birthday and there was a lot of tap-dancing in the show. She loved it.'

'I remember. She wanted dancing lessons after that.'

'If Peggy wanted something, your dad would do anything to get it for her.'

That made Beth think back to the time when Dad had brought a special present home for Peggy. It was not unusual for him to bring her a box of crayons or new ribbons for her hair but never before had there been anything quite like this.

Peggy had let out a cry of wonder when she opened up the big cardboard box he'd put in her arms. They'd crowded round to see the

41

china doll, with eyes that closed when she was laid flat and eyelashes curving over her cheeks.

Mam had made their dolls, with buttons for eyes and wool for hair, but to get a shop doll, brand new and still in its box, was very special. And it wasn't even Peggy's birthday.

In her mind's eye, Beth could see Peggy as a child now, totally enthralled, nursing the doll in her arms, while she and Jenny had looked on enviously. Jenny's fingers had gripped hers with a force that told of passionate longing. Their father never brought anything for them.

He'd asked, 'Are you pleased with it, Peggy?'

Peggy was radiant. To be pleased clearly understated how she felt.

'It's so lovely.' She could hardly speak, she was astounded. They'd never seen a child in the Blocks with a doll like this.

'You can say thank you by making me a cup of tea.'

Peggy had flung herself into the scullery to fill the kettle and when she'd put the cup of tea beside him, he'd said, 'Run down to the paper shop for me, there's a good girl. Get me ten Gold Flake.'

When Peggy rushed out to the shop, Jenny had put a tentative hand out to touch the doll.

Dad had shouted, 'Leave that. It's not yours. Peggy won't be pleased if you spoil it. You've got to earn these things, Jenny. You think about that. And you too, Betty. You've got to work for what you get in this world.' Jenny had backed away.

'You two can get the table cleared for your mam.' Mam was down in the washroom doing the family wash.

They'd done what he asked, wiping down the oilcloth and washing up as well, but it hadn't earned them any praise or presents from Dad. Mum had rewarded them with thanks and kisses.

'Dad indulged Peggy,' Beth said.

'When he brought her home, after her twelfth birthday treat, Peggy said, "Wouldn't it be lovely if I could earn my living that way? If I could dance at the Argyle Theatre in a show like that?" Her eyes sparkled, we thought that if any child could do it, Peggy could.'

'No other child in the Blocks ever had dancing lessons. How could you afford them?'

'Your dad swore he'd find the money somehow. For the first few lessons he did.'

'Then I suppose you had to scrape the fees together by cutting down on what you ate yourself?'

Her mother smiled to herself. 'Peggy really enjoyed those lessons.

When the School of Dance put on a little show, they always gave her a big part and she performed well.'

'You took me and Jenny to see her.'

'After a couple of years she wanted to change to learn ballroom dancing.'

'She did change.'

'Once she left school and could pay for the lessons herself.'

Beth thought of Seppy handing over all the money he earned at his Saturday job. Of the way she and John and Lottie chipped in part of their wages to help support the family. They couldn't spend the money they earned on themselves. It had been different for the firstborn.

'I suppose the trouble started when she had to take a job in the tapestry works.'

Beth knew that many of the girls in Peggy's class at school had found jobs there, but Peggy had been aiming higher than them. She'd wanted to go on the stage. Dancing was what she was good at.

'She was disappointed but she settled down quite well. The tapestry factory is a good place to work. They look after their girls, train them to do high-class hand work in this age of machine-made furnishings. And it's so near.'

It was just a bit further down Stanley Road behind the high walls of old brick and corrugated iron sheets.

'Jenny loves it there,' Beth said. 'She says they do needlework and crewel embroidery and weave Jacquard tapestries by hand. And they can copy designs made hundreds of years ago.'

'Jenny brags that the work she does sells to royalty and the aristocracy.'

'Was Peggy all right until she took up with Sidney O'Connell?' Beth asked.

'I don't know, you and Jenny always seemed happier. You needed less.'

'We got less. We thought Peggy was very lucky.'

'We all got less as the family grew. I don't know how Peggy will manage with another baby to look after.'

'She looked a bit down tonight,' Beth agreed.

'She has since number five's been on the way. She doesn't get time to recover in between.'

'There'll be fifteen months between these last two.' Her first two were only eleven months apart.

'Fifteen months isn't nearly long enough, Beth.' There was heartfelt sadness in her voice. 'Poor Peggy, she's going to have a big family just like me.' Mam took out her handkerchief. She was raw with emotion

43

again, just as she'd been last night. Beth thought she'd calmed her then; that she was accepting her bad prognosis in the way she'd accepted everything else in her life.

'Oh Beth!' Tears were shimmering in her eyes. 'If only . . .'

'You're tired and upset now,' Beth told her firmly. 'After a week's rest you'll feel better. You'll be able to do a bit about the house. Life will seem more normal.'

'It's not me . . . I'm not worried about . . . It's Peggy.'

'She's just a bit down. She'll be fine once the baby's born.'

'That's what everybody said about me, but she won't. I feel so guilty.'

'You've done all you could for her, always have. If anything, you did too much. You've nothing to feel guilty about.'

'My father said,' her mother's voice shook, 'you've made your bed and . . . you'll have to lie on it. At first I thought I was going to have a wonderful married life, but later . . . we didn't have enough money and we had to live in this place . . .' Beth hardly dared breathe, she was transfixed. She didn't think Mam had ever told anybody how she really felt before.

'D'you know what drove it home to me? My mother kept open house for all her relatives on Boxing Day. I'd take you children and pretend we all enjoyed the festivities.'

Beth remembered those rare outings. She'd loved them when she was a child. 'I remember Grandma in that big comfortable house. The table groaning with delicious food and Aunt Lily making such a fuss of me and Peggy.'

There were tears on her mother's cheeks. 'I could see . . . what I'd lost, how much better my life would have been if . . . I'd obeyed my father. He never showed me any . . . affection after that but my sisters are still very happy at home. They want . . . for nothing.'

Mam looked so sad. Beth took her hand between both of her own.

'I told myself . . . it was my choice . . . to be a wife and mother, but it was many years . . . before I saw that I'd made the choice for all you children too. It isn't just me that's had to put up with it.'

'We've been happy enough, Mam. We've never known anything else.'

'I hoped you'd all get away from here . . . I was certain Peggy would, and now look at her.'

There was nothing Beth could say to that.

'She's following in my footsteps, isn't she? Doing . . . what I did, and believing . . . that if it was right for me it'll be right for her. Twenty years from now she'll be ill like—'

'No, Mam! There's no reason to think that. Her heart could be stronger, she might be able to take it all in her stride.'

'She might not. What I did . . . fixed her here. It's fixed all of you here. I feel so . . . bad that she didn't get her dancing school. I was so sure . . . my children would have a better life . . . than I've had.'

Beth gulped. That sounded as though she accepted her life was virtually over.

'We were so certain Peggy would marry well. She feels a drudge, I'm sure.'

'No . . .'

'I know how she feels because I've felt that way too.'

'She could do more to help herself.' Beth had never had too much sympathy for Peggy.

'She can't make the effort. Not now. Promise me, Beth, you won't do what we've done.'

'Mam! I haven't got married, have I? I'm already free of Dock Cottages, I only come back to see you and the kids.'

'There's Ken Clover. I get nervous when I see you so friendly.'

'That's all we are, friendly. I've grown up with him, known him all my life. He treats me like he does Maggie, like a little sister.'

Once in a while, she went to the pictures with Ken, but she usually had to pay for herself because he was broke. When they got back, he always asked her in to have a cup of tea with his family.

'His mother's been hinting that Ken . . . Well, you know, that he rather fancies you.'

Beth straightened up. 'I don't think—'

'You'd be in the same boat if you married him.'

'Don't worry, Mam. He hasn't got round to asking me. It might be what his mother wants, but not Ken. He'll have other ideas. Anyway, he isn't likely to get married. He can't afford any more dependants, not when he's supporting his mother and his younger brother and sister.'

'You can do better than him, Beth. I wouldn't encourage him if I were you.'

Beth laughed. 'I thought you liked the Clovers.'

'I do . . . lovely people. Mary Clover's . . . been a good friend to me. They'd do anything . . . to help you, but if you tie yourself to him, you're going to find yourself counting the ha'pennies . . . to make everything stretch. The Clovers would pull you down. You'll end up like our Peggy.'

'I'm not likely to, Mam.'

'This Andrew . . . he'll be much better for you. He can give you an easier life. You'll never be scratching around for the last penny if you marry him.'

'He hasn't asked me either.'

'He will though.'

'Perhaps,' Beth conceded. She hoped so, it brought her pleasure to think of Andrew.

Mam's eyes had shone when Beth had told her she was entitled to call herself a registered nurse. But she'd been absolutely thrilled when she heard Beth had a boyfriend at the hospital.

'Marry him and you'll never look back,' she said, and her cheeks had glowed. 'He'll take you up in the world. A wife takes her husband's social position as well as his name.'

'You should know.' Beth had smiled.

It was true that since the war there had been a levelling of the classes. For the tenants of Dock Cottages the social barriers couldn't break down soon enough.

'Be patient,' Mam advised now. 'These things . . . are better not rushed. You need to get to know each other.'

'I've known him for two years,' Beth said. 'That's not rushing.'

'It'll happen . . . sooner or later, I'm sure. You behave like a lady. Never discuss . . . money or let him know just how poor we are.'

'I haven't.'

'Don't be . . . nosy about . . . well, what he earns. Don't do anything to upset him.'

Beth was afraid she had already upset him by refusing to meet him this week. She felt uneasy about that, and hoped he'd have got over it by the time her holiday was over.

'But you'll have lots of free time on holiday,' he'd protested. 'We could go to the pictures one night, and I'll take you to the theatre on another.' He'd laughed in anticipation.

'No, Andrew, thank you.'

'We could go over to Liverpool if you prefer, there's a good play on at—'

'I shall be busy. My mother needs real help with the family.' Beth had told him about her many brothers and sisters. 'I feel so sorry for her. I need to get things more organised at home, I'd like to concentrate on that.'

'You'll have the daytime for that.' He'd been unable to understand and looked unhappy about it.

Andrew had the manners of a gentleman, he always escorted her back to the nurses' home when they went out. She knew he'd want to bring her safely back here and she hadn't yet told him her family lived in Dock Cottages.

Beth wished she'd told him everything so she could have gone out with him this week. It was such a waste to have all these free evenings and spend them at home.

Andrew wasn't the first boyfriend she'd had, but he was the first she'd been really interested in. The others hadn't lasted long and none had had a good job like Andrew. He was certainly the best looking of them all; her fellow nurses thought him handsome and highly desirable. When she went back to work next week, it would be lovely to be able to concentrate on him.

Mam said, 'You've done so well for yourself up to now, don't throw it away. Don't do what I did, Beth, there's no way back afterwards. I do hope you get right away, that nothing goes wrong.'

'It won't. I'll end up a hospital sister at the very least, won't I?'

Beth couldn't sleep that night. Some of Mam's agony had rubbed off on her, but it was only her heightened emotions that were new. Mam had handed out the same advice many times. Beth thought she didn't need it, but she understood why Mam felt as she did.

Chapter Five

Beth sat in front of the dying fire waiting for her father to come home. He'd be five minutes after the last drinkers were turfed out of the pub. The rest of the family were already in bed. Usually Seppy exercised his right as the eldest child living at home to sleep on the living-room couch. Tonight, Beth had claimed that for herself and sent him back to his bunk in the children's bedroom. There was little privacy to be had in Dock Cottages wherever one chose to bed down.

She heard her father's heavy tread coming along the landing and the scrape of the front door.

'You still here?' He was blinking at her.

'I've got a week's holiday, Dad. I told you.'

'So you did.' He hiccuped as he shed his coat on the couch and made his way to the scullery, banging doors. He came back just as noisily.

'Mam's been asleep since ten,' she reminded him. 'Good night, Dad.'

He had wakened Mam, Beth could hear the murmur of their voices, but at least Bobby was still snoring gently in his cot. She made her way to the scullery and filled the bucket they kept under the sink, then carried it to the water closet which was in a tiny brick cubicle. The door had to be closed before anyone could use it, which shut off the last glimmer of light from the living room.

At first glance it looked like any other lavatory; a seat in the centre of a wooden bench set against the outer wall, but there was no chain and no cistern above it, just a pipe going down to infinity. She picked up the bucket of water and threw it with all her might into the hole; the more force, the quicker the waste would go down the outlet pipe. Dad rarely bothered after he'd used it.

The lavatory was something all the tenants complained about but when the tenements were built it would have been a luxury for each one to have its own, together with its own unlimited water supply. It had been common then to have one communal tap outside in the street, and one water closet shared by many families.

'But this is the twentieth century,' the tenants protested often to the landlord's agent, who always countered that by saying the toilets still functioned well. There was nothing to go wrong.

Beth washed at the sandstone sink, turned down the gaslight and lay down on her makeshift bed. It was all achingly familiar, she'd wanted to get away but Dock Cottages were closing round her, making it all too easy to settle back here.

Once again she found it impossible to get to sleep. The cinders were giving off a faint glow in the grate, Bobby was snuffling softly, but she was worried about her mother and afraid she'd upset Andrew. He was her lifeline out of here. Her mind wouldn't stop going round.

Violet felt better knowing Beth would be here with her for the whole week. When she'd said good night, shooing the younger ones out of her room, Vi felt herself relax, halfway between sleep and wakefulness. Beth knew how to make her comfortable in bed, she felt pampered and cared for in a way she hadn't since she'd left her childhood home in Meols all those years ago. She ached with nostalgia when she thought of those long gone days.

Her family had rented a large Victorian house, some distance from any other building and surrounded by its own twelve acres of market garden. The land was rich and black and they'd earned their living growing vegetables and soft fruit for the markets in the nearby towns.

Her father's first love had been flowers and he'd grown those for sale too. Violet had been the eldest of a big family; she had two sisters and four brothers. They were a different class of people to those she knew here; independent small businessmen who went cap in hand to no one.

Her family still lived at Knebworth Nursery, though her father had died five years ago. Her eldest brother Jim carried on the market garden, living there with his wife and growing family of four. The house was big enough to accommodate them in comfort as well as her two sisters and her mother. Lily and Iris had never married, they'd been happy to stay at home helping a little with the business and taking care of their mother and the home. They'd had a much more comfortable life than she'd had.

When she'd been seventeen, her father had employed Wilfred Hubble to do the heavy digging and carrying in the market garden. At that time, Wilf had been a strong and healthy 24-year-old, all rippling muscles and suntanned skin. His dark eyes flirted with hers whenever she went near him. He awakened such feelings within her that she could think of nothing else.

She'd been scared when he'd first tried to kiss and fondle her. 'You'll get me into trouble,' she'd said.

'All the better if I do,' he dared. 'Then your dad will let me marry you.'

'But will you?'

He'd laughed. 'I promise that if I get you in the family way, we'll be married straight away. You know I'd jump at the chance.'

To be pursued with such obvious ardour by an older man made her tingle all over, but her parents had been horrified and ordered her not to speak to him.

But Violet couldn't help herself, Wilf made her feel special and she thought him great fun. She'd defied her father and continued to search Wilf out whether he was working in the greenhouses, the nursery or the far field. Her sister Lily told their mother that she'd seen them kissing.

Her father had been furious and said, 'I warned you both, Violet, this affair had to end. I'm going to sack Wilfred Hubble. He's not a suitable person for you to be involved with. You're getting yourself talked about.'

He'd been replaced by an elderly man near retirement age, but she'd continued to meet Wilfred in secret. That summer he'd taken her for walks across the surrounding fields to lie in the long grass where prying eyes could not see them. Violet had seen herself as daring and adventurous and very much in love.

She recognised now that her parents had had her welfare at heart and that she'd been wilful and headstrong to go against their orders. The fun went out of the affair when she'd found herself pregnant.

'We'll get married,' Wilf said. 'I'll come with you to tell your parents. They'll be glad to give their consent now.'

'Oh no! No! I'd rather do it on my own.'

To take Wilf into their living room would bring her father's temper to boiling point before they even opened their mouths. Vi had put off saying anything for as long as she'd dared.

'You'll have to tell them,' he'd urged. 'We can't do anything until you do. They might even help us set up home.'

'Dad certainly won't do that.'

'He won't want you to starve, will he? Not his own flesh and blood.'

'He's very strict with us. He'll be raving . . .'

Eventually she could put it off no longer, she was afraid the baby was beginning to show. Her mother was in the habit of taking a rest on her bed after their midday dinner. Violet had crept up after her, and leaning back on the door with her hand still on the knob, she'd closed her eyes and uttered the words she'd rehearsed. Her mother had sat up

51

slowly, looking appalled. Before the questions started, Vi fled downstairs and out into the garden. That same evening, she found herself at the centre of a terrible row. While her mother sobbed into her handkerchief, her father had roared at her and told her she was a disgrace and a bad example to her two younger sisters.

'You've made your bed and you'll have to lie in it,' he'd said. 'You'll have a hard life with that fellow, don't expect otherwise. Don't ever forget that you brought this on yourself.'

From the day of her wedding, he'd never let Wilfred near the rest of her family. She was married with considerable haste when six months pregnant and still seventeen. Wilf said he was thrilled to have her as his wife and the coming baby was their little blessing. For a time Violet had believed they'd live happily ever after.

She soon found he wanted to make love to her every night and at Dock Cottages there was no space, no air and no money. The drunkenness, bawdiness and noise of the crowd she lived amongst came as a shock. It wasn't long before she felt trapped.

It had taken her a year or two to accept that her father had been right, Wilfred Hubble was physically strong but weak-willed and self-indulgent; he had no push and earned little.

But it hadn't all been bad. She'd been thrilled when her first daughter had been born, and even Wilf had been completely bowled over by the soft down on her tiny head and her plump waving limbs. Vi had wanted to call her Margaret.

'Too much of a mouthful for every day,' Wilf had laughed, 'but we can shorten it to Peggy.'

Violet had been against that. 'We could shorten it to Greta. Isn't that nicer?'

'A bit too fancy. Peggy's more down-to-earth.'

Violet had always regretted that she hadn't stood out against Wilf's choice. She'd never liked the name Peggy, but her pretty baby was stuck with it. Before long, even she thought of her as Peggy.

Peggy had the sort of looks that caught everybody's eye and had grown up to be a real beauty. Vi had been so sure she'd have a good life. It upset her that she hadn't done as well as expected, not as well as Beth.

At first, Violet had been a little disappointed in her second daughter. She'd expected her to be as beautiful as the first but Beth had taken after her side of the family. Beth's face was noticeably like her own; not plain by any means, but with her gingery hair and green eyes, she was no great beauty either.

However, in addition to her looks, Beth had also inherited her family's drive and energy, and she'd climbed the social ladder back to the position in which Violet felt she'd been born. So now she thought of her as the star of the family. Jenny had married young but seemed happy enough, and Lottie, though a domestic servant, also seemed happy, but Vi had hoped they'd both do better.

Violet's family hadn't cut her off entirely. Her mother invited her to bring the children home to Meols every Boxing Day, and also for her sisters' birthday celebrations. But it was made quite clear to her that she must not bring Wilfred, he wouldn't be welcome.

When her father lifted the main potato crop in the autumn, he sent the hired help round with the cart to deliver two sacks of potatoes, together with a supply of carrots, onions, swedes and some green vegetables. Her sisters gave her their coats and dresses as they cast them off. More recently, her brother's wives packed up the clothes their children grew out of and gave them to her. After the first few years, she'd been grateful for anything, but Vi no longer felt she belonged in the family.

The next morning, Beth was woken by Colin climbing on top of her. She opened her eyes to the living-room ceiling which was badly in need of a coat of whitewash. She got dressed quickly, the children would soon all be up and wanting their breakfast. She took cups of tea in to her parents. Dad liked a lie-in on Sunday mornings, he was an inert mound on the bed, but Mam wanted to get up and help. Beth insisted she take things easy and stay where she was.

She got her brothers and sisters to help tidy up and get their Sunday dinner in the oven. It was their biggest meal of the week. Afterwards, Beth made sure that the young ones were all clean and dressed in their best and sent them off to Sunday School. It was what Mam usually did. In the soporific atmosphere, her parents dozed, Mam on the couch and Dad in his armchair by the fire. Beth sat quietly at the table, darning socks so as not to disturb them.

She felt at a loose end. She'd already been down to see Mrs Clover and learned that Ken wasn't home but might be in a couple of days. She thought of visiting Jenny, but didn't like to on the only day of the week her husband was at home.

Beth put Bobby in his pushchair and took him out, walking for miles along Vyner Road where she could see half across the Wirral Peninsula. It rained and they both got wet.

53

On Monday morning, she was up early to get the fire lit so her father could have a cooked meal before he went to work. Getting breakfast for her school-age siblings was more hectic, even though they only had bread and marge.

She kept Mam in bed until the flat emptied, when she could see to her and little Bobby in peace. Colin had been the first out of bed and she'd had to stop him going out to play.

'I'm taking you down to the school,' she told him. She sponged his face and combed his hair and looked for a clean jersey for him. Most of his jerseys were hand-me-downs from Ivor, which although shrunk were still too big for him. Beth found a jumper belonging to Esther but it was pink and he refused to wear it.

'It's sissy. Anyway, she'll kill me if she sees me wearing that. It's her best.'

He settled for one of Ivor's which was at least clean. Beth couldn't find any socks for him, and he had only plimsolls to wear on this cold January morning.

'We'll go to the shops first,' Beth said. 'I'll get some more socks.'

'The girls need knickers too.' Her mother sighed. 'And you'll need to get something for your dad's sandwiches tomorrow while you're out. Take the housekeeping purse. It's not fair that you use your own money all the time.'

Beth did so. There was eight shillings and tenpence in it to last until pay day on Friday.

It started to rain and Colin's feet were soon wet. She took him into a shop on Laird Street and bought six pairs of socks and then a pair of strong boots for him; buying a size too big so he'd get his wear out of them. Then when his feet were adequately shod she took him by the hand and they walked down to the school that the whole family had attended. The smell of chalk and plimsolls took her back to her own schooldays as she went along the corridor to the headmistress's office.

Miss Thompson remembered Beth. When she explained that her mother was ill and she needed Seppy to leave at the end of the week so he could be at home to help her, Miss Thompson agreed to take Colin into school early so that he wouldn't be running wild around the Blocks.

'Leave him here now and we'll see how he gets on,' she said. 'I'll make sure Esther takes him home at dinner time.'

'I can find my way home by myself,' Colin assured her. 'I'm a big boy now.' Beth didn't doubt he could. They were not far from St James's Church which was a clear landmark.

Miss Thompson smiled. 'I was so pleased to hear you'd trained as a nurse. I feel proud when I hear of a former pupil achieving a professional qualification.'

Beth said, 'Do many of us?'

'No, sadly very few.'

'It's hard if you come from Dock Cottages.'

'I know. I grew up there myself. Block B.'

Beth hadn't known that, she was all smiles. 'You're one of the few who managed to get right away.'

'I haven't gone far,' Miss Thompson said gently. 'I don't live there any more but I chose to come back to teach the next generation. Esther is another bright little girl, she's doing very well.'

Beth headed back home feeling triumphant. For Mam, having Colin in school would remove the worry of wondering where he'd gone and what he was getting up to, and it would have been asking a lot of Seppy to cope with him as well as the household chores.

All the local streets were lined with small shops and most were doing a brisk trade. Beth passed a chip shop, and the scent of frying fish made her mouth water, but they couldn't afford that. She went into the homemade brawn shop to get some for her dad's sandwiches, and bought two large loaves from the baker. Past the cobblers and the scrap metal merchant then to the butchers. The last of Sunday's joint would go at lunchtime. She'd make a big stew for tonight and she'd need to buy vegetables for that before she went home.

Dad was right about the air not being fresh. There was a terrible stench coming from the nearby knackers yard in Beaufort Road. Officially it was known as the Wirral Refinery. When a horse was fatally injured or killed on the roads or the docks, it was taken there to retrieve everything of value from the carcass. The meat was sold as pet food, though she'd heard some of their neighbours say they ate it themselves. Glue and bone meal were produced from the bones and hooves.

In the greengrocer's, Beth met Mrs Clover. 'How's your mam getting on, love?'

Beth told her. 'You saw how difficult she found it to get up the stairs. I wish we were on the ground floor like you.'

'There's an empty flat in the next lobby to ours. The tenants did a midnight flit on Saturday.'

'Really? I'd like to move Mam down. All those stairs aren't good for her. Does it need much doing to it?'

'It will. I've never been in, but I don't think Mrs Brand kept the cleanest house.'

'Being home this week, I could clean it up, give the walls a coat of whitewash first.'

They walked back to the Blocks together. Three rough men with dogs were lifting a cover to the dust cellar, into which each tenement had a chute to get rid of the rubbish. It was a breeding ground for rats, although the muck cart came to empty it weekly. The dogs were sniffing eagerly and the men were anticipating some sport. Dogs that were good ratters were highly prized.

'You'd be much closer to this sort of thing.' Mrs Clover pulled her skirts closer to her legs. 'Up on the top floor you don't have to worry about rats or smells. Here we are, this is the empty flat. I hear they didn't even bother to lock the door.'

In fact, the lock had been taken right out of the front door. It couldn't even be closed properly.

'They must have taken it out themselves,' Beth said, examining the chisel marks round the gaping hole.

'Sold it, I expect.'

All the cottages were built to the same plan and were the same size. Beth thought she knew what to expect but she was appalled when she stepped inside.

Mrs Clover gasped. 'What a shambles.'

In each of the two bedrooms, there was a decomposing mattress, together with a heap of rags and a strong smell of urine. In the living room, the gas bracket was broken and two internal doors were missing.

'Chopped them up to make a bit of fire in the grate, I shouldn't wonder.' Mrs Clover shook her head. 'Don't stand too close to the wall, love, there'll be bugs behind that paper.'

Beth jerked herself away. 'We can't move here.'

'Pity, it would have been nice to have your mam this close. She could have popped in and had a cup of tea when she wanted to.'

Beth was tight-lipped. 'That's kind of you, but . . . If only we could get right away from here.'

'That's what we'd all like, love.'

Wilfred Hubble eased his arms into his new jacket; the comfortable fit over his shoulders brought a surge of satisfaction. The checked material of fawns and browns felt soft, even luxurious. Once, it must have been expensive. He left the bedroom to get Vi's opinion. She was still sitting at the living-room table. Beth was clearing the dishes away after their evening meal.

'Nice, isn't it, Vi? D'you like it?'

56

Her tired eyes looked him over at length. 'Is that check a bit loud?' she ventured.

Beth looked him in the eye. 'Much too loud,' she said.

'I didn't ask you,' he retorted. 'I like it and it suits me.' The girl always had to rub him up the wrong way.

He went back to his room and slammed the door. It wasn't difficult to get a decent jacket at a knockdown price because trousers always wore out first. There were rails of suit jackets without the trousers in Fuller's second-hand shop.

He combed his hair and tried to see himself in the mirror. The years had been much kinder to him than they had to Vi. She was beginning to look like an old woman, while he could still be pleased with what he saw in the mirror. Middle age suited him, he'd filled out, as most men did in time. He still had a full head of glossy hair, his shoulders were broad and his belly wasn't too bad. He rubbed at his upper lip and wondered whether he should grow a moustache.

At forty-nine he was in good shape; even now women turned to look at him. He could still have a good time, it was only at work that he didn't get what he wanted. He was fed up with dock labouring. There wasn't enough work. Most of them got no more than two or three days a week, and had to go cap in hand to the Public Assistance for help.

Since the war had ended they kept reducing the wages; it was no wonder the men were bolshy and always threatening to strike. Often they did, but it didn't get them far. Thank heavens he had plenty of energy. He could get out and about and do things after work. He didn't just sit at home like many of those he worked with. Tonight he was off to the New Dock Hotel. It was only a stone's throw from E Block and to Wilf it was like a second home.

On the way out he pecked at Vi's cheek and said, 'Get some more coal for the fire, Seppy, before it goes out.'

The pub was commonly known as the Blood Tub because of the frequent arguments and fights that started inside. At the behest of the licensee, most of these were concluded outside. The combatants often stripped to the waist and fought with their fists on the cinder patch on the opposite corner of the street, while the customers went out with full glasses in their hand to cheer them on.

Sidney was drawing pints of bitter behind the bar when Wilf arrived, his battered straw boater at a jaunty angle and wearing new braces over his shirt.

'A pint of mild for me,' Wilfred called to him. He liked his son-in-law, Sidney; thought of him as a friend and felt closer to him than he did to his own sons.

Sidney took the money from the customer he was serving but before ringing up the till, he swung Wilfred's pint of mild up on the bar in front of him.

'Have this on me, Pa.'

Wilf drank with deep satisfaction as the till pinged noisily and Sidney slapped change on the counter in front of the other customer.

Wilfred knew Sidney hadn't put any money in to pay for his drink, it was the licensee who was standing him this. It happened regularly.

At twenty-eight Sidney was slim and lithe and moved around the bar with graceful ease. He was a good-looking young man with wavy fair hair and a rather shaggy straw-coloured moustache. Wilf saw a lot of himself in Sidney. He believed in enjoying life and his belly laugh often rang out across the bar of the Blood Tub.

Everybody said Sidney was a live wire with just the right personality to work in a bar. Wilf admired his musical ability, he could play the banjo and was trying to teach him, but he wasn't making much progress. Wilf didn't understand how to read music, but he didn't let that stop him. He played the mouth organ with great gusto, he'd taught himself years ago when he was a lad, playing by ear. There were several others in the Blood Tub who could play the mouth organ. It was the most easily affordable instrument.

Wilf could manage a few tunes on the saxophone too, but he wanted to learn to play it really well. He'd bought a second-hand one in a junk shop off Exmouth Street, but he knew of nobody who could teach him. There was a demand for saxophone players. Ballroom dancing was becoming more and more popular and dance bands were being formed to play in church halls on Friday and Saturday nights. It would be an enjoyable way of earning a bit more cash.

Once Sidney had been keen on ballroom dancing, but he could also tap dance and clog dance and on nights in the pub when argument was falling flat, Wilfred would take out his mouth organ and Sidney could be persuaded to dance in the bar.

Sidney had a job he really enjoyed. He was well suited to it. Wilf was envious of that. He hated the docks.

Chapter Six

For Beth, the days of her holiday began to fly. Each one drew her more firmly into her family and their concerns.

She decided to spring-clean, and on the spur of the moment she bought whitewash to freshen up the ceiling and walls in the living room. With her mother ill, Jenny at work, Peggy on the point of giving birth and the youngsters at school, there seemed nobody to help her. When Mrs Clover heard she'd started on the job alone, she offered to send Ken round when he came home that evening.

There was nobody like Ken for roping other people in – Seppy and Ivor were quite keen on the job after he'd had a chat with them, and Jenny left her children with her husband and came round too. Ken brought his younger brother Billy, who was Ivor's age, with him.

Ken's mother offered to look after Colin and Bobby in her flat and Beth told her mother that the best thing for her was to go to bed early.

'I'll be out of the way there,' she agreed.

'I'm afraid we might be noisy, Ken will make it fun rather than hard work. He's that sort.'

They started painting as soon as the evening meal was cleared away, and such was the workforce that they repainted the living room, the back kitchen and the tiny passages and cubicles out at the back. However, the ceilings were so darkened with smoke from the fire that they had to come and put a second coat on the living room the following evening.

Beth scrubbed the stone floors and blackleaded the grate until it shone and felt the whole place had had a face lift. Her mother was delighted with the result.

'Doesn't it look clean? You've worked miracles, Beth. The place is always so crowded with family and neighbours, I found it almost impossible to sweep the floor.'

Beth saw a good deal of her married sisters, they called in at Dock Cottages almost every day although they said they didn't like the place.

Family ties wouldn't let them go. As the days went on, Mam began to look and feel better.

By Wednesday, the housekeeping money was running out and Beth knew there would be no more from Dad until Friday night after he'd been paid.

Over their evening meal of liver and onions, she said, 'Dad, John's postal order hasn't come.' Every month, her brother sent money home to Mam. 'I've got only twopence left. I won't be able to get anything for tea tomorrow.'

'John won't forget. His postal order will be here in the morning.'

'What if it isn't? Could you give me a bit more to tide us over? I need it.'

'Last week was a bad week.'

'There's no bread left for your sandwiches tomorrow.'

'You said you still had twopence left.' Her father was angry. 'Seppy, get yourself down to the bakers with it before they close.'

'What about tomorrow? We'll all go hungry if John's postal order—'

'What have you spent the housekeeping on? You've been extravagant.'

'Dad, you tip up only half your wages to Mam. It isn't enough to put food on the table for all of us.'

'You're here this week, eating your head off. There's no reason why I should feed you now.'

'Wilf!' her mother protested. 'You know Beth more than pays her way. She's bought new boots for our Colin, and socks and—'

'All right. I hand over eight shillings for the rent as well as half my wages, don't I? It's been enough up to now. Your mother's always managed.'

'She hasn't. She's too soft with you. Those of us in work contribute. John and Lottie and me.'

'And so you should. You were fed and clothed out of my wages for years.'

'You spend too much on your own beer and fags. What you hand over has to cover coal and clothes and food—'

'Damn and blast. You can't manage anything. Your mother's always coped.' He flung a florin on the table with bad grace. It fell to the floor and rolled noisily. 'Mind you put some of that homemade brawn from Jones's in my carry-out.'

Beth groped for the coin and found Seppy's hand covering it first.

'I'll go for a loaf.'

'Two loaves,' Beth said.

'And brawn?'

'The shop will be closed now. He'll have to have bread and dripping.'

On Thursday night, her father came home from work with his coat swinging heavily round him, and began to turn his pockets out on the table that Beth had set for their meal.

'Oranges for you kids,' he told Colin and Esther who crowded round excitedly. For once he was in a good mood. He brought out a bottle of brandy. 'For you, Vi. This should get you on your feet again.' He opened it and poured a generous measure into a tumbler for her. 'Gifts from the gods.'

Beth said, 'Stolen property, you mean. You're always knocking things off.'

'The others, not me.'

'Give over, Beth,' her mother murmured.

'It's no good throwing up your arms and going on at me about honesty. If there's stuff going begging, dockers will help themselves. We have to, we can't live on the wages.'

Beth knew that well enough.

'I get my share when I can, I'd be a fool not to. If it's something we can use, I bring it home. It's a perk of the job.'

She began dishing up the pan of scouse she'd made.

'Anyway, if it makes you feel any better, this was an accident. Somebody dropped the case on its corner, it burst open and the oranges were rolling everywhere. No shop will take a broken case, will they?'

'Here's your tea, Dad.'

'You don't have to touch the oranges,' he flared at her. 'I'm sure they'd choke you if you did.'

The family fell on their plates of scouse and as soon as they'd scraped them clean were reaching for the oranges. The delicious fresh tang filled the room, making Beth's mouth water. She reached for the biggest orange and cut it in half, then handed one half to her mother and sank her teeth into the other.

Her father leered at her across the table. 'You see, it's not just money I provide. You've forgotten all the other things I bring home.'

When her holiday came to an end Beth was quite pleased to be going back to her other life. It was nine at night when she returned to the nurses' home. There was an envelope addressed to her in the letter rack. She recognised Andrew's writing and, suddenly nervous, hurried to her room to read it.

'I've missed you,' he wrote. 'It's been a long week without so much as a glimpse of you. Can I meet you when you come off duty at eight tomorrow?'

She felt a rush of pleasure and relief that Andrew seemed to have forgiven her for refusing to see him. She heard other nurses laughing outside in the corridor, and laughed with them, thrilled that she could pick up with Andrew where she'd left off.

All week she'd been longing for a long hot soak in the bath to wash the grime of Dock Cottages away. After that she put on a clean nightdress and a blue satin dressing gown she never took home, and went down to the sitting room to catch up on the news.

Later, settling down to sleep in a bed which was far more comfortable than the couch at home, her mind was on Andrew. She thought him gentle, modest and unassuming; he had a slight stutter which was more marked when he was nervous.

She rarely saw him in the hospital except by prior arrangement. The nurses ate in their own dining room and Matron did not approve of them socialising during working hours. Beth needed a good reason to visit his laboratory, but the next morning she happened to meet him in the corridor when she was going for her coffee break. She felt quite fluttery but he was all smiles, delighted to see her.

'How was your holiday?'

'Fine. I did what I'd intended.' She'd told him she was worried about her mother. She brought him up to date quickly, self-conscious about being seen talking to him here. There could be ward sisters about.

'You don't look . . .' His mild dark eyes were studying her. 'Well, as though you've had a holiday.'

'A change is as good as a rest.' She laughed nervously. 'I worked quite hard.'

'I've been thinking . . .' He smiled down at her. 'Is this a good time to ask you to come and meet my parents? My mother has suggested I bring you home to supper.'

Beth's heart leapt and tumbled. This was wonderfully unexpected.

'When is your evening off this week?'

'Friday night.' Staff were passing in both directions. They stepped back and she felt his fingers brush her arm, it made her shiver.

'Can I tell Mother you'll come?'

She nodded. 'I'd love to, thank you.' This was a huge step forward; an important one. Confirmation that Andrew loved her and wanted to make their relationship permanent.

'I'll come back tonight, at eight o'clock, shall I? So we can have a long talk.'

Her head whirled while she drank her coffee. She assured people who asked that she'd had a good holiday even though it had been filled with hard work and anxiety about so many things. Suddenly everything seemed so much brighter.

She went back to work on Ward 3, the women's surgical ward, beaming at everybody, feeling full of love for Andrew. For the rest of the week she felt little shivers, half nerves and half excitement, every time she thought of meeting his parents.

At four thirty on Friday afternoon, she went down to the nurses' dining room where the second serving of afternoon tea had just begun. By then, she'd worked herself up into such a state she couldn't eat. It was very rare for anybody who'd been brought up in Dock Cottages to miss a meal. She had a quick cup of tea and then ran over to the nurses' home to have a bath.

She felt refreshed as she changed into her best green dress. Andrew had seen it many times before and she wished she had another. She combed out her hair. Should she leave it loose about her shoulders or put it up in a French pleat? She decided on the French pleat.

Andrew, too, had worked all day. He'd arranged to meet Beth at the bus stop at five fifteen, which allowed her time to get herself ready. It was almost dark and starting to rain; there was quite a long line of people waiting for the bus. He stepped out of the shadows and kissed her cheek.

'You smell lovely,' he told her, taking her hand in his and pushing them together into his greatcoat pocket. Beth shivered.

'Are you cold?'

'No, just a bit nervous. It's a big thing, meeting your parents . . .' And being taken to his home. She'd wondered about it often enough, tried to imagine what it was like. Nothing like Dock Cottages, she was sure.

'No need to be. They've been at me for years, telling me it's time I got married and settled down.' He still lived at home although he was over thirty. 'Always asking their friends with daughters of the right age round to meet me. It was a relief to tell them I'd found exactly the girl I was looking for without their help.'

Beth was brimming with happiness. The bus came, and though there were many passengers they got a seat together. The window was covered with moisture.

He squeezed her hand. 'I was never any good with girls, until I met you.'

Andrew had said his father was a doctor in general practice and that he didn't get on too well with his parents. It had taken him a long time to tell her that he felt he'd been a disappointment to them. His father had told him that with a little more effort on his part, he could have been a doctor too.

'I'm afraid they expected more of me than I've been able to achieve.'

To Beth, they sounded fearsome. She was afraid they'd guess her origins. They certainly wouldn't approve of her if they knew where she came from.

'They'll love you as much as . . .' He looked at her and smiled, then with a little rush added, 'They'll love you as much as I do. There, I've said it. I do love you, Beth.'

She felt a warmth spreading through her and couldn't stop smiling. She murmured her response. This was what she'd been hoping for. He did love her!

'You understand all my worries and you never put me down.'

'Why should I put you down? I think to work in the lab as you do, well, it's an interesting career, isn't it? About on a par with being a nurse.'

'My mother was a . . . was a nurse.'

Beth's heart lurched. 'Where did she train?'

'The same place as you. Liverpool Royal. Long before your time, of course.'

But she would have known the two-tier system as it used to exist. No doubt she'd have been one of the lady pupils. Everybody was saying that these days social divisions were disappearing but to Beth it didn't seem so; she hoped Mrs Langford wouldn't ask if she'd been a lady pupil.

Andrew turned to her, his eyes met hers. 'Beth, will you . . . will you marry me?'

What she'd longed for had come so easily, so quickly. She felt a hot flush run up her cheeks. 'Oh yes. Yes, I'd like that.'

His hand tightened round hers, he still held it in his pocket, while a tide of blissful happiness ran through Beth. Everything she'd always wanted seemed suddenly possible.

Andrew was happy too, she could see it in his smile.

'Come on,' he said, hurriedly pulling her to her feet. 'We get off here.'

Thrilled and overjoyed, Beth walked beside him down a pleasant tree-lined road. The houses seemed big and were set in their own gardens. Lights beamed out of hall windows and showed round the chinks of thick curtains.

Andrew whispered, 'Shall we tell my mother and father? That you've agreed to marry me?'

Beth nodded, almost too full to speak. 'Why not?' This would be a tonic for her own mother. She was marrying out of Dock Cottages to somewhere like this. It was what Mam wanted for her, above everything else.

'They'll be pleased.' He was leading her through the front gate of a detached house and putting his key in the front door. She felt warmth close round her as she was drawn inside. His mother came fussing up the hall to greet them, elegantly dressed in grey with faultlessly groomed hair. Beth felt a stirring of compassion for her own mother, she couldn't bear to compare them.

'This is Beth,' Andrew was saying and she heard pride in his voice. Her hand was grasped and shaken.

His father had prominent eyes and a disdainful mouth. His forceful manner soon had them organised in front of a warm fire in the sitting room, with glasses of sherry to sip.

Dr and Mrs Langford seemed pleasant people, and there was no mistaking their pleasure that Andrew had made up his mind to marry and settle down. They were very welcoming.

'I understand from Andrew that you're a local girl.'

'Yes.' Beth smiled. She'd foreseen that questions like this would have to be answered. 'Meols,' she said. 'My family run a market garden and nursery there.'

She was skipping a generation. It was what she usually did when anybody at the hospital asked her that question.

'Not that big place just off Birkenhead Road?' Dr Langford's razor eyes met hers.

'The Knebworth Nurseries, yes.' Beth was disconcerted. Nobody at the hospital had ever heard of the place.

Mrs Langford turned to her husband. 'Isn't that where you stop to get cut flowers?' Her eyes went to an impressive vase of yellow daffodils on a side table. Their sharp, crisp scent filled the room.

'Yes, I know it well. I bought some shrubs from there last spring. Forsythia. I put them in near our front gate. They've done very well.'

Beth's heart sank. They were both looking at her, expecting her to tell them more about herself.

'My aunts look after the flowers.' She knew she was speaking too quickly. 'My grandfather was so fond of flowers that he gave all his daughters flower names. Lily and Iris are my aunts, my mother's name is Violet. I have an uncle who deals with the market gardening side, the cabbages and lettuce and that.'

Before the words were out of her mouth, she realised she'd passed from fiction to truth and felt herself blushing. She was afraid they might know the nursery too well.

'They're patients of mine.' Dr Langford was smiling at her. 'Fancy that!'

Beth froze. If he mentioned to her aunts that he knew her, they'd soon set him right about where her side of the family lived.

'They've called me out to see the little girl several times recently.'

Beth panicked. 'Rose?'

'Yes, Rickerby, Rose Rickerby.'

'My mother's name was Rickerby before she married.' What a silly thing to say, it would have to be. What was she getting herself into? Beth felt her head reel. She could no longer think clearly.

'There are three little girls. I think they have flower names too.'

'Marigold and Jonquil. It's a sort of family tradition.'

'Yes, well, what a small world.'

Beth knew she was in too deep now. Rose was a frail child, it would only be a matter of time before she was ill again, and they'd call Dr Langford out to see her. Then the fact that she'd lied would be only too obvious to him. How could she get out of this now?

His piercing eyes were on her again. 'And what does your father look after, Beth?' What she dreaded most were questions about her father's work, she knew she'd implied he worked in the nursery too.

She swallowed hard. 'He works on the docks – Mersey Docks and Harbour Board.'

She'd already said much the same to Andrew and couldn't change her story now. She knew she was giving the impression he had a job of some status and wasn't just a labourer who wheeled bales and crates about the docks on a hand truck, hired for the day to load and unload the ships.

'You must bring them to meet us,' Andrew's mother said as she led them to the dining room.

Beth looked round at the table set with a starched white cloth, sparkling silver and cut glass, and felt overwhelmed. This was the way she used to set the table when she was a housemaid in service. At Knebworth Nursery they didn't sit down to a table anything like this. She shook out a table napkin that had been fashioned into the water lily shape. She'd learned to fold them herself.

She couldn't imagine her parents here, and she knew her mother would be horrified if she thought she had to return hospitality to this standard.

Beth felt even worse when a housemaid appeared to serve the meal. She wondered if they had help with the cooking too. All the same, she realised Andrew's family had gone to a lot of trouble to entertain her.

Later, she couldn't have said what she'd eaten, there were several courses but her appetite had vanished, it was for once an effort to swallow the food. The dainty coffee cups of strong black coffee she'd learned to make but never tasted were no easier to manage.

Andrew was attentive and very kind but Beth felt she'd let him down. She found the rest of the evening difficult to get through. At last, she heard the grandfather clock in the hall strike ten o'clock and felt she could take her leave.

'Andrew can run you home in my car,' Dr Langford said. 'It's not far, after all. Only down the road.'

She had to say, 'I need to go back to the nurses' home,' knowing it must seem odd to them since she'd mentioned she had a day off tomorrow.

'No matter, we can't let you find your way back by bus at this time of night.'

'It's very kind of you.' Beth did her best to sound grateful. 'Thank you, the dinner was lovely and I've very much enjoyed meeting you and seeing where Andrew lives.'

But what she most wanted now was to get away from them all, even Andrew. She needed to think about the lies she'd told and the disastrous effect they could have. At any other time she'd have been thrilled with a car ride. She couldn't remember when she'd last had one.

'Why are you going all the way back to the hospital?' Andrew asked as they set off. 'Wouldn't it be more convenient to go straight home?'

Of course it would have been if her home really was in Meols. The whole point had been to avoid Andrew escorting her back to Dock Cottages.

'I should have packed my case and brought it with me,' she said. But it upset her more to have him question her reasons. He took his eyes off the road for a moment to smile at her.

'Can we meet tomorrow? It's Saturday and I don't have to go to work either.'

She made her mother's illness an excuse to say no.

'Just for an hour or so,' he tried to persuade. 'I could take you to choose the ring.'

'I feel terrible saying this, Andrew, but I'd like to leave things as they are for the moment. It's all happening so quickly. I need to think.'

'You're not changing your mind?' There was alarm in his voice.

To be honest, she didn't know what she wanted other than to free herself from this web of lies. She'd said too much already, she felt she'd only dig herself into a deeper hole if she said more now. She could feel him drawing back from her.

'With your two maiden aunts there, surely they can give your mother all the help she needs?'

Beth shook her head in misery. He pulled up in front of the nurses' home and said sadly, 'I feel as though you've suddenly erected a wall round yourself and I can't get through.'

'I'm sorry.' She wanted to get out and run for the privacy of her own room, but Andrew was pulling her into his arms and kissing her. She knew she wasn't responding as she usually did. The thrill she normally felt was missing. She pulled away, but Andrew tried to hold on to her.

'What's happened? You've changed since we set out tonight.' She could see he was puzzled and upset. 'I know my father can be heavy-going but Mother isn't that bad. Didn't you like them?'

She stifled a sob and said with her hand on the door handle, 'It's not them, Andrew, it's me. Forgive me.'

Beth rushed to her room, unable to take any more of his company, but found no comfort when she reached it. What a fool she'd been! She should have realised it was impossible to hide such things from the man she meant to marry. And it wasn't just to Andrew she'd told lies, it was to his parents too. She was afraid she'd ruined everything and she'd lose the man she loved.

She didn't sleep well, she tossed and turned for half the night, dozing intermittently. She told herself she could sleep in in the morning, it wouldn't matter.

She was wide awake when the other staff were getting up to go on duty but had drifted off again when the maid brought her breakfast tray. She usually enjoyed this luxury on her days off. Then after another leisurely doze, she got dressed and walked up to Dock Cottages.

She knew she should feel rested and ready to help where she could at home, but her mind was still reeling. She'd been telling herself that what she wanted most in life was to marry Andrew, but just when it was within reach, she'd ruined everything. Better if she'd told him the truth from the beginning. If he didn't think she was good enough for him, well, so be it.

As she walked down Stanley Road towards E Block, she was afraid the truth was that she belonged here. She couldn't cut herself off.

Jenny had arrived before her and was sweeping up. Colin and Noreen were rolling together on the hearth rug.

She said, 'Hello, Mam, how are you?'

'Feeling better, love. Our Jenny's brought us a cake.'

'That was kind.' Beth looked at the light fruitcake still in its wrappings on the table; it was what they called cut-and-come-again cake, a big one. Jenny understood what they needed.

'We were wondering what had happened to you.'

'I slept in, had a leisurely start this morning,' Beth told her.

'Mam's looking better, isn't she?' Jenny put the kettle on to make tea. It was only just poured when Peggy arrived with two more toddlers.

Jenny patted her stomach. 'How much longer to wait?'

Peggy looked jiggered after climbing four flights of stairs and almost fell on a chair.

'Two weeks today, if I go my time.'

She looked as though she already had. Her walk was reduced to a waddle. Another cup of tea was poured for her.

Jenny bit into a piece of her own cake and said to Beth, 'Come on then, didn't your Andrew take you home to meet his parents last night? What were they like? Did you have a good time?'

Beth knew her whole family were interested in Andrew, they were always asking for news of him, but she was too full of misery to do more than nod.

'Is he any nearer asking you to marry him?'

'He did last night,' she choked.

There were whoops of delight from her sisters. Mam's face lit up. 'That's wonderful news.'

'You said yes of course?'

'I did, but . . . His home, you should have seen it.'

'Posh?'

'You'd think so, Peg. A bit like the Wisharts' house, though I think theirs was larger. They see it as just a normal comfortable house.'

'The sort of house Andrew would expect to have when he got married?'

'Eventually, yes. I expect we'd start in something smaller.'

'Isn't that what you want?'

'It's what I thought I wanted.'

'Well then?'

69

'I've told him and his family such lies, Mam. I feel awful about it. They asked where my home was and I told them Knebworth Nursery.'

'Well, it was my home. You're not far wrong there.'

'Mam! Andrew's father is not only a customer but he's Rose's doctor. He'll probably mention me next time he's called to see her. He knows Uncle Jim quite well. He'll find out I've told lies. What will they think of me?'

'He'll understand.'

'I doubt it. Will they trust me after this? Will Andrew? You have to be able to trust the person you marry.'

Beth watched her mother's face crumple.

'It's my fault. Haven't I been on at you? I'm ashamed of having to tell people where we live.'

'We all are,' Beth agreed. 'But I shouldn't have made a secret of it.'

'You can't give him up because you've told him a white lie. You can't, Beth. There's no sense in that. I'd be so disappointed.'

'We all would.' Jenny cut herself another slice of cake.

'If you can't get away from here, none of us can,' Peggy puffed.

'I love him,' Beth wailed.

'Beth,' her mother said, 'I'm sorry. I shouldn't have suggested—'

'We all said say nothing about Dock Cottages,' Jenny chipped in.

Beth sighed. 'It's my own fault, I didn't have to take your advice, did I?'

'Usually you don't,' Jenny told her.

'I don't talk about Dock Cottages at the hospital,' Beth said sadly. 'Sometimes Sister makes comments when a patient is being admitted, like, "You see where this one comes from, make sure she hasn't got head lice or body lice." Sometimes I worry that someone I know will come in. I didn't want to tell Andrew, not at first, but I should have done. Long ago. I could feel it like a stone between us, something I had to confess but couldn't, and it was stopping me going out with him. I was a fool to hide it.'

Mam put her teacup down on the floor. 'How big a family does he come from?'

'Just Andrew and one sister. She's already married; happily, I believe. They think he should marry too.'

'There you are then.'

Beth bit her lip. 'Would he see it as a white lie? Would his father?'

'Only two children,' her mother ruminated from the couch. Her cheeks were flushed but had a bluish tinge. 'That proves it. The doctors all manage to limit their own families but they won't tell the rest of us how to do it.'

'That's right. Andrew would be a wonderful husband,' Jenny said. 'Not only will you get a posh house but he won't give you a baby every year.'

Peggy gave a hollow sigh. 'I wish this was over. I feel I can't stand another day of feeling like a whale.'

'Just make sure, Peg, that you aren't in the same condition next year.'

'I will,' she said with feeling. 'I will.'

Chapter Seven

Beth decided there was no point in worrying about the lies she'd told. The only sensible thing to do now was to tell Andrew the truth as soon as possible and try to explain. At least then she'd know where she stood. She'd always known she'd have to tell him the truth before they were married.

She felt calmer once she'd made up her mind to do it. She loved him, he was a kind and considerate person; she hoped he'd forgive this lapse. She wanted to think he would.

She'd refused to meet him although it was a Saturday and he'd be off work this afternoon, and the problem was she didn't know when her next day off would be. Sister worked out the off-duty rota on Sundays. After lunch, while the mood was still on her, Beth walked down to the post office and telephoned him at home. She was eager now to get her confession over.

'Meet you in Birkenhead? Of course, what time?'

'Two o'clock? Can you make that?'

'I told Dad I'd have a round of golf with him this afternoon. Can we make it later?'

'Of course. Four o'clock then, or five?'

'Better make it five. I hear there's a good play on at the Gaiety, we could go there tonight.'

'I want to talk, Andrew.'

'Right. I'll come on the train.'

'I'll meet you at Hamilton Square then.' Beth felt better now the time and place was set. She was committed to it.

It was a dark overcast day and by twenty to five when Beth caught the bus into town, it looked as though the rain had set in for the night. As she waited in the station ticket hall, she felt shivery as much from nerves as from cold. So much depended on how Andrew reacted. He might feel strongly about people who told lies and want no more to do with her.

A lift came up from the underground and disgorged a crowd of passengers. She caught sight of Andrew in the midst of them, looking rather staid in his mackintosh with a furled umbrella on his arm. His face broke into a radiant smile the moment he saw her and he came striding over to peck her cheek.

'Lovely to see you. I'm glad you changed your mind about tonight.'

Beth took his arm as they went to the entrance. The rain was coming down in sheets. Andrew put up his umbrella. 'Where shall we go?'

Beth had envisaged making her confession while they walked in Hamilton Square gardens. It was hardly possible in this downpour.

'A cup of tea? Five o'clock is rather a difficult time.'

'Good idea,' he said. 'We'll have to walk down to Woodside. There's that little cafe near the ferry or the refreshment room in the railway station.'

They could see that the cafe was closed as they hurried down. Andrew swept her straight into the mainline station. There were not many people in the refreshment room. It was warm and moist and the tea urn hissed comfortingly.

'Do you want to take your coat off?' He carefully shook the raindrops off it and hung it on the bentwood stand, then did the same with his mackintosh. Beth watched, her throat tight with tension.

'A cake too?' There was little left under the glass domes on the counter, and what there was looked dry.

'Better not, we'll need something more substantial soon.'

His eyes were playing with hers. 'What did you want to tell me?'

The tea was too hot to drink. It burned her tongue. 'I know you think I was acting strangely last night, not wanting to choose the engagement ring, putting it off.' She'd rehearsed that much.

'You wanted to think about what you were committing yourself to . . .'

'No, I need to explain a few things.'

'Yes?'

Beth took a deep breath, she'd known she wouldn't find this easy. 'Have you heard of Dock Cottages?'

'Yes, I've seen them from the bus. Coming to work, I catch one that goes past St James's Church.'

Of course he did, what was she thinking about. 'I was brought up there. That's where my family lives.'

'I thought you said Meols?'

She could see from his face he didn't understand and launched into a long and halting explanation. 'I come from a poor family.'

'Well . . . we aren't rich.'

'You are by our standards.'

'Is that all?' He was trying to control the smile hovering on his lips. 'You worried me, Beth. When you had a whole week off and wouldn't come out with me. It made me think. I had to know where we stood.'

'You'd have wanted to see me home. You always do. You'd have seen where I came from.'

'I don't care where you come from. Why should I? You agreed to marry me last night and afterwards it seemed you'd changed your mind. I was afraid you had.'

'No, no . . . It was just . . . I felt I was getting caught up in a web of lies. I had to put you straight before we went any further.'

'Thank goodness that's all it was.'

'What about your parents? I told them too. Your father knows Uncle Jim, he's one of his patients.'

'He'll think he misunderstood. About where you lived, I mean. Nothing to worry about. Come on, let's walk up to the Woodside Hotel and have a drink and something to eat. We've got something to celebrate now.'

Beth felt she'd had a wonderful evening. Andrew was in high spirits. After a meal at the Woodside Hotel, he took her to see a play at the Gaiety Theatre. She felt relief as well as happiness; she hadn't expected to be forgiven so easily and thought herself very fortunate that her lies seemed to have brought them closer rather than driven them apart.

'I could forgive you anything,' he'd said when he took her back to the nurses' home. 'I love you, Beth. I want us to get the ring next week. That makes it official, doesn't it? Then we can start thinking about looking for a house and setting the date.'

Beth was spellbound. This was what she'd always wanted. It had been her dream.

'Just to think of it . . .' Her wedding and her very own home. She was tingling all over, with anticipation and love. It would be a whole house with a garden just for the two of them. Andrew would make a wonderful husband. She was so proud of him, possessive even. 'In the summer, do you think? July perhaps or August?'

'Wonderful! No point in putting it off. Not when we've made up our minds. Shall we say July?'

Beth nodded, feeling her cup was brimming over. How could she have doubted him for one minute?

'You must come and meet my family,' she told him. Of course he must, now they were about to be married. 'They keep asking about you.'

75

'I hope they'll like me.'

'I've already told them you're wonderful.' She smiled. 'How about afternoon tea one Sunday? I can't ask you for dinner, I'm afraid.'

'That'll be fine. After all, you don't really live there.'

'I'll be due for my next Sunday afternoon off two weeks tomorrow.'

'I'll look forward to it. What about the ring? When can we buy that?'

'I don't know yet.'

Her off-duty was still a day off every week, but it depended largely on Sister's whim as to what day it would be. Almost certainly it would be a weekday when Andrew would be working.

'I've had today off, and Sister usually takes Saturdays herself. I'll have to ask for another, because I work opposite her.'

'Let me know which day you're given and I'll ask for an afternoon off.'

'You'll be able to do that?'

Mostly Andrew worked nine to five and had Saturday afternoon and Sunday off, but the lab staff had to take turns to cover the weekend.

'I think I might.'

Beth felt a little frisson of pleasure.

The off-duty list for the week was done the next morning. Beth had been given a day off on Thursday.

'Early closing day in Birkenhead,' she said to Andrew.

'We'll go to Liverpool then. Might as well make a celebration of it. Have a meal out and go to a show. Yes?'

It sounded wonderful to Beth. She felt she was living in a fizz of excitement. Andrew seemed in the same state. He asked, 'What sort of a ring would you like?'

'Any sort, I've never owned a ring. I'd like what you choose for me, I'm sure.'

'Oh no! You might not. I want you to choose it.'

Beth, always very conscious of money, said awkwardly, 'I don't want to choose one that costs more than you want to pay.'

He smiled. 'I want you to have the best. You're going to wear it, so you must be there when we buy it.'

When on Tuesday Beth had a few hours off duty in the morning she went into town and gazed in the windows of Pyke's the jewellers. Diamonds, sapphires, emeralds and rubies glittered back at her. She couldn't make up her mind which she liked best. He planned on giving her a real stone, she knew that. Jenny had a ring, but it wasn't a real diamond. Nobody in her family had ever owned a precious stone.

She couldn't stop thinking about Andrew and the huge change she'd be making in her life when she married him. She'd have to resign from her job. It was one of the rules, married women couldn't be nurses. In a way she'd be sorry, but she'd have many other exciting things with which to occupy herself.

On Thursday, Beth dressed herself in her best green hat and coat and at half past one went to meet Andrew outside the hospital. They caught the underground train to James Street Station on the Liverpool side of the river.

'The best jewellers are near there,' Andrew told her. He took her to Boodle and Dunthorne's which she'd heard was the most expensive jewellers in the city. They stood looking at the rings in the window for a time. It was Andrew who decided that diamonds would be the wisest choice.

'Mother says they go with clothes of any colour.'

He left her there for a few moments while he went in to settle the price range. When he came out to fetch her, he'd already picked out a solitaire in which Beth could see every colour in the rainbow. It felt heavy on her finger.

'I like this one,' he said, 'but do say if you'd rather have one with three stones.'

A black velvet tray of rings had been brought to the counter. An elegantly dressed assistant in a black jacket and high winged collar removed the solitaire and slid a three stone ring on her finger.

'Which do you like?' Andrew murmured beside her.

'I like the solitaire.' The price tag hadn't been removed, it took her breath away. 'I love it. It's magnificent.'

They walked to the Playhouse and booked seats for that evening, and then because it began to rain and it was too early to have a meal, he took her to the museum for an hour or so. Beth hadn't been before; there was plenty to interest her but she couldn't concentrate. Andrew held her hand and kept twisting the ring on her finger. They were both in a ferment, laughing at everything and nothing.

He asked, 'What sort of a wedding do you want?'

'Quiet, no fuss.'

'That suits me down to the ground. The reception?'

Beth felt rooted to the spot. Mam had put on a big help-yourself spread for both Peggy and Jenny. Mrs Clover had helped with the baking and Dad had bought firkins of beer. The whole lobby had joined

77

in and most of the male guests had gone down to the pub afterwards. For Andrew's family, it wouldn't be right.

She said, 'It wouldn't be possible to have it at my home.'

'No, not with your mother being ill. We could go to a hotel – unless my mother wants to do it.'

Beth imagined her family in Andrew's home and quailed. Her father there? And Peggy's husband?

Beth often went home when she had a few hours off duty and the very next morning she went to show Mam her ring.

'It's absolutely beautiful,' Mam breathed, holding on to her wrist and moving her hand so that the diamond caught the light and flashed with fiery colours.

Seppy propped the broom he was wielding against the table and came to stare at it.

'This means you're engaged then?'

'Yes,' Beth told him. 'Isn't it wonderful?'

'I don't know. We don't know this Andrew. When are we going to meet him?'

'We would like to.' Mam smiled up at her from the couch. 'We must now. Once he becomes your husband, he's part of the family.'

'Of course. I've invited him to tea to meet you all. On a Sunday, the next time I have the afternoon off. I hope that's all right.'

'That'll be lovely. But you'll have to get the cake.'

'I'll see to all that, don't worry.'

Beth felt excited all day. When she went off duty at eight o'clock she showed off her new ring to all the nurses in the sitting room. Some of them knew Andrew and spoke highly of him, saying he was quite a catch.

At nine o'clock, she wished she'd called round at Jenny's house and shown her the ring. She lived only a few minutes' walk away so she decided to go now. She was too restless to settle to her book.

As soon as Beth turned into Newling Street, she could see light shining through the front bedroom curtains of Jenny's house and was afraid she was going to bed. She knocked on the front door and a moment later heard footsteps running downstairs. Jenny's honey-blonde head came round the door.

'Beth!' The door opened wider. 'Come in.'

'I'm not too late? You're not on the way to bed?'

'No, Tom went early, his leg's bothering him.'

Beth followed her sister to the kitchen and watched her fill the kettle. She expected Jenny to ask about the ring; she'd told her Andrew was taking her to buy it.

She asked, 'Are you all right?'

Jenny turned round under the light and for the first time Beth saw traces of tears on her cheeks. 'You're not.' Beth put an arm round her shoulders. 'What is it? Not Tom?'

Jenny shook her head. 'His leg's playing up and he's a bit depressed as well. We've another little blessing on the way, Beth.' She jerked free of her arms and too quickly began getting teacups from the cupboard.

'You're having another baby?'

'Oh, I know you're going to say it's only the second and we always intended to have two so what's the problem.' She mopped at her eyes with a tea towel.

Beth hated to see her sister like this, Jenny normally had a sunny temperament. 'It's coming at the wrong time?'

'That's about it.' Jenny sighed. 'The rent here is a good bit more than it was at Morpeth Buildings and we wanted to get on our feet first. I love my job and Noreen will be starting school in September. Only last month, Mr Lee said my embroidery was top notch and he'd be glad to have me back full-time once Noreen was in school. A year or so with both of us working – that would make such a difference.'

Beth could feel Jenny's anguish, and because she'd come to share her own joy and good fortune, it made it seem worse.

Jenny said fiercely, 'I suppose you think that compared with our Peg I haven't much to worry about.'

'You haven't.'

'Me and Tom, well, we wanted just two, so we could bring them up properly. We want to have a decent house, dress them well and be able to enjoy things.'

'You will, Jenny.'

The tea was in the cups, Jenny was leading the way to their living room.

'What about Tom's tea?'

'Oh! This has knocked me for six, I hardly know what I'm doing. I won't be a minute.' She ran upstairs.

Beth took the two remaining cups into the living room and poked up the dying fire. She'd never seen Jenny so upset. It wasn't as though she was asking for the earth, all she wanted was the chance to work and save for a better life. Instead, she'd be looking after another baby.

Her sister came back and sank down on a stool. 'I know Peggy thinks I'm lucky to have gone this long without . . .'

'When is it due?'

'October.'

'You'll love it once it's born.'

'Probably.'

'Mam always does, and so does Peggy.'

'If only we could have put it off for a couple more years. We thought we could, Tom being in the army and that; he thought he knew how to stop them coming, he said the men were always talking about it. He's been getting some things from the barber's shop in Cleveland Street, but they're not that reliable. This is a right setback for us.'

Beth felt full of sympathy for Jenny.

'Tom says we have to accept it now, and I'm coming round to it, but I don't want to start a third right off.' There was desperation in her voice. 'You've got to help us, Beth. There's nobody else I can turn to. I mean, you're a nurse. Don't you know how to stop babies coming?'

Beth was shocked. 'No, nobody talks about such things. They don't believe it's a good thing for nurses to know.'

'Tom thinks there's something better. Than what we've used, I mean. Something for women. Couldn't you find out what it is and where I can get it? I mean the doctors in the hospital must know.'

'Jenny, you know more about it than I do. I can't believe . . . Mam asked me the same thing not so long ago. In almost the same words.'

For years it seemed nobody dared mention such a possibility as interfering with nature. Beth had heard it whispered that if the masses got to know, it would lead to decadence and evil, and weaken the human race. There would be more disease and more prostitution. And now Mam and Jenny had both mentioned it, expecting her to know all about it.

'Mam asked?' Jenny was staring at her. She had mauve shadows under her blue eyes; Beth thought she'd never seen her look so pretty.

She gave a forced laugh. 'Do you remember years ago when we were growing up, we wondered where babies came from? You said you thought God sent them, that He was asked to do so in the marriage service.'

'I wish we could ask Him to send this one somewhere else! What a family we are for having babies.' Her smile was sardonic. 'But you'll be all right with Andrew.'

It was only then that Beth put out her hand to show Jenny her new ring.

When Beth was taking her leave, Jenny said, 'You will try and find out for me, Beth?'

She gave her a quick hug. 'You know I'll do my best.'

Beth walked back to the hospital feeling desperately sorry for Jenny. She'd driven home to her how badly her family needed to know how to limit the number of children they had. There was Peggy, whose family was burgeoning out of control, Jenny and Tom who had hoped for a better life only to have their plans swept aside with another baby on the way, and Mam, who had to avoid another pregnancy to protect her health, to save her very life.

Beth could feel anger burning in her throat. She knew it wasn't just her family, there were many others in Dock Cottages in exactly the same position, equally in need. How could it be so very wrong? Surely the whole population would be healthier and happier if knowledge of birth control was available for those wanting it? The babies who were born would be loved and wanted. Their parents would be able to afford to feed and clothe them adequately. Yet the churches preached unanimously against family planning and the medical profession jealously kept this knowledge to themselves. Denying it even to Mam and those like her was criminal.

Why should it be such a big secret? Beth felt a growing curiosity and now she'd agreed to marry Andrew she'd soon need to know these things for herself.

Andrew had never mentioned the subject but she felt he must know. If he didn't, he could easily find out, his father was a doctor. Mam believed all doctors knew how to manage these things for themselves even if they weren't prepared to divulge the secret to their patients. No doubt he'd be happy to enlighten his son.

She didn't know what Andrew's feelings were about having a family. They'd never talked about it but surely they should? She sensed he didn't approve of large families like hers, but soon he was going to want what Jenny said all men wanted. She made up her mind to broach the subject when next she saw him. He'd agreed to meet her at eight o'clock the following night.

It was already dark when she was coming off duty. Beth didn't usually bother to change out of her uniform if she was running up to Jenny's house or even going to Dock Cottages for an hour. She would just remove her apron and white cap and put on her gaberdine raincoat. But Andrew had let her know that he preferred her to change into her own clothes. So she ran across to the home and changed as quickly as possible. She recognised the tall figure wearing a bowler hat and light rubberised raincoat waiting under the street lamps at the gates.

'Hello, Beth.' He bent to kiss her cheek. 'What would you like to do?'

There was little they could do. Beth had to be back indoors before ten thirty. Everywhere was wet though the rain was no more than a light drizzle. He took off his chamois gloves, tucked her arm through his and clasped her hand. She could feel his fingers twisting her ring.

They walked up to a small cafe near Park Station, where they sat for more than an hour over cups of tea and sandwiches of potted meat.

Beth couldn't say what they talked about, her mind was on Jenny's problem. She'd do anything to help her family but was nervous of raising the subject with Andrew, and knew she must choose the right moment. It was the forbidden subject, especially for unmarried girls; very few wanted to talk about it. The inference was that girls who were interested in such things were not quite nice. They were said to be rather fast. She didn't want Andrew to think that about her.

He was talking earnestly about the sort of house he had in mind. His father advised buying one, but his mother had seen a very nice house to rent that she thought would suit them for the first year or two.

'It's in West Kirby, but a reasonable walk from home. It has a nice garden and three bedrooms. Everything we'd need.' His face was only a yard away from hers across the blue gingham cloth.

'Everything we'd need for a family?' Beth asked. 'How do you feel about having children? Is that what you want?'

He was evasive. 'We'll want them if they come.'

Beth didn't doubt they'd come, they had for her sisters. 'Do you want to start a family straight away?'

'Well, we'll have to see if it happens.' His mild brown eyes wouldn't meet hers. 'Is it time we went?' He got to his feet.

Outside, with the darkness to cover her blushes, Beth felt she had to carry on. She had to know.

'That's exactly what my family have done, they've accepted the babies as they came. They've done nothing about it, just waited to see what happened.'

'You don't want a family then?' He was stepping out briskly, Beth found it hard to keep up. 'You've been brought up in such a big family, you don't like the idea of having children?'

'It's not that. I would like a baby of my own, but not one every year.'

'I don't suppose we could achieve a baby every year.' He was smiling, making a joke of it.

That riled Beth, she pulled him to a standstill. 'Andrew, in this day and age, there's such a thing as birth control. With a little forethought we can have what we want.'

He looked taken aback. 'I don't know anything about that.'

'Don't you?' According to Jenny most men took a great interest in the matter.

'What about you? Do you know?' He was staring down at her.

'No, but your father must. Don't you feel you could ask him?'

'Don't be disgusting,' he said. 'No! It's not something an unmarried girl like you should concern yourself with.'

Beth felt shaken and disappointed in Andrew for the first time. She couldn't believe he didn't want to talk about having a family when they were thinking of being married. And, worse, family planning embarrassed him. It made him seem something of a namby-pamby. It told her, too, that she might find herself with a big family like Peggy's because she wouldn't be able to rely on him to prevent it.

After more than two years, she thought she knew him well but now it seemed she didn't. She'd have to find out how to limit her family herself, and take responsibility for doing it. It was no longer just a question of helping her family, she would need to know herself very soon.

When Sister Jones was off duty, Beth was in charge and used the ward office. She saw a lot of Dr McCormick the house surgeon, who was about the ward every day. He often came in the office to read files, seek information about patients or add to their notes on the edge of the desk. Occasionally, he came just for a chat. He was young and Irish, not overly friendly but approachable.

He came today when Beth had just finished serving dinners, and the scent of fish and stewed prunes was still heavy in the air. He closed the door to shut out the clatter of plates being collected and sat on the second chair. The light glinted on his gold-rimmed spectacles as he spoke earnestly about one of the patients and her treatment. Beth knew that for once she had privacy and steeled herself to ask him about birth control. In the end, she had to come straight out with it.

'I need to know more about family planning,' she said, letting it all come out in a rush. 'Would you explain it to me? What's available and where to get it, I mean, and how it works.'

Dr McCormick's pale eyes were staring at her in surprise. He seemed to be seeing her in quite a different light.

Beth pushed on. 'I'm one of ten children, my mother has cardiac failure and is worried about having another baby.'

It sounded too dramatically awful to be true. As though she was trying to give him a reason for wanting to know. She was afraid he, too, would think her fast. Single girls must not have information of that sort, even if they did say it was to help their sick mothers. It would take away their innocence. To want to know such things was a sin. Different perhaps for a married person, except nurses were expected to give in their notice before they walked to the altar.

'I'm getting married in the summer,' she added hurriedly. 'I need to know . . .'

'I don't believe you do. It's not nice, and anyway, it can do you a lot of harm.'

'What sort of harm?' she gasped.

'I've heard it causes mental illness, and also a terrible degenerative disease of the sex organs. You might never bear a normal child afterwards. It wouldn't be safe to use anything.'

'Marie Stopes says—'

'A dreadful woman! Such filth. You mustn't fill your mind with what she writes. It's against all the teachings of the church. Much better if you leave things to nature.' He got up and went out without another word.

Beth was deflated and shocked at his response. His reaction was much the same as Andrew's, but he was more positively against it. She'd been a fool, she should have known he was not the right person to approach. She hadn't considered his religion, she should have guessed he'd be a Catholic. She'd heard they were more strongly opposed to birth control than anyone else; that other denominations were beginning to take a more liberal view.

Chapter Eight

Beth had many misgivings about taking Andrew to tea at Dock Cottages. She knew he was going to see the place through eyes that were used to very different surroundings. It was some comfort that her home looked cleaner than it had for some time.

'I'll go round that Sunday morning to make sure everything's tidy.' Jenny seemed to have accepted her pregnancy and was more her sunny self. 'And I'll be there in the afternoon too. I'm dying to meet him. I'll make a cake. Pity our Peg's laid up in bed with a new daughter, she'll be sorry to miss this.'

Beth asked, 'Should we have sandwiches as well?'

'Yes, one cake won't be enough, not for our lot. Not even the cut-and-come-again sort.'

On the day itself, Beth ate Sunday lunch at the hospital. She always did, no point in going home to eat food that her family needed; besides, the hospital meal was timed to be ready when she came off duty and she was always hungry. There were white tablecloths too, and maids to serve it. The lady pupils had expected this standard and now all the nurses enjoyed it. She reached home in time to help with their washing-up.

'Dad, do you mind if I put your hook out of sight in your bedroom?' Beth asked. 'It looks . . . Well, you know.'

Her father looked grim, but returned to his Sunday paper without saying anything. Beth took down the hook and also his belt with the big brass buckle – she felt threatened by that. Both were put out of sight on Mam's dressing table.

Beth made sure all her family changed into the best clothes they had; and all but Seppy, who considered himself too old for Sunday School, were sent there as usual. She bathed and changed Bobby, curling his hair round her fingers, thinking he looked very sweet.

'I'm going out,' her father said.

'No,' Violet objected. 'This is our Beth's intended. You've got to stay in and meet him. Wear a tie and put on a clean shirt.'

He did what she suggested without complaint.

Mam seemed quite excited. Beth helped her wash and change into her best black dress, then settled her on the couch.

'I'll wear my cameo brooch, Beth. It's in the top drawer of my dressing table.'

'A good idea.' Once it had been Grandma's cameo, it was the only real piece of jewellery Mam had apart from her wedding ring, and fastened to the high neck of her dress it took away the look of poverty.

Beth was shaking the folds out of Mam's best tablecloth, a wedding present, when Jenny arrived with a basket on each arm. She'd come alone; they'd already decided if she brought her husband and child the room would be packed to suffocation. Beth helped her unpack from her baskets a matching set of six cups and saucers which Mam didn't possess, a fruitcake, a Madeira cake and some scones.

Seppy was gloating over the unaccustomed spread. 'As well as the chocolate biscuits you brought, Beth. It looks marvellous.'

'All this fuss,' their father grunted. 'You'd think he was royalty.'

Beth had consulted the bus timetables and agreed with Andrew that she would meet him off the three fifteen at St James's Church. She felt on edge as she walked up to the bus stop.

As the bus pulled in, she could see a knot of passengers already on their feet preparing to get off. Andrew was amongst them, looking noticeably middle-class in his overcoat and new trilby. He kissed her cheek as he usually did and she took his arm and drew him down Stanley Road.

Dock Cottages was at its quietest at this time on a Sunday afternoon, but there were plenty of thinly clad children playing hopscotch and many more with spinning tops, bats, balls and homemade carts. They shouted noisily to each other and to the better clad children streaming out of Sunday School. As always there were plenty of dogs about, some collecting in packs.

Andrew eyed the dogs warily, and trod gingerly round the chalked marks on the pavements. He paused to peer down one of the streets that separated the blocks.

'Aren't the streets narrow here,' he exclaimed. The gaunt buildings looked more oppressive than usual on this grey afternoon. Beth felt him draw back as she led him towards her lobby in E Block.

'This is it,' she told him, urging him through the door.

'Hello, love, is this your young man then?' Mrs Clover was standing at her door, chatting with Mrs Brown who leaned against her own doorpost opposite. Both had arms akimbo and were wearing their usual floral pinafores and carpet slippers.

Beth introduced him. Andrew put out a faltering hand in response. 'Mam's friends,' she told him. They were both good-hearted, looking after Bobby and Colin when needed and going up to keep Mam company. But they were staring at Andrew with too obvious an interest.

As she led him off to the first flight of stone steps, Beth heard them say, 'A very nice young man.'

'She'll do well for herself there. That she will.'

She felt the heat run up her cheeks as she hurried him along the landing towards the second flight of steps. Suddenly, the children released from Sunday School caught them up and surrounded them. Not only her siblings but children from other families living on this lobby.

'Is this him, Beth? Is this the gentleman?'

'Is this your intended?'

'He looks nice.'

Andrew stumbled at the bottom of the fourth flight; there was little light here on this overcast afternoon.

'These steps are steep,' he puffed.

There were fewer children now. Esther giggled. 'You aren't used to them.'

Jenny had heard them coming and opened the door before they reached it. Then with the whole family on their feet, Beth went round the circle introducing them. Her dad's hands were callused and his nails none too clean, but he'd shaved and was on his best behaviour.

'I've started school,' Colin told Andrew proudly. 'I'm a big boy now.'

His three-quarter socks had collapsed in rolls on top of his boots and his laces were undone, but otherwise her young brothers and sisters looked like little angels. Each brandished a colourful card with a religious text on it. Colin had given his to baby Bobby who was chewing it. Beth removed it surreptitiously.

They all sat down, the smallest children on the floor because there weren't enough seats to go round. The conversation seemed stilted and Beth thought the adults looked ill at ease. The children were all interested in Andrew and bombarded him with questions.

'Where do you live?'

'I'd like to work in a hospital too when I'm grown up.'

'How old were you when you left school?'

'Eighteen? Goodness that's old. Did you stay on to teach the little ones?'

There was a knock on the front door and when Seppy opened it, their neighbour Mrs O'Malley from across the lobby came in.

'Can I borrow a cup of sugar, Vi? Can you spare it? We're right out.'

Beth took the proffered cup. 'Of course.'

Mrs O'Malley always returned what she borrowed, and occasionally they needed to borrow from her. Neighbours had to rely on each other here.

The fire was blazing in the grate. Jenny swung the kettle back to come to the boil again. Beth thought their living room had never looked so bright and clean, but of course any room thirteen feet by nine would seem cramped with so many people in it. The seat of the velvet armchair could be seen sagging, and the horsehair couch was shabby.

A moment later, there was another knock on the door. 'No,' she heard Seppy say. 'You can't come in to play, and Esther can't come out. We've got an important visitor today.'

She saw Andrew wince and knew he'd heard the exchange too. Jenny was trying to be her vivacious self, telling him about the hand embroidery she did at the tapestry works of A.H. Lee.

He nodded. 'I've heard of them.'

'We're world famous.' She beamed. 'We make beautiful tapestries and furnishing fabrics all by hand.'

'My mother has a fire screen that was made there.'

'Really? Is it crewel work? I do that sometimes. She must have paid a lot for it, everything's very expensive. We make things for royalty, you know.'

Beth had never seen any of it and busied herself filling cups and passing them round. The plates of cakes and biscuits emptied fast, as always here. Small silences fell, and Beth did her best to fill them but it was becoming an effort. At half past five, Dad pulled himself to his feet to bank up the fire.

Andrew stood up and said it was time he went. He thanked her parents politely for their hospitality, and asked Beth if he might use the bathroom before he went. She'd been hoping he wouldn't ask, although the ceiling had been whitewashed, the brick outside wall brushed to remove cobwebs and the floor scrubbed. Esther had cut several newspapers into squares to hang on the nail there.

He didn't ask how he should flush it, and she was too embarrassed to explain. She just showed him to the sink in the back kitchen where she'd put out the tablet of Lux toilet soap she'd bought specially, together with a clean towel.

Violet was on her feet when they got back to the living room. 'I'm so glad we've met you,' she said, taking his hand in both of hers.

Her father said, 'Our Betty will be all right with you.'

'Betty?' Andrew's jaw dropped in alarm.

Her father corrected himself. 'Beth I mean.' Beth felt Andrew's eyes examining her. 'She likes to be called Beth now.'

'Dad called me Betty when I was a child,' she choked. 'I'll walk you back to the bus stop.' She was putting on her hat and coat.

'I can find my own way,' he said, with none of his usual warmth. 'I don't want to trouble you.'

Beth was taken aback. She'd expected him to stay longer and to be asked to go out with him afterwards. She had a precious free evening still ahead of her and tomorrow was her day off.

'It's no trouble,' she said.

She borrowed Mam's torch to light him down the stairs. Very little light came through the small windows at the best of times. On this dark afternoon, daylight was already going. He hung on, both to her and the iron handrail.

'Isn't there a light?'

'No.'

'It's dangerous. These steps are steep.'

Beth bit back the words, 'We have to manage.' The tenants all cleaned their own landing and flight of stairs. Here in this lobby, each step had been donkey-stoned to a depth of two inches along its edge to make it more visible.

Andrew paused at the street door. There were more people about now. Maudie Everett, a raddled street walker, was dawdling past. Maudie fixed her smile on him.

'My, my, mister, how about it?' she cackled as she hitched her skirt up a couple of inches.

Beth saw him freeze. 'Please go,' she said.

'I'm looking for my friend Fanny. Have you seen her? Fanny Kershaw?'

'No.'

Her bad teeth flashed again at Andrew. 'You won't get it from her, darlin',' she sniggered and then hiccuped. 'Bye Beth.'

'Come on.' Beth took his arm. He seemed speechless with embarrassment. 'She's drunk.'

'Do you know her?'

'Everybody knows her round here.'

There was a large group of youths fooling about on the next corner and laughing together.

He stopped. 'Should you come with me? I mean, is it safe? You'll be coming back alone.'

Again, Beth was taken aback. She could see that the district was making him nervous.

'Why shouldn't it be safe?' She knew most of the lads by name. 'We go up and down these streets all the time.'

Constable Cummins was coming towards them on his beat, his familiar figure was like a plump apple, widest round his waist.

'Come on, lads,' he said. 'If you want to fool about like that, go down to the cinder patch.' They went obediently without a word. The cinder patch had swings and seesaws at one end and provided enough space for games of football.

Beth said, 'You see, it's as safe as anywhere else.'

'It's not what I expected.' Andrew's face looked drawn.

'I didn't think it would be. I can see you don't like Dock Cottages.' Who would? The poverty must be hard to take when he wasn't used to it. Things here were clearly much worse than he had imagined when she first told him where she lived. 'It's put you off, hasn't it?'

'No, no, of course not.' But Beth was sure it had. 'You're a very good-looking family. Such attractive children.' Beth felt he was trying to placate her. 'But so many of them. Such a handful for your mother.'

'She loves us all.' Beth was defensive.

'I'm sure.'

He was avoiding eye contact with her, she didn't like that. 'You haven't seen all of us. John's away at sea. Charlotte's in service and Peggy's married.'

He asked faintly, 'How many does that make?'

'Ten, I told you.' Beth tossed caution to the winds. 'Ten of us living, that is. Two more have died and Mam had two miscarriages. But only the five youngest live at home now.'

He whistled through his teeth. 'A big family.'

'Huge,' she agreed.

'My mother was wondering . . .'

Beth guessed what was coming and felt sick.

'Well, you trained as a nurse before the Registration Act, didn't you? She wondered whether you were a pupil nurse and had the proper training or whether you – worked your passage.'

'Need you ask? You've seen my home.' She summoned all the dignity she could muster. 'You must know my parents couldn't have afforded to pay for me. In a family like mine, we all have to stand on our own feet once we leave school. In fact, we're expected to help our parents, not the other way round.'

He heard the hurt in her voice. 'Beth, I need to get things straight, that's all.' He sounded a little testy.

She took a deep breath, she must stay calm, not show her displeasure. 'It's my day off tomorrow – I told you. Can I meet you outside the hospital when you finish work at five?'

'Monday?' His reluctance was only too obvious; it was hurtful.

'Yes, it makes a long break to have my half-day and day off together, but I might have to work for a fortnight before I get another. It could be Friday or Saturday next week.'

'Yes,' he said at last.

That made her wince. She had to ask, 'Yes, we'll go out?'

'All right.'

'We could go to the pictures,' she suggested hurriedly. 'I'll find out what's on.'

When the bus had come to carry him off to his comfortable home, Beth walked slowly back. She was afraid he did mind where she came from. It did make a difference, even though he'd said it wouldn't.

Beth felt heavy with disappointment and was fighting tears as she climbed the steps in E Block. The ring on her finger was no longer a reassurance of Andrew's love. She let herself in to find the living room quiet. Jenny had cleared away and washed up. She was packing her own crockery back in her basket.

'Andrew's nice,' she said, keeping her voice low. 'I liked him but he's very quiet.'

'He isn't usually that quiet.'

'I thought you'd be going out with him tonight.'

Beth sighed, so had she. 'I think Dock Cottages came as a shock to him.' She couldn't say any more. Couldn't tell Jenny what she feared. Not yet.

Jenny was indignant. 'Our place is as good as any of them. Better than most. You worked hard on it during your holiday.'

Seppy was playing his mouth organ softly, curled up on a cushion in the corner. Mam was dozing on the couch, Bobby asleep in her arms. The others had gone out.

'Esther's downstairs with the Browns, and Ivor's taken Colin out to kick a ball about.'

91

'What about Dad? The pubs aren't open yet.'

'Shot out somewhere the minute you went. I'm going home, I've left Tom looking after Noreen.' She lowered her voice further. 'I think Mam's feeling tired.'

Beth felt depressed, she was afraid all her plans would come to nothing.

'You've seen to everything here, I'd better go round and see our Peggy. Haven't seen the new baby yet.' She needed something to fill her evening and take her mind off her own problem.

'She's three days old already. Quite a shrimp, not quite five pounds.' Jenny's eyes went anxiously to their mother. 'We'll let her sleep, Seppy. No point in disturbing her just to say goodbye.'

They let themselves out quietly and felt their way down the dark stairs.

'How is Peggy?' Beth asked.

'A bit low. Fed up.'

'Oh dear. The baby's all right?'

'Slow to feed, difficult to settle.'

'I'll try and cheer her up.'

'Her place is a right tip. Sidney never lifts a finger to help. You'd think he would, especially at a time like this. I made a hot meal for them all and took a load of her washing home. Sidney wanted me to take their two youngest home with me, but he's there a lot of the time, I can't see why he shouldn't look after them.'

They reached St James's Church and went their separate ways. Beth headed up Tollemache Road. When Peggy and Sidney were married six and a half years ago, they'd rented two rooms in a small terraced house in Powell Street. As their family grew and they could no longer fit into one bedroom, they moved three doors up the street where they now rented a whole house and had it to themselves. Even so, it had only two bedrooms and was a squash for a family with five children.

Beth couldn't help but notice that Peggy's house was the only one in the row that hadn't had its step holystoned. She knocked on the door. The torn net curtain on the downstairs window hung askew; suddenly it swung up, and Beth saw her five-year-old niece May press her nose against the glass. The curtain swung back and she came scampering to open the front door. The scent of recently fried bacon was heavy in the air, it made Beth's mouth water.

'Hello, May. How's your new sister then?' May was a pretty ash blonde nymph with a dirty face.

'She's crying.'

Above the noise from the living room, Beth could hear the thin fretful mewl coming from upstairs. Within seconds she was surrounded by a slavering brown mongrel and Peggy's toddlers. Frankie was eating a bacon butty.

'Oh, it's you.' Sidney came out of the scullery with a scowl on his face. 'I'm just going to work.' The Blood Tub opened its doors in the evening at six o'clock. 'Where's my jacket?'

Beth followed the family into their living room. It was sparsely furnished but a chaotic mess. 'How's the new baby?'

'She's giving us a hard time.'

'All right if I go up and see her?'

'That's what you've come for, isn't it? I've got to go.' He pushed past her, and a moment later the front door slammed behind him.

Beth climbed the steep stairs with May and Hilda bounding up ahead and Frankie following on all fours. The bedroom was dusty and untidy and was almost filled by the wardrobe and a double bed.

'How are you, Peggy?'

Peggy had raised herself on her elbow, her face was hot and sweaty and twisting with anger.

'Has he gone? He said he'd see to Eric first.' Fifteen-month-old Eric was lying on one side of her in the rumpled bed, the new baby on the other. Both were grizzling.

'He's gone, Mammy.' May was climbing on the bed too.

Peggy turned on her, fuming. 'I told you not to let him go until he'd come up here. He has no thought for anyone but himself. I keep telling him I'm supposed to lie in for a month and can't do much. Now Eric's had no tea.'

May looked close to tears. 'Daddy made a bacon butty for him, but Bonny took Frankie's out of his hand.' Bonny was the dog. 'And he screamed and screamed so Dad gave Eric's to him.'

Beth said, 'Shall I make something for Eric? Sidney had to go to work, Peg.' She wanted to soothe her sister's anger.

May tugged on Beth's skirt. 'This is her, the new baby. Her name's Rita. D'you like her?'

'She's lovely.' Beth went to the other side of the bed to scoop her up. 'Let's have a proper look at you.' She took her nearer the window. 'I like the name Rita, very modern. I thought you wanted to call her Alice?'

'I don't much care what her name is.'

Beth froze. Surely every mother took pleasure in naming her new baby?

93

'It was Daddy's idea to call her Rita,' May piped up. 'Isn't her face red?'

The baby was wrapped in an old piece of flannelette sheet. Beth could feel the damp leaking through.

'I think she needs changing, Peggy. I'll do it, shall I?' The pile of clean napkins on the shelf in the wardrobe was pitifully low. Beth had to say, 'Her nightie's wet too and there isn't another here.'

'May, what did you do with it?' Peggy's voice was shrill. 'You were playing with it.'

'My teddy's wearing it.'

'Rita needs it, get it off. Hurry up.' Peggy was out of bed and pulling her coat on over her shabby nightdress. 'Has Sidney made the fire up downstairs?'

Beth finished dressing the baby and carried both her and Eric downstairs. He was wet too and now crying noisily. The fire was almost out. Beth took the scuttle out to the yard to fill it.

Within five minutes of going down to the living room the children were romping with Bonny the dog. May was trying to ride on her back, Frankie was pulling her by the piece of rope round her neck that served as a collar. Suddenly Bonny growled and bared her teeth. May slid off, giggling and screaming with delight. Frankie shot away.

'Shut up, you lot,' Peggy screamed. 'For goodness' sake shut up.' Beth didn't need to be told her sister was at the end of her tether.

'Peggy,' Beth burst out. 'With all these children, why do you have to have a great brute of a dog as well? I bet it takes some feeding.'

'It's Sidney's.' Peggy shooed it out to the back yard and slammed the door on it. Rita was kicking and screaming, making more noise than seemed possible by one so puny. Eric was crying noisily too. 'I've got to feed Eric,' Peggy said, heading into the scullery.

'Feed the baby,' Beth said, alarmed. 'I'll see to Eric.' There was no way she could feed Rita. She pushed her into Peggy's arms. Her sister collapsed on a chair near the fire and started undoing the buttons on her nightdress.

Beth found a dry napkin on the fire guard; it had a faint yellow stain on it and an unmistakable aroma.

'It was only just damp,' Peggy said, somewhat shamefaced. Beth took Eric to the kitchen sink and washed and changed him as best she could.

'What can I give him to eat?' she called. There was half a loaf on the table and a jug with some milk in it.

'Don't give him that milk,' Peggy commanded. 'We need it for our tea.'

'Want butty. Want butty,' Eric raged. He had his mother's blonde hair, it was damp with tears of anger. Beth cut him a slice of bread and spread it with plum jam, it was all there was.

May pulled herself up on the edge of the table to watch. 'I want a jam butty too.'

'No you don't,' Peggy screamed at her. 'You've already had your share.'

Beth had to pull Eric on her knee while he ate, to stop his siblings taking the food from him. She couldn't see how her sister was going to cope with five children under six. They were squabbling all the time.

Peggy looked at her. 'Sometimes I think the best thing would be to put a pillow over this one and snuff her out before she gets any bigger.'

'Peggy! You can't mean that! She's a lovely baby.'

'A bit puny.'

'She'll put weight on, get more rounded. Get prettier, they all do.'

'She's one too many. Well, so was Eric.'

'You're just tired. Things will look better in a day or two.' Beth was shocked. She'd heard that mothers could be depressed after childbirth but Peggy had never been like this before.

'I often think I'd like to run away. I could leave the lot of them then. Sidney would have to get on with it.'

'No, Peg!' She was afraid her sister needed help. 'There's nowhere you can run to.'

'If there was I'd have gone by now.'

'You wouldn't. I think you should see the doctor.'

'Don't be daft, Beth. I'll have a bill for thirty shillings from the midwife by next week. We can't afford to pay that, I can't run up any more.'

Beth silently hugged Eric until she felt him squirm in her arms. He'd finished eating and wanted to get down.

'Put him in his cot,' Peggy said irritably. 'It's time he went to sleep.' Beth carried him upstairs and did so.

'No,' Eric wailed. 'No bed, no bed.' Beth had to harden her heart to him.

Back in the living room downstairs, they could all hear him screaming and furiously rattling his cot sides.

'Kids.' Peggy shrugged. 'He'll shut up soon.'

'I'll make us some tea,' Beth said.

While they drank it she studied her elder sister and found it hard to understand what had happened to her.

95

'Peggy, in a week or two, when you're feeling stronger, I'll come and help you get on top of things here. We'll give this place a spring-clean and get the kid's clothes washed and mended.' There were tiny garments spread on every surface.

'You and whose army?'

'We could do it. You need to get your strength back and get a grip on things. Give yourself a break from having babies so you've got time for other things.'

'And how d'you think I'm going to do that?' Peggy barked at her.

Eric kept up the noise for another half-hour, during which time the older children squabbled noisily. It was only when Frankie fell on the stairs and added screams of pain to the general racket that Peggy lost her temper and whacked at the table with a cane. Beth flinched. Dad used to do that with his belt when he was cross with them. She tried to comfort Frankie.

'Upstairs and into bed, all of you, this minute,' Peggy yelled. 'You too, Frankie. Put a sock in it.' The cane sang through the air and the children rushed for the stairs. 'Not another sound from any of you or you'll feel this on your legs.'

Peggy sank back in her chair, still holding the baby. She looked exhausted. Her sudden burst of fury had produced immediate silence. Even Eric was quiet. All that could be heard was a soft scuttling on the floor above.

'Will they get themselves into bed?' Beth whispered. 'Undress themselves?'

'They'll take some of their clothes off.' Peggy shrugged. 'They'll go to sleep and give me a bit of peace.'

'Should I—'

'No! For goodness' sake sit down and have another cup of this tea you've made. You're on the go all the time. It gets on my nerves.'

'I want to help.'

'You don't have to. Nothing you do will really help. The work's never done here.'

'It could be if . . . Peggy, you'll be fine. You'll get over this. All you need is a rest.'

'A rest! That'll be the day.' The baby had fallen asleep in her arms. 'At least she's here, that part's over and done with. I've told Sidney enough's enough. I can't be doing with any more.'

Beth could see tears glistening on her sister's lashes, and was left in no doubt that she was very unhappy with her lot.

She meant to comfort when she put out her hand, but the light caught her diamond, making it flash. When she'd first shown it to Peggy, she'd thought her manner a little strange, now she blazed out, 'It's all right for you, Beth. You're going to escape all this. You're going to get a posh house and a small family. You've got it made. You'll never know what it's like to have a baby every year, with your body not your own.'

Beth wanted to yell back at her that Andrew was breaking her heart. That he thought she wasn't good enough for him. She was afraid he was about to break the engagement. But she couldn't stand any show of sympathy, not now, when they were both so near to tears.

'You're going to be rich, aren't you? You won't have to worry about where the next shilling is coming from.' There was envy in every line of Peggy's body.

Beth couldn't bear to hear any more. 'I've got to go,' she said. 'It's getting late.'

If Andrew had changed his mind, she didn't know what the future held for her, and it was frightening to see Peggy like this.

When the door closed behind Beth, Peggy dragged herself upstairs, put Rita down for the night and collapsed on her bed. The tears she'd been holding back in front of her sister came flooding out to wet her pillow. That Beth had offered to help her spring-clean the house made her feel hopeless and helpless.

But there was one thing she felt very firm about, she was determined to have no more babies. Whatever happened, Rita was going to be her last. As it was, life was hardly worth living with five of them. People gave her pitying looks when she went out with all the kids clinging round her skirts. She was fighting a losing battle to keep them clean and fed. She wasn't going to be like Mam and go on to have ten and work herself into an early grave.

She was still awake when Sidney came home. 'You're crying, Peg. What's the matter?'

For once he seemed stone cold sober and in an affable mood. He got undressed and into bed beside her, taking her into his arms. Peggy drew away from him. She hated any show of affection, it could lead only too easily to sex.

'I don't want any more babies,' she told him. 'I couldn't cope if I had another.'

'Course not,' he said. 'Five is more than enough, we've got to stop now.'

'You agree then? You'll use those things Jenny brought up?'

97

'I'll have to get used to them,' he said. 'Don't you worry. Try and go to sleep now.'

He was asleep within minutes but Peggy lay there, glad she'd caught a good moment to speak to him. Rita was snuffling and sighing, she hoped she wasn't going to howl for another feed just yet. She ached for sleep to come.

Beth felt near to boiling point and almost ran down to Jenny's house. Peggy had always irritated her, she'd wanted to shake her today, but she'd been stung to sympathy too. When she'd seen her sister's desperate tears, she'd almost taken her into her arms to comfort her but Peggy had brushed her off.

Peggy had to stop having babies. She couldn't cope with those she had. There was Jenny too and Mam. They had to have the help they needed to limit their families. She mustn't stop trying because she'd failed on her first two attempts. She'd been made to feel brazen, a bit of a hussy. Coming from Andrew, it had been very hard to accept.

But Peggy needed help and Beth didn't know how to give it. She feared for her sister's mental state. Mam would be the best person to help with that but she was ill, and Beth didn't think she should be burdened with extra trouble. There was Sidney of course, but he wasn't the sort to help anybody. It would have to be her and Jenny.

Peggy was so changed!

When they'd been young, Beth had been envious of Peggy's good looks and the fuss everybody made of her. Jenny had too. Dad had told them that his eldest daughter outclassed them in every way.

As the family grew, Beth understood that Mam did her best for them all, but she'd had less energy and her money had to stretch further. Beth had worn Peggy's clothes when she grew out of them, but she hadn't suited pink frills. Jenny had shared her dislike of Peggy's hand-me-downs, and by the time she was wearing them they were shabby. They'd both understood there was no possibility of dancing classes for them.

'Teach us to dance, Peggy,' they'd begged, hoping to share a smattering of her pleasure. To be fair, she did try, but had soon given up.

'You've both got two left feet,' she'd laughed. 'I'm wasting my time.'

'I can bake better cakes than you,' Jenny had spat back. At times there was antipathy between them as well as rivalry, and the three of them had fought and quarrelled.

'You're both jealous of me,' Peggy accused and Beth was afraid she might be right. 'Specially you, Betty. You're so jealous your eyes have turned green.'

'They've always been green.'

'No, they were blue once like mine, they turned green. Green for jealousy.'

Beth found it hard to understand how Peggy had fallen to her present state when she'd shown such promise. Beth felt no envy for her now. She was sorry for her.

Jenny and Tom were on the point of going to bed when she got there. Beth couldn't hold back her fears.

'I'm worried about Peggy. She's in a terrible state, talking about suffocating the new baby. I'm going to have nightmares about that. She really needs help.'

Tom put the kettle on. 'She's alone too much with those children.'

Jenny led the way to the dying fire. 'She's never very welcoming when I do go round. She says, "What have you come for?" It's off-putting.'

'She's scared about getting pregnant again. Says she couldn't cope with a sixth. Perhaps you could . . . ?'

'Beth, I already have! I've talked about how to avoid pregnancy till I'm blue in the face. I've even taken some of Tom's things there so Sidney can see them and try them. She says he doesn't like them, and anyway, since I've fallen for it again, it's obvious they're no good.'

'Nothing's a hundred per cent safe,' Tom sighed.

'Talk to her again, Jenny, please.'

'OK, but there must be a more sure way. You've got to find out for us, Beth.'

'I'll do my best, honest I will.'

'And I'll try and persuade her to take the baby to the clinic next week. I'll go with her. I've suggested it before but she's never wanted to go, says she hasn't the time.'

'Make her go. It'll get her out of that house and the walk will do her good.'

'And the company,' Tom said.

'She'll never say how much money Sidney gives her, but the very poor can apply for a free pint of milk every day until the baby's a year old.'

'Those kids of hers could certainly do with that.'

'It's for the mother, to help her get her strength back, and if the doctor thinks she's anaemic she'll give her a free iron tonic.'

'She's probably in need of that too. I'll go round to see her more often.'

'You've got to work, Beth, and you're up at Mam's nearly every day.'

'Yes, well, we've got to get Peggy back on her feet, haven't we? Who's going to look after all those kids if she can't?'

'Not me I hope.' Jenny giggled.

On Monday afternoon, Beth couldn't stop thinking about Andrew. She was sure that if she hadn't pushed him, he wouldn't have suggested taking her out. She told herself she'd been through this before, worried when she'd refused to see him during her holiday, but all had been well when they'd met again. All might still be well. His memories of Dock Cottages might be pushed to the back of his mind.

She walked down to the hospital gates and got there a few minutes before five. Andrew was late coming out and she was getting the jitters before he came. But he kissed her cheek as usual and took her arm.

'A bite to eat first?'

He was quieter than usual, subdued, not smiling on the bus going into town.

Facing him across the small table in the cafe, Beth knew she couldn't put off what she had to say any longer.

'It's Dock Cottages, isn't it? Because my home's there?'

He was embarrassed, his gaze on his plate. 'Well . . .'

'I didn't expect you to like the place. I don't myself. We'd all like to move somewhere better.'

Andrew was concentrating on his fish and chips, looking as though he hadn't eaten in days.

'You said you didn't mind where I came from.' But that was before he'd seen the place.

His eyes met hers for an instant. He said, 'I don't suppose it makes that much difference. After all, you don't live there any more. Let's go to the Scala, shall we? There's a good cowboy film on.'

Beth could see he wanted to drop the subject. She felt defeated. He couldn't talk about it, but he'd said it made no difference. She should be glad about that.

She fell in with his wishes, although she wasn't keen on cowboy films, and it wasn't very good. Andrew was restless, it didn't take her long to realise it wasn't holding his interest either.

They sat through it to the end and when they came out it was raining heavily. Outside the nurses' home he kissed her, but she could have been his maiden aunt for all the passion in it. Beth shivered as she went up to her room.

100

Chapter Nine

Wilfred Hubble yawned as he joined the early morning line of workmen heading in twos and threes down Corporation Road on their way to work. Most looked half asleep, many were sallow-faced and coughing, warming their hands round a Woodbine or a Gold Flake as they shuffled along. It was easy to pick out the dockers even if he didn't know them, because their hooks made bulges under their coats. Few strode out with Wilf's vigour. He was making his way to Vittoria Dock where a Brocklebank ship would load this morning.

When he arrived, a huge number of dock labourers were waiting on the stand to be hired for the day's work. Far more than would be needed. The Mersey Docks and Harbour Board licensed private firms to load and unload ships and handle cargo on the quay. Master stevedores and their gangs loaded and unloaded ships and master porters took charge of the unloaded cargo and hired men to move goods from the quay to the warehouses.

Wilfred joined the jostling and swearing pool of labourers seeking work. This morning he didn't have to wait, already gangs of stevedores were being picked from one end and quay hands were being chosen from the other. He edged near the end for quay hands, preferring to work between the warehouse and the quay rather than load the ship. Quay work offered better opportunities, and he had an understanding with Larry Bilton, the gaffer who was picking out the men for work. Since many would be turned away without work, this was a big advantage.

It was a cold and blustery March morning, and the river was being whipped up into white horses. The buildings on the Liverpool waterfront stood out stark and black against an anthracite sky. Lascar seamen off the ships, well wrapped up in scarves, stepped cautiously over black oily puddles and the crisscross of hawsers and ropes holding their ships to the rusting bollards.

'Morning, Mr Bilton.' Wilfred doffed his cap as he was picked out for the gang. Larry Bilton had done that well, not too obviously, not as

101

though he was his first choice, though Wilf knew he was.

Bilton was almost as old as Wilf, but he'd kept a youthful figure. He had the exotic good looks of his Spanish forebears: a waxed moustache with dark curly hair and a bronzed complexion that did not depend on being out in the sun. He was rather a dandy and wore his bowler at a jaunty angle. He had a voice that resounded through the warehouses and a laugh that was heard often.

Wilf had been working with these dockers for years. He couldn't say he'd made close friends of any of them, but there were plenty with whom he was happy to pass the time of day; he knew those who could take a joke, those who played an honest game of poker and those who were ready to help themselves to some of the cargo if they thought they could get away with it. The dockers who drank at the Blood Tub he knew even better. He knew their wives and children too.

Wilf stamped with the rest of the gang and did busman's warm-ups until Bilton's sidekick, Charlie Hogan, a rather haughty youth, led them off to the warehouse and got the sliding doors open. There was a collection of hand trucks in the entrance, and they each took one.

'Railway siding,' they were told. Wilfred trundled his truck across to where a line of waggons was waiting. Two of the gang were given the job of boarding the goods train and moving the crates to the door; that was Wilf's favourite job. It was under cover on this bleak morning and there were few eyes to see what went on inside. Two more of the gang swung the crates onto the hand trucks.

'What we loading today, Mr Hogan?' he asked. That was the all-important question.

'Mixed cargo.' It usually was. 'This is jam.'

He was disappointed, jam was heavy stuff and not worth much. It was refined sugar in the next waggon and that was no better. They were like ants, scurrying back and fore between the goods siding and the quay in front of the *Nomad*, an eight-thousand-ton tramp which would sail for Cape Town when loading and coaling had been completed. The stevedores were making up netted loads of the crates for the ship's derricks to swing over the hold. Wilfred hadn't liked working on the ships, not since the day he'd seen a net of crates accidentally nudge a man into the yawning depths where he broke his back.

Later, they were directed to number one warehouse, where part of the cargo was being stored whilst in transit. It was chemicals, sulphate of ammonia, no use again.

Wilfred was used to it but it was hard and boring work. It would be even more dreary if this was all that would happen until knocking off time. The morning passed slowly. What kept Wilf alert was knowing more interesting goods could come to hand, that the boss would choose the moment and he'd have to rise to it.

When he caught sight of Bilton waving his clipboard at him from the entrance to another warehouse, Wilf knew the moment had come. The boss was sheltering from the sharp wind just inside the door and gave him a wink as he directed him to a stack of crates at the back. He felt the adrenaline begin to race round his body. Larry Bilton was following behind him.

'Here,' he said.

Large cardboard cartons, each with a protective wooden casing round it, were stacked three high. Wilf halted his truck in front of one.

'Start over here.' Bilton waved him on to a position where they would not be so easily seen.

Wilf moved his truck. 'This?'

'Yes.' Bilton put a helping hand to one end, Wilf lifted the other. It felt much lighter than the jam.

'Clocks and watches?' He wasn't very good at reading labels.

Bilton nodded. Just what they wanted. Wilf felt galvanised, electricity was running through him. He knew what he was expected to do; he knew he had to be careful. He mustn't be seen deliberately damaging a case, particularly not by the dock police or the haughty Charlie Hogan, who was known for his high moral stance.

'Take your time,' Bilton said from the corner of his mouth as they settled the first case on the hand truck. Other quay hands were coming to move this cargo out to the quay. There were too many men about just now.

The trucks trundled out of sight behind the stacked cases. Wilf watched the gaffer, who he knew was keeping a lookout for him.

When he turned and gave him the nod, Wilf let the next case fall on its corner. It survived undamaged. Bilton pulled a face and helped him lift it on top of the first.

'Right,' he prompted, when they had the next case. 'Now.'

Wilf lifted this one higher and threw it crashing to the floor with all the force he could muster; he heard the crack as the wooden casing burst open. The cardboard carton was crumpled on the corner but it stayed intact.

'Go on,' Bilton hissed impatiently.

Wilf's heart was thumping wildly as he gave one deft jab with his hook and opened the carton along its fastening seam. Then the boss bounced the whole thing on the crumpled corner again to make it look like accidental damage.

Wilf was sweating now. There was a lot of packing inside between the smaller boxes. His hand was shaking. Surely with a gang this size somebody would catch them at it.

'Hurry up,' Bilton grated between his teeth. 'For God's sake get on with it.'

Wilfred got two smaller boxes out and opened one up.

'Alarm clocks!' The gaffer grunted with disappointment. They'd both been hoping for something more expensive.

'Better than nothing.' They were just the thing for flogging off in the Blood Tub. Sidney would have no trouble raising a bit of cash on them.

'I was hoping for watches,' Bilton sniffed. Suddenly he raised his voice. 'Look what you're doing, can't you? Be careful, you've damaged this crate.'

Wilf didn't look round, he knew someone must be near. He busied himself loading his truck.

'Get going,' Bilton urged, impatient again. 'I'll see to this now.'

Wilf pushed his truck out and along the quay, taking things slowly. Their first attempt had not been a great success, but he knew his cheeks would be scarlet with the thrill of trying and was glad of the cold air against them. He must not seem excited. The open crate would be noted, some of its contents would be found to be missing, but others were at the same game, the blame must not be put on him. God help him if it fell on Mr Bilton. Their agreement was that they'd watch each other's backs.

When he returned for another load, all the gang were heading for the crates of watches and clocks. The refined sugar was now all out on the quay. The crate he'd damaged had been put against the wall, its internal packing hanging out. The job went on hour after hour. Another broken crate joined the first. The gaffer yelled at them all to be more careful. His voice resounded round the warehouse but Wilf knew it was all for show.

Each time he returned to the warehouse, he avoided young Mr Hogan and kept his eye on Bilton. He could hear his laugh and was sure he'd try again. At last he was waving him over to one of the hoists. Wilf felt his heart begin to beat faster. Crates and boxes could be damaged in the hoist as they were brought down from the upper floors.

Bilton yelled at the warehouseman. The hoist thudded down with a load of boxes. Others in the gang dragged them off and loaded them three high on each hand truck as it was pushed forward. Close by was a large square stack of bales making a convenient wall.

There were two trucks waiting ahead of Wilf when he saw Bilton move back to get a wider view of the warehouse. Was he going to give the signal? Wilfred didn't take his eyes off him, his chest felt tight with anticipation. Yes, the gaffer was making jabbing movements with his finger. Wilf knew what that meant. He turned his truck round and pushed it towards Bilton, who began pointing with his elbow.

Wilf turned behind the stack of bales. Two or three more steps and he could see a single crate hidden between the warehouse wall and the stack. A sack had been thrown alongside it. He knew what that meant too. He couldn't be seen either from the hoist or from across the warehouse, the gaffer had arranged it so.

He wasted no time. He threw himself at the crate and levered it open, hoping there was enough background noise to cover the splintering sounds. He could feel the blood pounding in his head.

This time it was wristwatches, the latest craze. Wilfred rather fancied one to replace his old pocket watch. He took one out of its box. Ethel had fixed a new headband inside his flat cap and altered the lining so it would cover small objects, though it wasn't often he got something small enough to hide in there.

He was tossing as many of the small boxes as he could into the sack that had been left in readiness. He was at fever pitch as he peeped round the end of the stack. He could see Hogan way across the other side of the warehouse by another hoist with his own gang, hugging an important looking clipboard to his chest.

Wilfred pushed the sack under his coat. To keep it in place, he had to bend double and hang over the shafts of his hand truck as he went to get it loaded. With only one truck waiting ahead of him, he tried to jerk the sack higher. Three crates were swung on, jolting his truck three times. The sack dropped again. He'd put too much in it, it was too heavy and too bulky to manage. He was heading towards the entrance where he could see Bilton watching him. He'd indicate where he wanted him to put the watches.

Suddenly, Wilfred realised Hogan had joined the gaffer. He had his back to him but was waving his arms about as he explained something. Bilton lifted his eyes to meet Wilfred's for a second: almost imperceptibly he shook his head. That meant keep away from us, you're on your own. Wilfred felt the sack slipping. He bent further over the shafts of the truck and hoped no one would notice.

Panic was drying his mouth. He'd seen others caught for theft and the dock police sent for. He was scared it might happen to him. He told himself that pilfering went on all the time and most got away with it.

But it wouldn't do to keep the stuff on him while he went on working. The sack was too heavy for him to cope with and the broken case would probably be found before long and inquiries started. Somebody might remember seeing him near it and he might be questioned and searched. He had to hide the sack, but where? Some other bugger would help themselves to his loot if they saw him do it.

The porter who'd been next in line to have his truck loaded came past at full speed. He shouted, 'Come on Wilf, get going. Pull your weight, man.'

The sack was banging against his knees, he was afraid it must be showing beneath his coat. Wilf risked a quick look all round before he stopped, yanked the sack out and shoved as much as he could of it between the crates on his truck. At least he could move now. It came to him then what he must do. He headed as fast as he could down the side of the warehouse, dreading to hear another shout as the next porter came out with his truck.

His heart was pounding like an engine. He could hear the blood pumping in his ears. He was sweating but he made it round the back and out of sight. There was a good bit of rubbish here; broken crates and boxes, empty drums rusting and battered, and such like. He rammed the sack under a wooden box and pushed it hard against the wall. He had an urgent pee alongside it, stress always had this effect on him. He headed back towards his hand truck doing up his flies.

He had to get out of here now without being seen. At the corner, he looked cautiously up the side of the warehouse and just jumped back in time. One truck was heading towards the quay, another going inside. Another peep and he set off pushing his truck to the quay. The weight of it was pulling his arms out of their sockets. The quay was a hive of activity, the ship's derricks were swinging back and fore.

'Cold enough to freeze a brass monkey,' one of the gang said as he helped him swing the crates off.

Wilf was sweating again, though the sky was leaden and it looked as though a storm was coming. He returned to the warehouse taking things more slowly, savouring his triumph. He'd kept his head and hidden the stuff. He didn't think anybody had seen him. It would be a good haul, and there was no reason why they shouldn't get away with it.

Mr Bilton was alone now, waiting for him at the entrance to the warehouse. He was making a great play with his arms as though directing him somewhere, but Wilf knew he wanted to hear what he'd done with the sack.

'Good man, it'll do there for now. I'll see to it.'

Wilf calmed down as he trundled his handcart back and forth. The morning seemed neverending, his back felt as though it was breaking.

At last his dinner hour came and they knocked off. His stomach craved food and his brawn sandwiches tasted good. He had his bottle of cold tea and, as always, he wished it was hot. Even so, he felt buoyed up with success.

Afterwards he took the opportunity of having another pee behind the back warehouse wall. It was what they all did. He checked that the sack was still where he'd hidden it and had a look at the wristwatch he'd commandeered. He'd hoped for an expensive gold one, but it was chromium-plated and of cheap quality. Just the sort of stuff they'd send out for the natives of Cape Town.

He rejoined his gang in the corner of the warehouse. One or two walked to the nearest dockland pub for a pint but many didn't bother, preferring instead to have a smoke, a game of cards or a rest. There were some old sacks lying about; Wilf lay back on them and closed his eyes. He was pleased with himself.

Their dinner hour was cut short by the need to go back on the stand to be picked out again for the afternoon shift. By then, three heavy drays had arrived, pulled by teams of carthorses. Wilf was put to unloading drums of treacle from them while the horses munched from nosebags. Loading was complete by late afternoon, the *Nomad* was getting ready to move to the coaling berth when Bilton dismissed the gang.

Wilf was glad to walk up to a cafe in Cleveland Street and sit in the window with a cup of hot tea and a bun. He watched the street outside for Larry Bilton who arrived shortly afterwards on his motorbike. He waved but didn't come in; he'd told Wilf he didn't want them to be seen together, not near to the docks. Wilf hurried out, and saw Bilton a few yards further up the road.

Wilf pushed his cap in his pocket and mounted the seat behind. They were off in a burst of noise and a cloud of blue smoke. He loved the rush of wind in his hair as he clung on. He could see the cover over the sidecar bulging with its contents.

Bilton found a quiet spot where they could share out their haul. It was somewhere different every time; today it was the park. There weren't many people about on this cold, damp day. Bilton left his motorbike on the road and they carried the sacks into the bushes.

Wilf was pleased to see a few alarm clocks as well as some more expensive timepieces meant for the mantelpiece. There were lots of watches.

'Not a bad day's work.' Larry Bilton beamed at him. 'And we get a bit of a kick out of taking the stuff from under their noses, don't we?'

'Yes,' Wilf agreed, because he wanted to be thought the sort of man who enjoyed danger, but there were times when the whole business scared the living daylights out of him. He had to do it, he had to do something to get a bit more money.

At work, he was at the bottom of the pile. For years, he'd been done down by the gaffers who'd taken a dislike to him for no reason and who only picked him out if there was no one else.

Bilton did him down in his own way, he took two-thirds of their haul, while Wilf took two-thirds of the risk. Bilton had also impressed upon him that if he was caught, Wilf was on his own, he would not protect him if things went wrong.

Wilf scooped up his share, stuffing a handful into each of his pockets. Ethel had sewn extra large poacher's pockets inside the lining of his coat especially for occasions like this.

He went straight to Powell Street to see Sidney with the contents of his pockets banging against his knees. May came rushing to the door and flung herself in his arms.

'Hello, Grandpa.'

'Hello, Queen.' Usually he brought sweets for Peggy's kids, but he'd not had time to get any. They all came rushing to him, expecting them. Peggy's resentful eyes met his across the room.

'Hello, Dad. Have you come to see the new baby then?' She was feeding her.

He'd forgotten all about the new baby! 'Yes, love,' he said. Sidney had been going on about it in the pub the other night, letting everybody know the midwife had been here all day and kept him on the run boiling kettles and chasing round after the other kids. Wilf had meant to come round the following day but it had left his mind. He'd gone to Ethel's instead.

'A girl, isn't it? What you calling her?'

'Sidney said he'd told you. It's Rita.'

'Very nice. How are you feeling, then?'

He saw tears start to her eyes. Women were always so emotional when they had babies.

'I'm all right,' she said angrily.

'Let's have a look then.' She parted the tight wrappings of old flannelette sheeting to show a crumpled red face.

108

'She's lovely. Isn't she lovely, May?' He patted Peggy's shoulder in a show of comfort. 'Is Sidney in?'

'He's in bed. You know him, says he needs a rest in the afternoon. Though I can't see why he needs it more than I do.' She put her head back and yelled at the ceiling, 'Sidney? Dad's here. He wants you.'

He knew Sidney had heard; the ceiling creaked as he walked about above them.

'I'd better cross the baby's palm with silver,' he said, 'to bring her luck.' He took from his pocket what he thought to be a florin. It turned out to be half-a-crown. Still, he mustn't look mean. He folded the baby's tiny hand round it.

He looked at Peggy, expecting her to thank him, but she just glared back at him. He didn't understand what was upsetting her. Poor girl, she looked terrible. Really washed out.

She was growing more like her mother, but she was bitter in a way Vi had never been. And she wasn't coping with the housework the way Vi had; the place was a real mess.

He could hear her husband coming downstairs at a great pace. Sidney knew why he'd come. He took his arm and led him out to the back yard. May tried to follow them.

'Where you taking Grandpa?'

'Go back to your mam,' Sidney thundered and pushed her back inside the scullery and slammed the back door on her.

In the wash house, Wilf started bringing out his haul. 'I think I'll keep one of these alarm clocks for myself.'

'Clocks and watches.' Sidney whistled through his shaggy moustache. 'They'll go well. That fellow Sandy from Block A was asking if I could get any watches. What shall I ask for them then?'

There were four different styles of clocks and several more of watches, it took some time to sort out the asking prices. Sidney pencilled double each price on the boxes, so he could offer them as bargains. Then he put a few of each sort into a shopping bag.

'That's enough to take with me tonight. Give us a hand to push this mangle over, Pa.'

'What for?'

'You'll see.'

He'd made a very secure hiding place by lifting one of the flagstones in the floor, and digging out some of the packed earth beneath.

'What a good idea,' Wilf said. 'The stuff will never be found there.'

'Had to. The kids are into everything. The less they know, the better.'

They dropped the flagstone back and swung the mangle over it before they went away.

The following day, Beth had a morning off. When she went home to see her mother, Violet said, 'Maggie Clover's been up here looking for you. She's got a few days' holiday.'

Maggie, her old friend from schooldays, had gone into domestic service in Southport. Beth ran straight down to the Clovers' flat. Maggie answered her knock and threw her arms round her in an excited bear hug. 'Lovely to see you.'

'I didn't know you were coming.'

'Neither did I. The family have gone to visit relatives in London, so no work for the cook. I've got an unexpected holiday. Aren't I lucky?'

Once Maggie had had long dark pigtails. Now she had the latest short bob. With her robust build and red cheeks, she looked a typical country girl though she'd spent her childhood in Dock Cottages. She wore a fashionable cream wool dress, the bodice all tucks and cross-overs.

'You look wonderful, Maggie. Very smart.'

'Given to me by the daughter of the house.' She laughed. 'She wears the very latest styles. It doesn't take her long to tire of them and I get them when she throws them out. I'm lucky there because I'm her size. I copy what she does and try to look fashionable too.'

'You do. Very fashionable.'

Maggie was great fun and had tremendous energy, she was always suggesting outings. When Beth had to return to the hospital, Maggie walked up to the bus stop with her.

'I've got four days off, but I stayed in Southport for the first so I could go out with my new boyfriend. His name's Len and he's lovely.'

Beth heard a great deal more about him; Maggie was in love, she had no doubts about that. She hoped things would work out for her. She hardly mentioned Andrew, she couldn't bring herself to talk about him. Couldn't forget him and give herself up to enjoying Maggie's company either.

The bus came and all the way down to the hospital Beth thought of him. Neither she nor Andrew had enjoyed last night. She just had to hope that they'd both get back to feeling about each other as they had. As Maggie did about Len.

Maggie met her outside the hospital when she came off duty at eight o'clock. 'Let's go down to New Brighton on the ferry. It's lovely at night.'

Beth asked herself why she and Andrew hadn't done this, instead of drinking tea in local cafes. With the moonlight shining on the water, everything looked so beautiful.

'I really miss the river.'

'You've got the sea at Southport.'

'Not the same.'

Maggie filled the following days for her. She and Beth had always had long heart-to-heart chats in their schooldays. Beth told her how worried the family was about her mother, and about Peggy having so many babies.

'I don't see why women don't just say no to their husbands,' she said. 'Surely they don't have to make love if they don't want to.'

Maggie giggled. 'Then they risk the husband looking elsewhere for it.'

'But if they're worn out like our Peggy . . . Surely abstinence is the answer?'

'Perhaps for a short time, but you know what men are, sooner or later they have to have it.'

They took a picnic up to Bidston Hill just as they used to in their schooldays, and laughed about the jam sandwiches wrapped in newspaper that they used to take.

'We're expecting Ken home any time now,' Maggie said, but he didn't arrive until the day came for her to return to Southport. Beth had an afternoon off and both she and Ken went to see her off on the train. Ken kissed his sister more than once.

'I wish you could stay a bit longer,' he mourned.

She shook her head. 'Family's coming back, they'll want supper tonight.'

'I was so sure I'd get the old rust bucket back in time to see something of you.'

'So what kept you? You promised me a night out.'

'Couldn't get the cargo on in time.' Ken pushed his thatch of curly hair off his forehead. His mother trimmed his hair for him, he was not groomed in the way Andrew was.

The train jolted and Maggie said, 'You'll have to take Beth instead then, won't you? Goodbye.' They watched it pull out of the station, then turned to go.

'How about it?' Ken asked.

'What?'

'The night out? Will you come? It was going to be a treat for Maggie. I missed her birthday.'

111

Beth had been to the pictures many times with Ken, even more often in a group with other members of the Clover family.

'What did you have in mind, the pictures? I've got an evening off on Friday.'

'A dancc, if you fancy it.'

Beth wished it was Andrew inviting her out with such eagerness. Should she go? What would he think? But Ken was almost family.

'Yes, why not?' She was rewarded by a smacking kiss on her cheek.

'We'll have a good time,' he said. 'I know just the place. Put your glad rags on. I'll come up and collect you about seven.'

Beth was glad to be going out with Ken Clover, it might help to keep her mind off Andrew. He was as cheerful as ever when he came to pick her up on Friday. He meant to enjoy himself and his mood lifted hers.

Ken couldn't keep his steps in time to the music, not like Andrew. She and Maggie had tried to teach him to dance years ago; he hadn't improved much. But there was nothing aloof about him; he held her close when they danced and she didn't have to make conversation. Ken never stopped chatting – about his family, about Maggie, and in particular about himself. Beth heard all about life on board the coastal tramp.

'I'd love a shore job,' he said. 'With all those ships in the river, there must be something I could do and sleep in my own bed at night.'

'Such as what?'

'What I'd really like,' his head was on one side, his eyes shone with enthusiasm, 'is to lift wrecks from the deep. That would be really exciting. To lift ships that sank years ago.'

'Are there any in the Mersey?'

'Yes, but unless they were vessels of importance, nobody bothers.'

'Or were carrying a valuable cargo?'

'Yes, or they're in the shipping channels and causing a nuisance.'

When he took Beth back to the hospital, he held her in his arms and kissed her in a more than friendly manner. 'I've had a great time tonight,' he told her.

'Do you always kiss girls like this?' She laughed.

'Yes, every chance I get. I have to spend a lot of time on that tramp and there aren't any there.' He smiled down at her. 'We always have a good time together, Beth. I wish I could spend more time with you. I've applied for a dozen shore jobs. The trouble is that all the other sailors want them. After a few years at sea many would rather stay home with their families.'

Beth felt a pang of guilt. Hadn't Mary Clover told Mam that Ken fancied her? She thought of Ken as a friend, almost as much a friend as Maggie. She mustn't lead him on to think . . . Not when her mind was so full of Andrew, it wouldn't be fair.

Chapter Ten

The days began to pass without any word from Andrew. Beth had another evening off on Friday, one of the perks of being a staff nurse. She wrote him a note, sealed it into an envelope and took it on duty with her so she could put it with the specimens to go up to the lab. At the last minute she retrieved it, feeling she couldn't again ask Andrew to take her out. Neither could she bring herself to use the phone in the entrance hall to call him at home.

Whenever she went to the dining room she looked in the rack where letters were left for staff to collect. There was never one for her.

She became more uneasy as another weekend went by. She'd been given Thursday off, and she had a free evening on Wednesday too. She felt she had to know definitely one way or the other, she couldn't stand this uncertainty. She didn't know where she stood and was beginning to fear Andrew didn't want to tell her to her face and was going to leave things as they were.

On Tuesday morning, she wrote him a note and one of the junior nurses took it up to the laboratory with the ward specimens. She said she wanted to speak to him and she'd meet him at his bus stop at five o'clock the next day. When she went for her tea, she found a note from him waiting for her in the rack.

Dear Beth,

I've had several attempts at writing to you but there's no easy way to say this. I think perhaps I was too hasty when I spoke of marriage. I think our backgrounds are too different and we wouldn't be happy together. I hope you won't think too badly of me if I ask you to release me from the engagement.

This being the situation, I don't think there's any point in our meeting.

I'm sorry, Beth. Truly sorry. Please forgive me.
Andrew.

Beth felt the heat surge up her cheeks. She groped her way to a chair and slumped down at the table. A maid appeared with the large teapot and filled her cup.

She was angry. A note like that to end their engagement? He hadn't the guts to tell her to her face. He was a wimp. She ran over to her bedroom where she scribbled a reply. She said she needed to speak to him and she wanted to return his ring, and that she'd be waiting for him tomorrow as suggested in her earlier note. She added, sarcastically, that she hoped he could spare her a few minutes.

She was shaking when she returned to the ward. She was in charge that evening and found it hard to keep her mind away from her own problems long enough to write the report for the night staff.

She didn't sleep well, she tossed and turned for half the night. He'd said he loved her and she'd been so certain of her own feelings. She felt that, for all his gentlemanly ways, Andrew had treated her badly.

The next evening, she missed tea in order to change out of her uniform and was waiting by his bus stop opposite the hospital from before five o'clock. The staff came surging out shortly afterwards and the crowd waiting for buses grew. Beth stood back against the park railings out of the way. Buses came and filled up and the line of waiting passengers began to grow again.

All day she'd been distracted and upset. She felt torn apart. Should she ask him to go into the park for a few minutes? It was quite a pleasant evening. Or should she just hand back his ring and let him go home?

While she was working, she usually wore her ring on her imitation pearl necklace round her neck. The collar of her uniform dress came up high and hid it completely. Her ring was now in its box in her pocket, ready to return to him. She fingered it as she watched the hospital gates for his tall figure.

He was late coming out. She looked at her watch. She'd paid only half-a-crown for it and it lost between five and ten minutes each day, so it wasn't much help.

She saw two young trainees from the laboratory coming out.

She asked, 'Is Mr Langford still in the lab?'

'No, he's gone. He left early today.'

'Oh!' That rooted Beth to the spot. 'At what time?'

'Before five, about quarter to.'

She couldn't believe it! He'd done it deliberately, knowing she'd be waiting here for him. He couldn't face her!

'Said he was taking his mother somewhere and needed to get away quickly.'

As the two youths turned away to join the queue at the bus stop, she heard one say to the other, 'All right for Mr High and Mighty, but we have to stay on to put everything away.'

Beth was absolutely furious. She turned away and rushed to the park gates, wanting to be alone. She could feel the tears on her cheeks and brushed them away, but they kept welling up. It was a struggle to hold them back.

There were not many people about at this time. She reached the lake and sank down on one of the benches. She'd been half expecting Andrew to break their engagement since he'd left Dock Cottages with such haste. All the same, it was a shock and she felt he could have found a kinder way to tell her. She wondered if he'd have bothered to write a note at all if she hadn't written to him first. Or did he think that if he avoided her for long enough the message would sink in? How could he say he loved her and then treat her like this?

It was hard to believe he'd left work early tonight to avoid seeing her, and told white lies to hide what he was doing. Andrew was not the person she'd thought him. He was a coward, a terrible coward if he couldn't tell her to her face. And what about his ring? He'd rather let it go than face her?

She took the ring box from her pocket. Opened it up and studied the ring he'd given her, feeling a powerful urge to toss it into the lake, to throw it off as he'd thrown her off. But it was eighteen carat gold, and a real diamond, a sizeable one, set in platinum shoulders. It was the most expensive thing she'd ever owned and she couldn't bring herself to throw it away. He'd surely want it back.

On her next evening off she'd catch him on his way home at five o'clock. No note to warn him this time. She'd throw the ring back at him, tell him no gentleman would act in this way. She hoped half the lab staff would be at the bus stop within hearing. She'd let them all know just what she thought of him. He wouldn't like that, she knew. He prided himself on being upright, a pillar of society. He was so turned in on himself, he couldn't mix with people, be on easy terms with anybody. He stayed aloof and kept his distance. He wasn't popular with the laboratory staff, and he'd told her he didn't get on with his parents. Yet at thirty-one years of age, he was still living with them. He didn't seem to have any friends. He couldn't relate to other people, not even her. He wasn't a happy man.

Perhaps it was better to find out now rather than marry him and be unhappy later. But it was all so hurtful; she was sick with

117

disappointment. Her big plans for the future were shattered.

Beth sat there alone, getting colder and colder as dusk fell. Then she started walking. There were tree-lined roads running through the park; she went up and down and round, plodding on and on.

She was exhausted and hungry, ready to drop, before she felt she could control her tears. She needed to tell somebody, get it off her chest, to stop herself fulminating like this. She thought of Jenny who lived quite close, and crossed the road to Newling Street.

Jenny's house seemed to offer security and contentment. The living room felt cosy, Tom was sitting one side of the fireplace, Jenny's chair was pulled up on the other. To Beth, it seemed a picture of domestic happiness. She'd have preferred to catch Jenny on her own so they could have a long heart-to-heart chat, but Tom's presence couldn't stop her now.

'Andrew's broken it off. It seems he couldn't stomach Dock Cottages.'

'Oh Beth! How awful for you. You were afraid . . . half expecting it, weren't you?'

'A cup of tea?' Tom got to his feet.

'Please.'

Jenny's blue eyes were full of sympathy. 'So he thinks you're not good enough because you come from Dock Cottages? Forget him.'

'There's nothing else I can do.'

'What a rotten snob he is. All that trouble we took when you invited him to tea to meet us all. You're better off without him.'

'He wouldn't tell me to my face.' Beth was getting out the note he'd written to show her when Tom came back with the tea and the cake tin.

'A piece of Jenny's cake? It's fresh today.'

'Please. I missed both tea and supper.'

Jenny's arms went round her then in a comforting hug. 'Poor Beth, no wonder you're upset.'

Tom said rather stiffly, 'I'm sorry about Andrew.'

'I shouldn't have set my hopes so high.'

'Not high enough.' Tom was patting her shoulder. 'Believe me, you're worth two of him. He's no good if he does that.'

Jenny put a teacup in her hand and pulled up another chair to the hearth for her.

'You have Tom and all this,' Beth choked, 'and I have nothing now.'

Tom gave her knee a gentle slap. 'Better fish left in the sea than ever came out of it.'

Beth sighed. 'No, it's fished out. There are two million more young women than there are men in Britain as a result of the war. I might never get another chance.'

Tom smiled at her. 'You read too many newspapers.'

Jenny said softly, 'The trouble is we're all brought up to think marriage is the only way of life for us girls. We're not expected to do anything on our own. We need a man to keep us. But you have a career, Beth, you were very keen on that before you met Andrew.'

'I was.' She'd grown greedy. 'I wanted more.'

'You can earn your own living. You can still have a good life without a husband.'

Of course she could. Beth felt comforted. She'd thought of doing midwifery, getting another qualification. She could still do that. She had to stop thinking her life was at an end because Andrew no longer wanted her.

She smiled wryly at her sister. 'All the same, I think I'd like to have a husband too. I feel I'd be missing a lot if I—'

'You'll get one,' Tom assured her. 'I know lots who'd jump at the chance. But what's important is getting the right one.'

Just before five o'clock the next Friday, Beth was waiting at the bus stop for Andrew to come out. She felt cold, her anger with him had evaporated with the passage of time. People were drifting out in twos and threes, their day's work over. At last she saw his stiff, erect figure striding towards her. He was wearing his white mac and was alone as usual. She didn't move until he joined the group waiting for a bus.

'Hello, Andrew.' He jerked back, she'd taken him by surprise this time. He was backing off, his voice a harsh whisper.

'What d'you want? I thought we'd ended . . . It's over.'

She had to follow him into the shadows, away from the crowd.

'Don't you want your ring back?' She held out the little box between her finger and thumb as though it was too hot to hold. 'I'm no longer entitled to wear it, am I?'

He couldn't look at her. 'No, no. I can't . . . What would I do with it?'

'You could give it to your next girl friend.' She doubted he'd ever manage to get engaged again, he kept everyone at arm's length.

She heard his agonised intake of breath. He was acutely embarrassed. 'You keep it.' So he was ashamed of the way he'd treated her.

'Here's my bus.' It lumbered to the stop and pulled up with a squeal of brakes. He couldn't wait to shake her off. Beth followed him onto the bus, most of them went past Dock Cottages. He wasn't going to escape her that easily. He'd found an empty seat and she slid down beside him before he realised she was on the bus. The look he gave her was almost of hatred. It made Beth feel totally rejected.

'What did I do that made you change your mind? Did it upset you to meet my family?'

'Well, yes . . . It made me realise . . . Most upsetting, the district . . . It was worse . . . A nightmare, I couldn't sleep that night.'

'Poor you.' There was contempt in her voice.

'Now I see the address everywhere. It's a slum.'

'I know, I was brought up there.'

'It should be bulldozed. Every time I pick up a newspaper, there's trouble reported there. It's a hotbed of crime.'

She flinched. 'Are we all to be branded by that? I know lots of decent people who live there. Poverty is their only crime.'

It was what Beth had always feared. Why her mother had advised her to keep quiet about where she lived. Andrew was deeply entrenched in the comfortable middle classes. She'd developed a finely tuned sense of social status and despite the talk about the levelling of classes she knew there was a great divide between his family and hers. Class had come between them and it wasn't just a question of whether she could bridge it, but whether he could too. It looked as though he was too set in his ways.

She got up abruptly at St James's Church and left without another word. She almost ran home, her fingers closing on the ring box in her pocket. She'd never wear it again, she couldn't.

She'd keep the ring by her. If she was really in need of money she could sell it. She'd think of it as a nest egg.

One night, when Sidney came home at midnight after the Blood Tub closed its doors, Peggy knew immediately he wanted more than a cuddle. She reckoned he was fired up by the randy talk that went on in the bar. Although he'd promised her she'd have no more babies, it seemed he expected things to be exactly as they'd always been.

'Give over, Sid. Wives are supposed to get six weeks' peace after they've had a baby. You know that.'

'I've heard it before,' he murmured, running his lips up her cheek.

She'd never been able to keep him away for more than two or three weeks, but this time Peggy was determined to be firm.

He whispered, 'Come on, Peg, don't let's fight every time I want a bit of you know what.'

Peggy felt life was one long fight; a fight to make the kids behave, a fight to make ends meet and pay for food and fuel, and a running battle to keep Sidney at a safe distance.

'You enjoy it too.'

'How can I enjoy it? We're risking another baby. I'm scared.'

'It's safe enough right now. It's too soon after Rita to start another.'

'It's not a month yet. It's too soon for sex too.'

Peggy managed to choke him off that night, but he didn't stop bothering her. Another week went by and Sidney became hostile in a way he never had before – bad-tempered and vicious. The following night he hit her. Afterwards he was contrite.

'I'm not myself, I'm all on edge. You get me all wound up. I'm sorry, I didn't mean to hurt you. I don't want to do that, but you can't just refuse me.'

'All right, but only if you use those sheaths.'

'Peggy!'

'I'm not going to have another baby. I'm not that motherly and you aren't a good father. We're dragging them up. If we had just May and Hilda we'd have done a good job. Enjoyed having them.'

'You don't enjoy anything, Peggy. That's your trouble.'

'You're making me unhappy, really miserable.'

'Damn it, Peggy, you're making me miserable too.'

'Surely nothing is worth the risk of having another?'

'Why can't you relax and have a bit of fun?'

'Fun! I hate it! Can't you see I'm scared stiff? Where's the fun in that?'

'You're turning yourself into a shrew.'

'I'm not going through another nine months of backache and bleeding piles and feeling tired, only to end up with another mouth to feed.'

She managed to hold him at bay for another couple of weeks. One night he got into bed with her and immediately started unbuttoning her nightdress. She knew what that meant.

'You won't forget, Sid?'

'What?' His lips came down hard on hers so she couldn't answer straight away.

'What you promised. That you'd use those things.' She was edging away from him.

'Oh, them? Nah, they don't work, do they? Look at your Jenny.'

'Jenny says complete abstinence is the only guaranteed way not to make another baby.' Peggy was scared, she managed to put six inches of sheet between them.

121

Sidney was shocked. 'You can't say total abstinence, I'm your husband. It's my right.'

'You've got to do something. You won't even withdraw before the end. I'm not letting you near me unless you use those things our Jenny recommends.'

'Right,' he said. 'That's what I'll do if you want it that bad.'

'They're on your bedside table. I'm not going through all that again, I've told you.'

He pulled himself up the bed and she heard him tear the packet. 'You won't have to, luv. I'll see it's all right.'

Peggy was instantly back into his arms. It was only later when she lit the candle to get up that she saw the unused condom on his bedside table, and realised he hadn't put the thing on.

'You cheated! You lied!'

'It doesn't feel right, Peg. Not with that on.'

Peggy was crying with fear and frustration but he was laughing.

She screamed at him, 'You think it's funny, some sort of a joke you've managed to play. You're totally irresponsible. I can't rely on you for anything.'

'I'm sorry,' he said, looking contrite now.

'Never again,' she spat. 'I can't trust you. It's total abstinence from now on.'

Peggy boiled with rage over the following days. She felt Sidney had betrayed her. She couldn't see any reason why he shouldn't use those things. According to Jenny, other men did.

Beth and Jenny were coming round all the time, but she couldn't tell them what Sidney had done to her, it cut too deep, she was still hurting. But that didn't stop her talking about her other dissatisfactions. They made a pot of tea and sat round talking about old times.

'Think of Mam bringing up ten of us on the fourth floor. Having to carry all the food up.'

'And the pram. The women suffer most in Dock Cottages. The men go out to work and get away from the place.'

'They have beer and their friends at the pub while the women have to stay home to look after the children. They have all the problems of looking after large families on very little money.'

'It's all right until their health goes.'

Peggy said, 'I thought Mam was wonderful when I was small.'

'You thought Dad was wonderful too,' Beth told her.

'Yes, they were both so loving and kind. Mam couldn't do enough for me. She used to read me a bedtime story every night.'

'I remember her doing that,' Beth said.

'I don't,' Jenny retorted.

Peggy said, 'By the time you were old enough to remember anything, she had too much to do. Things were better for me before the rest of you came along. I had the happiest childhood of anyone in Dock Cottages.'

'You were spoiled,' Jenny said. 'You got everything you wanted.'

'But when I left school everything fell apart.'

'I thought you liked the tapestry works,' Jenny said. 'You talked me into working there anyway.'

'In a way I did, but I expected ... That was when I first realised lessons at the North End Academy of Dance weren't going to lead to professional stage work. Dad promised I could train for the stage, but I had no idea how to go about doing it.'

'Neither had he.'

'I felt let down. I was at war with him when I was in my teens, then when I was seventeen I met Sidney.' Peggy felt the lump growing in her throat. It hurt even to talk about her disappointments.

'Mam wanted me home by half ten when I went out with him, but it was impossible if we went dancing over in Liverpool. I couldn't see why I should cut my evenings short and neither did Sidney. I used to fly into rages at Mam, defy her and refuse to pull my weight about the house or look after the babies or anything. I wouldn't do anything she asked. I was a bad example to the rest of you.'

'I remember that,' Beth said. 'I remember finding Mam in tears over something you'd done.'

Peggy was blinking back her distress. 'Mam wasn't keen on Sidney, she thought I could do better.'

'Dad liked him.'

'I know, and I wouldn't hear a word against him.'

Beth said, 'She didn't want you to get married at eighteen.'

'I could see no reason to wait. I wanted to be grown up too. I must have been a devil to live with.'

'Mam said you were,' Beth agreed.

'It took having children of my own to make me realise what Mam had had to put up with.' Peggy blew her nose. 'I should have listened to her.' She knew that now. 'You didn't give her any trouble, Beth.'

'I was away, working at the Wisharts'.'

'You were at home, Jenny. You caused no trouble either.'

Peggy knew she wasn't talking about the things that were really upsetting her, but to talk of lesser hurts of years ago released some of her anguish and made Beth and Jenny think they were helping her.

Peggy dreaded the weekends and school holidays when all the kids were at home. Today was Saturday and worse than usual. Rita had vomited twice and wouldn't stop whingeing. She was sobbing and nothing would soothe her. Usually, she was a good baby, she slept through the night and the other kids kept her chortling happily during the day.

Now she was four months old and beginning to take an interest in what was going on round her. She smiled at everybody, and Peggy was beginning to feel attached to her. She was still adamant about wanting no more babies, but she was accepting Rita.

May was hanging over her pram. 'She's poohed her nappy again, Mam, she stinks.'

Peggy felt fear shaft through her. Rita had filled her nappy three or four times already, or was it five?

'Take her to the clinic,' May said.

'The clinic was yesterday, they aren't open today.'

Peggy cleaned her up but the baby didn't stop howling. This wasn't like Rita.

'I know, we'll go up to Grandma's,' she told May. 'She'll know what to do. Perhaps Auntie Beth will be there. Get Eric's boots tied for him.'

It bothered Peggy when her children were ill, it wasn't as though she could afford to get medicine from the doctor for them.

Jenny opened Mam's front door when she knocked and Peggy was glad to see Beth there too.

'You changed her to the bottle, didn't you?' Beth was biting her lip.

'My milk went,' Peggy said. She hated breast-feeding, it made her feel like a cow.

'But bottles—'

'I'm very careful. I do wash them out properly.'

'Stop all feeds,' Beth said. 'Nothing but boiled water to drink, give her plenty of that.'

Her mother said, 'Have you got a bottle with you? There's water that's been boiled in the kettle here, she could have some of that now.'

Peggy retrieved a bottle half full of milk from the bottom of the pram and didn't miss her sister's grimace. 'She doesn't like water, she won't take it.'

'She doesn't like milk either today.' Beth poured it into a cup and gave it to Eric, and then scrubbed the bottle viciously. That made Peggy feel inadequate.

'How long must she have just water?'

'Until she's over all this. If you put her back on milk too soon, the diarrhoea will start up again.'

'But she'll be hungry soon. She'll really howl then.'

'It's what the doctor would tell you,' Beth said.

Jenny cuddled Rita and gave her the water. She took a long drink and fell asleep in her arms. It made Peggy see both her sisters as stronger than she was, better organised and more determined.

The place seemed full of children. Mam was dozing.

'She isn't feeling too good today,' Beth said. 'I'll walk back home with you, though I've got to go back on duty at five.'

'I'll come too,' Jenny said. 'We've got meals organised here for today and tomorrow.' It didn't help that Jenny was able to do things like that even though she was six months pregnant.

Beth said, 'The vegetables from your allotment were a great help, Jenny. Do tell Tom how much they're appreciated.'

They set off. The pram wheels squeaked irritatingly, Peggy had meant to look for some oil for them. Eric wouldn't walk and had to be lifted to sit on the end of the pram. Peggy was sweating, it was heavy to push.

'Wouldn't Sidney like an allotment, Peg?' Jenny asked. 'It helps a lot with the housekeeping.'

'Can't see him doing anything like that. He'd rather read a newspaper and rest on his bed.'

'That's where he is now,' May said.

'He's like Dad. And I suppose I'm more like Mam.'

Jenny said gently, 'Mam's well-organised, Peggy. Or she was until she got ill. She always had a good grip on the household. Everything was as clean and tidy as it was possible to be. Hot meals were on the table at regular times. Mam had strength.'

'But not where Dad was concerned. I'm not going to be as soft with Sidney as Mam was with Dad.'

'Good,' Jenny said. 'Have you kept that stockpot going?'

'Yes, I boil it up every day on the trivet like you said and throw in bits of this and that, so there's always hot soup for the children at dinner time.'

'Dad likes the soup,' May put in. 'So do I.'

'I've tried hard to keep the house tidy too.' They'd both come and spring-cleaned the place for her as Beth had promised. Jenny had made her new curtains for the living room, but Peggy knew her sisters thought she was letting things slide again, and that she ought to make more effort.

'There's so much to do. All the beds need changing again and I spend so much time trying to find clothes for them to wear.'

'It needn't. It's a question of getting on top of things, of taking control.'

'I never stop . . .'

'Do the important things first.'

'I do, Beth.' She unlocked her front door and they lifted the pram inside. Bonny got up from the hearth rug and leapt round the table, barking her head off. 'I do try, but my life's a mess, I'm going down the drain.'

Beth sat down. 'Look at the time you waste fussing over that great slobbering dog. Think of the work she makes. On a wet day she comes in making paw marks everywhere. And as for the food she eats . . .'

'You need the time and energy for other things,' Jenny told her. 'The children need the food. You've got to get your priorities right.'

'Bonny licks your plates, I've seen her.' Peggy saw Beth curling her nose up. 'She's a source of infection for the kids, like Rita being ill now.'

Peggy cringed, Beth was making her feel guilty about that. She had to justify keeping Bonny.

'Sidney says she's a good guard dog. That we won't get anything stolen while she's about. She's better than a lock on the door.'

'But a lot more trouble.'

Beth said more gently, 'I've got a morning off on Monday. Shall I come up and help you change the beds and wash the sheets? If there's time, we could look through the children's clothes and get them sorted.'

'They'll need more than sorting,' Peggy complained. 'May needs new boots, she's growing out of the ones she's got.'

'I don't know what we can do about that,' Jenny said. 'But I'll come and help with the washing, you'll feel better when you're straight.'

Monday turned out to be a good drying day, it was fine with cool sunshine and a blustery wind. Rita was better, only two dirty napkins yesterday and not sick at all. She was whimpering a lot, Peggy thought she was hungry and wanted to give her milk but thought she'd better ask Beth's opinion first.

Peggy hated wash day, but it wasn't such a bind when there were fewer kids underfoot and three adults to do the work. She had to heat all the water on the stove in the scullery and carry kettles and pans out to the wash house. Beth and Jenny were taking turns to wield the posher in the zinc tub. Putting the flannelette sheets through the mangle

126

afterwards was an awful job, but with Beth to turn the handle, Peggy didn't find it too bad.

'It would be easier if the whole thing didn't rock,' Beth said. 'Give us a hand, Jenny, let's move the mangle over a bit.'

As Jenny put her weight on the flagstone under the mangle, she felt it move. 'What's underneath here?' she asked.

Peggy didn't know. 'Nothing.'

It was Beth who noticed the metal bar standing in the corner, and used it to lever the flagstone up.

'It looks as though this has been done many times before. Look at these scratch marks.'

Jenny held the stone upright. 'There's boxes of something here. It looks like a hidey-hole.'

Peggy felt weak at the knees. 'Sidney's always coming out here. And so is Dad.' She lifted one of the boxes out and opened it up. 'Watches!'

Beth and Jenny were crowding close to look, their eyes round with surprise.

Jenny said, 'I bet Dad's pinched them from the docks.'

Peggy could feel herself going cold with horror. 'And Sidney probably sells them in the pub.'

'There's that biscuit tin I gave you for Christmas,' Beth said. 'Not last Christmas, the one before. Such a pretty tin with those dogs on it.'

'Pekinese,' Peggy said, hooking it out. 'May wanted it to keep her bits and pieces in, but when it was empty it just disappeared.'

'It rattles.'

'It's heavy.' Peggy took the lid off. 'It's full of money!'

'Blimey,' Jenny said. 'Does he tell you how much he makes?'

'No, never. Never gives me any either. This is between him and Dad.'

'Old meanies. This is all beer money then.'

'Looks like it. I wonder if they know how much is here?' Peggy trawled her fingers through it. It was a long time since she'd seen so much money.

'It's a treasure trove.' Jenny giggled.

'Feels like Christmas over again.' Peggy giggled with her. 'I'm going to take some and buy new boots for May.'

'Should you? I mean . . .'

'For heaven's sake, Beth! Hilda can have May's old ones, they aren't in bad nick yet, just too small. I'll buy a pair for Frankie too, and Eric can have his old ones. Then they'll all be well shod.' Peggy took a

127

handful of coins. There was a golden guinea amongst them. She picked out another. 'I could get them new socks and—'

'If you take too much they'll miss it,' Jenny said.

Peggy threw one of the guineas back. 'Better if they notice nothing. Then I can come back when I'm short. It'll all go on booze and fags otherwise. Why shouldn't I?'

When Beth had to go back to the hospital, Jenny left with her, and Peggy sat on in the bed chair fingering the money she'd taken. She felt disgusted with Sidney. He was so selfish, he cared more about enjoying himself than getting clothes and food for his kids.

Chapter Eleven

Now that she no longer went on outings with Andrew, Beth went home almost every day when she was off duty. She told herself it was to make sure Seppy was coping and her mother was all right.

Tonight she had an evening off and she wished she had something interesting to do. She felt restless if she spent an evening off in the nurses' home. That was considered a terrible waste by her colleagues, who all seemed to have no shortage of friends and places to go. Beth thought of going to the pictures by herself but then decided she was feeling low and wasn't in the mood, she'd go home again.

The light drizzle when Beth started to walk up from the hospital turned to a downpour when she reached St James's Church and she ran the rest of the way. She let the lobby door bang behind her, and felt out of breath as she climbed the stairs.

'Beth.' She'd reached the first landing when she heard Ken call. 'Hang on a minute.'

He bounded up the stairs and stood towering over her. 'You're soaking! Here, let's have that wet coat off before you go in, it needs a shake.' It was done before she found the breath to protest. Her hat was lifted off too and raindrops scattered down the stairwell. 'I wanted a word.'

'Yes?' Ken always treated her as though she was six years old and in need of his care.

'Mam's just told me you're no longer engaged, you changed your mind about him.'

'It wasn't quite like that,' she choked. At the hospital she'd let it be known that her engagement was off and had heard the pros and cons dissected so many times, she felt she could stand no more. 'Your mam's being kind.'

'I want you to know . . . I was very unhappy when I heard you were serious about him. Good-looking, Mam said, and a real gent. Rich too.' There was intensity in Ken's gaze now. 'If I said nothing, it doesn't mean I didn't care. It cut deep, Beth.' He sighed. 'I stood back because I had nothing to offer you.'

Beth said, 'It wasn't me that changed my mind, it was Andrew. I reckon Dock Cottages put him off.'

'That's awful! It didn't put my mother off.' Ken was leaning against the wall, her coat over his arm. 'And she had to come and live here. She said love sees everything through rose-tinted specs, even Dock Cottages.'

'My mother too,' Beth agreed.

'You're better off without him if he held that against you.'

'Yes, well, it's all over now.'

'It's his loss and my gain. I couldn't compete with him, could I? Not when he could improve your lot in life so much. I'm glad he's not in the running any more.'

'Ken . . .'

'Anyway, your mam was against me.'

'She said you were good-hearted and would do anything to help, like all the Clovers.'

'But I'd never be able to give you what that other fellow could.'

Beth turned to go, she couldn't take any more, this was bringing it all back. He put a hand on her arm and stopped her. She choked out, 'I loved him, Ken.'

He sighed. 'I'm sorry, I'm not doing this right, am I?'

'I'm not ready. Can't think of anyone but him.'

'No, you're still hurting. You must think I'm heartless. Selfish too. I should have had the sense to wait. I will wait.'

Beth tried to pull herself together. 'Thank you for telling me. It's good to know you care.' It was. 'I'm fond of you, Ken, but not in the way . . .'

'I understand,' he said softly, then bent and kissed her cheek. 'I'll wait. I have to anyway, I've still nothing to offer you. I'm caught fast for the next couple of years. Mam's got nobody but me and Maggie to give her anything. She takes in a bit of washing and looks after old Mr Jackson but it's not enough.'

Beth understood poverty only too well. 'It'll be easier when the younger two are earning.'

'I wanted you to know how I feel. I mean, well, I always fancied you, Beth. We can be friends, can't we?'

'We've always been friends.'

'When's your next evening off? We could go to the pictures. That's if you can pay your own way.'

Beth smiled. 'Thursday.'

'Sod's law. My ship sails Thursday morning.'

'Next time?'

'Yes, next time.' He draped her coat over her arm and plonked her hat on her head. She listened as he clattered back to the ground floor and his front door slammed. Then she pulled her hat straight and went on up. Ken was a good sort, kind-hearted and selfless. He'd had to look after his mother and family since his father died. He was outgoing and jolly too. She'd never have to worry about what he was thinking, because he'd tell her straight out. She always knew where she stood with him. He was attuned to the feelings of others and wouldn't hurt anybody. It was a great pity she'd fallen in love with Andrew instead of him.

As soon as she started to climb the last flight of stairs, her nose told her Seppy was cooking liver and onions. When she reached the living room, the usual evening flurry was in full flood. Dad was already at the table shovelling his meal down, Mam was there too but was pushing hers round her plate. Beth had not told them she'd be coming.

'You must have half of my liver,' Mam said. 'I'm not hungry.'

'No, Mam.' Beth would be embarrassed to take it. 'I've had my tea already.'

She always prepared herself for an evening at home by eating more than she normally would at teatime in the hospital, but there was only bread and jam and either a biscuit or a piece of cake on offer. It meant she missed hospital supper which was a more substantial cooked meal, but it didn't hurt her to be hungry now and then, she usually had an apple in her room.

She busied herself taking over the cooking from Seppy, making him sit down with his meal. The children were clamouring for food but the pans weren't large enough to cook for everybody all at once, and anyway, it was a squash if they all sat at the table together. It meant that the job of cooking was spun out over a longer time. The young ones fell on their food when it was ready, all except Bobby.

'What's the matter?' Beth cut up his share of liver, and softened his potatoes with a little milk. 'Come on, Bobby.'

Her mother sighed. 'He hasn't seemed himself all day. I'm afraid he's sickening for something.'

Beth tried to coax him to eat, but he wouldn't have it. She felt his forehead, he was hot. 'It could be just a cold he's getting.'

She shared his meal between Colin and Ivor. To give Seppy a break, Beth sent him out to find his friends and Esther disappeared in search of hers. Ivor promised to look after Colin and took him out to play football, and Dad never stayed in. Within an hour, peace was regained.

131

Violet got up on shaky legs and felt her way to the couch to lie down. Bobby crawled after her, and pulled himself to his feet on her cardigan. Beth lifted him up on the couch before Mam could do it herself and watched her arms close round him.

It was only then she realised her mother was feeling down too. She didn't say so, Mam rarely complained about anything. She never had a bad word to say about Dad and never discussed her own problems with Beth. Problems with the children, yes, and the perennial shortage of money, clothes and food. That sort of chatter went on all the time in Dock Cottages.

Mam usually asked about her day in the hospital, told her snippets of news about Jenny and Peggy, and things that the younger children had said and done. Tonight she was unusually silent. Beth could see an unaccustomed droop to her mouth. Bobby was dozing in the crook of her arm. Beth pulled a chair up to the couch, sat down beside her and felt for her hand.

Her mother said, 'Perhaps it's for the best. Would Andrew have made you happy? I'm not sure he would have been right for you.'

'I'll get over him.' Beth hadn't realised her own low spirits were so obvious.

'Of course you will.' Beth saw a tear leak out and run down her mother's cheek unheeded and felt a stab of compassion.

'What is it, Mam? You're really in the dumps tonight.'

'Whatever will become of the little ones? It frightens me to think of them being motherless. Bobby's only a baby.'

'You mustn't think like that.' Beth tried to sound firm. Mam had not mentioned her illness since the day she'd come home from the hospital when she'd learned how serious it was; the night Beth had embarrassed her father by telling him he must avoid making any more babies.

'Beth, I want you to have my cameo brooch.'

'No, Mam, I like to see it on you. It really makes your black dress look special.'

'Get it for me, love.'

Beth fetched the little box from her dressing table. Violet opened it. It was a larger than average brooch with a gold safety chain; finely carved in the traditional style in a gold filigree setting.

'It's a handsome ornament.'

'Your grandmother gave it to me just before I was married. She said she'd have liked to give me money, but she hadn't any. Instead, she gave me this. A gold bracelet and a locket on a gold chain too. She said I could raise money on them if I had to. I disappointed her, I'm afraid.

132

Poor Mother, she was very fond of this cameo and I've hung on to it through the thin times when everything else went. I want you to have a little nest egg, Beth. I'm afraid you might need it.'

'I have Andrew's ring, haven't I? I'd sell that first. It's not something I'd want to wear now.'

'Here.' The cameo was pushed into Beth's hand.

'I shall keep it. It reminds me of you.'

Mam gave a gusty sigh. 'I might not be here much longer. I'm dying, aren't I?'

'No,' Beth protested.

'I feel I am. I'm useless now, not able to look after Colin or Bobby.' Her arm tightened round the sleeping child. 'I wish I could get better, for my own sake and theirs.'

'You are getting better. You're stronger, putting on a bit of weight.' That was what she and Jenny told each other but Beth wasn't sure it was the truth.

'I can feel my strength ebbing away, Beth. It's terrible to know it's going to happen. My life shortened by twenty or thirty years.'

'You could be here for a long time yet, Mam.' Beth tried to sound convincing. 'It isn't going to happen for ages.'

'It's the thought of leaving him.' She was staring down at Bobby's sleeping face. 'And the rest of you.' Beth saw another tear roll down her mother's cheek. 'I can't bear to talk of it to any of you. It makes me think about it even more, makes it seem closer. Better if I don't.'

'Mam!' Beth's hand tightened on the frail fingers.

'How will you manage? So many young ones.'

'We'll manage somehow. They have plenty of grown-up sisters and brothers to look after them. I'll take care of Bobby.' The pain on Mam's face told Beth how much she was agonising about this. 'What's brought this on? You're usually so cheerful.'

'Mrs Gordon died today. You know her, from number eighteen.'

'She had cancer, Mam. Quite different.'

'I know a dicky heart is different. Nobody's saying I've got a year left or six months or whatever.'

'There then.'

'But I could go at any moment, couldn't I?'

Beth couldn't bring herself to agree. 'You're more rested now, Mam. You're better. You could be here for years.'

'I'm a trouble to you all like this.'

'No. You're still keeping the family together.'

'I want to live. I want the normal span.' There was anguish in her

133

voice. 'Three score years and ten. I don't want to leave you all.' Her eyes were tightly shut, her face screwing up; she was hugging Bobby tight.

Beth ached for her. Mam's troubles made her own seem as nothing. It must be a terrible thing to accept that death was close for oneself.

'What a fuss I'm making.' Mam dried her eyes. 'What a coward you must think me.'

'I think you're very brave, Mam.'

One morning in September, Beth was on the ward, setting up the trolley to do the dressing round. It was one of her regular duties to re-dress the patients' wounds following their operations. One of the nurses in training helped her with this, moving the screens from bed to bed and undoing bandages in readiness. If her helper was a probationer, she would watch Beth remove drains and stitches and clean wounds. The more senior nurses did the routine dressings under her supervision.

This morning, Beth asked Myrtle Harris to do the round with her. She was a pretty dark-haired girl in her second year of training.

Myrtle was pleased. 'I like the dressing round. Are there any stitches to come out today?'

'Yes, Miss Lewis's, if her wound's healed enough.'

'Can I take them out?'

'If you want to, but she's not an easy patient. She'll make a fuss.'

They'd all agreed that Miss Lewis was neurotic. She'd complained of such frequent abdominal pain that the surgeon had performed a laparotomy but had found nothing wrong. He'd removed her appendix but the laboratory report had confirmed that it was healthy.

'I could do with the practice,' Myrtle said.

'You were fine with that hysterectomy last week. I hope Miss Lewis isn't going to throw herself around the bed.'

Beth liked Myrtle Harris, they'd talked together about their plans, what they hoped the future would bring them. Myrtle was engaged.

'He's going to be a missionary,' she told Beth. 'He's undergoing training and hoping to be sent to China. I'd love to go out there with him, though I've got to finish my own training first. He says a nurse would be very useful to his mission.'

'What a wonderful adventure,' Beth breathed. 'You'll see another part of the world.' Her life would never be as exciting as that.

She'd noticed that few women on the ward bought themselves a newspaper. If they had the money, they preferred to keep it to spend on their families rather than themselves. As she pushed the dressing trolley to Miss Lewis's bed, Beth saw she was engrossed in the *Daily Mail*. She was able to see what she was reading, her eye caught the name Marie Stopes.

As Myrtle rattled the screens round her bed, Miss Lewis hastily folded the pages and pushed the paper guiltily into her locker.

The name had caught Myrtle's eye too. 'Was that an article by Marie Stopes?' she asked as she laid the patient flat on her back and turned back the bedclothes.

'Yes. Absolute filth. There's also letters from the public to her.' Miss Lewis was elderly, with a prudish mouth. 'They shouldn't be allowed to print such things in newspapers. I think it's disgusting.'

Myrtle was silent, refusing to meet Beth's gaze. They undid the bandages.

Miss Lewis said, 'What is England coming to? All this dirt in the papers.'

Beth said, 'Really she's trying to help women . . .'

'Nonsense! She should be put in prison.'

Beth had heard the clergy thunder from their pulpits about the pornographic nonsense Dr Stopes was spreading. She knew the medical profession denounced her ideas because she held a doctorate in fossil botany and not a medical degree. The newspapers printed articles by her and letters to her, to increase their circulation; her reputation had reached even to the inhabitants of Dock Cottages, though few had read her books. Like Beth's family, they couldn't afford the six shillings they cost.

'Are my stitches to come out today?'

Beth examined her wound and nodded to her colleague to go and scrub her hands at the washbowl. 'Yes, they're ready to come out.'

'I've been dreading this, it won't hurt, will it?'

'Hardly at all,' Beth told her.

She watched Myrtle Harris as she bent over the bed, carefully edging the suture scissors into position. She caught a glimpse of a necklace of blue beads showing at the neck of her uniform and knew she threaded her engagement ring onto her necklace, so she could keep it safe when she wasn't allowed to wear it on her finger, just as Beth had used her necklace of imitation pearls.

Before the snip could be made, Miss Lewis writhed on her bed. 'Oh, the scissors are so cold.' Her hands hovered over her abdomen, as though to protect her wound. She was making the fuss Beth had expected.

She said gently, 'Hold my hands. You can squeeze if it helps.' She kept them out of Myrtle's way and the scissors advanced more purposefully. They snipped and one stitch was removed.

'Oh, that really hurt. I knew it would.'

Myrtle paused to look at Beth who said, 'Your wound is well-healed, Miss Lewis. You shouldn't feel more than the catgut pulling through.' She nodded to Myrtle to continue, she was doing everything exactly as it should be done. Another snip and another.

'Ohhh! That hurt! This is awful.'

'Only three more to come out,' Myrtle murmured, and snipped another.

'Do try to keep still,' Beth urged. 'Nurse will be finished more quickly if you do. We can't leave them in any longer.'

'The scissors are wet! I can't stand cold wet steel on my stomach. It's torture.'

'We keep them in methylated spirit,' Beth said in her calm voice. 'To keep them sterile.'

Miss Lewis snatched her hands free. She was trying to hold Myrtle away from her, preventing her taking out the last two. 'Give me a minute's rest, I can't stand this. I really can't.'

Beth said, 'All right, we'll wait a moment.'

When she took firm hold of Miss Lewis's hands again, she said, 'Take a deep breath, Miss Lewis, and hold it.' She wanted to give her something else to concentrate on. But as the scissors went close, Beth couldn't hold on to her hands. She made a grab for Myrtle's wrist, but Myrtle raised the scissors out of the way. The patient's flailing hands caught at the bib of her apron, Myrtle stepped back and the patient hung on, pulling at her apron, dress, and the necklace of blue beads, which snapped. Beads began to drop through her clothes and roll across the floor.

'Oh, my necklace, it's broken!' Myrtle held her scrubbed up hands high and tried to stop the beads bouncing across the floor with her foot.

'I'll see to them. You get those last stitches out.' Beth moved to the other side of the bed.

The beads were rolling everywhere, through the wheels of the screens. The ring which had been strung on the necklace rolled too. Beth had to chase it under a locker. When she picked it up, she found she had a wedding ring not the engagement ring she'd expected. She popped it in her pocket.

'I'm sorry,' Miss Lewis wept. 'So sorry, I couldn't help it, such agony. I've ruined your necklace.'

Myrtle's shocked eyes stared over her mask at Beth. 'My ring?'

'I have it safe.'

'There's another bead over here, Nurse.'

'And another here.' Beth went to get them. She could hear Miss Lewis fretting away.

'Ough, ough.'

'They're all out now, Miss Lewis. Your wound is nice and dry, it's healed well. You'll be going home soon.'

'I'm not well enough to go yet. I don't think I could manage at home yet.'

Beth heard voices on the other side of the ward.

'Doesn't she fuss so? You'd think she was being murdered.'

'I had my stitches out yesterday and I hardly felt a thing.'

'You'll need a dry dressing only now, Miss Lewis,' Beth said, glad of the mask hiding her smile.

The moment the new dressing was in place and the screens removed, Myrtle set off up the ward with the dressing trolley at a furious pace.

'Hang on, there's still Mrs Owen and Miss Pringle to do,' Beth said, hurrying after her.

The trolley didn't stop until it was inside the clinic room. Myrtle whipped off her mask. There was desperation on her face. Beth closed the door carefully before offering the wedding ring back to her on the palm of her hand. 'You're married already?'

'Please don't say anything. Don't tell anybody.'

'I won't, don't worry.'

'I must finish my training. If Matron found out, she wouldn't let me carry on.'

'When did you get married?'

'Five months ago. When I had a week's holiday. Bill wanted it.'

'How romantic,' Beth breathed.

'I thought it was too at the time, but I only see Bill on my day off.'

'How much longer have you got before you sit your finals?'

'Eighteen months. I get collywobbles when I think of it. Anything could happen in that time. Bill will probably sail for China about then. I just hope I get my results in time to go with him. And I'll have to pass at the first attempt.'

'You will. You're keen.'

'I do hope so.' She smiled. 'The voyage out will be our belated honeymoon. I'm keeping my fingers crossed that it'll all work out.'

'You do live life to the full,' Beth said. 'Fancy you being married already.'

137

'You won't tell?'

'I won't breathe a word to anyone. Your secret's safe with me.'

'Thanks.' She was re-setting the trolley with more sterile dressings. 'Mrs Owen next?'

It was only later, when Beth was writing up the notes in Sister's office, that she realised Myrtle Harris must surely know about family planning. No new wife needed to avoid pregnancy more than she did. If she started a baby now, she wouldn't be allowed to finish her training here or to travel out to China with her husband. She'd have to stay in England without him until the baby was deemed old enough to travel, and the medical profession was unlikely to see China as a suitable place to bring up a young child. For her, it would be a disaster.

Beth went down the ward to look for her and said, 'Can I have a word in the office?' She had no reason to be nervous of Myrtle Harris. She sat down at the desk and indicated the other chair.

'Aren't you afraid of getting pregnant in the next eighteen months?' she asked.

Myrtle pulled a face. 'Yes, a bit.'

'But wouldn't that ruin all your plans? About going to China?'

'I'm more than a bit worried. Some missionaries leave their wives and children here. I wouldn't want that. I should hate to be left behind.'

'But you went ahead and got married all those months ago?'

'We put our faith in Marie Stopes.'

'And?'

She smiled. 'Fully justified up to now.'

'You've got to tell me how you do it,' Beth said and told her about her own family.

'It's all in Marie Stopes's book,' Myrtle whispered. 'We bought a copy of her *Wise Parenthood*. We had to save up for it, but it gave us the answers.'

'Everybody seems to be against her. What d'you think?'

'She's a godsend to us. People are against her because she dares to write openly about sex education and contraception, and up to now it's been a sin even to mention such things.'

'But it's what everybody needs.'

'Exactly. We started saving for her other book, *Married Love*, but we saw it in a chemist's shop and it's subtitled *A New Contribution to the Solution of Sex Difficulties*.' Myrtle stifled a laugh. 'We decided to spend our cash on something else.'

138

'So what does she advise, you know, by way of contraception?'

'She lists half a dozen ways, the safe period, or well-soaped sponges or vinegar douches.'

'I thought there was more to it than that. I read somewhere that she was keen on the latest scientific discoveries.'

'Those too. Sheaths, condoms, you know.'

'But isn't there something women can use?'

'Yes, the Dutch cap, but you have to be fitted for it and she says it's not easy to put in until you've had one baby.'

'Marie Stopes invented it?'

'Not exactly, the Dutch cap was invented ages ago. Marie Stopes has a smaller improved version.'

'Will you lend me her book? I want to read it myself and show it to my sisters and mother. They really need her help. I'll bring it back.'

'Yes, but I haven't got it here with me. I couldn't risk leaving it in my bedroom where the maids might see it. Bill's looking after it. I think he said he was lending it to a friend, but I'll get it for you.'

'You won't forget?'

'No, I promise. One favour deserves another.'

Chapter Twelve

'Mary Clover's been up,' Violet told Beth when she went home to see her one morning. 'Maggie will be home on Saturday night for a week's holiday. She asked me to tell you.'

'Good, it seems ages since I saw her.' Beth felt she needed taking out of herself. A week of Maggie's company would cheer her up. Maggie had so much energy and always wanted to be doing something.

Maggie loved New Brighton, and the fun of the beach and the fair. She loved trips on the ferry and going round the big Liverpool shops. They'd have a good time together. Beth looked forward to it.

She had Sunday morning off. As soon as she was off duty she went home, looked in on her mother, and then ran downstairs to the Clovers' flat. Maggie came to the door and threw her arms round Beth.

'Lovely to see you, I'm so glad to be back. I do miss you all.'

It was only when she sat down and Mrs Clover asked Maggie's little sister Pat to make a cup of tea that Beth noticed Maggie had lost her usual bounce. The ruddy glowing colour in her cheeks had gone too. She looked drained.

'Aren't you well, Maggie?' she asked.

'She doesn't look well, does she?' her mother said.

'Toothache,' Maggie said. 'It's nagging at me. I'll have to do something about it tomorrow.'

'She's rundown, that's what it is,' her mother said.

'Working too hard.' Maggie smiled.

'I'll get her an iron tonic tomorrow.'

Beth said, 'Let's go over to Liverpool on the ferry, I've got a couple of hours. A blow on the river will make you feel better.'

She was quite shocked when Maggie pulled a face. 'It's raining.'

'No, it's stopped.'

'It'll be cold on the river and I'm tired. I just want to take it easy today.'

'A walk then? We could have a good chinwag. We've a lot of catching up to do.'

Maggie gave her a wan smile. 'I'll walk up to the bus stop with you when you're going back.'

Beth sat on while Mrs Clover and Pat attended to their Sunday dinner, a roast in honour of Maggie's visit. She told her friend about Mam's illness and how they were managing. She heard about Ken, who was down in Cardiff and wasn't expected home in time to see Maggie.

When they had the living room to themselves, Beth asked, 'How's the boyfriend?'

Maggie's face showed distress. 'That's over, he's gone.'

'I know exactly how you feel.' Beth told her at length about Andrew and how bad she'd felt when he rejected her.

'It wasn't quite like that for me,' Maggie said, and started to talk about something else.

Beth felt she knew then why Maggie was so down. She'd had big expectations of Len. She'd talked about him the last time Beth had seen her, he had a good job in an insurance office. She'd seemed totally infatuated by him and now he'd let her down. It took time to get over that sort of thing.

When it was time for Beth to go back to the hospital for her own dinner, Maggie put on her hat and coat and strolled up to the church with her.

'You're still working split shifts, Beth? You'll be able to pop in again tomorrow?' Her big brown eyes implored. 'You cheer me up.'

'All right. I've an afternoon off.'

Maggie was not her usual self then but she was persuaded to go for a walk. Beth was disappointed that the visit she'd looked forward to was falling a little flat.

She didn't see her on Tuesday because Maggie said she'd arranged to go to the dentist. On Wednesday morning, Mrs Clover let her in and seemed distracted and upset.

'I'm glad you've called, Beth,' she said. 'I'm worried.' She lowered her voice. 'Maggie's not at all well. I've got to go out soon, it's my day to go to the Jacksons. I get a bit of dinner ready for them, and I push him to the shops or the park in his wheelchair for a bit of an outing.' They paid her a few shillings to do other little jobs around the house because his wife was frail now in old age, and could no longer manage.

Maggie was hunched in the only armchair. Her eyes were closed and her face was paper white.

'You're ill, Maggie, you must be.' Beth put a hand on her forehead. 'Do you feel sick?'

Maggie's eyelids shot up. She looked guilty, as though she'd been caught doing something wrong. 'No.'

'A pain?'

'I'm OK, Mam's tonic will soon have me right.'

Beth didn't think so. This wasn't the Maggie she knew.

Mrs Clover put the kettle on but Maggie didn't want any tea. When Beth had finished hers, she stood up to leave.

'I'll pop in again later,' she said. 'See how you are.'

Maggie pulled herself to her feet too. She'd taken only two or three steps towards the front door to see Beth out when she suddenly sank in a heap on the floor.

Her mother gave a little cry of shock. 'I knew she was ill. She wouldn't have it. Thank goodness you're a nurse. What should I do?'

Beth was aghast. 'She's fainted.'

'There's something very wrong with her, I know it. She went out yesterday afternoon and she's been terrible ever since.'

'She went to the dentist, didn't she?'

'So she said.'

Beth thought for a moment. 'I think we should take her down to the hospital. They'll see her in casualty.' She stopped. 'How are we going to get her there? She doesn't look as though she could walk up to the bus stop today.'

'Mr Jackson's wheelchair? We could push her up in that. I'll see if he'll lend it to me.'

Maggie was coming round.

'Lie still for a moment,' Beth told her. 'Until you feel better.'

She closed her eyes obediently and when she opened them again they were brimming with naked fear. 'Help me, Beth. Help me.'

'Of course I will. I'm going to take you to the hospital, I think that's the best thing. Tell me what's wrong. Why won't you say?'

There were tears in Maggie's eyes. 'Where's Mam?'

'She's trying to borrow a wheelchair. To get you up to the bus stop.'

'I didn't want anybody to know. Not Mam. I'm bleeding and it won't stop.'

Her mother had the wheelchair at the door. Beth found Maggie's hat and coat and together they helped her into it. Beth could see blood staining the back of Maggie's dress. She was horrified but said no more in front of Mrs Clover. She pushed Maggie up to the bus stop while her mother fussed and worried.

'I said I'd take the wheelchair back and take Mr Jackson out.'

'You do that,' Beth told her.

'But will you be able to manage without it?' Maggie was lying back in it now.

'Yes, the bus stop's almost outside.'

'You'll have to cross that courtyard in front.'

'We'll manage.'

'I ought to come with you, I want to know what's wrong.'

'It's easier for me because I work there, I know everybody. Don't worry, I'll take care of things. Here's the bus. Come on, Maggie, let's get you on.'

Seated beside her on the jolting bus, Beth said, 'What's happened? I have to know.'

'I was in such trouble . . . I was having a baby, Beth. I had it taken away.'

'Maggie!' Beth was shocked, her hands came up to cover her open mouth. Maggie having a baby? Maggie Clover, her best friend? How many times had they been told good girls saved themselves for marriage? Warned never to risk such a disaster. It would expose their sins to public gaze and they'd be treated harshly.

'The woman said I'd be all right.'

There were several women living on the Blocks who for a few shillings were known to help end unwanted pregnancies.

Beth whispered, 'Who was she? Which block?'

'I promised I wouldn't say anything. She could get into trouble.'

'It's illegal, that's why. The doctors will ask you in hospital, press you perhaps. They want to stop women like her doing it.'

'What am I going to say?'

'I don't know . . . Sometimes a miscarriage happens for no reason. You could deny doing anything to start it.'

'But will they believe me?'

'Maybe, maybe not. Depends whether you've been torn inside.'

Maggie covered her face with her hands. 'But I had to have it done.'

'It's dangerous. We get girls on the ward from time to time who . . .'
She was about to say they could be extremely ill after a botched abortion, but she couldn't say that to Maggie now.

'It was the only way. I have to work, I couldn't look after a baby, and I couldn't dump it on Mam, could I? I couldn't even ask her to help look after it. Not start again with another tiny baby. Not after what she's gone through trying to bring us up on her own.'

Beth knew what a struggle Mrs Clover had found it after her husband had been killed.

'Who was this woman? No, on second thoughts, don't tell me.

Better if I don't know. I know too much already.'

'I'm so ashamed,' Maggie moaned. 'I didn't want anyone to know.'

She managed to walk to casualty hanging on to Beth's arm. It wasn't busy at this time of the morning. Beth left her sitting on a chair and was relieved to find Staff Nurse Collins in charge. She occupied the next bedroom in the nurses' home and they were on good terms.

'A friend of yours?'

'Yes, my best friend.' Beth was filling out the card with Maggie's name and address.

'Here's a hospital gown. Get her undressed and into bed in the women's room. I'll get the doctor to look at her straight away.'

When the casualty officer came out from seeing Maggie, he was saying to Nurse Collins, 'It's Mr Cushing's morning in theatre, isn't it?' Mr Cushing was the gynaecologist.

'Yes, he's operating now.'

'I'll get a message to him, he'll probably come out between cases to see her.'

'Does she need to go to theatre?'

'I think so. She's bleeding profusely.'

Beth said, 'Will he put her on the end of his list?'

'Possibly. That's usually what happens.'

Beth went back to sit with Maggie and explain that in all probability her abortion was incomplete and that was why she'd continued to bleed so heavily.

She gripped Beth's hand. 'Don't tell Mam. She'll be so shocked. She'll give me a right bollocking for this.'

'Maggie, what am I to tell her?'

'Anything, but not that I was expecting a baby. She'd kill me.'

'No, she wouldn't. She's right worried about you. You're in good hands here, whatever's needed will be done.'

'Don't leave me . . .'

'I have to, Maggie. Your mother will be waiting to hear from me, and I have to get back here for dinner by half twelve. I'll need to get a move on. You'll be all right now, honest.'

Beth was just in time to catch a bus going back to Dock Cottages, but when she knocked on the Clovers' door, there was no answer. She went up the lobby to the Jacksons'.

It was Mrs Clover who came to the door. 'How did you get on? How's Maggie?'

'They're going to keep her in for a few days. She might need an operation.'

145

'An operation? What for?' Mary Clover was clearly agitated.

Beth felt she couldn't tell an out-and-out lie and say it was for appendix or anything like that. There'd be no scar, and besides . . .

'Not a big one. She'll be perfectly all right. No need to worry.'

'But I am worried. Maggie's never ill. What's wrong?'

'She'll probably be coming up to my ward. I'll be looking after her so I'll be able to keep you up to date with everything.'

Mrs Clover came further out into the lobby and closed the Jacksons' front door behind her.

She hissed, 'Was she having a baby? I think she went up to that Vera Stone on the middle landing yesterday, and afterwards . . .'

Beth had nothing to say to that. She knew her silence was telling.

'She tried to get rid of it, didn't she? I'm sure that's it. She was bleeding . . .'

'Maggie didn't want me to tell you.'

'Why not? She could have bled to death.'

'She's ashamed, very upset and she thought you'd be mad at her.'

'The poor love! If only she'd said . . . I could see she was in pain, writhing in the chair.'

'She'll be all right now.'

'I wish she'd told me. The baby's gone?'

'I believe so.'

'How far on was she?'

'Only a few weeks.'

'But what went wrong? That woman . . . She did something wrong, didn't she? Must have done to cause bleeding like that.'

'The usual reason is something's been left behind, but I don't really know. I couldn't wait for the consultant to see her, and I'll have to rush back now. I'm on duty at one o'clock.'

'What about your dinner?'

'Half twelve, I hope I'll make it in time.'

'You run along, love.' Mrs Clover gave her a hug. 'I don't know how to thank you.'

'You don't have to. Maggie's my best friend, you know that. I'll look after her once she comes up to my ward.'

'I don't know what we'd have done without you.'

'I'll come up after eight tonight. I'll be able to tell you more then.'

'I'm putting you to a lot of trouble.'

'No, I'll be able to spend an hour with Mam. There's no visiting at the hospital until Thursday night.'

It was five o'clock before Maggie was wheeled into her ward but she wasn't fully round from the anaesthetic.

Beth took her notes into the office to read. She'd had a D&C to remove products of conception. Nothing else. It seemed they hadn't found any cuts or tears. Beth kept an eye on her and by seven o'clock Maggie had recovered sufficiently to be able to talk. Already there was a little more colour in her cheeks.

Her first question was, 'Has the baby gone?'

'Yes, you'll be your old self in a day or two.'

Maggie took a deep breath. 'Such a weight off my mind.'

Beth bent over her and whispered, 'Your mother guessed. I couldn't deny it when she asked me straight out.'

'Oh no! Did she say anything . . . You know, that she was disappointed in me, that sort of thing?'

'No. She's upset of course, but she wants to help you. It's better that she knows.'

'At least I don't have to pretend it was something else. You won't tell anyone else?'

'It's written in your notes, so the nurses and doctors here will know. Nobody else needs to.'

'I'm very grateful, Beth.'

Later that evening, Beth was reading the annual statistics published in a newspaper that she'd taken from the pile cleared from the ward. She was horrified to see that fifteen per cent of maternal deaths occurred after illegal abortions. How close had Maggie been to that? If only she'd read Marie Stopes's books, she and her mother would have been saved so much anguish. Beth felt even more strongly that women should not be kept in ignorance of contraception. It caused so much unnecessary suffering.

When Maggie was discharged, Beth was going to tell her all she knew about it. She must never go through this again.

Wednesday was operation day on Ward 3 and always busy for Beth. Today's list was a long one. Sister Jones was concerned about one of the patients newly returned from theatre and was trying to get hold of Dr McCormick.

'There's something the matter with the phone in the doctors' sitting room,' she said to Beth. 'Pop down and see if he's there, will you? Find him if you can.'

Beth headed downstairs and along the main corridor and had almost reached the doctor's room when she saw Dr McCormick coming out of it.

He treated her with frosty formality these days. She said, 'Sister Jones would like you to take a look at Mrs Green, this morning's hysterectomy. She's been trying to ring you, she thinks your phone's been left off the hook.'

'I'll go straight up. Check the phone, would you?'

Beth knocked before pushing the door of the doctors' room open, but there was nobody in. It was how she imagined a gentleman's club would be, with large leather chesterfields and a faint cigarette haze. She'd never been further than the doorway before and had to look round for the telephone. She moved the handset and heard it click into place.

She was turning to go when she noticed the bookcase. The shelves were crammed tight and there were piles of books on top as well, and another pile beside it on the floor. There were books of every sort, even novels, but mostly medical reference and textbooks.

She crept closer. Dare she look to see if they had any books on birth control? Her heart was jumping, she mustn't be caught. Matron's office was almost opposite this room. The lift clanged across the corridor. Beth had left the door ajar but unless somebody stepped inside she couldn't be seen here. Her eyes perused the titles slowly. She made herself concentrate. There were books covering all aspects of medicine, orthopaedics, eyes and ears, general surgery; old volumes bound in calf, newer ones in fresh board covers. Nothing on the subject of birth control.

Would she find it under gynaecology? She took a heavy volume out and skimmed through the index. No, it would more likely be covered under midwifery. They didn't take midwifery cases here, there was a maternity hospital in town, but she found two textbooks on the subject.

She picked up the first. A name had been scrawled on the flyleaf, suggesting this had once been a personal possession, lost perhaps or abandoned. Her fingers were shaking so much she could hardly turn to the index page. It was all about midwifery and its complications. She rammed it back on the shelf and took out the other. As she did so, she saw another, smaller, volume that was half hidden between it and the end of the bookcase. Had it been deliberately hidden?

She took out the small volume and opened it, but her mind was hardly taking in what she was reading. She wasn't even sure the book would be all that helpful, it looked very old and was therefore less likely to have what she wanted. It seemed to be largely about . . . This was it! What she was looking for, birth control.

She was skimming through the pages when footsteps in regulation rubber soles squeaked up the stone corridor outside. Beth froze, and only started breathing again when they went past the door. She dared stay no longer. She wished she could borrow this, take it where she could settle down and read it in peace.

On the spur of the moment, she rammed the book into the large pocket that all nurses' uniforms had, conveniently hidden beneath her apron, and then shot back up to the ward. She was still shaking inside. She could hear voices in Sister's office, the door was ajar. She made herself push it open and tell Sister Jones and Dr McCormick that the telephone handset hadn't been replaced properly but was all right now.

For what was left of the morning she bounced about the ward in a fever of anticipation, the book banging against her knee with every step she took. She could barely sit still to eat her dinner.

She had an afternoon off, and when at last she could rush over to the nurses' home, tear off her cap and apron and throw herself on her bed to read, she realised the book she'd picked up was a real find.

It provided something of the development and history of birth control. She'd thought contraception was in its infancy but she could see now that she'd been wrong.

The methods were listed, including the Dutch cap. There was even a diagram of it, which gave Beth some of the answers she'd been seeking. She hadn't been able to imagine what a Dutch cap was.

It had been devised in Holland in the 1870s and consisted of a rubber disc with the rim reinforced by a watch spring. A free clinic had been opened in Holland in the 1880s, where this, as well as condoms and spermicides, had been prescribed – nearly forty years ago! Beth couldn't believe it.

She learned that this information originally came from a booklet called *The Wife's Handbook* which had been printed in Britain in 1886. It had cost sixpence and was written in a simple style that most women would be able to understand.

It had been a manual of practical advice on hygiene, pregnancy and childcare, with one chapter on contraception. It seemed that spermicides were then in mass production and available in chemist's shops. Quinine or cocoa butter were advised. It even suggested a homemade device: a tampon, a ball of cotton wool tied on a strong thread, soaked in vinegar. That, Beth thought, should suit Mam and Peggy and the women of

Dock Cottages, because it would cost little. The book would have been a boon to poor women everywhere.

She read on and learned that the medical profession had decided *The Wife's Handbook* was 'detrimental to public morals' and as an indecent publication it was withdrawn from sale. Its author, Dr Allbutt, a Leeds dermatologist, had his name removed from the British Register for 'infamous conduct in a professional respect'.

Beth was shocked. Mam need never have had such a large family if she'd known these things. But then there'd be no Colin who was a lovable little tinker, and no Bobby, who was adorable. She hated to think of her family being without the younger ones. She loved them all. Esther, who was so good, and Ivor who was fascinated by horses. But if she'd never known them, if they'd never existed, then it wouldn't have mattered. Certainly it would have been better for Mam.

When Beth finished the book she felt elated. She'd managed at last to find out most of what there was to know about contraception. Certainly enough to prevent her sisters having a baby every year as their mother had done.

She had twenty minutes before teatime and she wanted Jenny to read this all-important book. She took the large envelope in which she kept her nurses' certificates and slid the book into it. Then she ran up to Jenny's house with it. As she'd feared, Jenny was out and there was no answer, but the book would just go through the letter box. Beth scribbled her sister's name on it, together with the message, 'Read this urgently.'

She hurried back to the hospital dining room and felt she had really achieved something. She ate her tea and then went back on the ward for the evening shift.

The feeling of triumph was still there when she came off duty at eight o'clock. She went round to see what Jenny thought of the book.

'It's exactly what we need.' Jenny was enthusiastic. 'I haven't quite finished reading it yet . . .'

Tom laughed. 'She had to stop to get the tea ready but neither Noreen nor I are getting the usual attention.'

'Tom got Noreen ready for bed so I could carry on.'

He smiled. 'I'm dying to read it myself.'

Beth said, 'I want Mam to read it.'

'She must,' Jenny said. 'And Peggy.'

'Let's both take it to Peggy, she takes no notice of me because I'm not married. She thinks I haven't a clue.'

'When are you off tomorrow?'

150

'Evening. It's my day off the next day. But I think we should give it to Mam first.'

'Right. Tom can start reading it now, he'll finish it tonight. I'll finish it off in the morning and take it up to Mam. I'll talk to her about it and leave it for her to read, all right?'

'We'll leave Peggy till my day off.'

'Friday morning then?' Jenny said. 'I'd rather stay home with Tom and Noreen in the evenings.'

'Right.'

'What time does Sidney go to work?'

'He's at the Blood Tub by half ten. What if we get there just after that?'

'I'll go straight there. Better if she doesn't think we're ganging up on her about this.'

Violet could feel her toes screwing up with embarrassment. She couldn't bring herself to look at Jenny, it made her feel totally inhibited to hear her talk about contraception. Nobody ever had before, and Jenny looked so wide-eyed and fresh-faced, so innocent and pure. It was hard to believe she knew about such things. Violet patted her nose with Wilf's handkerchief, wanting to hide behind it. She should be explaining these things to her daughter, not the other way round.

Jenny put the book into her hands. 'Read it, Mam. It'll tell you all you need to know. I'll make a cup of tea.'

Violet was lying on the living-room couch. She closed her eyes, wanting to shut it all out.

'Grandma, read us a story.' Noreen was pulling on her skirt.

'No, love, Grandma's tired, and we aren't going to stay. I'll take Bobby out so you can rest, Mam.'

'He's not very well, been coughing all night.' She could hear his chest rasping as he breathed.

'I'll get some cough mixture for him.'

'I'm afraid Noreen might catch it.'

'She'll be all right, she's never ill.'

Violet sipped her tea, and watched Jenny button Bobby into a coat that was too big for him and wrap a scarf round his head and throat. Jenny was being very sweet.

'Seppy will be back from the shops soon, and Beth will be home at teatime.'

'Yes, and she's got a day off tomorrow.'

The door closed behind them and the room was quiet at last. Violet felt sleepy but Beth would be asking what she thought of this book, she had to read it.

It seemed hardly any time before Beth was smiling down at her and Seppy was cooking tea at the range. Violet had dozed off once or twice but she'd made herself keep on reading though she was finding it hard to concentrate now.

'Isn't it amazing,' Beth was saying, 'that all these things were known about and available years ago?'

That was the fact that had impressed Violet most. It made her feel quite sick. Beth and Jenny thought the book would help her but all it did really was underline the fact that she need never have had fourteen pregnancies and lost her health. She should have done more to help herself when she was young. If Beth could do it, why hadn't she? She hadn't tried, hadn't even thought of it.

Tears were prickling at her eyes but she mustn't let them show. It was no good being sorry for herself now.

Chapter Thirteen

Bobby had slept through the night and seemed better in the morning. Beth put him in his pushchair and walked up to Powell Street. Jenny and Noreen were already there. Bonny the dog had been shut out in the back yard. Peggy's living room seemed tidier and more peaceful than usual. Peggy was curled up in the bed chair giving Rita a bottle. She was using it as an armchair though it was designed for use as an occasional bed. May had slept in it for a time until they had found her a proper bed.

'Where's Hilda?' Beth asked.

Peggy smiled. 'In school.'

'I reminded her that Colin had been taken in early,' Jenny said.

'And made me go up to see the headmistress, with all four of them hanging round me. She agreed to take Hilda in straight away instead of waiting until after the summer holidays.'

'Things will be easier for you now,' Jenny told her. 'You'll soon have things under control and feel a new woman.'

'And you've had your hair cut,' Beth said. 'You look much better.'

'Jenny did it.'

'It's supposed to be the latest bob.'

'It looks very nice, Peg. Brighter too.'

Jenny smiled at them both. 'That's the camomile. She looks years younger, doesn't she?'

Beth realised that was to give Peggy encouragement. She was still stout and her face looked grey and exhausted.

'This book will help too.' Beth took it from her bag and put it on the arm of Peggy's chair.

'What's this?'

'It's a book I borrowed from the doctor's sitting room at the hospital. It tells you a lot about birth control.'

'It looks old. Is it the Marie Stopes book you've been on about?' Peggy picked it up and looked at the spine.

'No, but it is good. Mam's read it as well as us, and we've brought it for you now.'

153

Peggy slammed it down. 'I haven't got time to read all that.'

'Don't be daft, Peggy. You moan that you don't want to start another baby and then say you haven't time to read how to stop it.'

Jenny said, 'You've got to read it. All the answers are there.'

'There aren't any answers.'

Beth said as patiently as she could, 'Read the book, Peggy. You don't have to have another baby if you don't want to. Jenny will tell you.'

'Oh, Jenny!' Her tired eyes rolled towards her younger sister and back again. 'She's forever telling me. It's not about those sheath things again, is it? They didn't work for you, did they? You were so sure they would. You used to boast you only had Noreen and now look at you.'

'I hadn't read this book then.'

'Sidney says Tom knew all about those things from being in the army. They talk about them and about Marie Stopes in the Blood Tub all the time too. But if you're going to get pregnant anyway, I don't see the point.'

'You won't get pregnant so often,' Beth said. 'There's nothing invented that's one hundred per cent reliable.'

'Unless it's total abstinence.' Jenny laughed. 'We didn't know we should use spermicides as well as the sheaths.'

'Do you know what those things cost?'

'Less than another mouth to feed,' Beth retorted.

'Sidney says the sheaths are ten shillings for ten.'

'I know, but it's still cheaper,' Jenny said.

'He says we can't afford them, he doesn't like them, and he won't wear them.'

'You've got to make him, Peggy. You've got to insist. He doesn't want to add to your brood, does he?'

'No, he's always swearing at them. I think they get on his nerves.'

'Then he's got to make some effort. It's his responsibility too.'

'Didn't you say there was something that women can use?'

'Yes, but that's difficult. It's fitted inside you and you have to be measured for it. Marie Stopes fits them. I read in *John Bull* that she's opening a clinic in London to do it.'

'That's no good to us, is it? We can't go off to London.'

'In time—'

'Time isn't on my side,' Peggy said crossly. 'I need it now or it's going to be too late again.'

'There's a very cheap homemade device. Just vinegar and cotton wool.'

'That sounds a fat lot of good.'

'Read the book, Peggy. It can be made to work, I'm sure. I'll be back for it tomorrow, I've got to return it.'

Beth had decided the best time to do it would be before breakfast. The doctors wouldn't be in their sitting room then, she'd need only watch out for the cleaners.

'What about Marie Stopes's book?'

'I'll bring you that as soon as I get it.'

A few days later, it so happened that when Beth got up from the hospital tea table, she ran into Myrtle Harris at the dining room door.

'I was hoping to catch you,' she said in a low voice. 'I've brought that book you wanted to borrow.'

'Oh!' Beth was instantly aglow with anticipation. She'd been afraid Myrtle had forgotten. As a student nurse Myrtle was moved from ward to ward in order to widen her experience, and Beth hadn't seen much of her recently.

'It's in the cloakroom.' The student nurses' homes were in the park, ten minutes' walk away. They all used the cloakroom; it was small and busy at this time of the afternoon.

Myrtle unhooked a brown paper carrier bag from the peg under her gaberdine and gave it to Beth. Inside was a well-wrapped parcel. Beth put it into the pocket of her uniform.

'Thank you.' They left the crush in the cloakroom and retreated to the corridor.

Myrtle whispered, 'Have you heard that Marie Stopes has had more books and pamphlets published?'

'Yes, there was a list of her pamphlets in *Lloyd's News* last Sunday and I saw an article about her in the *Penny Magazine*.'

'She's got another book out called *A New Gospel*, which she claims was dictated to her by God. It's raising a storm of disgust in the churches and schools, that's why the newspapers are full of it all over again. Bill thinks she's wrong to keep herself in the headlines like this. His church thinks she must be going mad. They're very much against her. He doesn't want us to buy any more of her books.'

Marie Stopes was earning even more widespread notoriety for her openness in sex matters. Her name was known everywhere and if it had to be spoken, it was in hushed tones.

'But he's still willing to follow her advice . . . ?'

Myrtle looked troubled. 'He feels such guilt when he does. He's torn between what his church expects of him and what he calls our own selfish whims. I wish I could get fitted with one of those caps she talks about. Then Bill needn't know, it would be up to me, wouldn't it?'

'Is it all right if I keep the book for a week or so? I want my sisters to read it.'

'Of course. Keep it as long as you like.'

Beth had mixed feelings as she ran over to her room in the nurses' home. Somewhat awed, she unwrapped the book, keen to see it. Myrtle had already covered the jacket with plain brown paper so that nobody need know what she was reading. She flicked through the pages but she didn't have time to read it now. She wrapped it in her nightdress and rammed it under her pillow before going back on duty.

All evening, she looked forward to a good long read when she finished work. As soon as she reached the nurses' home, she had a bath then got into bed with the book. She'd managed to ferret out most of the facts about contraception by now, but had always felt this book would be right up-to-date and give her every known fact. It would be the icing on the cake.

It was after midnight when she turned the last page. All the forbidden subjects had been discussed: limitation to the safe period, cold baths, willpower and total abstinence, withdrawal before the end, as well as sheaths, diaphragms and spermicides, and Marie Stopes put forward her own preferences.

Beth put out her light and settled down to sleep, knowing the book would be a great help to her family and women like them, but she felt a certain amount of guilt too. As an unmarried girl with no immediate hope of changing that state, she was one of the people the churches felt should be protected from such publications. They said it would rob her of her innocence.

But the more she thought about it, the more she thought they were making a great fuss about nothing. She didn't feel diminished by any loss of innocence. If anything, she felt empowered by her new knowledge.

If this information could help women get what they wanted from life, then in her opinion it ought to be available for all. Why wouldn't doctors help their patients? Why should it be such a sin to know about these things?

As time went on, Mam was much more her old self. Her colour was better and she was beginning to do little jobs about the house.

'You and Seppy have given me a lovely rest,' she told Beth. 'I'm much better.'

'Don't do too much and overtire yourself. Tell Seppy what needs doing and let him get on with it.'

Seppy was out shopping, he liked doing that. He was managing the cooking and the washing very well, and he kept the fire going in the range.

'You concentrate on the mending and the darning for a bit longer.'

Beth went home almost every day when she had her two hours off in the morning or the afternoon. Peggy came with her brood as often as she could, and Mrs O'Malley from across the landing was in and out with cups of tea and all the gossip. Mam said she missed seeing Jenny every day. She wasn't able to come as often as she used to when she'd had a job in the tapestry works, and now in the last stages of pregnancy she didn't feel like doing so much.

Beth felt they were getting along well. She'd even taken Mam down to Mrs Clover's rooms once or twice. If the weather was good, she was able to sit by her door and chat to everyone who passed. Dad and Ken Clover joined their crossed hands to make a seat for her and carried her back upstairs when she got tired.

Old Mr Jackson told Mrs Clover she could borrow his wheelchair to take Mam out, and for days she'd looked forward to being pushed round the local shops, but the weather turned wet again. There was even talk of taking her to the pictures in it but so far that hadn't happened either.

Lottie came home for her annual week's holiday. Beth was there when she arrived; it seemed a long time since she'd seen her.

'Mam, I've brought you a pair of slippers. You take size five, don't you?' She was rummaging through the shopping bags in which she'd brought her clothes home. 'They aren't new, I'm afraid. Miss Wishart gave them to me.'

Mam's slippers were worn out. Seppy had cut new cardboard inner soles to put inside but the carpet uppers were going into holes too.

'They're very smart.' These were of red velvet.

Lottie knelt down, took off the old ones and pushed Mam's feet into the new. 'Do they fit?'

'Yes, yes.'

'Are they comfortable?'

Mam was holding her feet out. 'The most comfortable I've ever had. Thank you.'

'She's given me a dress too. She says it's too tight for her, but it's too big for me.'

'We'll take it in for you while you're home,' Mam said. 'Jenny's got a sewing machine, did she tell you? I'll fit it and put tacking stitches in, it won't take her a minute.'

157

Beth asked, 'Are you still happy there?'

'Like you said, it's a good place to work.' Lottie gave an excited giggle. 'Mr Wishart's taken on a new chauffeur cum gardener and he's lovely. He's taken me out to the pictures and for walks along the front.'

'So you've got a boyfriend?'

'Yes, his name's Peter Shaw.'

'And you can see each other every day since you work at the same house?'

'Well, he's either out driving or in the garden, but yes.'

Lottie looked very much like a younger Peggy. She had the same neat features, fine fair complexion and blonde hair. At eighteen, she was fresh-faced and slim. She moved about the flat with rapid grace and her mouth turned up at the corners in a ready smile. Beth looked at her younger sister and wondered if she'd follow Peggy's lifestyle, and if in a few years she'd be a sour and shabby matron with a large family and a depressed sneer.

Lottie said, 'Miss Wishart sends you her regards.'

'I thought she was living in London.'

'She's home on a visit. She asked after you, and said she was delighted to hear you were working as a staff nurse.'

'Does she still work?'

'Yes, as a nurse too. Beth, she knows the famous Marie Stopes who she says is going to set up a clinic in London for married women.'

'What sort of a clinic?'

'Birth control, silly.'

Beth looked at her sister in surprise. 'You know about that?'

'Everybody knows about Marie Stopes. Miss Wishart's got her books. She leaves them in her room and I have a little peep when I'm making her bed.'

Mam was a little shocked. 'You'll get into trouble if you're caught. I don't think she should leave them lying around.'

Lottie laughed. 'In her bedroom isn't exactly leaving them lying around. She told her father she was going to work in this clinic and Mr Wishart forbade it. "The woman's a disgrace," he thundered. "You must have nothing to do with her. You'll get a bad name."'

'What did she say?'

' "I'm not a child any more, Daddy. You can't order me about. I've made up my mind it's useful work and it's what I want to do. I'm going."'

'I bet that put him in a temper,' Beth said.

'Terrible, he's finding fault with everything, which isn't like him.'

They were all delighted to have Lottie at home. It so happened that

John's ship was in the Salthouse Dock over in Liverpool for three days and he was able to have a weekend at home too. Mam loved to have her grown-up children back. On Beth's night off, she went to the pictures with Lottie, John and Seppy.

Once John returned to his ship and Lottie went back to the Wishart house, Mam was more despondent again.

Everything seemed a little flat in the days that followed. Beth was popping in to see Jenny every day now because she was getting near her time.

Tom beamed at her this morning. 'Everything's ready. The midwife's just been, she's loaned us a rubber sheet to protect our mattress.'

'And told us to save all our old newspapers to put between that and the sheet.' Jenny giggled. 'I'm quite looking forward to having another now, and Tom's excited about it.'

'We've got used to the idea,' he said.

'It's really not such a bad time for us. Paula, next door, has said she'll take Noreen if Tom isn't home when I start, and Noreen's used to staying with her.'

'You always intended to have two.'

'It makes us a real family. Noreen's over the moon.'

'You've told her?'

'Yes. Mam never told us. Our first inkling was seeing the new baby in her arms. It was quite a shock when our John was born. I felt I'd been pushed out.'

'John was the first boy. They made a big fuss of him.'

'They made a bigger fuss of Peggy. Anyway, I don't want Noreen to feel pushed out.'

Sunday morning was very wet, and when Beth knocked on Jenny's door, it was opened by Noreen. Her voice was shrill with excitement.

'Our new baby's here at last. She's lovely, come and see her, Auntie Beth.'

She followed the scampering child upstairs. A smiling Jenny was sitting up in bed with her baby in her arms.

'Born just after midnight.' Tom was lolling on the foot of the bed. 'We've been up all night.'

'Another girl,' Jenny told her. 'Seven and a half pounds. Noreen, tell Auntie Beth what we're going to call her.'

'Amy Violet.' Noreen had a giggle just like her mother's.

Her father picked her up and gave her a hug. 'That's right, and if she turns out as well as you, we'll be very pleased.'

'Can I hold her?' Beth couldn't resist a close look at her new niece. 'She's very like you, Noreen, when you were first born. Isn't she wide awake?'

'She's the only one who is.' Jenny yawned. 'But everything went well. Easier this time.'

Beth said, 'Tom, what can I do to help? Would you like a couple of hours' sleep?'

'The midwife said she'd come back about eleven.'

'I'll be here to keep an eye on them all. I'll get your dinner on too, if you like.'

'Thanks, that would be wonderful.' Tom stifled another yawn. 'I'll bed down in Noreen's room. Sorry, love,' he said to Jenny, 'I can't stay awake any longer. Though I'm sure you did more work than I did last night.'

Chapter Fourteen

Beth was spending her day off with her mother. A year had gone by since her illness had been diagnosed. Violet had never recovered enough to do much in the house and today seemed low in spirits.

'Have you seen Peggy?' she asked. Beth knew she worried about Peggy being unhappy. 'She's not been round for a day or two. I hope she's all right.'

Beth said, 'Dad would know if she wasn't.' He spent his evenings in the Blood Tub where Sidney served behind the bar. 'Sidney would say.'

'Would Sidney even notice? You know what he's like. I'm afraid he's drinking more than he should.'

Beth was making potato soup for their lunch. 'I'll pop round and see her when we've had this.'

When she knocked on Peggy's door early in the afternoon, she was cutting rounds of bread and jam on the living-room table. Her children were chasing round with the butties in their hands, and Bonny the dog was joining in, waiting for her chance. The living room was as messy as it had ever been. Rita was walking now and wailing for attention above the noise of the others.

Peggy roared, 'Shut up, you kids, your dad's in bed. If you wake him up he'll thrash the living daylights out of you.'

Beth said, 'I'm surprised he can sleep through this.'

'He can sleep through anything.'

'Does Rita need feeding?' Beth asked. 'Can I do it for you?'

Peggy hoisted her up in the armchair and pushed a jam butty in her hand. 'She can feed herself with that, but you could fill her bottle with milky tea for me.'

Beth did so. 'Doesn't she drink from a cup?'

'She can, sort of. But she manages the bottle by herself and doesn't spill any.'

Peggy pushed the bottle between her hands, and mercifully nothing more was heard from Rita but vigorous sucking noises.

May and Hilda were at school, but Eric and Frankie were causing a

161

rumpus. In order to sit down, Beth took Rita on her knee.

'Shall I take them all out for a walk? So you can have a little rest?'

'Will you?' Peggy stifled a yawn. 'That would be lovely.'

'I'll collect the other two from school on the way back.'

'You don't have to worry about them, they know the way home.'

'Well, you go and have a sleep on your bed.'

'With Sidney there? No thanks, I'll curl up down here. I'll get some string for Bonny, otherwise she's likely to run away . . .'

'I'm not taking the dog, Peggy. A pram and two toddlers is as much as I can manage.'

'Bonny will bark all afternoon if I shut her in the yard.'

'Get a muzzle.'

'I'll keep her here with me, she'll probably go to sleep on the rug.'

To get to the park from Peggy's house was quite a pull up Sumner Road. Beth had to sit Eric on the bottom of the pram because he was dragging his feet and saying he wanted to stay with his mam. That made it heavy to push, but it was a bright afternoon and Rita went straight off to sleep. She thought it would do Peggy good to do this herself every day.

When she got back, Peggy put on the kettle for tea. She seemed more relaxed. There was still no sign of Sidney.

'Sleeping it off,' she said. 'He had quite a skinful this morning.'

'Is he drinking too much?' Beth asked.

'Oh, for God's sake! Don't start handing out any more advice.'

'Mam's worried about you.'

'About me? I'm all right.' Her hair was no longer bright, her cardigan needed a wash.

Beth drank her tea in silence. She'd go back and tell Mam that Peggy was irritable with everybody and best given a wide margin for a day or two.

Peggy asked in a very different voice, 'How's Mam?'

Beth sighed. 'I don't think she's feeling well. She seems quiet. A bit down.'

'She told you, did she?'

'Told me what?'

'She's fallen for it again.'

'What?' Beth felt her knees go weak. 'Not another baby? She can't be!'

'She is.'

'Oh my God! She said nothing to me. I've been there since teatime yesterday.'

162

'She wouldn't, would she?' Peggy sneered. 'She knew you'd be angry with her. She's scared of telling you.'

Beth felt tears stinging her eyes. 'It's not a question of my being angry. It could kill her. Her heart isn't strong enough. The specialist warned her . . .'

'I know.' Peggy nodded. 'She's terrified.'

'Poor Mam!' Beth felt sick. 'After all the trouble I took to find out. After I told her how to prevent it and gave her the books to read.'

'You told us all, Beth. You acted as though it was your mission in life, but nothing is guaranteed to work.'

'Why didn't she take care? She knew she mustn't let it happen again. And Dad?'

'He's upset.'

'So he damn well should be.' Beth felt a great tide of anger rising in her throat. 'I told him . . . I thought he understood . . .'

Peggy's face twisted. 'It's you who don't understand. You aren't married.'

'I understand what it means to Mam. Another baby! The one thing she's always had in abundance.'

'What you don't understand is that a husband expects his conjugal rights.'

'Surely Mam's wellbeing is more important? The last thing Dad wants is more children. He yells at us all and loses his temper often enough. Mam's health, her very life must mean more to him. Ten is enough for anyone to bring up. Too many. It's ruined her health.'

'Men don't think of the consequences. There's this need planted in them. It's all for that moment of pure pleasure. When I try to talk to Sidney about having too many kids, d'you know what he says?'

Beth shook her head.

'That marriage is ordained for the procreation of children. That it says so in the prayer book, and I agreed to it in the marriage service.'

'You've had five, you didn't agree to go on having them year after year. Anyway, whatever you're doing seems to be having the right effect.'

Beth saw the angry flush run up Peggy's face. 'You make out you know everything. You set yourself up in judgement over us, but really you know nothing. You've heard the saying, haven't you?'

'What saying?'

'Marriage is the price men pay for sex, and sex is the price women pay for marriage.'

'No . . .'

163

'Well, of course nobody would mention the word sex to you. You're not married. Probably you'll end up as an old maid. You're as innocent as a babe in arms.'

When the door slammed behind Beth, Peggy slumped down on a chair and cried bitter tears. They were all upset at Mam's news, of course they were. She'd wept in sympathy when Mam had told her. She understand only too well the feelings of anguish and frustration at finding herself pregnant again. And Mam's worries were much more than how she'd be able to afford the midwife's bill and feed and clothe another child. Peggy didn't dare think of what her mother was facing.

Mam had confided in her and not the others because they each understood what the other had to put up with. Peggy caught sight of her reflection in the mirror over the fireplace and winced. She looked an old harridan, worn out and ill, and no wonder, the life she led.

That her sisters were having a better time than she was was another cause of bitterness. Peggy thought of Jenny as succeeding where she'd failed. She'd believed Jenny's luck had run out when Tom had been badly injured in the war, but he had more guts than Sidney. He'd put himself out to learn something different and got himself a desk job. Jenny boasted that he was a white collar worker now. She boasted about her house which was bigger and better than this one, and she had some nice furniture too.

Jenny still spoke of Tom with affection and Peggy had often seen him put his arm round her sister's shoulders. He'd bought her a treadle sewing machine, a Singer at that. Jenny was running up curtains for their house and little dresses for Noreen, who always looked well turned out. She had to say that for Jenny, Noreen never looked a little scruff like May.

Peggy wiped away her tears as she thought of how Jenny had been taken down a peg by getting pregnant again. Noreen had remained a single child only because Tom had been away fighting the war, and come home a physical wreck. It had done Peggy good to see it happen to Jenny. She seemed to be coping all right with the new baby, taking it out in its smart pram to be admired, but after a few more years and a few more babies, she'd lose her pert girlish looks and the energy to keep her house nice and bake cakes and that.

Even Beth had got her comeuppance. She'd really thought herself a cut above the rest of them, as a State Registered Nurse on the same register as Dorinda Wishart. But the handsome rich boyfriend had tossed her off. Beth had been aiming for the moon anyway.

Nothing bad happened to Sidney, though, and Peggy felt her biggest gripe was with him. This wasn't how she'd seen herself spending her life, running round after a useless husband, and cleaning up after kids. She never had any fun, never went anywhere except to the shops, and there was no pleasure in trying to stretch a shilling to do the work of two.

She'd been a fool to tie herself to Sidney O'Connell when she could have had her pick of men. How could she have been so blind not to see what he was? All he'd ever wanted to do was enjoy himself, he was bone idle, never doing anything he could put off to another day.

Sidney had promised so much and delivered so little that she felt cheated. His big plans had come to nothing. He could dance, she had to give him that, but teach others? Now she knew him better, she knew he'd never been capable of that. It had been pie in the sky.

He'd also talked of them winning national dance competitions. That had seemed within their grasp when they'd done so well in Liverpool and it had sounded great fun. Peggy had realised her days of competition dancing were over when she was heavily pregnant with May. She'd had to sell her sequined dresses for a few shillings each when she'd been short. Her lot in life was poverty and a large family.

Sidney had conned her into marriage with his big ideas. Dad had made her believe she was a cut above the others and capable of doing anything she set her mind to. He'd taken to Sidney straight away, encouraged her to marry him. Peggy knew now she'd have been better off staying single like Beth. Much better off. She'd be having fun now, if she had.

Peggy was working herself up into a rage, wanting to blame everyone else for her plight. The baby had fallen asleep in the armchair. She carried her upstairs and tucked her into the cot and then stood looking down at Sidney.

He was heavily asleep on the bed, with his mouth open, and snoring so loud she'd been able to hear him in the living room below. He did this every day. Worked the morning shift in the pub and came home just after two slightly tipsy, and expecting a hot meal. Then he'd sleep like this, and she'd have to wake him with another meal in time to get him back to the Blood Tub by opening time. He never said thank you, but he was ready enough to complain if the food wasn't to his liking.

But what she could never forgive was the way he regularly pleasured himself on her and refused to take any precautions to stop her becoming pregnant. She hated him for that and for laughing and joking when she was so worried about it.

165

And neither could she forgive him for being in league with her father, making money on the side and never giving her any of it. Well, she helped herself from his little hoard from time to time, she was entitled to take a bit, it mostly went on necessities. He was a rotten husband and a rotten father. It was no good relying on him. Or Dad either, come to that. Men were worse than children, having no forethought and valuing the pleasures of the moment above everything else.

She'd had enough of it. She wasn't going to end up like Mam. She wished Sidney would have an accident and die so she could be rid of him. But he was fairly safe in the pub; the worst that was likely to happen was that he'd rick his ankle doing his silly clog dance.

If only there was something she could do to get him out of her life.

Beth hardly knew what she was doing. Mam having another baby? The very thought of it frightened her. Mam wouldn't be able to bear another child. Beth was furious with her father. She rushed straight back to Dock Cottages. Seppy was stirring a pan on the fire, Mam was sitting up to the table peeling potatoes.

'Mam, why didn't you tell me?' Beth knew from the look on her face that what Peggy had told her was true. 'How far on are you?'

'Not now, Beth.' She saw her mother look at Esther and Colin, who were having one of their mock fights and rolling on the hearth rug.

She looked exhausted, her eyes were moist, she was close to tears. Beth put her arms round her in an agonised hug. Her own cheeks were wet with tears. It was a disaster of the worst sort.

'What is it?' Seppy wanted to know. The younger two were quiet now, lying still with their arms round each other, listening. 'What's happened, Beth?'

She was cold with shock, with outrage, that this had happened. They all heard their father's step on the landing. Seppy jumped back towards the pan.

'He's home and the potatoes aren't in yet, he'll be cross.'

The door crashed open and Dad glowered down at them. They were turned to stone like rabbits caught in the light of a torch.

'What's up?' he asked suspiciously.

'Take Esther and Colin down to the Clovers,' Beth ordered Seppy. 'Go on, now.'

'The stew—'

'You go, I'll see to that later.'

166

'What are you playing at?' her father demanded as Seppy herded the two young ones away. 'I want my tea.'

'Mam, come on. Come and lie down.'

'No, Beth, give over,' she said gently. 'It's no good, this won't achieve anything. You'll only upset yourself and Dad.'

'Dad ought to be upset.' She flew at him in fury. 'Do you realise what you've done? I can't believe it, after what I said to you. I did my best to explain. What were you thinking of?'

Her father's face went puce. 'Don't you talk to me like that! I won't have it.' His voice carried to the neighbouring tenements. Often after one of her father's outbursts, Mrs O'Malley from across the landing would come in to see if they were all right.

Mam put a hand on her arm. 'Beth, stop it. It's too late anyway.'

She shook it off. 'Dad, why did you risk this? I told you Mam's heart wasn't strong enough to have another.'

'It stands to reason, your mother must be strong enough if she falls for another.'

'No! What are you trying to do, kill her?'

Beside her, Mam gasped. Beth knew she should never have said such a thing in her hearing. She was so wound up she was forgetting herself.

'Don't you dare say such things to me. I'm the head of this household.'

'Yes, and you ought to look after your family. You're utterly selfish. You expect to have your every whim satisfied, regardless to what it does to the rest of us.'

He was reaching for his army belt. Beth didn't care. Her rage was beyond control. 'You're no better than an animal.'

'You deserve a good thrashing for that.' His face was ugly.

Beth took a step back when he swished it through the air. Mam got up more quickly than she had for some time and moved away from the table. He brought the belt crashing down, the cutlery leapt and rattled. The bottle of brown sauce fell to the floor and broke.

Beth hissed, 'You use that on me and I'll never lift a finger for you again, so help me I won't. I'll never cross this threshold when you're home.'

Her father flung the belt on the floor and strode out.

'I hope you burn in hell!' she shouted. They could hear him crashing downstairs.

She sank down on a chair, put her arms on the table and let her head drop on them. It was a long time since she'd cried like this. She felt helpless, full of despair.

167

Mam's arm came across her shoulders. 'You shouldn't have, Beth,' she told her. 'After that, things can never be the same again.'

'I hate him!'

'No, love, you don't.'

Violet could feel the cold sweat breaking out on her forehead, her nerves were shattered. The thing she'd dreaded had happened again just as it always did. She hadn't the energy to fight Wilf, hadn't energy for anything any more.

She tried not to think what the coming year would bring. It terrified her; made her feel everything was hopeless but she couldn't keep her thoughts away from it.

Beth and Jenny didn't understand how this affected both body and mind. She couldn't throw off her black depression. She couldn't sleep, couldn't even rest. She wondered all the time whether this child would be all right. Surely her illness would affect it, damage it in some way? That's if she had the strength to carry it to term. The doctors had prophesied that she wouldn't. She couldn't believe she could die. How would her family manage without a mother? Who would look after Bobby? She could hardly find the strength to get dressed in the morning and when she did, she had to sit down for half an hour to get her breath back.

She was filled with a thousand worries that boiled away inside her, and there was so little she could do. Her varicose veins throbbed even though she was spending so much time with her legs up. It pained her to see all the jobs she used to do crying out for her attention.

Seppy was doing his best, but Violet had always prided herself on being on top of everything, and he certainly wasn't that.

If only this hadn't happened. But she'd known it would. It always did. Wilf never would take no for an answer.

Wilf turned over in bed. 'What's the matter, Vi?'

'Nothing, I can't get off to sleep, that's all.'

'You're tossing and turning and threshing about like a wild thing. You woke me up.'

'Sorry.'

He raised his head from the pillow. There was no light coming through the thin curtains. 'It's the middle of the night.'

He picked up the alarm clock. It had the very latest dial, the figures were of luminous paint and it was just possible to make out the time.

'It's ten to three! For God's sake! I've got to get up for work before

168

six.' He punched his pillow to a more comfortable shape. 'Let's get back to sleep.'

He heard her sigh heavily. 'Is something the matter?' he demanded.

'I want to spend a penny,' she said softly. 'I'm sorry.'

He heaved himself up the bed with a jerk. 'Can't be helped, I suppose.'

With the passing weeks, he was afraid that Beth was right. Vi was losing her strength, she was needing more help. Really, she needed a nurse to take care of her.

'Wait a moment while I light the candle.'

Wilf hated getting out of bed in the middle of the night. He'd never done it for his children, but now he had to for Vi. She was no longer steady on her feet. Quite feeble really, he couldn't trust her to get that far alone.

The floors were wood in the bedrooms but linoleum elsewhere and cold. He shivered, he had no slippers. Vi had hers on. He took her arm and felt he was half carrying her as he hurried her out to the lavatory. Seppy was asleep on the couch, nothing woke the young even though Wilf walked into a chair and it scraped along the floor. Vi stumbled, but he got her there and gave her the candle to take inside because otherwise it was a black airless cubbyhole.

He stood waiting, first on one foot and then on the other. Having an invalid wife was a terrible bind. He went to the scullery to get himself a drink of water, feeling his way through the blackness.

'Wilf?'

She'd come out and was swaying with the candle. He took it from her before she dropped it and made all speed to get her back to bed so he could creep back into its warmth too. She was almost too weak to walk, he could feel her swaying about. It was only his hold on her arm that was keeping her upright.

'Vi?' Suddenly he was scared. He could feel her sinking, she was going down on the floor, he couldn't hold her up with one hand. They were crossing the living room. He slid the candle on the table and lifted her up. Really, she was no weight at all despite the baby inside her. 'Vi, what are you doing?'

He carried her back to the bedroom and lowered her onto the bed. Then rushed to fetch the candle. He held it aloft over her and couldn't believe what he was seeing.

'Vi, wake up! For God's sake wake up.'

She couldn't be dead, could she? Not as suddenly as that? Her colour was grey and waxy . . .

'Seppy,' he screamed. 'Seppy, come here quick.'

169

* * *

Wilf was numb with disbelief. He'd had a terrible night. He'd woken Jim O'Malley who'd gone to fetch the doctor. As if there was anything a doctor could do for Violet.

'Don't panic,' he kept telling himself. 'Don't panic.' It had happened so suddenly; crept up on him when he least expected it, taken him completely by surprise.

Mrs O'Malley had fussed about, making tea for them though he needed something stronger. He remembered the brandy bottle under his bed and gave his cup a good spike, but it didn't help.

The world seemed a threatening place without Vi. How was he going to look after the kids? He needed her. Seppy's tear-stained face pushed close to his.

'What happened, Dad? Why did Mam die? She was all right when I was going to bed.'

'I don't know why, she just did. Collapsed and died. I couldn't hold her upright. There, on the floor.' He pointed out the exact place where she'd gone down.

Seppy gulped with distress. 'She was perfectly all right at bedtime. She drank the hot milk I made.'

'Well, she won't drink any more.'

Wilf could feel his neck and face suddenly burning with anger at Violet for dying, for leaving him to cope alone. The kids had woken, they were clamouring round him, asking questions and crying. All except Bobby who was screaming his head off in his cot.

Wilf quaked, guilt was making everything a thousand times worse. He'd loved Violet. He'd been so proud of her when they were first married. Such a cut above the rest. Just to see the curve of her breast brought on such craving, such a need. Until last year, Vi had always been kind to him, giving him what he wanted. She had tried to stem his passion, put up a half-hearted resistance. He should not have insisted on his marital rights, certainly not recently. Beth blamed him for that, everybody would if they knew; he blamed himself.

The doctor came and put his stethoscope to Violet's heart. His face was grave, his voice soft with sympathy.

'She just went down,' Wilf sobbed. 'What made her do that?'

'Her heart gave up, it just couldn't go on any longer. Not unexpected under the circumstances.'

But Wilf hadn't expected it, and that made him feel worse.

* * *

'Nurse Hubble, Matron wants to see you.'

Beth was surprised and then a little shocked. Sister had come down the ward and parted the screens to deliver the message.

'Now?' She was in the middle of preparing a patient for her operation, painting her skin with iodine. 'Or shall I finish . . .'

'No, you run along.' Was that sympathy she saw in Sister's stern, cold eyes? 'I'll scrub up and take over.'

'There's just Miss Parsons left to prepare.'

Beth washed her hands and wondered why she'd been summoned like this. It had never happened before and she'd never known it happen to anyone else. What had she done wrong?

In the mirror above the washbowl, she tucked some straying wisps of red hair under her cap. Should she change her apron? No, it didn't look too bad. She ran downstairs on legs that felt unsteady, knocked on the door of Matron's office and heard her call, 'Come in.'

Beth's knees almost gave way when she saw a quaking Seppy inside, gripping the arms of the chair with grubby fingers. She'd never known Matron to invite anyone to sit down, but she was directed to another chair. Matron's manner was different, more kindly, gentle almost. Beth couldn't contain herself.

'What is it, Seppy?'

'It's Mam.'

Beth went cold, she could guess what was coming. 'Has she . . . ?'

He nodded. His eyes were bright, his cheeks scarlet. 'Yes, in the night.'

Beth swallowed hard. She should have been prepared for the suddenness of it, but it stunned her.

Matron said, 'Your brother was found wandering about the hospital.' She took out a register and started leafing through it.

He sniffed. 'Dad sent me down to find you.'

'When are you due for your next holiday, Nurse?'

'Not for three months, Matron.'

'I think the best thing is to bring it forward. There'll be things you have to arrange.'

Seppy was nodding.

'Are you the eldest child?'

'I have one older sister but she has five children of her own. They're very young and she hasn't time to see to anything else.' Beth had a lump in her throat. She covered her face with her hands and rocked herself when she thought of Bobby. 'My youngest brother is only two.'

'I understand things will be difficult for you. You must talk it over with your father and decide on the best thing to do. If you start your holiday tomorrow, you will be due back on, let me see, yes, the twenty-third of the month. Sister is on the ward there now, isn't she?'

'Yes, Matron. It's Mr Jenkins's list this morning.' They'd be busy.

'How many for operation?'

'Six.'

'Yes, I have the list here. I'll tell Sister what's happened. You get off home to your family.'

Seppy held her hand as she went to the nurses' home. There were tearstains on his cheeks. Beth had remained dry-eyed throughout her interview with Matron but she felt as though she had a block of ice inside her. Poor Mam. What a life of hard work she'd had.

'Nurse! Who is that you're taking upstairs?'

Beth recognised Home Sister's harsh voice. 'My little brother, Sister. He's just brought me some bad news, our mother died in the night. I want to get a few clothes, Matron has given me a week's holiday.'

'I'm sorry to hear of your bereavement, Nurse Hubble, but you must remember there may be off-duty nurses walking about in their dressing gowns. It's only half past nine and they may not welcome young men as visitors.'

Beth felt Seppy's hand tighten in hers. 'I'll take him straight to my room and close the door,' she said. 'I'll only be five or ten minutes.'

'What an ogre she is,' Seppy breathed when the door was safely shut. 'I didn't know where you'd be or how to find you, it was awful.'

Beth was pulling off her uniform, tossing it into her laundry bag. Then she took her case from the wardrobe and started to pack the things she'd need. What about mourning? She had nothing black to wear for Mam.

'I didn't dare go up the front steps and come in through the main entrance. It looks so grand.'

'You used the staff entrance on the side? That was right.'

'I met a porter and told him what I wanted. He took me to one of the sisters who said she knew you.' Seppy was crying in a way he hadn't for years. Beth gave him a clean handkerchief from her drawer and found she was crying herself.

Beth found her home at Dock Cottages crowded with people. The neighbours were there in force. Mrs Clover had been down to the post office to telephone to the Wisharts and to the owners of John's ship. Ivor had been sent round to tell Peggy and Jenny. Peggy had already arrived with some of her brood.

'Our Jenny was out, I couldn't get any reply. Her next-door neighbour said she'd gone shopping. She said she'd tell her to come home straight away.'

Mrs Freeman and Mrs Clegg had just finished laying Mam out. Beth went into the cramped bedroom to see her, and closed the door to shut out some of the clamour of the living.

They had spread a clean sheet on the bed and Mam was lying on top, on her own side of the double bed. She was wearing her best nightdress, a Christmas gift years ago from her sister Lily. It was of fine cambric with tucks on the bodice and frills at the neck and wrists. It was worn thin in places, had been mended in others and all was fragile with age, but it had been freshly ironed.

Beth pulled out a chair and sat down beside her. She wished she'd been here when it had happened. She knew Mam had been deteriorating over the last few weeks. Beth had found that hard to accept and tried to turn a blind eye to it. Only yesterday she'd been here and Mam had talked of knitting a matinee coat for the coming baby. That had died too, of course.

Mam seemed at peace. Her hair had been made neat with more care than she'd been able to give it herself. Her face no longer seemed careworn; the lines had disappeared, she looked years younger, her mouth seemed to turn up in the slightest of smiles.

Beth felt full of love for her and wished she'd been able to say goodbye.

Chapter Fifteen

Wilfred curled into himself on the armchair, feeling there could be no deeper misery than this. He was touching bottom as he stared into the flickering flames in the grate, wondering how he was going to manage without Vi.

Jenny had brought some meat and she and Beth were chopping vegetables on the table to make a hot meal for them all. The kids were making their usual racket but he felt set apart, as though he was on his own.

Lottie arrived at that moment, decked out in an expensive looking black outfit: dress, coat, hat, gloves, everything. She was small and dainty and fragile looking, and turning into a real beauty. She reminded Wilf of Peggy at that age. Lottie would have to stay home and help. The babies would have to be looked after. Vi would want that.

In low voices, Beth and Jenny were telling her what had happened to Vi. He saw her wipe away a tear. They were all ignoring him.

Violet had had that same dainty build when she'd been young, and though she'd had red hair, she'd not had the ferocious personality that traditionally went with it. Not like Beth, who'd inherited her colouring but who was always ready to fight him.

Lottie would be the right one. She was less argumentative than Beth and didn't nag. Lottie was more easygoing, she'd take care of Bobby all right and put meals on the table for them all. She was eighteen now, old enough to do what was needed.

She was taking a sponge cake from the bag she'd brought with her. She carefully peeled the paper back from the well-risen dome that had been dusted with sugar.

'I made this, Dad. I'm learning to bake. Shall we try a slice now?'

'Would it be better to keep it for the funeral tea?' Jenny suggested. 'We'll have to offer cake.'

'No,' Wilf barked. 'We need something now.'

A slice of cake was little enough comfort. It tasted as good as it looked; if Lottie could put cakes like this on the table as well, they'd be all right. He got up and helped himself to the last slice from the plate.

'We were keeping that for Seppy,' Beth said in her tart manner.

'Where's he gone?'

'To bed, Dad. He was up half the night.'

'So was I. Lottie, you're needed at home now your mother's gone,' he told her. 'You'd better let the Wisharts know you won't be coming back.'

'What?' Her deep blue eyes looked mutinously into his.

'Somebody has to be here to look after Bobby.'

Her mouth had dropped open, she was choking with indignation. 'Why should it be me? I don't want to come back to Dock Cottages. I told you, I've got a boyfriend in West Kirby. I'm not leaving. Not for anything.'

Wilf was taken aback. Here at home he'd been all-powerful, Vi had never questioned his right to decide family matters. He felt a rush of anger, he wasn't having this.

'The little ones need you. I'm not asking you, Lottie, I'm telling you. You're to come home and look after us.'

He watched her straighten up to her full five feet two inches. 'Not on your Nellie. I'm not coming back to drudge for you. I'm better off where I am, Dad, and that's where I'm staying.'

'What about our Bobby?'

'He's your responsibility, not mine.'

'You're being utterly selfish.'

The look she gave him was full of scorn. 'I take after you then, don't I?'

'I'd have thought you'd be glad to help, especially at a time like this.' He was conscious of Beth and Jenny chopping away at carrots, keeping their heads down and saying nothing.

'But it wouldn't be just at this time, would it?' Lottie said sharply. 'If I came, it would be for ever. My whole future.'

The future! Yes, better if he thought of the future – the past was over and done with. For the first time, it occurred to Wilf that he was free to marry again. He wouldn't go far wrong if he hitched up with Ethel Byrne, she had a good business going. Such a union could turn out very well for him. But Vi's kids knew nothing of Ethel, and she certainly wouldn't want to look after them. Besides, her place would be more comfortable if he didn't take them. He'd had enough of screaming kids to last him a lifetime. Better wait a few weeks before he brought her into the picture.

176

He said, 'Just till our Bobby's old enough.'

Lottie hooted mirthlessly. 'As far as I'm concerned, that is for ever. Anyway, why pick on me?'

'I'm not picking—'

'What about you, Beth?' Lottie was angry now. 'You're unmarried and you're older than me. Why can't you do it?'

Wilf could see by Beth's flushed face that she felt Lottie had betrayed her. 'What makes you think I want to do it?'

'It's got nothing to do with wanting to,' Lottie told her. 'You're round here most of the time anyway and somebody's got to do it.'

Wilf listened to them arguing as if he wasn't there and felt diminished. It was for him to decide, not them.

He'd thought life would be easier with Lottie, but he'd probably be no worse off with Beth. By rights it should be Beth's job. She was the more thrifty; the more sensible. She'd be all right if he could turn a deaf ear to her nagging. Beth was too sure of herself by half.

For Beth, the finality of the parting came only when Dad asked her to look through Mam's things for her insurance policy. She hadn't known Mam had been paying a penny a week for years to cover the cost of her funeral, but she had, so that would be paid for. The undertakers came and put her into her coffin. It stood on a bier in her bedroom which meant Dad could sleep in the bed again.

When the family began to arrive, John had to sleep there too. The scent of flowers was overpowering in the flat. Friends and neighbours kept bringing more, together with gifts of food.

Beth had always known the neighbours rallied round those in trouble, but she knew how poor they were and was overwhelmed by their generosity. Mrs O'Malley sewed black armbands not only on Dad's clothes, but on those of all the boys. Mrs Clover loaned a mourning outfit to Peggy. Beth and Jenny were too slim to fit into her clothes and had to go to the second-hand shop for theirs. But they had a choice of black hats offered to them by the neighbours, who also outfitted the younger children in black.

Beth wished Ken would come home. She needed someone to lean on, to help her through these terrible days. His mother said his ship was in Cardiff and wouldn't be back in the Mersey until the funeral was over.

Dad, John and four other men carried Mam's coffin up the hill to Flaybrick Cemetery on a warm spring morning that somehow seemed quite wrong for a funeral. Beth could hear the birds singing in the trees around them. Across the river, the sun glinted on the Liverpool waterfront.

Mam had been only forty-three; her life had been pitifully short, and it needn't have been like this if only she'd known how to space her family. Beth was worried stiff about how they were going to cope without her. She'd promised Mam she'd take care of Bobby and only now that the moment was on her did she really think about what that would entail.

The neighbours had laid out refreshments on the table by the time they got back from the funeral. The kettles were kept boiling both in their flat and Mrs O'Malley's. It was a crush, they were all sagging, the room seemed hot and airless. The mourners spread out onto the landing. Friends told her again and again what a good woman her mother had been.

Then it was over at last, and the crowd in the living room began to thin out. Beth helped Mrs O'Malley wash up the teacups and return them to their owners. Even Peggy and Jenny left with their families.

Beth had seen her family and neighbours in tears and she could hardly control her own.

Her father was sitting in morose silence in the armchair; she'd never seen him shed tears before. Suddenly he stirred and said, 'Beth, it's your duty to stay home now and look after the kids.'

Beth wanted to do what Lottie had done. She had to stifle the urge to shout no; that she couldn't give up the job she'd spent so long training for, that the height of her ambition was to leave Dock Cottages, that she'd done it and she didn't want to come back.

'Seppy can't look after Bobby and do everything that's needed here. You know he can't.'

That had worked out fine while Mam had been here to nurse Bobby and tell Seppy what he should do. But on his own? He and Ivor were slouched one each end of the couch, both looking shattered.

Beth was struggling with blame and hate and anger. This was all Dad's fault. Mam needn't have died so young. The older members of the family had talked about it endlessly and were agreed that he'd hastened her death.

It was Seppy who had said directly to him over tea, 'You killed her, Dad. You must have realised years ago that you were giving her far too much work.'

'Fifteen pregnancies,' Jenny said. 'Sapping her strength and her health.'

'Did you really want us all, Dad?' John asked.

Beth added, 'Mam was never strong enough for the life you made her lead. And didn't I tell you? I went out of my way to tell you when she first went to the hospital that she shouldn't have any more babies.'

Dad had looked like a cornered animal, there was guilt in every line of his body. She too felt guilt, for being so reluctant to help her family now.

'It's your bounden duty,' Dad told her. 'You're the oldest without a husband and a family of your own to look after. If you came to live at home instead of down at that hospital, we could manage. It's not far, you could go down on the bus in the mornings.'

'I wouldn't be allowed to, Dad. I don't know anyone who lives out.'

'You could ask, couldn't you? Damn it, you've got responsibilities here.'

'If I'm to go on working at the hospital, I've got responsibilities there, and that's all Matron cares about. If I came home,' she said slowly, 'if I gave up my job, I'd want to know how much money you're going to hand over for housekeeping. I'd want it every week without fail.'

'You'd get it every week.'

'I've got to have more than you gave Mam.'

'I don't see why. Seppy can get a job if you're here. John thinks the company he works for will take him on. It's what he wants, to go to sea. That's one less mouth to feed. Then there's Ivor, he's leaving school this summer. He'll be working soon.'

'Dad, I'd have to give up my own job.'

'You ask about that. You're such a wonderful nurse, perhaps they won't want to lose you.'

Beth sniffed at his sarcasm. 'You walked all over Mam, and I'm not having you doing that to me.'

She felt there was no escape for her, she'd promised her mother she'd take care of Bobby and she'd have to do it. It wouldn't be possible to farm him out round the neighbours, not for all the years before he was old enough for school, and there was Colin and Esther to think of too. If it wasn't for the children, she'd refuse. She wouldn't come just to housekeep for Dad.

Wilfred was sitting on his bed with the door shut, polishing the brass of his second-hand saxophone on his sleeve. One of the keys was a bit dodgy, it didn't go down over the hole in the tube as smoothly as it should. There was a momentary delay before that note came, which made it difficult to keep to the strict tempo that dance music demanded.

179

'Just what you need to learn on,' the shopkeeper had assured him. 'That key is a bit stiff, but it'll loosen up when you use it. It's been here in my shop for a long time, hasn't been played. Apart from that, it's perfect.'

Wilf thought he'd done very well to buy it for seventeen shillings, and he'd been practising hard in his bedroom over the last few weeks to get the hang of it and loosen up that key.

Sidney had told him about a man called George, who had come into the Blood Tub one lunchtime, though he usually drank at Murphy's. He played the saxophone in a band called the Henchmen and said he was willing to teach Wilf for sixpence a lesson.

Wilf had shot round to Murphy's, or the Graving Dock Hotel to give it its proper name, and had already had his first lesson. George could really play. He'd said that if Wilf could learn to play reasonably well, he'd be snapped up by a band. There were lots of dance bands being formed. Dancing was becoming quite a craze. The Henchmen did jazz numbers as well as more sedate tunes. They could play for the Jog-Trot, the Shimmy and the Heebie-Jeebie.

Wilf took a deep breath and started again at the beginning of a fast jazz tune George had been teaching him. It was a catchy number and he'd got it now. He could play it by ear.

Beth put her head round the door, her face screwing with distress. 'Dad, do you have to play that thing so loud?'

'Don't you like it?'

'Not tonight, not that jazz.' She looked quite severe.

Wilf sighed. Beth was so like her mother. She wanted him to feel guilty, and he did.

John came to the door. 'Dad, it's not nice when we've just buried Mam. I'd have thought you'd want to show more respect.'

'Just trying to cheer myself up,' he said and started to play 'Lily of Laguna.' It had a plaintive note and was more in keeping with their sombre mood and it had been one of Vi's favourites. He played 'Danny Boy' too. He was improving no end, so was the dodgy key. He quite fancied himself on the saxophone.

If he took it to the Blood Tub, it made him the life and soul of the party, but that wasn't where he wanted to play. He wanted to join a band with regular bookings. It would be good fun and he'd be paid for playing. If he could join a famous band and play full-time, he'd never have to get on the stand down at the docks again. That was his ambition.

He shook the spit out of his saxophone and put it away. He'd go round and see Ethel, he'd told her he might come tonight to be cheered up.

Ethel's shop was still open. He could smell the rich aroma of cooked meats and hot pies before he reached the door. The shop was full of customers, and there were three people darting up and down behind the counter serving them, all neatly turned out in white caps and aprons over navy dresses. Mrs Watts, Ethel's assistant, was cutting thick slices off a joint of juicy roast beef; her maid Clara was packing up two steak and mushroom pies and two steak and kidney. Her daughter Molly was serving from a big tray of potatoes baked at the bottom of the ovens.

Wilf stood for a moment watching the busy scene. Coins were rattling into Ethel's till. She made pastry that melted in the mouth, crisp and brown, and many varieties of savoury pie, including Cornish pasties.

He let his eyes linger over the great joints of pork with crisp crackling and the boiled hams. There were pig's trotters too and dishes of homemade brawn. Ethel had started putting potatoes in to bake last year and had them ready at dinner time and teatime. She made pease pudding too and her trade had grown steadily since she'd moved out of the North End.

'Lazy housewives rely on me and buy their dinner ready cooked.' She smiled. It was good quality food, well cooked. The tenants of Dock Cottages couldn't afford the prices she charged.

There were more customers coming in. Wilf moved closer and caught Molly's eye; she laughed up at him, there was a sparkle about her. At fifteen she was a comely lass with a well-developed bust and slim waist that made her look nearer twenty. Glossy brown curls peeped out round her cap.

'Is your mother in?'

She lifted the flap that allowed him to go behind the counter. He knew he'd find Ethel in the room behind the shop.

She was doing her accounts at the table under the back window. Ethel had dark eyes like round buttons and rather a plump face; she'd never been as pretty as Vi but she had the same curly brown hair as her daughter, the same mouth that turned up at the corners and seemed ever ready to break into a smile. She was jolly by nature and had the energy and drive of a whirlwind. There was even something of the sparkle Molly had inherited. Ethel was thirty-nine but looked little older than Peggy.

She leapt to her feet and put her arms out to Wilf. 'You must have had a terrible day, you poor pet.'

He felt both comfort and lust as he kissed her. He'd already been spliced to Vi when he'd bought his first steak and kidney pie from Ethel

181

at her father's front door, but if he'd chosen to marry her he wouldn't have gone far wrong. Ethel had a bit of go about her, she said she'd started her business to support herself and her daughter Molly because it didn't look as though she could rely on anyone else to do it. She was the very opposite of poor Vi.

What Vi and her children had given him was a feeling of power. He'd decided everything for them until they'd grown up. Beth was doing her best to cut him down now, and Lottie had defied him, but with Vi he'd always been the boss.

There was none of that with Ethel. She was more independent and knew how to look after herself. The difference was he provided her with a bit of fun and she enjoyed his company. He had to do what she wanted most of the time, nobody could mess Ethel about. Duty wasn't her strong point. She was more like him, out to enjoy herself if she could.

'Come on.' She was peeling his mackintosh off his shoulders. 'They'll be busy in the shop for the best part of another hour, why don't we go upstairs?' Her dark eyes were looking up at him through her lashes, teasing and seductive. 'It'll do you good.'

He liked this about Ethel, she didn't wait to be asked. Today she was pushing him upstairs into her bedroom before he'd even thought of it. She had decent sized rooms over the shop, with solid walls. She turned the key in the door and her fingers began unknotting the tie he'd worn for Vi's funeral.

She let him undo the buttons of her dress and take it off. He could look with delight at the lacy things she wore underneath. Once under her eiderdown, she was much more fun than Vi, who always lay back as though she wanted nothing more than to get it over and done with.

Ethel said having Molly had taught her a thing or two and one child was as much as an unmarried woman needed. She was going to make sure it wouldn't happen again and it never had. For years, Ethel had been making him withdraw before he came and kicking him off if she thought he wasn't going to. Recently, she'd taken to buying condoms and making him wear one.

When they were spent, Ethel curled up and put her head on his shoulder to rest. Wilf closed his eyes and relaxed too, he wanted to shut out the awful moments he'd endured at Vi's funeral.

It wouldn't be a bad idea for him to marry Ethel now. She wouldn't want to come to Dock Cottages, but there was no reason why he couldn't move in here. Much more space and comfort and good food in plenty to be had.

Ethel had told him often enough that he was Molly's father, and made no secret of it in front of Molly. He wasn't sure that it was true. He supposed he could be, but she must have had other men when she was young. If it was true, Molly was nothing like Vi's children. She was dark while they were fair or red-headed; voluptuous in build while they were thin and slight. Lottie was the only one of Vi's who wasn't earnest and duty bound, but Molly wasn't like her either. She had a confident saucy manner and promised to be even more fun than her mother. Already the boys were chatting her up as she served behind the counter downstairs.

He was thinking about it as they sat round the table in the living room. Clara was eating with them, she lived in. He studied Molly as she tucked into the lamb chops with the baked potatoes and cabbage. It was hard to believe he'd sired her. But if it was true, and it could be, then marrying Ethel must be right. It would cement his other family. The more he thought about it, the more he liked the idea.

Molly brought a magnificent bread and butter pudding to the table. Ethel dished up bigger portions of everything than he was ever given at home. Beth was even meaner in the amount she put on his plate than Vi had been.

He couldn't ask Ethel now in front of the two girls, and it wouldn't hurt to sleep on the idea. Could there be any reason why not? Any disadvantage to him?

When Clara started clearing the dishes, Molly opened the piano. Ethel had paid for her to have lessons and she could play well. The girl could have inherited her musical talent from him. She started to sing, she was fond of the music hall stars like Marie Lloyd, and was particularly droll singing as she did now the Harry Lauder song 'Roaming In the Gloaming'. She had a strong, throaty voice, with a husky note. The voice of a mature woman, not a kid of fifteen.

Ethel said that had come from her side of the family. She'd had an uncle who used to work the music hall circuit. He'd sung at the Argyle Theatre here, as well as other theatres all over England.

Molly's voice soared, she sang with such exuberance. Wilf enjoyed listening and knew others would too. He knew she had ambitions to follow her uncle onto the stage. She had a pretty high opinion of her own talent and a low one of his. She'd laughed and told him he was an average amateur on both the saxophone and the mouth organ. Molly could be as difficult as his other daughters, but she was more fun. And she might just achieve what she wanted and make a lot of money. That must be another reason to marry her mother.

Ethel would jump at the chance, he was sure. Once she'd spoken of being unlucky that he'd been married when they met. He'd keep her hanging for a little while. She might even think of it herself and ask him.

Beth left Bobby with Jenny for a few hours and went back to see Matron. She explained that she'd have to live at home and look after her younger siblings.

'I was afraid this might happen, Nurse, when you said you had such young brothers and sisters. But it's your duty and I'm glad you see it that way.'

Beth felt desperate. 'I really need to work. We shall miss my salary. Would it be possible for me to stay on part-time? I have married sisters who might be able to look after Bobby for short periods.'

'Oh no, Nurse. Sister Jones couldn't possibly manage with a part-time staff nurse. Your mind wouldn't be fully on your work. Half the time you wouldn't know what was going on on the ward and the patients wouldn't know you.'

That was exactly what Beth had expected her to say. It was the fear of poverty that had given her the courage to ask.

'Part-time staff nurses would never do . . . Unless . . .' The stern eyes were assessing her with compassion. 'What about outpatients? Dr Williams wants to run a second clinic, so another part-time staff nurse would be useful. Just to look after some of the afternoon clinics, you understand. Would you like to do that?'

'Yes please, Matron.' It was better than she'd dared hope. 'That would be excellent. Suit me very well.'

'I'll have to speak to Sister Bentham, and we'll have to look at what clinics there are. It might not be every afternoon.'

'Anything, Matron, would be a help.' Beth was thrilled. 'I'd feel I was keeping my hand in, if you see what I mean. I'll want to come back to full-time nursing when the family is older.'

Beth was delighted to be offered five afternoons each week, working from one thirty to five o'clock. She would have preferred to continue on the ward but running the clinics in outpatients was better than anything else she might have been able to find. Jenny was working three days a week and suggested Paula, her next-door neighbour, might look after Bobby as well as her children, when Beth could not.

Beth was pleased with that. She could drop Bobby off on her way to the hospital and collect him on her way home.

As the weeks went by, she found home a sad place without her mother and she saw very little of her father. Colin and Esther were at school. She cleaned and cooked and looked after Bobby and enjoyed her afternoons running the clinics more than she'd expected. Ivor left school and wanted to work with horses. Dad wanted him to apply to the knacker's yard in Beaufort Road, where they were always advertising for help.

'Live horses, Dad,' he said angrily. 'I couldn't stand the knacker's yard.'

He'd always hung about the nearby stables. The horse drawing the bread van was stabled on Townsend Street, and the one drawing the milk float almost opposite. He'd made friends with the horses and the men in charge, but jobs were no longer easy to find in the deepening depression.

Ivor was glad to be offered a job by a coal merchant, who kept a stable of three horses. He'd be helping to look after them but most of his day would be spent out with the carts delivering sacks of coal.

'It's heavy work,' Beth said. Dirty work too.

Ivor pulled a face. 'I'd prefer the bread van, but I'll have to take it.'

'Something better may turn up, if you keep on looking.'

Beth had never known her home to be so quiet during the day. She missed her old life, the camaraderie of the nurses' home. She felt her horizons had closed in.

They were none of them happy, how could they be? Colin and Esther kept asking her about Mam. Why had she died? Was she in heaven? Even Dad was miserable. All his bombastic confidence seemed to have drained away. He wasn't eating as much and his sleep was disturbed. She heard him having a nightmare; he woke her up shouting Violet's name. They were all grieving for her.

It surprised Beth to find that on some nights her father didn't come home until after six in the morning. Today, she was up and getting the fire started when he came in.

'Where've you been until now?' she asked.

'Drowning my sorrows. Vi was the best wife anyone could ever have.'

'The Blood Tub closes at half eleven, Dad. What's open all night?'

'None of your business,' he retorted. 'But I've been walking about, thinking of your mam.'

Beth didn't think so. He was quite prepared to go to work, and seemed much as he did when he'd been in bed all night.

The things she had said about blaming him for Mam's death lay heavily between them, souring everything. Beth knew it was going to take a long time to put behind them the anger and the hurt and the loss.

Chapter Sixteen

Peggy felt she was having a hard time. She was missing her mother, and rarely went to Dock Cottages now Beth had taken over there. She was always tired but tonight she felt exhausted, the clock was striking ten as she went upstairs to her bed. In the candlelight, May and Hilda looked like sleeping angels, innocent and utterly delightful.

Peggy felt full of love for them, they were lovely when they were quiet and not demanding attention. They'd thought it a great treat to be allowed to sleep in Sidney's place in the double bed. She lifted Hilda over to give herself more room and crawled in beside her. She could feel herself drifting off the moment she pulled the eiderdown up round her shoulders. That was one advantage of having to work hard during the day.

Some time later she woke to the sound of the front door slamming below. It shook the whole house. She knew Sidney did that deliberately to wake her up when he came home. The street lights were still lit, so that meant it wasn't yet midnight. She peered at her alarm clock. Only half eleven; for Sidney this was unusually early. She could hear him coming up, and settled back against her pillow, pretending to be asleep. She saw the candle he brought lighten the room. Then heard him draw in his breath in surprise.

'Good God! What are the kids doing here?'

Peggy gave up the pretence of sleeping. 'I want them with me. You can sleep in their bed.'

That made him swear. She knew by the way he slurred his words that he'd had a skinful. She shivered, he was always worse when he was drunk.

'You're not putting me out of my own bed.' He was lighting the other candle. 'They're going back this minute. Get up and move Hilda.'

He was carrying the still sleeping May away. Peggy didn't move. He swore again when he came back. He dragged Hilda to the edge of the bed and hoisted her into his arms. She woke up and started to cry.

'Shut up, you! I can't be doing with all this now.'

Peggy got up wearily. She'd move Hilda into Frankie's bed and sleep with May, though it was only a single bed. Sidney stopped her at the door and turned her back none too gently.

'You bitch!' He was angry. 'Get back into bed. I know what your game is and I'm not having it.'

'Sidney, we don't want any more babies. We agreed on that, didn't we?'

He was tearing off his clothes in a savage manner. 'You're my wife. God damn you, you'll do what a wife should.'

'I don't want another baby. We can't afford it anyway, not on what you earn. Be reasonable.'

Without warning, Sidney's palm came crashing against her jaw, jerking her head back and making it jangle. Peggy knew there was no point in resisting further. Revulsion welled up inside her. Sidney was going to have his way because he was stronger than she was. Much stronger. She was tempted to bring her knee up hard against his goolies but she knew he'd retaliate and hurt her more if she did. Giving in was her only option if she wanted to avoid that. He forced himself on her. She gritted her teeth and let him get on with it, resisting the urge to bite and kick at him.

'That was rape,' she said bitterly when he rolled off.

He laughed unpleasantly. 'You're my wife. It isn't possible for a husband to rape his wife. It's your own fault if I have to insist on my rights.'

'I hate you,' she was vehement, 'hate you.' He laughed again, releasing a cloud of beery breath in her face. He smelled awful and he was rough. She got out of bed, relit the candle and went down to the kitchen. She'd learned from Jenny that it was better to douche straight away. Jenny had helped her find a second-hand douche can. Quassia or quinine was recommended and she had only vinegar, but that was better than nothing. There was no warm water and she was thoroughly cold, but she had to make every effort now while it might still be effective. If only she could get one of those cap things she'd read about in the books Beth had loaned her.

Peggy was crying with exhaustion as much as anything else as she crept back upstairs. She would have liked to move Hilda and spend the rest of the night in May's bed, but she hadn't the energy. It was easier to lie down beside Sidney, who was now snoring.

Over the last year or so, the ill feeling she felt for him had hardened to hate. No, what she felt was more than hate; she loathed him, detested him, and would give anything to get away from him.

188

She'd had her first heavy sleep out and, though she ached with fatigue, she couldn't get to sleep again. She tossed and turned and thought again about Sidney. It would be wonderful if she could get a full night's sleep without being woken up when he came to bed hours after her. If she didn't have to worry about getting pregnant again, if she could stop cooking his meals and washing his clothes, and if she could stop pretending to everybody that all was well between them, life might be bearable.

But she didn't dare leave him. He barely gave her enough for the family to exist, she'd have nothing if she left him. She was trapped. There was no way out for her. She felt she'd lost control of her life.

The following Friday afternoon, Wilfred caught the bus into town to see Ethel. She was behind the shop counter with Molly and he'd caught them at a slack moment. He asked: 'What about going to a dance tonight, Ethel? D'you fancy it?'

Her button eyes stared at him in surprise. 'I thought you weren't keen on dancing.'

'I'm not very, but this fellow George – I told you about him, didn't I? He's giving me lessons on the saxophone.'

'Yes, you said.'

'Well, he's in a band called the Henchmen and they're playing for a dance at the Jubilee Hall.'

'Where on earth's that?'

'West Kirby.'

Molly was grinning at him. 'I'll come with you.' She did a pirouette. 'I love dancing.'

'I wasn't asking you. It's your mother I want.'

'I wouldn't mind,' Ethel said slowly. 'It's probably the back of beyond but I could do with a change. What time?'

'It's seven till eleven thirty.'

'You'll keep the shop open for me, Molly, won't you? Just until the stuff's sold. Saturday's a good night for us.'

'Mam,' her voice was loud with protest, 'I want to come with you. When do I ever go anywhere? Can't Clara and Mrs Watts do the shop?'

'Well . . .'

'Please, Mam. It would be so nice to go out with both of you.'

Wilf wasn't keen on taking Molly, but he knew better than to say so. He said, 'I'll go and find out about the times of the trains.'

Ethel asked, 'Will you be back for your tea? It's boiled ham tonight.'

It pleased Wilf to be asked. 'Yes, I'd like that. I'll go home and get my best bib and tucker on first.'

Molly flashed a mischievous smile at him. 'And some dancing shoes, not those clodhoppers.'

'These are new,' he said indignantly. 'My best, all I've got.'

Ethel laughed. 'She's only teasing.'

Wilf could have done without Molly's company, but Ethel never denied her anything. He could hear the thrum of the band as he paid their entrance money, and went to the door of the hall to watch them play while he waited for the ladies to hand in their coats and powder their noses. George was here, one of the two saxophone players. There was no shortage of dancers swirling round the floor. They were playing a military two-step; the drums pounded out the beat, the melody twinkled out on the piano, the accordion put some bounce in it, and the saxophones soared above it all.

All the members of the band were playing with great verve and enthusiasm, except George. That so surprised Wilf that he watched him more closely. George's face seemed lifeless, his eyes were closed, and he certainly wasn't putting heart and soul into playing.

Wilf was tapping his feet to the music when Ethel and Molly came to join him. Ethel was wearing her best frock of royal blue; he'd seen it before and she looked well in it, it made her look slimmer than she really was, but Molly took his breath away. He had to look twice at her, she was a picture with her brown curls springing round her face and her frilly scarlet dress.

'Marvellous band,' he enthused. It was bloody marvellous. To be able to play with a band like this would suit him down to the ground. New dance bands were springing up by the dozen. Most of the musicians had day jobs too but they were hoping the band would get enough bookings to make them unnecessary. The beat changed to a waltz.

'Come on,' Ethel said. 'Let's have a dance.' He led her onto the floor. They circled it once.

'You're a bit rusty at this,' she murmured.

He never had been any good at dancing, never had had any lessons, rarely even tried it. He had to concentrate on putting his feet down in the right place. Wilf knew he wasn't doing very well. Molly whirled past them in the arms of an unknown partner who really could waltz.

The music ended and Ethel led the way back to the row of chairs. When the next dance was announced as a bunny-trot, Ethel said, 'We'd better sit this one out.'

Wilf was relieved. He felt a little older than most of the other dancers. Molly was really kicking up her heels to this one, she waved to them as she went by. When he looked again at George he seemed quite switched off, he looked ill. An interval was announced and Molly rejoined them.

'Good grief, it can't be half time already,' she complained.

The band was retiring except for the pianist. A vocalist in a tight purple dress was making her way onto the stage. She sang several old music hall favourites.

'I don't think much of her.' Molly was scornful. 'She's too old and too fat.' Under the stage lights, the singer's shiny satin dress accentuated the rolls of flesh round her middle. 'I could do much better.'

Then she was gone too and the stage empty. People were getting restive.

'This is a drag,' Molly complained.

There was noise outside, people were drawing back the curtains to see what was going on, others were streaming to the door.

'There's an ambulance outside,' Molly announced. Wilf wondered if it could possibly be for George, and made for the door at the back of the hall through which the band had disappeared. He was in time to see a stretcher covered with a red blanket being carried out. The singer followed, she was wearing her coat over the purple dress. Everybody seemed to be talking at once.

Wilf asked, 'Is that George?'

Nobody answered him.

The band leader called, 'Come on, let's get back to it. We've taken long enough.'

Wilf felt Molly push past him. 'Have you lost your singer?'

'Yes.'

'Was that George's wife?' Wilf asked.

'I can sing.' Molly was wildly excited. 'I can do her numbers. Let me fill in for her.'

Wilf heard one of them say, 'Give her a go. She'd be better than nobody.'

'She looks good, better than Monica.'

'I am good.' She whirled on them. 'I can sing all the popular tunes of the day as well as that music hall stuff. I'm better than her, you'll see.'

'OK, talk to the pianist about the numbers you'll sing. That's Ted over there.'

'I can play tenor sax,' Wilf said, jumping on the bandwagon. 'George is teaching me. Is that his sax over there? Let me take his place.'

The band were all wearing dark lounge suits and red bow ties.

'You can't wear that.' Somebody was pulling Wilf's jacket of loud fawn checks off him, another removing his tie.

'Where's George's bow? Somebody took it off him and unbuttoned his shirt.'

George's red bow tie was retrieved and clipped onto Wilf's shirt. He smoothed back his hair and George's saxophone was pushed into his hands.

'You don't look too bad,' somebody told him. 'You'll do in shirt sleeves. Come on.'

Wilf stumbled back into the hall in the wake of the other band members. He heard the band leader, a small, slight fellow, apologise for the delay and announce that Wilf Hubble had been kind enough to offer his services to the band in place of George Thompson who had been taken ill.

Wilf glowed with pride. He'd dreamed of being up on a stage with a saxophone in his hand. Adrenaline was shooting through him; he'd never felt so alive, so on top of everything. The alto saxophone player, a pimply youth, was arranging sheet music on the stand in front of him.

Wilf almost told him not to bother, that he couldn't read music, but stopped himself in time. If the lad could whisper the title of each piece before they began to play, that might be helpful, but he didn't like to ask. Wilf flipped through the sheet music studying the written titles. He didn't find words easy to read either, and even the first one defeated him.

He was sweating as he waited. There was a drum roll, he took a deep breath and raised the instrument to his lips. The leader gave the beat and the music burst forth. Wilf knew the tune well and relaxed a bit, he could play this. The instrument was much better than his own, it was a delight.

Beside him, the alto sax played with great confidence, his notes soaring ever louder and higher. Wilf tucked his notes in behind, feeling any small inadequacy on his part would not be noticed under the blaring alto. But he didn't know the second tune nearly so well; he'd never tried to play it before and his instrument was embarrassingly silent through many bars. Wilf felt his confidence seeping away when it happened again and again in the following tunes.

Molly came bounding on stage and was introduced as Veronica Eastly, 'a very talented eighteen-year-old who has sung with Henry Hall's dance band and is making a guest appearance with us here tonight'.

Molly was in front of him and was so excited she couldn't stand still. She was letting off little laughs like sparks. Starry-eyed, she turned to wink at him. Bubbling over as she was, she looked very attractive.

The band leader was indicating they should play more softly, but Molly's voice was strong enough to rise above the band. She had a knack of putting her laugh into her singing voice which was very jolly. The dancers were stopping to watch her. She was a bit of an actress too and pirouetted about the stage.

Even from behind her, Wilf could see Molly was rising to the occasion and giving the performance of her life. He was afraid nerves were having the opposite effect on him, as they always did.

Molly's scarlet dress of fancy frills was just right for a stage appearance, and she wasn't against showing a bit of leg. She needed a bit more flesh on her but time would take care of that. She was getting plenty of catcalls from the boys and was being applauded with far more enthusiasm than George's wife had been. Molly was right, she had a better voice.

Wilf let his eyes wander round the briskly applauding hands of the dancers. He was looking for Ethel to exchange proud parent glances. She would be thrilled for Molly. He noticed then, somebody waving at him as though trying to attract his attention. He held his breath, it was Lottie!

The heat was running up his cheeks as she smiled and waved again. He looked hurriedly away. He'd always known it was essential to keep his two families apart. He'd managed it up to now and prided himself on his skill. He'd never been found out doing anything wrong at home or at work, but with Molly just in front of him breaking into another song and Lottie waving from the hall, he felt threatened.

He gave Lottie a lift of the hand in cautious acknowledgement. He'd need to get out of here without Ethel and Molly coming face to face with her.

He looked round the hall for Ethel. She could be as quick as a load of monkeys and would tumble to the fact that Lottie was one of his daughters. She'd always known they existed but had never wanted to hear anything about them while Vi was alive. She'd kept herself aloof from his other family, but now, if she knew Lottie was here, he couldn't be sure she wouldn't introduce herself.

Molly was even more of a danger. As far as he knew she'd been kept more or less in ignorance, knowing only that he was married to someone else. She'd shown plenty of curiosity but he'd told her next to nothing. Molly would leap at the chance of talking to Lottie and he knew she'd extract every fact from her with ease.

Wilf felt worse as the evening went on. The alto sax was playing to a standard he couldn't reach. He tried to change over the sheet music in front of him when he saw the rest of the band doing it, to make it appear that he was reading it.

He had to listen intently to follow the tune by ear, and because he wasn't doing it well, it was sapping his confidence. He played a wrong note and felt he was going to pieces.

Lottie was still waving at him as though she wanted to tell him something. There was a lad beside her and he was waving too. Wilf didn't want to know, he counted it foul luck that they were here. He looked away. All this was really putting him off. He played another wrong note and the pimply-faced alto sax player turned and pulled a face at him.

At the same time, Molly's success was fuelling her efforts to excel. She was lifting her scarlet frills and doing a few high kicks. Ethel had paid for tap dancing lessons for her from a young age too. She was giving a good show.

He caught sight of Ethel, who was watching Molly over the shoulder of the man she was dancing with. Her face was full of pride. Ethel's dancing partner, Wilf noticed, was younger than he was, younger than Ethel too, he shouldn't wonder.

The evening was coming to a close. Wilf was glad, he was too tired to concentrate now. Molly gave an encore as calls for more came from the crowd. Then they played the last waltz and finally 'God Save the King'. The ladies flocked to the room set aside as their cloakroom.

Wilf followed the band in the other direction to the room they'd been using. He was patting the moisture out of George's saxophone, a really beautiful instrument, when the dapper band leader said, 'We'd better have that back now. To keep safe for George.' It was removed from Wilf's fingers. 'And his bow tie.' Reluctantly, Wilf pulled the clip-on from his collar.

'Thank you for helping us out.' His tone was formal, dismissive.

He would have turned away if Wilf hadn't spurred himself to ask, 'Another time? Will you need me again?'

The band leader was rubbing his chin.

Faltering now, Wilf said, 'George looked really ill. It could be some time before he can play again.'

'Yes, I'm afraid you're right about that.' His manner remained stiffly polite. 'But we need a player with more experience. You aren't quite good enough, not yet. Perhaps after more lessons . . .'

Wilf felt ready to sink into the ground. He'd blown it.

Molly was still letting off sparks. 'Wasn't that marvellous? Oh, I did love doing it.'

It didn't help Wilf's self-esteem to see the band leader press a silver coin into Molly's palm and tell her that she'd been wonderful and he wanted her again next week.

'We've got an engagement at the Floral Pavilion in New Brighton, starting next Monday. We'll be there Tuesday and Wednesday too. Fifteen minutes on stage in a variety show. Can you come and sing with us? How about it?'

Molly was ecstatic. A meeting on Sunday was fixed for a rehearsal. As Wilf struggled into his jacket, he felt aggrieved. It wasn't fair that success was coming instantly to Molly, she was just a kid. He'd been trying so hard for so long, and everything was staying out of his grasp. He rammed his tie into his pocket, feeling angry and humiliated.

'Let's find your mam and go for the train,' he choked.

'Mam's got a lift home in a car. She said to tell you.'

'What?'

'That man she's been dancing with, his name's Harry. He asked her.'

Wilf felt the bottom was dropping out of his world.

'What about you?'

'I don't want to play gooseberry, do I?'

That made him feel worse. Was Molly telling him her mother had found another man friend? It sounded like it.

'She can't just go off with a stranger like that.'

'I'm not sure he was a stranger, she said she knew him years ago.'

As far as Wilf was concerned, that sounded worse still.

'Mam said I was to get on the train with you. When you get off, it's only another minute or two into Hamilton Square.'

'Come on then, let's go.'

'My coat's in the cloakroom.'

There was still a crush down that end of the hall. 'I'll wait for you outside,' he said, thinking Lottie would be less likely to see him out in the dark, but even there the crowds were lingering. Somebody was whistling one of Molly's songs.

Wilf was so full of disappointment and envy he didn't see Lottie until she caught at his arm and pulled him round to face her.

'Dad, fancy seeing you playing here! I couldn't believe my eyes, I had to look twice.'

'A great band,' her companion said.

'This is Peter Shaw, Dad. I've been wanting you to meet him. We want to get engaged.' Only then did Wilf remember that the Wishart house where Lottie worked was in West Kirby.

'I'd like to ask your permission, Mr Hubble,' the lad said earnestly. 'I know this isn't the right place and that you'll want to know something about me—'

'Engaged?' It seemed no time at all since she was a babe in arms. 'Don't rush things, Lottie.'

'Dad!'

Her boyfriend looked appalled.

'You're only eighteen, plenty of time for—'

'Nineteen now, Dad. Mam was only seventeen when she married you, and our Peggy was . . .'

Molly pushed her way through the crush like a whirlwind to swing on his arm. 'They're saying in there that the last train leaves at midnight. We'd better get going. Wouldn't do to miss it. Where'd we sleep tonight?'

Molly was towing him forward; Wilf saw Lottie's mouth drop open in amazement.

'The singer! Do you know her?'

Molly laughed and swung on his arm. 'He certainly does.'

Lottie's horrified eyes swung to his. 'She's not . . .'

'No!' Wilf yelled above the noisy crowd, then wished he'd kept his mouth shut. It would be better if they thought she was his girlfriend. Anything was better than . . .

'Dad!' Lottie was frowning. 'You ought to be ashamed of yourself. A young girl like her.'

Molly collapsed in a fit of giggles and spluttered out, 'He's my dad.'

Wilf couldn't look at Lottie's face. Had she heard? He grabbed Molly's arm and bulldozed their way through the crush. Once on the road, they set off at the double. She couldn't have said anything worse!

'Who was that?' Molly demanded.

'Nobody to interest you.'

'Was it one of your other daughters?'

He'd thought Molly knew nothing of his other life. It came as a shock to find she did. 'Never you mind,' he told her.

'It was, wasn't it?' she wheedled.

Wilf quickened his pace. He couldn't stand another moment of this.

Chapter Seventeen

When Wilf got back to Dock Cottages, all the lights were out. Beth was a dark mound on the couch. He tried to creep past her to the lavatory, but when she stirred he knew he'd woken her up. When he came back she'd raised herself up on her elbow.

'Why didn't you say you wouldn't be home for your tea?' He could hear the condemnation in her voice. 'You knew I'd cook a meal for you. I tried to keep it hot.'

'What was it?'

'Irish stew.'

He was feeling hungry, it was a long time since he'd had the boiled ham. 'I'll have it now.'

'You're too late, Ivor and Esther ate it between them.' Beth turned over and pulled the blankets up round her chin.

Wilf felt really down as he went to his room to get undressed. It had been a terrible evening. Getting his big chance to play with a proper band and then having it messed up by Lottie. Once he'd seen her there, he'd been unable to concentrate. Rotten luck that she'd turned up like that. It wouldn't have been quite so bad if Molly had messed up her chance too, but she'd done amazingly well and that pointed up his failure.

Ethel going home with another man hadn't helped, and as for Lottie coming face to face with Molly, he'd had nightmares about such a thing happening. If only Lottie had gone away believing Molly was a new girlfriend, that might have given him kudos, a man of his age. But Molly had put paid to that.

Once in bed, he realised sleep was miles away. His head felt on fire after what had happened. He tossed and turned, worrying about what Lottie would do. Tell Beth no doubt, and the frost he was already feeling from her would harden. Life here would be unbearable.

He'd meant to take his time over asking Ethel to marry him, but it might be better if he got on with it so he had a bolt hole to go to if things turned sour here. He was uneasy, too, about the man who'd taken her home. He didn't want another to cut him out. Ethel provided a haven for him where he was always welcome, good food and a bit of fun on the side.

Ethel had had man friends before, they came and went, but he'd gone on and on. All the same, he'd better tell her that now he was free to marry her, he'd do it. He'd ask her to set the day.

It was very late when he finally fell asleep, and his alarm clock seemed to go off shortly afterwards. He felt sleep-sodden and couldn't be bothered getting up for work even though Larry Bilton would be picking his gang in Egerton Dock this morning. It was Saturday, he'd have an easy weekend and get his plans straightened out with Ethel.

What seemed like seconds later, Beth was hammering on his door. 'Dad, it's quarter to seven.' She put her head round the door. 'It's time you were up, your breakfast's on the table.' She'd woken him thoroughly now.

'Not going in today,' he gasped.

'What? You might have said last night. I could have had a lie-in too.'

'I didn't know then.'

'Why not?'

'Hadn't made up my mind. You can bring my breakfast in here. What is it?'

'Dad, if you want it, you can get up for it.'

His door closed quietly. The nerve of her! He could just do with a cup of tea and a bowl of porridge. It made him angry. No daughter should speak to her father like that. He definitely needed to find a more comfortable place to live. He'd walk out and leave Beth to get on with things. She could whistle for money, she didn't appreciate what he was handing over every week.

It was elevenish when Wilf did get up. By then, Beth was ironing on the table and all the food had been cleared away.

'Where's my breakfast?'

'Been eaten, bigger helpings for the rest of us.'

'You mean bitch!'

Wilf filled the kettle and put it on to boil. 'Iron my fawn shirt for me,' he ordered. He might as well look his best when he went down to see Ethel.

'I've done it. It's over in that pile there.'

'Thank you.'

'Will you be in for meals today?'

'I'll have something to eat now before I go out. I won't be in for tea.'

198

'You might at least let me know when you're going to be out, Dad.'

'I've said, haven't I? I won't be back for tea.' Ethel hadn't invited him, but she always did if he turned up at the shop. Beth took the other flat iron out of the fire and replaced it with the one she'd been using. He could see a pile of ironing waiting to be done.

'What about it then?' he asked.

She turned round to look at him. 'What d'you mean?'

'I want something to eat now. My dinner, before I go out.'

'You'll find the sandwiches I cut for your dinner in the meat safe,' she said shortly. 'You insist on taking them with you even when you're hoping for a half day.'

'How do I know what time the ship'll finish loading?' Wilf's stomach felt empty. He'd been hungry last night and had missed his breakfast this morning. He felt in need of a hot meal, but clearly he wasn't going to get one. 'You could try being civil,' he complained.

He made himself a pot of tea and found the sandwiches. They were filled with his favourite brawn. He took them back to his armchair by the fire and started to eat.

'You know I like mustard. You've forgotten to put it on.'

'I didn't forget, Dad. We've run out of it.'

'Then get some more.' Wilf felt he had a lot to put up with. The sooner he could get away from Beth, the better. She thought she ruled the roost here.

He went out as soon as he'd eaten. He'd have a pint in the Blood Tub before going down to Ethel's. Saturday lunchtime was busy in the shop. Mid-afternoon would be the best time to catch her on her own. He'd pop the question and she'd invite him to eat with them tonight. He'd take her out somewhere afterwards, she'd want to celebrate.

When the pub closed, he took the tram down to Ethel's. As he'd supposed, there were few customers about. Only Clara was behind the counter. He'd expected to find Ethel in the room behind the shop, but she was in the big kitchen beyond, pushing luscious stuffing into a fat chicken. The scent of sage and onion was strong.

'Hello,' he said, putting his arms round her. 'You got home all right last night then?'

She looked up, smiling. 'You can see I did. Wasn't it a marvellous night? I can't get over Molly. She did wonderfully well, didn't she? She's over the moon. We were up half the night, too excited to go to bed. She had her chance and grabbed it with both hands. We can't get over her luck.'

199

Wilf hadn't come to glory in Molly's success. He hated to hear Ethel speaking of it with such obvious joy. It cut into him that it had happened to Molly but not to him. He wanted to forget last night, it was too painful to dwell on.

Ethel asked, 'Have you heard what happened to your friend? The one who was taken ill?'

'George Thompson? Somebody told me in the pub that he'd been rushed to hospital in West Kirby and had had his appendix out.'

'Isn't it awful? The way we're pleased because he was taken ill? But if he and his wife hadn't rushed away, Molly wouldn't have had her chance.'

Wilf swallowed hard, he could feel anger welling up inside him. Lottie had ruined everything for him by being there. He'd lost his chance with the band and he was worried about what was still to come. She was probably going to blow his life apart. He must get on with what he'd come to do.

He took a deep breath and said, 'I'm glad I've caught you alone. There's something I want to ask you.'

'Go ahead.' She started stringing the chicken for the oven.

'You're making a good meal for tonight.'

'Yes.'

He waited. Usually she'd say, 'D'you want to eat with us?' The invitation didn't come.

'I wanted to ask you . . .' He hadn't envisaged it happening like this, her tying up a chicken. She should be in his arms. He got out the little ring box of tooled leather he'd found in the sideboard drawer and put it on the table beside her.

'What's this?'

'Will you marry me, Ethel?'

Her dark eyes came slowly up to meet his. Her hand reached for the ring box and opened it. He heard her gasp with surprise at the sight of Beth's ring. It was an impressive diamond.

'Marry you?' Was that a giggle he heard her suppress? She was pressing her lips together. He took the ring from its box and went to push it on her finger.

'No, Wilf!' She leapt back. 'You're sixteen years too late.'

'I know, but I couldn't marry you then. Now I can, how about it?'

'Not likely. I'm not keeping you for the rest of your life. I wouldn't want you under my feet permanently. Why should I?'

'I love you, you love me.'

She didn't answer. It came to him then that she might not want to marry him.

200

He began to plead. 'We've stayed together all this time. It's lasted. You keep inviting me for meals and . . .'

'I thought I should. I thought you'd want to keep in touch with Molly. I did it for her too, so she'd know her own father.'

'But you also want a bit of lovemaking. You can't wait to get me upstairs.'

Ethel grinned at him. 'Just a bit of fun, Wilf. Where else could I get that?'

'You could have it all the time if you married me.'

'No. I'd get other things too.' She took the ring from his hand, put it back in the box, clipped it shut and handed it back.

'I don't want this either. I'd be scared it would get me into trouble. Did you steal it?'

'Of course not.' Wilf was taken aback. 'Would I give you something that might get you into trouble?'

Beth had come by it honestly and she no longer wanted it. You couldn't call something stolen if it belonged to your daughter.

Ethel's button eyes were almost lost in her plump face when she laughed. 'I'm sure you already have, several times.'

Wilf was shocked. Ethel really meant to refuse him. If he couldn't come and live with her, the future looked bleak.

'I'd be a good husband to you.'

'I know exactly what you'd be, Wilf, I know you well. You'd expect me to support you and that tribe of kids you've got back in Dock Cottages. I'm not going to do it.'

'No I wouldn't, I'd keep on my job.'

'Don't even think of giving that up.' The kettle was boiling on the stove. She reached for her teapot and made tea before collapsing onto a chair.

Wilf felt as though the ground was being cut from under him. 'Take pity on me, Ethel.'

'You didn't take pity on me when I told you Molly was on the way. I'd have gone under before you'd have lifted a finger to help.'

'I did my best, I gave you a cot and—'

'Yes, you already had a wife and family, there was nothing you could do for me.'

'You had your dad.'

'He was mad at me, absolutely furious. He said he was disgusted and I should have had more sense. He said a lot of nasty things about you, a married man playing away from home, when you already had a wife and kids.'

Wilf was indignant, he'd done his best. 'I'd have helped more if I could. I've always been right fond of you,'

'I know, but it was a very unhappy time.' Ethel got up and poured two cups of tea. She pushed one across the table to him. Wilf pulled out a chair and sat down.

'I'm sorry.'

'Fortunately, Dad couldn't throw me out, he needed me. Mam had died a year or two before and he was dying of cancer, I was looking after him. He didn't want me to have anything more to do with you.'

'But you did. You still wanted to see me.'

'I needed support and affection as well as help.' Her voice trembled. 'I'd already given up my job at the moneylenders in Stanley Road. I was earning only a few shillings a week anyway, not enough to feed three of us and pay the rent. When Dad got too ill to get up at half three in the morning to go to work up at Wilkinson's bakery, we were desperate.

'It was a bad time for both of us,' he said.

'Dad hated the thought of me having a baby when I wasn't married and it would be another mouth to feed.' She drew in a deep breath, she sounded as though she had a lump in her throat. 'When we started making pies to sell from our front room, he said people wouldn't come and buy them because of the baby, but he was wrong.'

'You said he was fond of Molly.'

'Yes, once she was born. He used to feed and change her for me. I reckon looking after her lengthened his life, he was able to sit and feed her right up to the end. Even the day before . . .' He could see she could barely control her feelings. 'I had so many other things to do, I was glad of his help.'

She stood up with a jerk and got out a roasting tin for the chicken.

'It's time I got this in the oven. I don't like peeling potatoes, I'll get Clara to come and do that while I stand in the shop.'

Wilf felt he was being dismissed. He had to push his teacup away and stand up. 'We have good memories too. We had some good times.'

Ethel didn't answer.

'Are you going to invite me to tea?'

She always did, always had. He didn't doubt she would now even though she didn't want marriage.

Her eyes met his. 'Not tonight, Wilf. I've already asked Harry – he's the man I met at the dance last night.'

Wilf shivered. He felt as if a bucket of cold water had been thrown over him. Ethel was going into the shop and he had to follow her. Why did all the good things in life go to other people? Ethel was his, she'd been his lady friend for sixteen years, he valued her, he loved her.

There was a customer in the shop and Ethel went to serve her. Wilf let himself out into Bridge Street and started walking home, boiling with frustration. Had Ethel really found somebody else? If he didn't have her, he'd be truly bereaved. He'd have no one.

By Monday morning, Wilf felt very depressed. Ethel wasn't a good-looking woman, it had never occurred to him that she'd find someone to replace him. She'd been a cushion against bereavement when Vi died. He'd been so sure he could have a new life with her, a better life, and that he'd be able to get away from hard work and poverty at long last.

Wilf's shoulders were hunched as he slouched down to join the pool of labour collecting on the dock before the sun was up. They were standing about, grey-faced and sleep-sodden, dragging on their cigarettes. Nothing was happening yet. Wilf lit a Gold Flake and prepared to wait.

He was fifty now, almost fifty-one. Not the best age for a docker; he still had strength but his stamina was no longer what it used to be. Everybody knew stamina declined with age, he wouldn't be picked out for work so often now if it wasn't for Larry Bilton.

The gang of stevedores was being selected when Bilton came to pick for the portering gang. Wilf knew by the glances coming his way that he wasn't pleased. Bilton kept him waiting, picked him out last for the morning's work.

'You didn't turn up on Saturday,' he said accusingly.

'Did it matter?'

'Silverware.'

'My back was playing up. Could hardly straighten up, never mind lift anything.'

Bilton pursed his lips. Wilf wasn't sure whether that showed disapproval or disbelief, but he was on the gang again.

The stevedores were unloading the *Katherine May*. The derricks of the seven-thousand-ton tramp were swinging sacks of new potatoes onto the quay. It was hard graft wheeling them on his hand truck into the far warehouse. There were sacks of onions and boxes of oranges, which according to the labels had come from Majorca.

'Where's that?' he asked another docker.

'Spain. A Spanish island.'

Wilf knew a box of oranges would be broken open and they'd all fill their pockets before going home, but there wasn't much to be made from oranges and onions. Bilton was ignoring him, he wasn't planning to dirty his fingers on fruit and vegetables. In-coming cargoes never seemed to be of such high value as those being exported.

Before noon all the cargo was off and Bilton and his sidekick opened up another warehouse where the cargo they were to load was stacked. Wilf wheeled out several loads of the boxes before he found out what was in them.

'Fountain pens and propelling pencils,' Mr Bilton mouthed as he directed Wilf to a new stack of boxes. 'There you go, be careful now.' Wilf saw the sacks left in readiness for him to use.

When the moment came, it always gave him a jolt and made his heart race. His nerves were raw after the trampling they'd had over the weekend, but he broke open the case, and divided up the contents into the sacks. Each time he took a full truck to the wharf he moved one sack to the place Bilton had designated. From there, he would pick them up and take them through the dock gates.

Wilf was jumpy but everything went to plan until he realised that the crates containing fountain pens had been taken from the warehouse more quickly than he'd expected. They were still stacked in piles on the quay waiting for the stevedores to load but he could see that the warehouse doors were about to be closed and locked. The last three wooden crates were loaded on his truck, together with the last sack of contraband and he headed out of the warehouse. Wilf looked to see if Bilton had removed the sacks he'd left for him. They'd gone all right but he'd have to hide the one he still had somewhere else.

The warehouse door clanged shut behind him. Outside, he saw Bilton astride his motorbike. It was ticking over while he spoke to one of the dock police. Wilf knew instantly what he must do with the sack. He leaned forward and gripped it as he pushed the truck along, watching carefully until Bilton's body hid him from the policeman. With one quick jerk, he tucked the sack into Bilton's sidecar.

Wilf was glad to get rid of it, the gateman would turn a blind eye to a pocket full of oranges but he wouldn't want to be caught with fountain pens on him. They were Waterman's, good ones, and would fetch a tidy price.

He had to wait until they were signed off, but then set off walking to the cafe to meet the gaffer. He heard Bilton's motorbike coming before he reached it and it pulled up beside him. 'Get on,' he grated.

It was obvious the gaffer wasn't happy with him. The bike swooped into the park. The afternoon had turned out pleasantly sunny and there were plenty of people about. Wilf could feel Bilton clucking with impatience. They had to go to Vyner Road and up into Taylor's Wood to find a quiet enough spot to share out their spoils.

When he switched the engine off, Bilton turned on him in fury. 'What made you dump that last sack on me? I couldn't believe you'd do such a thing under the very eyes of the dock police.'

'Your body hid what I did.'

'There were people all round us. Anyone could have seen you.'

'Did anybody?'

'Damn dangerous. You could have landed me in it. Don't ever do such a thing again.'

He shared out the fountain pens with less generosity than usual. 'Perhaps we're overdoing this. Better if we give it a rest. It was a miracle I wasn't caught this time.'

Wilf said, 'What d'you mean?'

'What I say. Let's play it straight for a few months while we're still winning.'

Bilton was pushing his share back into the sacks. Wilf pushed his into his big poacher's pockets. It depressed him further to see yet another part of his life close off to him. Bilton didn't even offer to run him nearer to Dock Cottages. Wilf had to think about the best way to go. He headed straight through the wood to the cemetery at Flaybrick. From there it was only a stone's throw.

It occurred to him that as he had to pass the end of Powell Street where Peggy lived, he might as well drop off his haul. The sooner Sidney started selling them in the Blood Tub, the sooner he'd have money in his pocket.

He'd come at a good time. Sidney answered his knock at the door and led him through the living room.

'Hello, love,' he said to Peggy who was stretched out on a chair. As usual the toddlers were noisily teasing the dog. He just avoided tripping over Eric who was crawling round the floor.

Out to the back yard then and into the wash house. Sidney locked the door moments before the kids tried to join them.

'I want to see Grandpa.' Frankie was thumping on the door to be let in.

'In a minute.'

Sidney was opening the boxes. 'I'll have no trouble getting rid of these.' He was enthusiastic. 'Go like hot cakes.'

205

He packed a selection in a shopping bag, then they moved the mangle and hid the rest in his hidey-hole.

'What's in that tin?' Wilfred asked.

Sidney picked it up and shook it, coins rattled inside. 'My spends, my private bank. I keep my share there.' He chortled. 'Too dangerous to keep it in my pockets with Peggy about, you know what she's like.'

'Yes, always asking for more.'

With their business completed, they went back to the living room. Peggy was still stretched out on the armchair, reading a newspaper.

'Haven't you started to cook my tea?' Sidney tapped the mantelpiece clock. 'You know I have to be at work before the doors open at six.'

She struggled obediently to her feet. Wilf slid into the armchair in her place.

'What's to eat?' Sidney sounded impatient.

'I meant to buy some stewing steak . . .' Peggy looked confused, 'but I didn't get out to the shops.'

'For heaven's sake!'

'I haven't had time.'

'Is there any of that bacon left? The stuff your pa brought last week?'

'I think so.'

'Make me a bacon sandwich,' Sidney ordered, 'and you'll have to be quick.'

The frying pan had stood on the stove since breakfast. Peggy lit the gas under it and flopped slices of bacon on top of the congealed fat.

Wilf said, 'Count me in, Peg. I wouldn't mind a bacon sandwich.'

'Honestly, Dad!'

'Why not? I got the bacon for you. Real good Danish stuff.'

Peggy gave him a peeved look. 'As if I haven't enough mouths to feed. Won't Beth be cooking your tea at home?'

'I'm hungry enough for both.'

'Don't be mean to your pa.'

Eventually, Frankie brought him the bacon sandwich on a plate. He said, 'Delicious bacon, just what I need.' Sidney was biting into his, fat dripped down his chin. The tea was strong and sweet. Peggy went on cooking bacon for her children.

'I've got to go.' Sidney combed his wavy fair hair in front of the mirror over the fire. 'Where's my banjo, Peggy? I feel like a bit of music tonight.'

'How would I know?' Peggy retorted from the scullery. He went upstairs to look for it himself.

'Be seeing you,' Wilf said as Sidney made for the door. 'I'll be down later.'

He heard Peggy's sigh above the crackle of frying bacon. What was the matter with her? She was always in a foul mood these days. Without Sidney, he felt less welcome here which was silly, Peggy was his own flesh and blood.

'I wouldn't mind another of those butties, Peggy, and another cup of tea.'

Peggy spun round from the stove. 'For God's sake, Dad, I haven't got the time to wait on you. Can't you see I've got this string of kids to feed?' Eric's baby face crumpled at her anger, he began to cry noisily.

'Don't get shirty with me.'

'I'm tired,' she complained. 'Dead dog tired. You and Sidney, you're both alike. You think only of yourselves.'

'He's gone to work, Peggy.'

'He doesn't know what work is. He took his banjo. He's going to play it. He thinks of nothing but enjoying himself.'

'He's earning your living. It's that sort of job.'

'Here am I, on the go all day. I wish I had the energy to play the banjo.'

'You've got to take things easier.'

'Don't be daft, how can I? The kids screaming for this and that all the time, and when they give over, it's you or Sidney.'

'He's doing his best for you.'

'He never does anything for me, Dad. Never gives me anything either. I've had to sell all my own things to feed the kids, even my dance dresses. Not one left now.'

He had his own worries, he was fed up trying to keep her sweet. He said with a touch of spite, 'If you'd kept them you wouldn't be able to get into them now.'

The tears were rolling down her face. Perhaps he shouldn't have pointed out how stout she'd grown.

'What's the matter with you?'

'I wish my mam was still with us.'

That was like a needle in his side. Peggy abandoned the cooking and threw herself down on a chair by the table, putting her head down on her arms.

Within moments, the kids were out in the scullery, foraging for food. He heard a chair scrape as they moved it up to the stove. Frankie was at the frying pan.

207

Wilf swore. 'D'you want those kids to burn themselves, Peggy? Sometimes I wonder if you know what you're doing.'

Peggy shot back to the scullery, took a few swipes at her children and started to push pieces of bacon between thick slices of bread. Wilf poured himself another cup of tea, and poured one for Peggy in Sidney's cup. It was strong and thick now, and only lukewarm.

'You men, you're downright selfish, all of you.'

'I brought you all that bacon. Nothing selfish about that.'

She sniffed. 'It wouldn't hurt either of you to give a hand about the house.'

Chapter Eighteen

It was Esther who told Beth that on the way home from school she'd seen Mrs Clover in the lobby and she'd told her they were moving out of Dock Cottages. Beth left her to get a snack for herself and Colin, and ran down to the Clovers' flat.

'What's this about moving out?' she wanted to know. 'Have you found a house?'

'Our Ken has.' Mary Clover was all smiles. 'It's a terraced two up and two down, the rent's only a bob more than it is here. I'm made up, I really am.'

'How marvellous!'

She beamed. 'I'll have to give up my little job doing for the Jacksons though.'

'Couldn't you come back to do that?'

'Haven't you heard? They're going to live with their daughter in Liverpool. Otherwise I would. Have a cup of tea? The kettle's just boiled.'

'I'd love one, thanks. So what's it like, the house?'

'It's down in town, Taylor Street.'

'Where's that?'

'It's just off Bridge Street, near Hamilton Square.'

'You'll be able to get another job down there. I hear they're always looking for help on the market stalls.'

'What I'd really like is to work in a posh shop, selling clothes or shoes. Somewhere where I can dress up and feel smart.'

'There'll be plenty of those within walking distance.'

'I'm going to try.'

'And it's much more convenient than up here in the North End.'

'Yes, for the ferry and the market and shops and that. The house is no bigger than this place, except perhaps for the scullery. That's bigger. Then there's a living room on the ground floor, with two bedrooms upstairs. The lavatory's out in the back yard and it's got a chain to pull. Oh, and there's a wash house and a place for coal.'

'And it's in good order?'

'Well, not bad. It needs a coat of paint and I've bought a few rolls of paper for the living room.' She put a cup of tea in Beth's hand. 'I've been scrubbing out and cleaning windows down there today. I'd like to get it right before we move the furniture in.'

'When are you moving?' Beth asked.

'Day after tomorrow. Our Ken's coming home tonight. His ship'll be in dock for a few days. I'm hoping he'll get the new paper up before we move in. Maybe even a bit of painting.'

'I'll give him a hand.'

'You've got to work, Beth.'

'Only in the afternoons. I could come in the mornings.'

'That's kind of you, love. Very kind. I'll tell him when he gets here.'

'Must be exciting for you, moving out. A house. It's what everyone wants.'

'Yes, I am pleased. I've waited a long time for this.' Mrs Clover's eyes were shining.

Beth couldn't help but think sadly of her own mother, who'd waited just as long, and for her it had never come.

'Would your family want to move in here?' Mary Clover asked. 'You thought of moving downstairs once.'

Beth's eyes went round the room. It was clean and well cared for. 'If Mam were still with us . . . But if Ken can find a house, why can't I? I'm going to start looking.' To get out of Dock Cottages was the thing. It would benefit not only herself and the younger ones, but Dad too.

'Our Maggie wanted to come and help us move, but she can't get away.'

'How is she?'

'She's fine now. Over all that, thanks to you. She's going out and about again when she gets a few hours off, but no steady boyfriend, as far as I know.'

'She's settled down again, that's the main thing.'

'She writes that she's dying to come and see our new place. I told her right at the start that Southport was too far away, that she'd get home oftener if she stayed nearer like you, but she wouldn't listen. Still, she's the cook now and happy enough in her place.'

'That counts for a lot.'

Mrs Clover nodded. 'Things are looking up for us. It's easier now they're all growing up. Our Billy will be leaving school this summer, and even Pat's old enough to make herself useful.'

'I see you've started to pack.'

210

'The ornaments and things we don't use every day.'

Beth went home and started cooking their evening meal. Dad didn't turn up for his, which could mean he was working late. She and the children had finished eating when Ken knocked on the door. She was just pouring tea; she filled her father's cup for him and he sat down at the table with them, pushing their empty plates into the middle. Beth knew she was much more at ease with Ken than she'd ever been with Andrew.

He was strong-jawed and she liked the way his curly dark hair fell all over his forehead. It seemed a long time since she'd seen him.

'It must have been a big change for you, Beth. Coming back to look after the little ones and keep house for your dad.'

'It was.' Beth sighed, feeling she'd given up a much more comfortable way of life. 'I thought I'd got away from here for good.'

Ken said softly, 'I know why you came back. Didn't I have to do it for the same reason?' He'd broadened out, looked more of a man now. 'How are you managing?'

'So so.' She didn't like being back. She missed having a bedroom of her own, meals cooked for her and a hot bath whenever she felt like one.

'I expect you work harder here looking after the family than you did when you were working full-time at the hospital?'

She smiled. 'There's always something else that needs doing here, but I wouldn't mind helping with your wallpapering. It'll make a change.' So would working with Ken.

'You're sure?'

'Of course. Didn't you help me paint our place once? I'll have to get breakfast for the kids and see them off to school first. I'll ask our Jenny if she'll look after Bobby. She won't mind.'

'It sounds as though I'm putting on you.'

'No, Ken. As I said, it'll make a change. Anyway, I want to see this new house of yours. I'm quite envious. I must start looking for one for us.'

The next morning, Ken called for Beth just as she was buttoning Bobby into his coat. She was going to drop him off at Jenny's on the way.

On the walk down, Ken told her that he thought his mother was doing too much. 'I've persuaded her to have an easy morning. She'll come down about twelve and bring us a bite to eat.' Ken had a long loping stride and Beth had difficulty keeping up with him.

'Billy's taking a day off school to fetch and carry for us. I've sent him on ahead to open up and get the paste mixed.' He was in a buoyant mood. 'We all feel that getting this house will give us a new lease of life. Everything suddenly looks so much brighter for us.'

Beth could hardly bring herself to think of her own future. It looked grim. She shivered.

'Beth, I'm sorry.' Ken was clutching her arm.

She was biting her lip. 'Mam's death meant I had to come home, a disaster for me. I'm not over Mam yet, none of us are.'

'Of course you aren't. Forgive me, I was forgetting. You must think me a heartless brute.'

'No, Ken, that's the last thing you are.'

'Here, this is our new place.'

It was the last house in Taylor Street, on the corner with Bridge Street, a busy road, and close to the docks and the ferries. It was as Mary Clover had told her, a small house with the front door leading straight off the pavement. Every doorstep along the terrace had been holystoned, the curtains at every window looked clean. The front door was open, and they stepped straight into a living room that was much the same size as at Dock Cottages.

'I like it.' Beth looked round. 'A big improvement.'

'Mam's determined to get the place clean. We all came down last night and were here until eleven. Mam spent over an hour blackleading the grate.'

It shone and so did the brass fitments. The old wallpaper had been stripped off and the skirting board and picture rail repainted in green, but even in this state the room had a comfortable feel to it. The stairs went up inside a green cupboard in the corner. Beth ran up to see the two upstairs rooms. They were bigger than those at home.

Ken erected the pasting table he'd borrowed and they unrolled the wallpaper. It had full-blown roses all over it in a big pattern that was hard to match.

'Mam chose it.' Ken smiled. 'She's absolutely thrilled with this place. She's getting on a bit now, it's her fifty-fifth birthday tomorrow. She says this new house is the best birthday present she's ever had.'

Beth was better at pattern matching than Ken. She cut and helped paste. Billy made tea for them and helped Beth with the pasting. Slowly the transformation took place. Mrs Clover arrived with sandwiches and cake at lunchtime.

'Ee, it's going to be lovely,' she breathed, looking round at what they'd done. Beth had to go off to work before the room was finished.

'Thanks for helping,' Ken said. 'You've been great.'

'What about tomorrow?' Beth asked. 'I'll be glad to help again. I can't wait to see everything finished and all your furniture in.'

'You're a treasure,' Mary Clover told her, and Ken kissed her cheek as she turned to go. Hurrying up the road, Beth reflected that she really had enjoyed her morning.

After a busy afternoon, she called at Jenny's on her way home to pick up Bobby.

'What's the house like?' Jenny asked. 'I'm dying to hear all about it. Sit down and have a cup of tea.'

'I'd love to,' Beth said, 'but I've got to buy something and cook it before Dad gets home. Will you look after Bobby again tomorrow? I've offered to help them move.'

Jenny giggled. 'You must be keen on Ken! I'll walk up and get Bobby, shall I? I'm working tomorrow afternoon so you'll need to collect him from next door.'

'Right, and thanks a million.'

'You're going to be exhausted by bedtime.'

'I am now, dead beat.'

'You still haven't told me about their new house.' Beth did so in a hurry and then rushed up to the shops.

The next morning, when she went down to help the Clovers move, the handcart, which had been ordered for half eight, was already outside their door and a man was loading it with furniture from the pile building up on the pavement.

Ken and Billy were carrying out a bed. Pat, who looked very like her sister Maggie, was off school today and bringing out the coal scuttle and shovel. Beth joined in, helping to carry out the lighter pieces of furniture and the boxes and bags that had already been packed. Slowly, the flat was cleared.

'Thank goodness we've got a fine morning for this,' Mrs Clover said. 'It would be awful if it was raining.'

They walked down behind the handcart and started to carry the things into the new house. Beth looked round the newly decorated living room.

'Lovely now it's finished,' she said.

'Look at the stairs, we did that high wall last night. It really makes a difference.' The whole place smelled of fresh paint.

The Clovers' new home began to take shape. The curtains were put up and the mats put down. Billy lit their first fire in the grate.

At lunchtime, Ken said to Billy and Pat, 'There's a pie shop further along Bridge Street. Why don't you walk up and get us a steak and kidney pie each?'

His mother added, 'Baked potatoes too, I think, and mushy peas. We're all hungry, we need a proper meal to keep us going.'

When they brought back the parcels, Mary Clover set the food out on plates and they all sat round the table, tucking into the warm lush pies.

'I'm starving,' Beth said, 'and very grateful for such a good meal.'

'Beth, feeding you is the least we can do.'

Ken looked up and smiled at her. 'I must treat you too after all you've done for us. How about coming to the pictures with me?'

'Tonight?'

'No, I'm shattered now, aren't you? And there's still a lot to do here. I'll be falling into bed good and early. I was thinking of tomorrow.'

'I'd love to, but I'll have to arrange something for Bobby. I know he's nearly four, but I don't like leaving him with Ivor. Poor Ivor's tired out when he gets home, sometimes he falls asleep in the chair.'

'How's he liking the job?'

'Not that much. He's only fourteen and has to heave sacks of coal about all day. He comes home looking like a miner, covered in coal dust. He's applied for a job as a stable boy – at a riding stables in Irby. I do hope he gets it.'

'You could bring Bobby down here,' Ken said. 'Our Pat's good with kids, she wants to be a nanny. You'll look after him, won't you, Pat?'

Pat was a rather shy thirteen-year-old. Before she could say anything, her mother cut in. 'I'll be glad to do that for you, Beth. It's the least I can do. In fact I could go up and see them all into their beds.'

Beth hesitated. 'It's Dad . . . He can be . . . You know, rude and bad-tempered if he found you there. He doesn't like visitors in the flat. Didn't Mam ever tell you what he was like?'

'She never said a word against him but I know she didn't invite people in if he was about. He can't expect you to stay in every night to look after the young ones.'

Beth knew he did. 'Better if I bring Bobby down here.'

'If you'd rather.'

'Yes. Dad might come home for his tea and be gone again, but l can't be sure.'

'You ought to stand up to him, love. Why can't he stay in for once?'

'He never stays in. I don't know where he is half the time. I'm afraid he'd upset you. He can be quite nasty if he's had a bad day.'

'What about Colin and Esther?'

'Ivor will keep an eye on Colin, and Esther's no trouble to anyone. I suppose I could trust her to look after Bobby now.'

Ken said, 'Bring him down here. As soon as you can after tea. Tomorrow night's my last one. Got to rejoin my ship the next morning.'

When Beth knocked on the Clovers' front door the following evening, the family were waiting for her. Ken helped her lift Bobby inside, still in his pushchair.

They set out straight away. Ken took her arm. He was striding out at his usual fast pace. 'There's somewhere I want to take you first.' He brought her to a sudden halt in Market Street. 'This is the place and it's still open.'

'What place?' Beth could see it was an estate agent's shop. She started to look at the typed notices in the window.

'Those are all for sale. But they have houses for rent on a board inside.'

Ken had her through the door and in front of the board in moments. 'This is where we found ours; it's where we pay our rent.'

'Oh Ken! I've been meaning . . .'

'I know, you've been busy with other things.'

'Thank you, thank you, for doing this for me.'

She told the youth behind the counter what she was looking for. 'I'll take almost any house.' What she wanted was get out of Dock Cottages.

'I'd like Cleveland Street if possible, or close by.'

'In town, you mean, not out in the suburbs?'

'Yes, in town, with a rent of not more than ten shillings a week.'

'That's the difficult part. There's not much on the market since the war. Nothing was built for those four years.'

'But they are building now,' Ken said.

'For sale mostly.'

Beth came away with particulars of a house near the park. It sounded lovely and had three bedrooms, but she knew they could never afford the pound a week rent that was being asked.

'You've got your name on their books,' Ken said. 'If something comes up, they'll write to you. That's how we got the chance of our house.'

'I'd love one like yours.'

'I'd go round all the other estate agents if I were you. Houses do come up for rent from time to time.'

In the cinema Beth sank gratefully into the comfortable seat in the dark auditorium. 'Wonderful to sit back and be entertained for a change.'

'I haven't recovered yet.' Ken laughed. 'All that decorating and lifting furniture around.'

They saw Charlie Chaplin and Jackie Coogan in *The Kid*. Jackie Coogan was a young boy, a real heartbreaker.

'Reminds me of your Colin,' Ken whispered.

Beth laughed until her sides ached at their antics. Afterwards, they walked back to Ken's home, where his mother provided a cup of tea and a piece of cake. Bobby had gone to sleep on her bed.

'It seems a pity to wake him,' she said. 'He looks blissful.'

Bobby grizzled a little as Beth strapped him in his pushchair, but he went back to sleep three minutes later.

Ken said, 'I'll see you home.' He propelled the pushchair and kept her entertained with anecdotes about his life on board ship. Once inside the lobby of E Block, he lifted one end of the pushchair so they could carry Bobby upstairs without waking him.

On the landing outside her front door he whispered, 'Can I see you when I next come home? Take you to the pictures again?'

'I'd like that,' she said. His hand came on her shoulder in the pitch darkness. His kiss landed low on her cheek.

'See you then. Take care.'

She let herself into her home feeling closer to Ken. Closer in fact to the whole Clover family.

One morning, a week later, Jenny called round for Beth and they walked up to visit Peggy.

'She's not getting any better,' Jenny said as she pushed Amy's pram.

'It bothers me too, I wish we could do more. She doesn't look well.'

'It doesn't matter how many times we help her spring-clean, her house is always a tip the next time we go.'

'Perhaps today . . .'

When Peggy let them in, the living room was as bad as ever. Jenny sent Noreen and Eric upstairs to play, while Beth shut the dog out in the yard and put the kettle on for tea. They'd barely sat down to drink it when there was a knock on the front door.

'Who can that be?' Peggy looked round helplessly. Beth got up to answer it. She was closest.

'Oh, Lottie! Hello, what a surprise!'

She came in. She was glowing, there was a new sheen on her; Beth thought she'd never looked more beautiful.

'It's my day off. I thought I'd come and see you.'

'Why didn't you come home last night? You always used to when Mam was here. I'd love you to come just the same.'

'I've been home to see you now, there was nobody in.' Lottie laughed. 'I went out with Peter last night. Peter Shaw, I told you about him. We're engaged.' She held out her left hand in front of each of them in turn. A new ring sparkled on her third finger.

There were cries of amazement. 'Engaged!'

'Tell us about him,' Beth said.

'I already have. He works for the Wisharts too. He's their chauffeur cum gardener cum general handyman. There's only me and Mildred left inside now.'

Beth remembered Mildred the cook. She'd been working there for years.

'You didn't tell me, I didn't realise it was as serious as this.'

'Well, it is.'

Beth said, 'You're not twenty-one yet, hadn't you better ask Dad for his permission before you flash that ring about? You know what he's like.'

Jenny giggled. 'He'll play hell if you don't.'

'We have. Peter asked him when we met.'

'Dad's met him already? He knows?' Beth was surprised. 'He's said nothing to me. You told him you wanted to get engaged?'

'Yes. We showed him the ring.'

'And he agreed?'

'He didn't say we couldn't.'

'Well, really!' Beth was shocked. 'Why didn't he tell me?'

'He didn't tell me either,' Peggy said in a peeved voice. 'He's here often enough cadging something to eat. Where did you see him?'

'Peter took me to a dance at the Jubilee Hall in West Kirby not long ago. It was a Friday night. Dad was playing in the band.'

'Oh gosh.' Jenny laughed. 'Playing his mouth organ?'

'His saxophone, silly. It was a dance band.'

They stared at her in stunned silence.

'He's not that good on the saxophone,' Beth said. 'He practises in his bedroom sometimes, though I haven't heard him recently. The same tune over and over, generally with a few wrong notes.'

Jenny said, 'I've heard him, he's awful.'

'It was a really good band,' Lottie told them. 'Strict tempo.'

'He didn't tell us about that either.' Beth couldn't believe it. 'You'd think he'd be so proud of himself getting into a band that he'd tell everybody.'

'Their saxophone player was taken ill.' Lottie frowned as she tried to remember. 'They sent for an ambulance. The singer was his wife and she took him to hospital.'

'So Dad stepped into his place?'

'I suppose so.'

'Then he must have been at the dance.'

'Yes, I suppose so.'

'I didn't know he went to dances.' Peggy was up in arms. 'He might have asked me, I'd have loved to go with him.'

'I think he had a girl with him. He didn't need you.'

'What?'

'She sang with the band in place of the one who took her husband to hospital. Her name was Veronica something. Veronica Eastly, that's it, and she was absolutely top notch. She seemed to know Dad well, they left together to catch the train home.' Lottie's face puckered. 'She said she was Dad's daughter.'

Jenny giggled into the sudden silence. 'You must have got that wrong. She was probably asking if you were his daughter.'

'That's what Peter said.'

'Who was she then, a new girl friend?'

'Of Dad's?' Lottie laughed then. 'No, she wasn't the sort to be interested in Dad, not in that way. Too young, eighteen I think they said.'

'We've never heard of Dad doing anything like that.' Beth was astonished. 'Never heard of him playing in a band.'

'He wanted to, I know that,' Peggy said. 'He asked Sidney to find him a teacher so he could improve.'

'Did this girl look like us?' Beth asked.

'We're all a bit different.'

'Like you and Peggy?'

'No, she was dark and voluptuous, not really pretty. But she was bubbly and outgoing and she had a wonderful voice.'

'Perhaps she was teasing you,' Jenny said.

'What about a cup of tea?' Lottie suggested.

'There's some in the pot if you can find another cup,' Peggy told her.

'When are you going to get married?' Jenny wanted to know.

Lottie shook her head. 'We haven't made up our minds yet. I'm still walking on air because I'm engaged.'

'So when are you bringing him home? We want to see him, get to know him.'

218

'It's a bit difficult. We hardly ever get our days off together. If the Wisharts are staying home then they want me there to serve the meals. If they're going out, then Peter has to drive them. You know what it's like.'

'What about one evening?'

'Peter gets lots of evenings off. But they want to eat most nights, I'm the one who's short of free evenings.'

Chapter Nineteen

Wilfred Hubble felt he'd had a very hard week. Now that he couldn't rely on Larry Bilton picking him off the stand, he wasn't getting nearly enough work. On Thursday morning, he'd pushed himself forward to every gaffer who'd come to pick, but in the end he'd been left on the stand. Other men who were left had talked of going over to Liverpool and trying their luck there. Wilf decided he'd try again at lunchtime for half a day's work and went home with a newspaper, thinking he'd have a restful morning on his armchair.

Beth was sweeping up the hearth and didn't seem all that pleased to see him. 'Where were you last night? Why didn't you come home?'

She was too damn nosy, was Beth. He didn't like her suspicious eyes or the way she shot questions at him.

'I've been working all night,' he told her. 'It's all I can get. I could do with a cup of tea, and what about a bit of toast?'

She went without a word to fill the kettle. He noticed that everything had been cleared from the table and it had been scrubbed. He felt he had little hope of toast, but Beth came back from the scullery with a thick piece of bread which she pierced on the end of the toasting fork and handed to him.

'Dad, why didn't you tell us Lottie was engaged?' Beth was standing over him. 'She said she'd seen you and introduced her boyfriend to you, yet you never said a word to us about it.'

Wilf bent nearer the glow from the fire. He'd never given it another thought! 'I forgot.'

'Forgot! How could you forget that?'

He'd had a lot on his mind that night. A lot of more important things. He asked cautiously, 'Have you seen Lottie?'

'She had a day off yesterday and came home.'

That made him cringe, wondering what else she'd told Beth. He could hear the toast searing and it smelled good, he made a big play of turning the slice over.

'She said you were playing in a dance band.'

'Yes, I thought it might be a good way of earning a bit of extra cash. I told you that when I bought my saxophone.'

Her face told him she didn't think he was good enough for that. 'Lottie said it was a very good band.'

'They did me down. Didn't pay me, even though I stepped in when their sax player was taken ill. I'm having nothing more to do with bands like that. I'm giving up the sax, not worth the trouble.'

Beth's eyes were sharp and bright. 'The girl singer . . .'

Wilf felt his heart turn over. 'What about her?'

'Lottie said she was very good. That she's been singing at the Floral Hall ever since and is quite a hit.'

It was the last thing Wilf wanted to hear. If Molly could seize a chance like that, it made him feel a bigger failure by comparison. He'd have been all right if Lottie hadn't been there.

Beth's eyes didn't leave his face. 'According to Lottie, that girl said she was your daughter.'

He'd been bracing himself for that but it still made him tingle with shock. He tittered nervously. 'My daughter? Don't be daft.'

He was glad to take his hot toast to the scullery to spread it with the last of the marge. It got him away from her prying questions.

He almost fell over Bobby when he came back to the fire. The child screamed, of course, but got up with such speed to run to Beth that Wilf was surprised at how well he was coming on.

'Putting on a bit of weight now,' he said. 'And not always ill as he used to be.'

The morning seemed to pass in a flash. He had to be down on the stand by twenty to one if he was going to have any chance of working this afternoon. He'd have loved to stay where he was in comfort, especially as Beth would be out at work.

He was on the stand in time to be picked to unload a grain ship from North America. These tied up on the West Float in front of the grain warehouses. The grain was carried loose in the hold and was sucked up by a pump into the elevator. Wilf had thought this would make life easier for dockers, until he tried it. The gang had to go down into the hold and drag boards through the grain to move it towards the pump. When there was less than fifteen tons left in the hold, they had to shovel it into the elevators. It was very dusty work. The men covered their heads and faces with muslin, but Wilf hadn't brought his piece of cloth. He was covered in dust, it was in his hair, his nose and even his mouth, and bits of grain inside his shirt made him itch.

He was thoroughly fed up when the time came to knock off. He went home and had a wash down and a clean shirt. Beth complained she had to sweep the grain out of the scullery afterwards but she had a good plate of scouse waiting. He felt better once he had that inside him and decided to go down to see Ethel again.

She hadn't been in a very good mood last night but she wasn't the sort to hold out against him. She could have been having an off day. He'd go down and see if he was more welcome there tonight.

The evening meal was eaten much later at Ethel's, which suited Wilf. The customers were thinning out by the time he arrived. Ethel and Molly were about to go to the room behind the shop.

'You going to have something to eat with us?' Ethel asked, just as she always had.

He chose a steak and mushroom pie and had half of Molly's baked potato with plenty of butter on it. It was scrumptious, but they would keep talking about Molly's success and he didn't like that.

'I'm singing at the Floral Hall every Monday, Tuesday and Wednesday for the summer season,' Molly said. 'Doing a turn on stage.'

'That's much better for her than singing with a dance band.' Ethel cast fond eyes on Molly. 'Everybody listening just to her. There's talk she might get more of that sort of work.'

'I can hardly believe my luck.' Molly looked at Wilf. 'You must come and see me. It's a variety show and we do oldtime songs.'

'And Molly's now a regular with that band on Friday and Saturday nights in dance halls.'

'Your friend is back playing tenor sax but they didn't want his wife any more. They reckon I'm better.'

Wilf wanted to know if Ethel was still seeing her new man friend but though he tried to ask she brushed his question aside. All she wanted to talk about was Molly's success.

He left early. Yes, he was back in with Ethel when it came to meals, but she hadn't asked him upstairs, and both Ethel and Molly had seemed more remote than they used to. It seemed she didn't want him to stop visiting, but he no longer felt sure of her affections. Tonight had done nothing to restore his sense of security there.

He wanted to call at the Blood Tub to see Sidney. He was running short of money, and Sidney should have some for him. Wilf took the bus up to the North End, looking forward to a pint to cheer himself up.

He could hear the noise coming from the public bar as he walked down Ilchester Road. It was a jolly noise, voices were raised in song which was unusual for a Thursday night. Friday and Saturday tended to be better, when the customers had their week's wage in their pockets.

The atmosphere seemed electric when he pushed his way through the crowd to the bar. Immediately, his spirits lifted.

The Blood Tub was a roughish place with sawdust on the floor and spittoons placed at strategic intervals all round. Sidney was in good form, with his straw boater at a rakish angle and his face running with perspiration. Wilf's pint of mild arrived on the counter in front of him within moments of his arriving, and he heard that Jack O'Leary, a regular customer, had at last received his compensation for the accident he'd had at work five years ago.

Sidney looked the part of a jolly barman with a red neckerchief and braces worn over his shirt. Wilf relaxed and joined in. He hadn't brought his mouth organ and wished he had. When another customer tired of playing his and put it down to drink, Wilf borrowed it. This he could play. He'd started practising when he was twelve and was one of the best in the pub. He thoroughly enjoyed the evening.

It was only when the licensee called time that he remembered why he'd come. He hung around, finished his pint at a leisurely pace and decided to wait until Sidney was ready to walk up with him. He had to hang about for quite a while, it was getting late and Sidney didn't seem too pleased to see him still on the doorstep.

'What about my money?' Wilf asked. 'How much have you got for me?' Usually, Sidney had it all counted out and slipped the coins directly into his fist as though it was change from paying for a pint.

'The pens didn't go as well as I thought.'

'But you must have got rid of some of them.'

'Yes, but I haven't worked out the money.'

'I'm skint. I want my share.' Wilf felt indignant. He'd taken all the chances and now he wasn't getting his pay-off. Sidney had done this to him before, kept him waiting for his share, and then it had been less than he'd expected. Suddenly he realised Sidney was taking a road which cut between the blocks of Dock Cottages. 'Aren't you going home?'

'Not yet.'

'I was going to come with you to get my money.'

'Not tonight, Pa.'

'Where you going then?'

'I'm going to see a friend.'

'It's half eleven.'

'Yes, I know.'

'Everybody's going to bed.' The gas lights were being turned off in Dock Cottages. 'You don't mean . . . Not that Maudie Everett?'

He'd have to pay to visit Maudie. She charged half-a-crown for an hour.

Sidney laughed. 'I haven't come to that yet.'

'Where then?'

'This is the place.' He was heading for a lobby door in Block F.

'You haven't got a lady friend?' Wilf was trying to remember if there were any ladies living alone in Block F.

'What if I have?'

Wilf was put out. 'What about our Peggy?'

'What about her? You've had a lady friend for years. Why shouldn't I? Look, I'll bring the money to the pub tomorrow. See you then.'

'I wanted it now.'

But Sidney had swung himself silently up the dark stairs. Wilf went on to Block E, feeling quite shocked. He was curious too, wanting to know who the woman was. It shouldn't be too difficult to find out.

The months were passing, Beth was getting used to her new life. One afternoon when she went to the hospital, she could hear voices shrill with excitement before she even opened the cloakroom door. Today, she knew, the most senior of the student nurses would have received the results of their final examination. Those who'd been successful were bubbling over with joy, those who'd failed were distraught.

She asked, 'Has Myrtle Harris passed?'

'I think so.'

Beth went to the dining room before going over to the outpatients department. She knew the list would be posted on the board there. She was glad to see Myrtle's name on it.

At teatime in the dining room, the same subject was still being discussed. She heard Myrtle Harris's laugh before she saw her in the crowd. It was a laugh of triumph.

'Congratulations,' Beth said. 'I'm delighted you did it at the first attempt.'

'I'm so relieved.'

'I didn't doubt you'd pass.'

'I had plenty of doubts. The written papers weren't all that easy and there was so much hanging on it.' Her cheeks were flushed and her eyes danced.

'Are things going to work out for you?'

Another radiant smile. Myrtle moved closer and whispered, 'Yes, the ship's sailing for China from Tilbury in five weeks' time. I'm giving in my month's notice tomorrow, and we'll go down to London a

225

few days early so I can get to Marie Stopes's clinic first. I'm so thrilled, Beth. Everything's working out splendidly for me. Thanks for keeping quiet all these months – about you know what.'

'I've a lot to thank you for too. I hope you'll be very happy in China.'

'I'm sure I shall. Hope things turn out well for you in the future.'

Time sped by, and almost before Beth knew it another year had passed. Every morning, as soon as she'd got the children off to school, she cleaned and dusted around her home for an hour or so. But she avoided her father's bedroom, having told him he should be capable of keeping it tidy and making his own bed.

This morning he'd gone to work leaving his door open and it was only too obvious he was making no effort at all. The eiderdown was on the floor on one side of the bed and there was a twisted mound of blankets and sheets on the other.

Beth could stand the mess no longer. The clean sheets she'd handed to him last week were still folded on the dressing table. It made her cross that he wouldn't lift a finger to do anything for himself. She'd offered to help him make his bed up clean but he was sitting back and leaving everything to her, just as he'd left everything to Mam. Beth was determined not to be used in that way. She felt that if Ivor and Esther could make their beds, then so could Dad. It was her need for cleanliness and order that was making her give in. His room was fetid with cigarette ash flicked straight from the bed to the floor. She threw open his window.

She noticed the pawn tickets on his dressing table when she took the clean sheets to make up his bed, but it was only when she took a damp cloth to the dust that she picked them up. The first was for fifteen shillings on his saxophone, the second for five pounds on a diamond ring.

Beth felt the blood rush to her cheeks in a wave of fury so intense she couldn't move. She stared at the ticket for what seemed an age, then whirled to the dresser in the living room and opened the tin in which she kept her valuables. It stood on top, in pride of place, a fancy gilt casket with a picture on top of George V and Queen Mary. Once it had been a gift to the Wishart family and had held fancy biscuits. They hadn't wanted the empty tin.

She pulled out the reference they'd given her, together with her school report and nurse's certificates. There was the broken fob watch which Dorinda Wishart had thrown out but Beth had thought too pretty to discard.

226

Tears of vexation were blinding her. How could he pawn her ring without even mentioning it to her? The tin was packed tight with her personal odds and ends, but she couldn't find the little leather box. Her imitation pearls, on which she used to thread the ring, were here but of the ring itself there was no sign.

She pulled her case out from under the couch. She had to keep her underclothes in it, there was nowhere else. There was a chest of drawers in the children's bedroom but all their belongings were stuffed into three small drawers, and they rummaged through them frequently for clean clothes. Beth felt carefully through the clothes she'd ironed, but the ring wasn't there. Anyway, she was sure she'd put it into her tin. She went back to it.

Another thought came into her mind. What had happened to Mam's cameo brooch? Had Dad taken that too? Panic made her empty out the contents on the table; the little prayer book Grandma had given her one Boxing Day, an embroidered handkerchief, a small bottle of scent, pencils, and yes, thank goodness, her hand closed over the little cardboard box that held her mother's brooch. It was still inside and that brought some relief. But her ring had gone.

She took a deep breath and let the tears roll down her cheeks. Andrew had paid twenty-two pounds for that ring and Dad had pawned it for a quarter of its value. To get her hands on that sum to redeem it would be next to impossible. She earned just over three pounds a month for working five afternoons each week. They had to eat, she couldn't see any way of saving it. But if only she could, she could surely sell the ring for much more.

It took her half an hour to recover enough to return to cleaning out Dad's bedroom. Beth felt consumed with rage all day, even at work. What Dad had done festered in the forefront of her mind.

She was waiting for him to come home but he was later than usual. She dished up the meal she'd prepared for herself and the children. They were all eating at the table when she heard him coming along the landing. Usually Beth waited until the children were asleep in bed before she had a confrontation with him, but today she couldn't wait.

'You've pawned my ring, Dad. You took it without saying a word to me.'

That pulled him up sharply. 'You didn't want it. You said you tried to give it back to the chap.'

'You stole it. You knew it was mine.'

'You can get it back.'

'I can't! Where would I get five pounds from? You know that isn't possible. And what did you spend the money on? You know both Esther and Colin will need winter coats.'

He had the grace to look shamefaced until she said, 'I can't believe anybody would be so stupid. It cost twenty-two pounds, only a fool would let it go for five. It's the pawnbroker who'll get the value of it, not us. You might as well have tossed the money into the Mersey. You've no sense. None at all.'

Her father was bristling with rage. 'How was I to know how much it cost? You never said.'

'Why should I? You didn't ask and I didn't know you were going to pawn it.' Beth slapped his helping of scouse on a plate. 'I used to wear it round my neck to keep it safe when I lived at the hospital. I was a fool to imagine I wouldn't need to here.'

Her father was silent.

'I should have known you'd steal it. You steal everything you can get your hands on, don't you? I wish I'd never come back here to live.'

Esther pushed up against her, looking anguished. 'What about us?'

Beth was in tears again and put her arms round Esther. She wished she could ask Dad to leave, but without the money he usually contributed, she didn't think they could survive.

Beth banked up the fire and had her housework done early. She was expecting Lottie, and Beth looked forward to seeing her. She used to come home every day off she had when Mam had been alive, but now she was coming less and less, preferring to spend the time with her fiancé.

When Beth heard her quick step on the landing, she had the kettle on the boil. Lottie was all smiles and there was a flush of excitement on her cheeks. Her blonde hair had been newly cut in the latest bob, and there was just enough curl in it to frame her pretty face becomingly.

'Hello, Beth, hello, Bobby. My, how you're growing. We used to say you were small for your age, but not any longer.'

'I'll be big enough for school soon,' he told her in his piping voice.

Lottie's dark blue eyes lifted to meet Beth's. 'Will you go back to work full-time then? There'll be no problem with that?'

'I don't think so. There's a dressing clinic every morning. Patients stand in line to have their dressings changed, leg ulcers and all that.'

'You're lucky to have a proper career.'

'Well, I've kept my hand in this last couple of years, but if I'd stayed full time on Ward Three I'd probably have been a sister by now. I might ask to go back to a ward. What's the news from your end?'

'Marvellous news!' Since her engagement Lottie had seemed so happy, Beth thought her easily the best looking of her sisters now.

'Peter and me, we asked Mrs Wishart if we could get married and work as a couple. It took her a while to say one way or the other. I think she had to discuss it with her husband, but the answer was yes.'

'So you'll get married soon?'

'I'll wait and see Dad tonight, to ask for his permission and agree a date.'

'You'll not wait until you're twenty-one?'

Lottie laughed. 'This is the exciting part. We'll both have our holiday in August and we want to do it then.'

'When the family take their holiday? Are they going to Anglesey as usual?'

'Yes, for the whole month. Well, Mrs Wishart and Dorinda are. Mr Wishart will come back after two weeks to work, so we'll have to be back to take care of him. But he'll spend his weekends with them, so we'll have it easy for the rest of the month.'

'Dorinda's home again then? I thought she was working in London for Marie Stopes. At that clinic she started in the East End. There's always something about it in the newspapers.'

'Yes, Dorinda's had her name in the papers too. That was the last straw for her parents. Her father ordered her to come home or he'd cut her off completely. She's been here for the last six weeks.'

'She's not working any more then?'

'Her father forbids her to have anything more to do with Marie Stopes. "You'll bring the same notoriety to our family name." He bellows at her when he's cross so the whole house knows what's going on. "You are to have absolutely nothing more to do with that woman. I can't trust you any more, you'll stay at home where we can keep an eye on you. Disgraceful behaviour, you ought to be ashamed of yourself." '

'Poor Miss Wishart,' Beth said. 'Kept at home in disgrace.'

Lottie giggled. 'She's staying at home but when her parents go out, I've heard her pick up the phone and ask for Dr Stopes. Talks to her for ages, she does. I think she's still working for her. Oh! She gave me a letter to give to you.'

'What's she writing to me about?'

Lottie took it from her handbag. 'Open it and see. She's been asking about you. How you are, and what you're doing. If you're able to work, that sort of thing.'

Beth tore open the envelope and read:

Dear Beth,

Would you be able to meet me for coffee at Cottle's Cafe in Grange Road? There's something I want to talk to you about. I suggest eleven o'clock next Friday morning. If this doesn't suit you, send a note back with Lottie giving an alternative date.

She passed the note over to Lottie.

'Golly, she's signed it Dorinda. We always call her Miss Wishart to her face.'

'So did I.'

'And Cottle's Cafe! That's a posh place.'

'I wonder what she wants.'

'Have you been before?'

'No, I can't afford Cottle's. Friday's fine for me, I'd better write a note to say so.'

'Food of the daintiest. Cooking of the best. That's what the adverts say about Cottle's.'

'But what does Dorinda Wishart want to talk to me about?'

'You'll find out on Friday.'

Beth pushed her curiosity to the back of her mind. 'So you're going to be married in August?'

'Yes, if Dad agrees. Peter has the bedsitter over the garage. I'm going to move in with him.'

'It's very small. I was sent to clean it out once.'

'It'll be fine to start. We'll be able to save our wages because we have everything found.'

Beth pondered this. 'So you'll not be wanting babies?'

'Not yet. Plenty of time for babies. I want a bit of fun first.' Lottie giggled. 'Such a bit of luck, Miss Wishart working with Marie Stopes. She has all her books. I borrowed them one at a time and showed them to Peter. I think we'll manage it.'

'Good for you. Will you be married at St James's? I could put on a bit of a do for you here, but it won't be fancy.'

Lottie pulled a face. 'Thanks, but no. We thought we'd go to the register office and invite just the families, but Peter's mother was dead against that. She wants him to be married in church and says she'll put on the wedding breakfast for us – seeing as I haven't a mother to do it for me. She lives in West Kirby, so we'll be married at her church. Better to do it all in one place.'

'She has a house then?'

'Yes, a terraced house near the centre and within easy walking

230

distance of the station. She's a widow and takes in lodgers. It's got two living rooms bigger than this, as well as a scullery and a wide hall. Much better than here for a crowd. Oh Beth, I can hardly wait.'

'Lottie, we've none of us met Peter yet.'

'Dad has, remember?'

'Yes, but what about the rest of us?'

'It's not easy, as I said.'

'Can't you get a few hours off one Sunday?'

'They usually have guests on Sunday evenings, you know that, so they want me there. But they're more generous with evenings off than they used to be, and I go out with Peter. They give me an evening off every Tuesday, and often I get others because they've been invited out to dinner themselves.

'Next Tuesday now, why don't you come out with us? We're going to the Floral Hall in New Brighton to see . . . Well, it's a sort of oldtime variety show. D'you remember me telling you ages ago about a girl singer we saw in West Kirby? When Dad played the saxophone? Well, she's in this too. You could get somebody to look after Bobby for one night, couldn't you?'

Beth thought about it. 'I don't often go out like that.'

'You could meet Peter and see a bit of life too. Two good reasons to make the effort.'

'Yes,' Beth said cautiously.

'Esther can look after Bobby.'

'Better if I ask Mrs Clover. Did you know the Clovers have moved? They've got a house in Taylor Street.'

'You told me. Walk down now and ask her then,' Lottie urged. 'I'll come with you and go to Jenny's afterwards.'

Mary Clover was welcoming and wanted to give them tea. 'Course I'll look after Bobby, love,' she said. 'I must tell you, I'm so pleased. I've got myself a little job, Fridays and Saturdays in Clegg's, the hat shop in Grange Road. I started last week and really enjoyed it.'

'That's a lovely shop.'

'You should see the prices. I'd like more hours but it's a start. Yes, I'll be glad to have Bobby on Tuesday night. I can put him to bed here if you like. Save you coming back down here afterwards. He'll be all right with me and Pat. Our Ken too, he'll be home on Tuesday morning.'

'Will he? I wonder if he'd like to come with me?' Beth explained where she planned to go and why.

'Course he would, love. Ken doesn't have much fun. Do him good to go out with you.'

Lottie said, 'There'll be four of us then, good. Peter and me, we'll wait by the box office and not buy our tickets until we meet up. Then we'll be able to sit together.'

It was lunchtime on Tuesday when Ken knocked on Beth's door. The children had just come home from school and were clamouring for food. Beth had set out a piece of cheese and an apple for each one and was cutting bread and marge to go with it.

'I'm really looking forward to tonight.' Ken grinned at her. 'I'm glad you didn't forget me.'

'We could both do with a night out. The show's called *Thirty Years of Music Hall Favourites*. D'you want some bread and cheese?'

'I wouldn't mind. Then I can walk you down to the hospital on my way home.'

That evening, they took the bus to New Brighton, sitting upstairs on the front seat. Ken looked smart in his merchant navy uniform and was in a cheerful mood. As they walked up to the Floral Hall, Beth could see Lottie and her fiancé waiting outside in the evening sun.

'He looks very nice,' Beth said to Ken. 'Good-looking.'

'So's Lottie,' Ken whispered just before they joined them.

'This is Peter,' Lottie said. 'I've told you about him.' He was tall and slim and smiling.

As they went in, the band was taking its place in the orchestra pit. Beth found herself sitting between Ken and Lottie. She sighed with satisfaction, it was a rare treat to be out like this. The lights slowly faded and the buzz of chatter became an expectant hush.

The band struck up and the curtains parted. The opening turn was a line of six dancing girls. Lottie's elbow dug into her ribs.

'That's the girl I told you about, second from the right. She was with Dad the night he played the sax and sang with the band.'

Beth watched her dark hair bouncing to the beat of a jolly tune. She was kicking up her legs in perfect time with the others, but her smile was broader, her skirts were lifted higher and she danced with just that bit more verve than the others. She was enjoying herself and it was infectious. Beth's feet tapped too, it was the sort of tune that lifted everybody's mood another notch.

A man in a kilt sang three Harry Lauder songs, and then came a pair of Egyptian sand dancers who made the audience roar with laughter.

Afterwards, Molly came on dressed as a bride with flowers in her hair and sang about being left in the lurch at the church. Her voice was strong and deep, rising above the band in a parody of sorrowful lament. Her diction was clear as she told the tale through several verses

232

pretending to be more and more upset, desperately waving her bridal bouquet in one hand. She had the audience screaming with delight and holding their sides. As the curtain came down at the end, she broke into noisy sobs.

Beth clapped hard, her stomach ached she'd laughed so much. The audience gave Molly such an ovation she returned to sing the last few verses and the chorus over again.

'I told you she was good,' Lottie whispered. 'Hasn't she got a marvellous voice?'

'And that's the girl who was with Dad?'

'Yes, the one who said he was her father.'

'Must be her idea of a joke.'

'She's a blooming marvellous singer.' Ken had tears of merriment in his eyes. 'It's not just her voice, it's the way she sings, bit of an actress too. She's so pert and—'

'Does she look familiar to you?' Beth asked. 'I've got the feeling I've seen her before.'

'So have I.' Ken was frowning.

'You've heard her sing?'

'No, it's just her face . . .'

'She can't be from Dock Cottages.'

'No,' he laughed. 'I don't think so.'

'Our dad knows her, so we could too.'

The rest of the show was just as good. Molly came back in the second half to do some Marie Lloyd numbers. Ken was still chuckling as the audience streamed into the cool night air.

'I haven't enjoyed anything so much for a long time.'

Peter said, 'Let's go to the Grand for a drink.'

Beth wasn't sure she and Lottie should, and she was worried about what they'd charge.

'It's not like the Blood Tub,' Lottie told her, 'where only men go. I've been before, it's a hotel.'

Ken took Beth's arm and bustled her inside. 'No point in coming to meet Lottie's boyfriend if you don't stop to talk to him.'

'I'm paying,' said Peter. 'Lottie and I have something to celebrate. Starting married life at the Wisharts' makes it easy for us.'

'What if you get the sack?' Beth asked.

'We won't.' Lottie laughed. 'You know what the Wisharts are like.'

'If we did, my mother would have us as lodgers until we found somewhere else,' Peter said. 'She's got plenty of room.'

'We must do this again,' Ken said.

'You should bring Beth to the Jubilee Hall for a dance on a Friday night. A foursome there would be good fun.' Lottie looked at her sister. 'Come on, Beth, you've got to try and enjoy yourself. You're far too intent on work and duty. Relax and have a good time, the kids will be all right without you once in a while. Honest, it'll make you feel better.'

Ken waved down the last bus back to Birkenhead. Beth was tired now but knew he was still buoyed up by the events of the evening. She stared out into the darkness feeling sleepy.

'Next stop.' Ken nudged her. 'You're dozing off.'

'I'd almost gone.' She smiled and shook her head to clear it. As she got to her feet, Ken followed. 'No need for you to get off too.'

'Of course there is.'

'This is the last bus. If you stay on, it will take you home.'

'Beth, I'm coming. This could be the best part.'

'Best part of what?'

'The night out.' He was beaming down at her.

When they began to walk down Stanley Road, he put his arm round her waist and hugged her to his side. It was a dark night and the gas lights had been turned off. The Blood Tub had closed its doors. Its customers had gone home and the streets were quiet. There were very few lights to be seen at the windows of the Blocks.

Just inside the doorway of E Block, Ken took her into his arms.

'It's time I showed you I was serious.'

His lips came down on hers. Beth felt something within herself leap to life. She hadn't known Ken could make her feel like this.

234

Chapter Twenty

It was a bright and blustery April morning, and Friday, the day Beth had arranged to meet Dorinda Wishart. She walked into town to save the fare, leaving Bobby with Jenny on the way. She knew where the cafe was. The entrance looked very grand, all marble. Beth pushed open the massive door and went in.

She was aware of the delicious scent of coffee and of a hand waving to her. Miss Wishart was seated at a table facing the door and Beth's feet sank into the deep carpet as she crossed the room. Miss Wishart stood up and offered her hand. It was definitely not a mistress to maid greeting. She seemed a little nervous and spoke quickly.

'Coffee all right for you? Good, I'll order a pot then. What about something to eat? They do good toasted teacakes here.'

It was a long time since Beth had seen her but she hadn't changed much. Her manner seemed more diffident, but she was more smartly dressed.

'What did you want to talk to me about?' Beth asked. 'I'm curious.'

'Your sister Lottie told me . . .' Her kindly eyes surveyed Beth seriously. 'Just say no if you don't want to do it. Everybody else has.'

'Do what?'

'I've been working with a most wonderful person. You've heard of Marie Stopes? Did you know she'd opened a clinic in Holloway in London?'

'For birth control, yes.'

'We call it the Mother's Clinic for Constructive Birth Control. Well, I've been helping there.'

Beth was riveted. 'Lottie told me. You're still working for Dr Stopes?'

'Yes. You're in favour of what she does? So many are against her.'

Beth smiled. 'Yes, I'm very much in favour. She's a pioneer in her teaching and her openness in such matters. Her books have been a godsend to my sisters, I only wish they could have helped my mother.'

'Your mother was exactly the sort of person we want to help. I was sorry to hear about your loss.'

Beth said, 'I have a friend, too, who was let down by her boyfriend after he'd made her pregnant. If only she'd known how to avoid it, it would have saved her so much anguish.'

'Beth! We can have nothing to do with unmarried girls. They must not be encouraged . . . We'd get pilloried by the press if we allowed . . . We are accused of being immoral as it is, if we treated unmarried girls, they'd make mincemeat of us and say we were encouraging prostitution. Total abstinence is right for us unmarried women.'

Beth felt rebuked. 'I understand.'

'It's for married women only, Dr Stopes is very strict about that. There's more than enough married women to keep us all busy.'

'Yes.' Beth had to pull herself together. 'You know I come from a big family. My eldest sister Peggy had five children very close together. She can't cope with any more, nor afford them either. She's managed to avoid it over the last three years, which is a relief.'

'Lottie told me.'

'And Jenny, did she tell you about Jenny? She says the Marie Stopes books have changed her life. Made things possible for her that would otherwise not have been. She's very grateful.'

'Many women tell me that. Especially those who come to the clinic and are fitted with the cap. You see, for everything else the women have to rely upon the co-operation of their husbands.'

'My sisters would both like the cap. If only Dr Stopes would open a clinic here,' Beth said.

'That's exactly what she plans. She wants to open clinics in all the big cities. I've been looking for suitable premises in Liverpool.'

'That's marvellous!'

'I'm trying to find suitable staff. We have a midwife and a lady doctor, both are down in Holloway at the moment learning the techniques, but I need nurses.'

'I'd love to have a job like that,' Beth breathed. 'That's if you're asking me.'

'Yes, you know I am.' Her horsy face broke into a broad smile. 'But I must warn you, we expect trouble. There were crowds barracking outside our North London clinic when we first opened.'

'I read about that in the newspapers.'

'Marie, well, she's a celebrity and attracts attention from every politician and church dignitary in the land. The newspapers keep printing these scurrilous articles condemning what she does; and she keeps writing further books as well as pamphlets and articles and it all serves to keep her in the public eye. She brought out a book called *A New Gospel*. Have you read it?'

Beth shook her head.

'I'll lend you a copy. Well, Marie claimed that it had been dictated to her by God. That really caused a furore. She's about to bring a libel action against Halliday Sutherland, a Roman Catholic doctor who accuses her of "experimenting on the poor". That will make headlines in the national papers, you can be sure.'

'It must be very worrying for you.'

'Yes, the work would be much easier if we didn't have to cope with all this condemnation.'

'I can't see why people should be so against it.' Beth frowned.

'Marie isn't a qualified doctor and those who are feel she's usurping them. After all, they charge fees for delivering babies, it's how they earn their living.'

'But she calls herself Dr Stopes.'

'She's entitled to because she holds a doctorate in fossil biology, but she's not a medical practitioner and she's condemned for that.'

'She knows so much about it, she must be clever.'

'She's very clever. We've been trying to persuade her to qualify as a medical practitioner, that would cut out objections from that profession. What about a bit of lunch? On me, of course. They do very nice soups and salads here.'

'That would be a lovely treat for me.' Beth was overwhelmed, she hadn't expected such friendliness. 'Did you know I'd want to take this job?'

'I gathered from your sister that you might. I've been looking for married nurses but their husbands stop them working and others have children and don't want to work. Not in this sort of clinic, anyway.'

Beth said, 'I've been working part-time, doing outpatient clinics, because I had to look after my youngest brother Bobby, but he'll be starting school in September. I was hoping to get a full-time job then.'

Miss Wishart outlined the hours she'd want Beth to work, and the salary that Marie Stopes offered. 'You'll be taught all about it, of course.'

'I read somewhere that Dr Stopes expected her staff to work for nothing, like the wartime VADs.'

'Some do, those who can afford to. She funds the project herself. You're very necessary, I've not been able to persuade anyone else.'

'I don't need persuading.'

237

'Would you like to see the premises I've rented? Where you'll be working?'

'Yes, very much.'

'This afternoon? We could go over now.'

Beth looked at the clock. 'Oh no! Is that the time? Gosh, I'll have to hurry, I start work at half one. Do forgive me.'

'Another time then. I'm going back to London for a week or two but I'll be in touch. We hope to open in Liverpool in July. We'd like you to start work at least a week beforehand, say the end of June, so you can get the hang of what's required of you. I'll let you know the exact date later.'

'I'm so pleased.' Beth put out her hand. 'Thank you for thinking of me and for the lovely lunch.'

'You're the answer to my problem. Please keep mum about all this for the time being. I don't want the newspapers to get hold of the story just yet. We'll have to advertise what we're doing before we open the doors, of course, to let prospective clients know.'

It was Colin who heard the postman come, he brought the letter to Beth who was pouring their breakfast tea. She yawned. 'Who's it from?'

She put the teapot down and tore it open. Seconds later her sleepiness was banished and she was laughing.

Ivor said, 'What is it, Beth? Something good?'

'I'll say! I put my name down with an estate agent – oh, ages ago, when the Clovers got their house – and—'

'Has he found one for us?'

'They say there's a small house to rent in Bridge Street at nine shillings and sixpence a week, payable weekly in advance.' Beth felt suddenly at fever pitch and began to read the details aloud. 'It has two bedrooms, a living room and a kitchen with stone sink and larder, and a back yard, with wash house and lavatory.'

'Are we moving?' Esther was all smiles too. 'Leaving Dock Cottages?'

'Wow,' Colin screamed. 'When?'

Beth was all of a flutter. 'I'll go straight down and see it this morning. It's near the Clovers' house. It sounds . . . Just right.'

'I'll believe it when it happens.' Ivor spooned up his porridge. 'It might need a lot doing to it. To make it habitable, I mean.'

Beth was in raptures. 'Oh, I can't believe it! We could be leaving Dock Cottages at last.'

'You've got to see it first,' Ivor insisted, but he was showing every tooth in his head in a beaming smile. Beth knew he was as excited as the rest of them. They all helped her wash up so she could get down to the estate agent's shop as soon as possible.

She dumped Bobby's clothes in front of him. 'Dress yourself this morning. Come on, we're in a hurry.' For once he managed it though Esther had to tie his bootlaces and do up some buttons. Beth was ready to leave as Colin and Esther set off for school. She had the pushchair almost flying over the pavements and was outside the shop as an assistant was opening up. She showed him the letter.

'Bridge Street, yes. The previous tenants moved out yesterday.'

'Is it in . . . good order?' Beth remembered the empty tenement she'd looked at in Dock Cottages.

'Fair – not bad.'

'What about cooking? Is there a range?'

He frowned. 'I'm not sure. It doesn't say here.'

'I'll go and see it. It sounds just what I'm looking for.'

A key was put on the counter in front of her. 'You'll have to sign for it.'

'Right.'

'Please bring it back as soon as possible, we sent out four letters and we've only got two keys.'

'Four letters?' Beth was alarmed, that could mean competition to get it. 'Am I the first to come?'

'Yes.'

He was giving her directions to find it. Beth knew she'd have no trouble with that, it was close to the Clovers' house. Out in the pale sunshine again, her feet flew even faster, she was all of a fizz inside. She'd know the moment she opened the front door if she didn't want to live there.

From the opposite side of the road, the house didn't look clean as she approached. The pink curtains were closed and the door hard to open. She stepped straight into the living room, blinking in the gloom after the morning brightness. The place smelled fusty. She drew back the dirty curtains and wasn't sure she liked what she saw.

Bobby was kicking his heels against his pushchair and shouting, 'Beth, Beth, I want to come with you. Want to see.'

She ran out to undo the straps and lift him out, and he shot inside. She was about to follow but decided to lift in the pushchair too.

The living room seemed smaller than their present one, but the grate was a kitchen range with an oven. She walked through to the scullery behind. The stairs went up in one corner but it was a good-sized room and would take their table so they could eat here. Both bedrooms were bigger than those at Dock Cottages, but the whole place was shabby and needed redecorating.

'Outside,' Bobby said, trying to open the back door.

Beth unlocked it and he ran out into the yard. There was rubbish that should have been cleared away, a broken tea chest and some parts of a rusting bike frame. Bobby poked his head round the lavatory door and turned round to scream, 'It's a real one, it's got a chain. Come and see.' His voice was shrill with excitement.

Beth knew this would clinch it for all of them, they could overlook its drawbacks. She pulled the chain and the water roared through the cistern.

'Are we coming to live here, Beth?' Bobby was in the wash house. He touched a battered table and it lurched sideways on a broken leg.

'Careful. We don't want you hurt. Yes, yes, if Dad agrees.'

'He will, won't he?'

Dad wouldn't be home until teatime and she wanted to tell the agent she'd have it before somebody else did. She thought of going to look for her father. She knew some of the dockers had their children deliver billy cans of tea to them, well wrapped in old woollens to keep them warm. But Dad never spoke much about his work, she didn't know where he'd be working today. Beth felt she needed another opinion.

'Let's go and see if Mrs Clover's in. Her place is just round the corner.'

The Clovers' house looked clean and comfortable by comparison. Mary Clover was almost as excited as Beth when she heard the news.

'I'll be right glad to have you as neighbours again.' She put on her hat and coat straight away and went back with Beth to see it.

'My place was filthy when I first saw it.'

'It's very much like yours.'

'Don't let the dirt put you off, we'll soon scrub the place out. A lick of distemper upstairs, and wallpaper down and it'll be like a little palace.'

'It's even got a range in the living room.'

But Mrs Clover shook her head when she saw it. 'It's the same sort I have. It's no good for cooking. I put some sausages in the first night and three hours later they were still half raw. I had to get a gas stove.'

'No good?' Beth was disappointed.

'Our Ken worked on the flues and cleaned it all out but it still wouldn't cook. It'll heat water though.' She lifted the lid of a tank on one side of the grate. 'You pour it in here and when the fire's been going a while, you get hot water from this brass tap. It's a boon, always having hot water.'

Beth considered the cost of two weeks' rent in advance, of wallpaper and paint and of getting a gas stove.

'You can rent one for sixpence a week. That's what I do. Ken will be home the day after tomorrow. He'll help you decorate. That's only fair. You helped us.'

Beth decided. 'I've got to take it.' It was their chance to get away for good, it could be a long time before she got another.

Mrs Clover's plump face creased into a smile. 'Of course you must. We've been very happy in our little house. You will be, once you get straight.'

She was glad of Mary Clover's support but wished Ken was here too. Still, he would be soon. They paid the rent at Dock Cottages a week in advance, which meant they could stay there for a week without paying more. It would give her time to clean up the other place before they moved in.

After a bad week in which he'd had only three days' work and those spent working in the bowels of ships, Wilfred Hubble felt he'd had a better than average day. During the morning, while unloading the *Baltimore*, he'd seen other stevedores pilfering from a case that held gold watches and they'd given him a share to ensure he kept his mouth shut. He'd hidden the three gent's watches and three lady's watches in his hat band, and carried on with the job.

He'd meant to take them home during his dinner hour, but he hadn't had time. He'd been taken on to work on the *Katherine Mary* in the afternoon, unloading brandy, and just before knocking off time he'd managed to break open a case himself and put two bottles in each of his pockets, and he'd done it without help from anybody else. The other stevedores had fallen on the broken case and within minutes he'd seen it emptied.

Wilf had gone straight to Peggy's place and given three of the bottles to Sidney, keeping one for himself. The landlord of a nearby pub took booze if the price was right. He decided to keep one of the watches for himself too, it was better than the chromium-plated one he'd been using for some time – he left that one for Sidney to sell on. And Sidney had given him the money he was due for the fountain pens.

Wilf was pleased with himself and whistling as he went up the stairs. He was further cheered by the good smell of Irish stew when he let himself in. Beth was beaming at him, she looked in a good mood for once. 'Dad, I've found us a house.'

'A house, where?' This stepped up his feeling of wellbeing. To move out of the Blocks had been what Vi had wanted most. It would do them all good to get away.

'Bridge Street.'

'What?' That hit him like a kick in the stomach. Bridge Street was where Ethel had her pie shop. It was the last place he wanted to move to. It would put his family too near her for his peace of mind.

'It's off Hamilton Street down by the ferry.'

'I know where it is.'

The kids were all talking at once, trying to tell him about it. There was no mistaking how keen they were. He could feel the crackle in the atmosphere before he'd even hung up his hook.

Wilf moistened his lips. 'Which end of Bridge Street? It's quite long.'

'The end nearest here. The other end is all shops.' He didn't like it, it was still too near.

Ivor said, 'Nearer to the docks, Dad. They'll be right on your doorstep there.'

Beth was radiant. 'When I start my new job, it'll be just a short walk to the ferry. That'll be a great help.'

She'd told him about the new job she was hoping to start at the end of June. He'd approved, just as she'd known he would because it was full-time work and she'd earn more. That was all he cared about. Now he said irritably, 'I don't know why you want to go over to Liverpool every day. It costs, you know. You'd be better off getting a full-time job at the Borough.'

'I'm changing because it's a job I really want to do.'

'Isn't that stew ready to dish up?'

She set out the plates and found the ladle. 'Aren't you pleased about the new house?'

'No,' he said. 'We'll stay here.'

They were all shocked and looked at him open-mouthed.

'Dad! Why? You've always wanted to move.'

'I like this place better. It's home.'

'How d'you know this is better?' Beth turned on him. 'You haven't seen the other yet. I was going to take you all down tonight.'

Wilf knew he'd been too quick, that had been a mistake.

'Anyway, I've said we'll take it. I've paid the first two weeks' rent.'

'What? It's up to me whether we move or not.' He was head of this

242

household and he hadn't even been asked. 'Where'd you get the money for that?'

'I borrowed it from Mrs Clover. We'll be quite close to her again.'

'Her!'

'She was Mam's friend.'

'Well, I hope you can pay her back because we're not moving.'

There were no smiles after that. Beth's eyes were full of anguish now.

'I had to say we'd take it straight away. There were others after it and you know how hard it is to find anywhere at this rent.'

'What about my tea? Get on with it.'

Ivor took the ladle from Beth and started dishing up.

'Dad, you've got to come and see it. We'll have our own front door straight onto the street. Mam would have given her eye teeth for this. It needs wallpaper and paint, but not much else.'

'And who's going to do all that?'

'The Clovers will help me.'

This was making him nervous. 'It'll cause a big upheaval. You kids will have to change schools.'

Beth spoke slowly with a look of pained patience on her face. 'There's a school quite close. Bobby will be able to start there. It's only Colin and Esther who'll have to change.'

'I want to,' Colin muttered.

'We can't afford it,' Wilf complained. 'It'll get us into debt,' but he could see Beth wasn't having that.

'Come and see it.' She was poker-faced now. 'We'll all go as soon as we've eaten.'

Wilf felt better when a plate of stew was pushed in front of him and they all began to eat. He knew he'd have to go. He'd be able to see exactly where it was. With a bit of luck it wouldn't be too close. He'd had one fiasco when Molly had come face to face with Lottie, and even now he couldn't understand why he'd got away with that. He certainly didn't want to risk anything like that happening again.

Beth couldn't understand why her father didn't want to move. Once, he'd told her to go out and look for a house for them. She'd expected him to be pleased. It was what everybody talked about, dreamed about. But now he'd turned against it she felt as though the ground had been cut away from under her feet.

She insisted on taking him to see it. He came with very bad grace, while the kids couldn't get there fast enough.

'It'll be far more convenient to live down here,' she told him.

Dock Cottages was almost two miles from the centre of town. She could sense her father was turning more against it before the house was even in view. He complained about the area, all factories and goods yards and docks.

'I thought you'd like to be closer to the docks,' she said. He was acting like a spoilt child.

When she unlocked the front door and they all went in, he stamped round the house, giving each room one cursory glance.

'This place is a pigsty. What d'you want to bring us here for?'

'It's what you said you wanted, Dad.' Beth was seething inside but trying not to lose her temper.

'It's like the Clovers' house,' Ivor said. 'We were envious when we saw theirs, weren't we, Beth? They've made it nice.'

'Nothing would make this nice. It's filthy.'

'It'll clean up. We could start now.' She'd brought a broom, some soap and a scrubbing brush.

'I'm not coming to live here,' her father said as he headed back to the front door.

Beth stood with her back against it, her anger welling up. 'Well, I am,' she retorted.

He stared at her in disbelief.

'I'm coming too,' Ivor said.

Her father turned on her then, it was a long time since she'd seen him look so savage. 'You're going to walk out on Bobby and the others, aren't you? You promised your mother you'd look after them.'

'No, they can come here with me and Ivor.'

'You wouldn't dare. You'll never manage by yourselves. Out of my way.' He pushed Beth aside and slammed the front door as he went out. Beth and Ivor looked at each other, appalled. If Dad didn't move with them, it meant they'd have no furniture to bring here. Beth was cold with shock at the enormity of what she'd done.

Ivor said, 'I can't see him staying there by himself. Cooking his own meals and that.'

Neither could Beth, but all the same, it was worrying.

Ivor said, 'We might as well make a start. Come on, Colin, we'll pick up the rubbish in the yard. I'll borrow a handcart tomorrow and take it to the tip.'

Ivor was right, work would calm her jitters. Beth took Esther upstairs and began to sweep down the walls. It frightened her, the money she'd had to borrow for this and she needed more for paint and paper, and possibly furniture too. She hadn't expected Dad to push her into doing

244

this on her own. Thank goodness Ken would be here soon. At least she could rely on him for help.

The next day Beth spent every hour she could spare scrubbing out the new house. Her mind was working even harder. She was planning how to manage the move, but she was spending even longer daydreaming about Ken.

She'd known for years he had a soft spot for her but she'd set her mind on Andrew and shied away from him because that suited her. Her mother had warned her off Ken because, like them, he had no money, though she approved of him as a person, everybody did.

Her affair with Andrew had taught her that personality and character were far more important than good looks and status. She'd always valued Ken as a friend and companion, she admired him for what he was doing for his own family, but when he'd kissed her after their night out with Lottie and Peter, she'd felt the first prickles of desire. It was an effort to keep her mind on moving house.

She got out the pawn ticket for her ring; it was still in date, but wouldn't be for much longer. She looked at her mother's cameo brooch. She didn't want to sell that, it was all she had left of Mam. But she might have to.

In the evening after tea, Ivor went down and worked on the house. He mended the leg on the table in the wash house, threw buckets of water down the yard and spring-cleaned the lavatory.

The day after that they went down together. Beth had blackleaded the grate and he'd cleaned the flues and lit a fire in it. It was getting late and she felt ready to drop, they were sitting on the floor, enjoying the rest, when Ken knocked on the front door.

She whooped, 'Am I glad to see you,' and pulled him inside.

He swung her into a welcoming hug so she felt his strong firm body against her own. 'Marvellous, you've got a house near ours.' He landed his usual smacking kiss on her cheek. Not a serious kiss, but they were not alone. He was looking round the living room over her head. 'Hello, Ivor. This is pretty much the same as ours.'

'I'm in trouble over it.' Beth told him about her father's refusal to come. 'That means he'll need to keep the furniture and I don't know where to turn for money to buy wallpaper and paint.'

'I'll help you.'

'Ken! I've already borrowed the rent money from your mother.'

'I know. It's all right, I was paid before coming home.'

'You do so much for us.'

'I want to. Haven't you done a lot for us in the past?'

245

Beth met his gaze. She had to try. 'I don't suppose you could lend me five pounds?'

He shook his head. 'I was thinking of two or three. I pay Mam's rent and we've got to live.'

'I know, Ken. You're very generous.' She took the pawn ticket from her handbag to show him. 'If I could get the ring out of pawn and sell it, I'd have enough left over to pay for what we need.'

'This is your engagement ring? Your dad pawned it? The old devil!' He stood looking down at her. 'Is there nobody else you could borrow the money from?'

Beth sighed. 'I've been thinking, I suppose I could ask Dorinda Wishart. It's just that . . . it's easier to ask you. Less embarrassing.'

Ken laughed. 'In the meantime, better if you let me pay for the wallpaper and paint. If you choose it tomorrow morning, we can get on with the job.'

'No, tomorrow I've arranged to meet Dorinda, she's taking me to see the new clinic. How long will you be home?'

'Four days. Beth, you're not the only one thinking of a new job. I saw one advertised in the *Echo* on the night we left Liverpool. It's just what I want.' He was bubbling with elation. 'I wrote and applied from Morecambe a fortnight ago, and I've been for an interview this morning.'

'You've got a new job?'

'Waiting to hear, but I'm hopeful. They said they'd write.'

'A shore job? That's what you want, isn't it?'

'It's on a salvage boat that's going to lift a wreck from the bed of the Mersey. But I'll be home every night – well, most nights.'

'But . . . it won't be permanent, will it? It won't take for ever to lift a wreck.'

'They're expecting to lift others. I might be working elsewhere, but I won't be out of a job.'

Beth smiled. 'I'll keep my fingers crossed. Be nice to have you home every night.'

'Hope I'll see more of you.' His dark eyes held hers for a long moment.

'Course you will.'

That made him plant another kiss on her cheek. 'I'm going home to borrow Mam's kettle,' he said. 'It'll soon boil on that fire. We could make a first cup of tea here. By way of celebration.'

Chapter Twenty-One

Beth had arranged to meet Dorinda Wishart at the Pier Head in Liverpool. Before leaving home, she pinned her mother's cameo brooch on her best coat and made sure the pawn ticket was in her handbag. She felt nervous about asking Dorinda to lend her money but she had to do it. She had to get money from somewhere and she knew nobody else who could lend such a sum. She was afraid Dorinda would think it the most awful cheek.

Beth was keen to see the premises being converted to make the birth control clinic in Liverpool. Newspaper coverage of Dr Stopes's activities was burgeoning since she'd started her libel action against Halliday Sutherland. Every newspaper carried reports and photographs under banner headlines. Every periodical had articles about Dr Stopes. Beth read every word about her that she could, and knew most of the population of Britain was doing the same.

She was looking out for Miss Wishart as soon as she reached the Woodside ferry, she walked all round the boat that took her over, but there was no sign of her. Nor was she waiting on the Pier Head when she reached Liverpool. Beth had to wait and that made her more nervous.

Miss Wishart came at last, bareheaded with her hair cut in the latest Eton crop style, and wearing a smart blue costume. She was full of apologies for keeping her waiting.

'We can walk from here, it isn't far.'

'That's very handy.'

Beth told her about her new house and how she could walk to Woodside from there.

'I'll only need to catch the boat over.' That meant she'd not have to spend too much on fares.

She couldn't stop talking about the house and how worried she was that her father had refused to come.

'Fathers! They can be so difficult. I'm glad you didn't hear what my father said about poor Marie. He forbade me to have anything

247

more to do with her, but I can't let him stop me now.'

'Won't he be cross when he finds out about the Liverpool clinic?'

'Furious. I have a cousin who says I can stay with her. But I'm trying to make him understand how important this is to the poor of this world. How strongly I feel about it and how much I need something worthwhile to do. All this publicity is very hard to take.' She asked anxiously, 'You haven't changed your mind about working for us?'

'Nothing would make me change my mind,' Beth said.

Miss Wishart shuddered. 'Poor Marie, it's the sort of publicity we can all do without. I feel ill every time I think about it. Everybody in the land knows her name. Nobody has ever achieved notoriety on this scale before. I've had one nurse change her mind about coming to work for us, so I'm grateful you haven't.'

Beth said, 'The more I think about it, the more strongly I feel. Advice and help with birth control should be available to all women.' She glimpsed Miss Wishart's face and added, 'Well, all married women. There are so many wanting help and unable to find it.'

'We think it a right and proper thing to do, but that doesn't alter the fact that many people consider it a sin to interfere with nature.'

'If the people who are against it could have seen and understood what my mother's life was like, I'm sure it would change their minds.'

'Here we are then.'

The clinic was taking shape in what had been built as a church hall in James Street. Even with new paint on windows and doors, it still looked like a church hall from the outside.

'It's a rough part of the city, but that's where the women live who need us most.'

Beth was shown round. The place smelled of fresh paint and sparkled with cleanliness. Much of the hall remained to serve as a waiting room.

'I'm going to get some toys to put in this corner for the children, and there'll be volunteers to keep an eye on them. Many mothers coming to the Holloway Clinic say they have nowhere to leave their children.'

There were rooms where consultations could take place in private, an office and a clinic room where mothers could be measured and the device fitted.

'The furniture is on order. It's mostly chairs but also examination couches and desks, and some glass-fronted shelves for instruments.'

The toilet facilities had been renovated and so had the kitchen. Miss Wishart said, 'I'll make us a cup of tea. We need to settle a few details.'

Beth felt she had to take over the tea-making; she'd worked in Miss

Wishart's home and knew she never made her own tea there. Her mind was only half on what she'd seen, she was screwing herself to ask the vital question. At last, with the tea steaming in bone china cups and the matters of working hours and uniform settled, the moment had come.

'I was wondering if I might ask a very great favour of you.'

'What is it?' Dorinda's expression was kindly.

'I need money to buy things for the new house, a gas stove . . .' Beth took out the pawn ticket and showed it to her. 'I need five pounds to redeem this ring. I could sell it for much more than that, I'm sure.'

'Well . . .' Dorinda studied the pawn ticket. 'A diamond ring?'

'A solitaire, my engagement ring.'

'I didn't know you were engaged.' She looked up as though about to offer congratulations.

Beth hastened to say, 'I'm not any more. My fiancé had second thoughts about me. After seeing where I lived.'

'So you pawned the ring he gave you?'

'No, my father did. He did it behind my back too. It came from Boodle and Dunthorne and I know Andrew paid twenty-two pounds for it. To let it go for a fiver is throwing money away. It's money I need.'

'Well . . .' She was still studying the ticket.

Beth felt desperate. 'I'll pay you back as soon as I've sold it and I'll give you my mother's cameo brooch as security. I don't know how much it's worth but . . .' She was unpinning it from her lapel.

'That won't be necessary, Beth.' Miss Wishart's horsy face broke into a smile. 'Though it's a handsome brooch. I can always arrange to have it stopped from your salary if you don't pay me.'

'You'll lend it?'

'We'll call at my bank when we've had this, and I'll draw it out for you.'

Beth felt such a rush of gratitude, she could feel her eyes prickling. She managed to thank her without breaking down in tears of relief. She thanked her again as she put the crisp new five pound note in her handbag.

Miss Wishart was going shopping in Liverpool so Beth went back on the ferry alone. She climbed to the top deck and surreptitiously opened out the large banknote. She'd never had a five pound note before, she couldn't remember even seeing one. She could do nothing more now. Time was going on, she had to go straight to the hospital to start work. She took no chances with the money, pinning the note inside her uniform pocket.

At five o'clock that evening she called at the pawnbroker's to redeem the ring on the way home. It was still in its leather box with the Boodle and Dunthorne name inside.

She'd intended taking the ring back there but decided the next morning she couldn't spare the time to go over to Liverpool again, and she'd try Pyke's in Grange Road instead.

This, too, was a very elegant shop and her nerve almost failed her when she got to the door. There were several customers inside, all of whom seemed to be buying not selling. A smartly dressed woman came out and held the door open for her. Beth swallowed hard and went in, towing Bobby by the hand.

Her finger shook a little as she opened the ring box for the sales assistant to see.

'Please take a seat,' she said. 'I'll have to ask the manager.'

Beth pulled Bobby onto her knee and looked round at the dazzling array of silver and jewellery. Her heart was in her mouth. It seemed a long time before she saw the manager returning with her ring box which he put on the counter in front of her.

'This is your ring?'

'Yes,' and then feeling she must offer some explanation, 'Broken engagement.'

'I understand you wish to sell it.' He put his eyepiece in and looked at it again. 'We could offer you eighteen guineas. Would that be acceptable to you?'

Beth had hoped for twenty pounds, but this was almost nineteen. Relief was flooding through her, she'd managed to do it. She'd have some money to pay for essentials.

She headed towards the new house to tell Ken and repay her debts. Ken was putting new window cords in so that all the windows could be opened.

Beth was up early the next morning. Ivor had asked for two days' holiday from work to help with the new house, as there was so much to do. They walked down together, and when Beth unlocked the front door, the place smelled of fresh paint. Ken had bought white distemper and had worked through the afternoons while she'd been at the hospital. It pleased her to see that not only had all the ceilings been done, but both bedrooms and the stair wall had had a first coat.

Ken and his mother arrived, laughing as they came in.

'I've got the job I told you about.' He grinned. 'This next trip will be my last on the tramp.'

'Ken, I'm so pleased for you.'

250

'He's over the moon,' his mother said. 'I am too, because I'll see more of him.'

'You'll all be seeing more of me.' He winked at Beth.

'Good. I miss you when you go away.'

'I've brought you some curtains,' Mrs Clover told her. 'Green velvet, not much wrong with them that I can see. They're big enough to go right down to the floor. Maggie got them from the family she works for, but by the time she brought them I'd already got my old ones up.'

They undid the bundle to show her. Beth was thrilled.

'They're lovely and heavy, lined too. They'll keep the winter draughts out. Come with me to choose the wallpaper,' she said. 'I must get something to go with these curtains.'

She chose a faint stripe in cream and green, and bought more white distemper and paint. Ken and Ivor had given the living-room ceiling another coat by the time they got back.

'Let's do the papering next. That's the biggest job.'

Beth cut it into lengths, and helped paste it. Ken put it on the walls. With four of them working, they were half finished by dinner time.

Beth had to go to work, but Ken and Ivor said they'd finish off the papering that afternoon.

'I'll come back after tea,' Beth told them. 'I can't wait to have it all finished. It's going to look lovely.'

Wilf was getting cold feet. He'd been left on the stand this afternoon without work and had gone to see Ethel instead. What he really wanted was to move into her place. She must surely see that was the best thing for them both.

She'd laughed at him. 'No, Wilf. I've told you, I'm not having you here. I don't want you sponging on me.'

'I wouldn't dream—'

'You already do. You never fail to fill your belly when you come.'

The biscuit and cup of tea she offered didn't soften the blow. He felt rebuffed, he'd hoped at least to be asked to a hot meal tonight, but couldn't ask after that. He was home earlier than usual, feeling anxious and irritable.

'What's for tea?' he asked Beth.

'It's not ready yet.'

'I can see that. I asked what it was.'

'I bought some sausages on the way home from the hospital.'

He watched Beth bundling up the children's belongings. 'You're not staying here then?' he asked.

'I told you we were moving, Dad.'

'You'll be in debt up to your eyes before you know it.'

'I don't think so. I got my ring back, the one you pawned for five pounds. I've sold it, so I've got a bit of cash.'

'How much did you get for it?'

Her green eyes were triumphant. This was doing his ego no good at all.

'I've still to pay back the fiver I had to borrow. But when I do, I'll have made thirteen pounds eighteen shillings.'

Wilf added it up and could hardly believe it. He certainly wouldn't pay nearly nineteen pounds for that ring. Diamonds they might be, but they looked no better than bits of glass.

'Lend me a pound,' he said. 'If you're so flush, you won't miss that.'

She was looking at him pityingly. 'Not likely, you owe me five pounds. You ought to pay me that back.'

He didn't like that. Beth's confidence seemed to be growing. He wouldn't admit it to her but now she had money, she had the upper hand.

Ivor was dishing up the tea. Heaped plates of sausage and mash were being put out on the table.

Beth picked up her knife and fork and demanded suddenly, 'Can I take the bedding from the children's room? And what about their chest of drawers? You won't be needing that.'

She was getting at him. 'You're not stripping this place bare. I'll not have that.'

'I'm not asking you to, not if you're staying by yourself. Is that what you're going to do?'

'I haven't made up my mind yet.'

'Then you'd better hurry up.'

'You're always in such a rush.'

Wilfred felt he'd been struggling for days, not so much with the decision but with how to climb down without losing face. It seemed his family were going to move close to Ethel's shop whether he liked it or not. It wouldn't make much difference whether he went too or stayed here. But if he did stay, there'd be nobody to cook and shop for him, nobody to do his washing and ironing either.

'Dad! Are you coming too or staying here?' Her hard green eyes were fixed on him. 'I have to know one way or the other. I'll need to buy my own furniture if you're staying here.'

'You won't be able to afford that.' He and Vi had spent years paying off the debt for furniture.

252

'The Clovers said I needn't worry about that. Ken knows where I can buy what we need second-hand. What are you going to do?'

'I suppose I might as well come too,' he said grudgingly.

'You don't have to, Dad, you have a choice. A free choice.'

Trust the little minx to rub his nose in. 'I'll come.'

'That means we take everything from here? All this furniture?'

He shrugged. 'Yes, why not? A lot cheaper than buying more.'

'You'd better start getting your things together then. We've almost finished papering and painting. We might as well move in as soon as we can.'

She was still staring at him. Suddenly her knife and fork clattered down on her plate and she was lifting a protesting Bobby out of his chair to get at the drawer in the table. By the time he realised what she was doing, she had the rent book open in her hand.

'I see you haven't paid any more rent.'

'No point in paying out till I'd made up my mind.'

'You've just been messing me around, haven't you, Dad? You meant to come all along.'

He didn't really want to live with her. She'd make him eat crow like this all the time. He'd no longer be boss in his own house. But if Ethel wouldn't have him, he couldn't see anything else for it. It was either Beth or he'd have to fend for himself.

'Have you given a week's notice to the landlord?'

'No, I hadn't decided, had I?'

'Then you'll probably have to pay another week's rent in lieu.'

'Not me!'

'You don't have to come for my sake, Dad. I'm not going to lose any sleep if you don't. In fact, it might be better if you stayed here, there'd be a spare bedroom for John and Seppy when they come home.'

Beth was tired by the time they were clearing up after the evening meal.

Ivor said, 'I'm shattered. Me and Ken finished papering the living room.'

'How does it look?'

'Good.'

'I'd love to go down and see it.'

'You go. I've had enough for one day, I'd rather stay here by the fire tonight.'

'Right.' Ken had said he'd be there, Beth was quite pleased they'd be alone. She was ready to set out when Mrs O'Malley knocked on the door.

'I've made a present for your new house,' she told Beth. 'A hearth rug.'

'That's very kind.' Beth unrolled the rug on the floor so she could see it. 'A rag rug and you've made it yourself?' She smiled. 'Thank you.'

'I started it – well you know I like making them, my place is full of rag rugs. But I ran out of bits.'

'That's why you came begging for our old woollen clothes?'

Esther was laughing too. 'That red border was my old coat and these blue diamond shapes were our mam's dress.'

Mrs O'Malley smiled. 'That's why I decided I'd better give it to you.'

Beth was overcome. 'It's just what we need. Everybody's being so kind.'

'You've been good neighbours, I hope you'll be happy in the new place.'

'Come down and see it when we move in. You must. I'll roll this up and take it with me now.'

When Beth let herself in the new house she was surprised to find Ken putting a row of tiles on the wall behind the kitchen sink. He put his arms round her in a hug of welcome.

'What energy you have – tiling now. Ivor's exhausted.'

'I want to finish it for you.'

'I don't know how to thank you. Have you eaten?'

'Yes, I went home for my tea. D'you like the living room now it's finished?'

Beth looked round her. 'I love it, Ken. It's a transformation, unbelievable. It's all so fresh and clean.'

'I've been out and bought a curtain pole. I unfolded those curtains and there's enough material to go from ceiling to floor right along the front wall. You'll be able to draw them across the front door too.'

'That'll look absolutely . . . The house is looking better than I ever imagined it could. You've done wonders, a marvellous job. And look what Mrs O'Malley's made for us.' She unrolled the rug before the fire. 'I'm glad you've lit it again.'

'It's chilly without a bit of fire at night. I thought we could have a quiet evening here together.'

'Lovely, I'm really tired. Couldn't do much more tonight.'

Ken had brought some cushions earlier, she piled them onto the rug and dropped down on them. She could feel the heat of the fire on her face. 'We deserve a rest, we've worked so hard the last few days.'

He stood looking down at her. 'There's something I want to talk to you about.'

'What?'

'Shall I make some tea first?'

'No, tell me. This place is so cosy now. I love it.'

'I was thinking . . . I'm going to be home much more in the future.'

'I'm thrilled about that too. Everything's coming up roses.'

'How would it be if . . .'

Ken dropped down beside her and kissed her full on the mouth. It took Beth by surprise and left her tingling. He drew back and his brown eyes were searching into hers. 'I love you, you know that?'

'I can see it. It's in your eyes, in the way you try to please me. You do so much for me.'

He laughed. 'I thought I'd schooled myself not to show it.'

'Why?'

'I couldn't follow it through, could I? Couldn't ask you to wait indefinitely.'

'I must have been a fool not to see . . . I love you too.' He was so honest, so transparent. 'Ken?' Tentatively she leaned forward to return his kiss and the next moment she found herself clasped in his arms. He was pulling her against his own body and this time she could feel his passion, hot and strong.

'I love you, Beth. Have for years. Even when I thought I was going to lose you to that fellow . . .' He was raining butterfly kisses all over her face. 'I've been thinking . . . Haven't been able to think of anything else for hours, to tell you the truth.' He ran his fingers through her hair. 'Such a lovely colour, bright red and gold, it glints in the firelight.'

'Carrots.' She smiled. 'Ginger.'

'I mean, you have this house . . .' His dark eyes were fixed on hers.

Beth gave him a nudge. 'What are you trying to say?'

'Will you marry me? Right away, now.' Her heart lurched at the very idea. 'I could move in with you here. I've wanted to ask you for years – you know why I haven't. Nobody could love you more, Beth.'

'Love is everything.' She couldn't stop smiling.

His eagerness was spilling over. 'You know our Pat will be leaving school next summer? Mam is better placed now she's got a proper job at Clegg's. She's happy there and they've asked her if she'll work full-time from next week. One of the girls has left. She'll be able to pay her own way. She says it's time I thought of myself for a change. Shall we get married?'

'But I can't!' She was thrilled to be asked. Thrilled to see he wanted it so badly, but . . . 'Ken, I have to think of Bobby and Colin and Esther.'

'I know that. I'll help you. I'll do my best for you, Beth. Don't you see? You've got this nice house, you've talked of moving in with the children and been worried about doing it on your salary and what Ivor can earn. But if we got married, and I came too, with my wages as well . . .'

'No, Ken!'

Beth felt the tears sting her eyes. She'd been upset when Dad had first refused to come, and frightened of coming without him, Ivor was still just a lad. But she'd faced that, screwed up her courage and decided they might just scrape by. Life would always be easier without Dad. She hadn't been all that pleased when he changed his mind. Now, it was a disaster.

She swallowed hard. 'Dad's decided to come too. He'll be here as well.'

'But just this dinner time you said—'

'I pressed him, over tea today, made him say whether he was coming or not. I had to know because of the furniture.' Beth's hands came up to cover her face. 'He needs me to do his washing and put hot meals on the table.' She felt bitter about that. 'I suppose I should have known. He was just messing me about.' She felt torn in two, sick with disappointment. 'Would you want to come if he's here? He'll boss you around.'

Ken sighed. 'Oh, Beth! I thought it was all within my grasp. That I could have you . . . He'll be taking up one of these bedrooms.'

'He most certainly won't. I'm going to insist on having a proper bed here. I'd decided Esther and I could share one room and Ivor and the boys would have the other. Dad's going to have the couch whether he likes it or not. He's always the last in anyway. Less likely to wake us up if he sleeps down here.'

Ken looked deflated. 'It doesn't leave much room for me.'

'You and I could have one room. Esther could go in with the little boys and Ivor could have the couch.'

'I've wanted it for a long time. You know why I kept quiet. My idea wasn't such a good one after all, was it?'

Beth knew she'd fallen in love with Ken almost without realising it. He was twice the man Andrew was. She knew she could rely on him. She put her arms round him and hugged him. She wanted marriage too.

'Shall I tell Dad he can't come? He's got a place of his own, after all.'

Ken straightened up. 'Would you? Would you want to?'

'Yes, he's not the easiest to live with. Oh dear, the last thing I said to him was he must be sure to give a week's notice on Block E.'

'He won't have had time yet.'

'Probably wouldn't anyway. He's the sort who'd just walk out and stop paying the rent. I think I'll tell him I've changed my mind. I'll suggest he stays where he is.'

Ken laughed and hugged her with glee. 'Would you dare do that and then marry me?'

She laughed too, feeling a little light-headed. 'There's nothing I'd like better. You're a lot more fun than Dad.'

He was drawing her into another embrace when she chuckled.

'You're nuts, Ken, d'you know? For years you say you can't get married because you're supporting your family. Now, as soon as they're off your back, you're ready to take on my responsibilities.'

A good hour later Beth was thinking it was time she went home when there was a loud *ratatat* on the front door. She and Ken jerked apart.

'Who can that be?'

'We'd better see.' He gave her another peck on her cheek before standing up. He had to draw back the heavy curtain from the door and there was an even louder knocking before he could open it. Her father bounded in the moment he did. Beth's spirits sank at the sight of his swaggering confidence.

'Oh, no.' This was on her before she was ready, but she'd have to stand up to him.

The news that Beth had sold her ring for so much money had made Wilf feel a complete fool. He'd thought she'd want him to move into the new house and had expected her to persuade him to do so. Her take it or leave it attitude had shaken him to the core. He'd thought he was surrounded by family and friends, but he was being pushed out, nobody wanted him. He went to the Blood Tub but drank silently in a corner, thinking about what he should do. For once he didn't join in the argument at the bar.

He knew he had to decide now. Beth was a pain in the neck, but he didn't fancy coming home to a cold flat every night and having to light the fire before he could start cooking his tea. And he'd have to buy himself a primus otherwise he'd not have a hot drink before he set off to work in the mornings.

Perhaps he could sleep in his own place and come to some arrangement with Beth or Jenny to provide a hot meal in the evenings. Mrs O'Malley took in washing, but he'd have to pay her. The girls would make him pay something for food too. It would be cheaper for him if he moved in with Beth and had everything by right as he did now. He'd be left out on his own if he didn't watch out.

His mind was made up, so the sooner he staked his claim in the new house the better. He would have liked another pint but he went home instead. The living room was warm but was not as clean as it used to be. There was ash all over the hearth. Beth's energy was going elsewhere.

Esther had put Bobby to bed, she and Colin were in their nightclothes drinking the cocoa Ivor had made for them all. The place would seem terribly empty if they went. Wilf went to his bedroom and began putting his clothes together, he was going to take some of his things down straight away.

He didn't know why Beth had had to create this crisis. Much better if they'd stayed as they were. He went down on the bus because it was getting late and he was half afraid she might have locked up and left the new house by now. He could see chinks of light between the curtains as he drew close, and relaxed. He was in time.

It shocked him to find Ken Clover opening the door. He'd no business to be there at this hour, alone with his daughter. Neither seemed welcoming. Wilf could guess what they'd been up to, he hoped Beth knew what she was doing.

He said, 'I thought I'd better start bringing some of my things down.' He had two bundles of clothes tied up with string. 'By jove, you've cleaned up this room nicely.'

Beth pulled herself to her feet. 'I said we would, didn't I? I said we'd make it comfortable.'

'Right then, I don't remember much about the bedrooms, I'll go up and see which one—'

'No, Dad!' Beth's eyes were burning into his. 'Look, you've got a place of your own. You don't need to come here.'

He was full of indignation. She didn't want him! 'You told me to get my things together. That you were nearly ready for us to move in. That's what I've done, brought some things down.'

'You said you didn't want to come.'

'You've done a good job here. You'll need me, Beth, to help pay for all this.'

'No I won't.' Beth's face was hardening the way it did when she was about to make a stand. Ken was looking apprehensive.

'A woman can't pay for all this on her own.'

'Ken and I are going to get married. He'll be here to help. We won't have room for you.'

That cut him deep, really hurt. It was out and out rejection.

'Don't be so silly! Of course there will.' He made for the stairs. 'I'll take these things up and decide which room I want.'

She said between her teeth, 'Listen to me, Dad. You won't be getting any bedroom. I don't want you to come.'

'But I'm your father,' Wilf protested. 'I've promised you all my furniture. How are you going to manage without that?'

'We will.'

'I'm head of the household . . .' He knew that was a mistake as soon as the words were out of his mouth. She jumped on him.

'Not this one, Dad. It's my name on the rent book. I decide what happens here.'

That shocked him. 'You don't know what you're saying. I don't want to be left up there by myself. You're even taking my little kids with you. I'd be lonely. You wouldn't shut your old dad out in his hour of need? I've given you a home for years, you can't just throw me out.' He gritted his teeth, he hadn't meant to wheedle.

He turned on Ken. 'I don't like what you're up to, lad. Turning a man out of his home.'

'I'd never do that, Mr Hubble.' Ken looked aghast. 'No, never.'

'But you are.' Wilf looked at his daughter's exasperated face.

'You stay where you are, Dad. You'll be more comfortable there than pushing in here with us.'

'You wanted me to come. You told me to give notice on Dock Cottages and I did.'

'You can't have, the rent office was closed then.'

'I wrote a letter and posted it. You have to put things like that in writing. You know that, don't you, lad?'

She was hesitating. Dad never wrote letters, she didn't think he could.

Ken looked uncomfortable. 'Beth? We can't say no, can we? Not to your father.'

Beth wanted to. She'd never wanted anything more. 'Why not?'

'Because I've always given you a home. Come on, old girl, don't be mean,' Wilf urged plaintively. 'You know I'll pay my whack.'

'I want to get married. Ken and—'

259

'Get married then. There's room for all of us here.'

There was a long drawn-out silence. 'If you come,' she choked, 'you'll have to sleep on the couch.'

Wilf began to breathe more easily. All was not lost after all.

Chapter Twenty-Two

Beth found moving day gruelling. Ken came to help and her father didn't go to work, but it was a Saturday morning which meant no school. Colin was underfoot and got in the way, but Esther took Bobby to the park and looked after him for most of the day.

Everything had to be carried down four flights of stairs to the handcart. It had to make two trips, mainly because of the wardrobe and dressing table from Dad's bedroom. In the new house, the only room with enough floor space to take them was the bedroom Beth had earmarked for herself and Esther.

'This will do nicely for me,' her father said, just as Beth had expected.

'Honestly, Dad, don't you listen to anything I say to you? You get the living room couch here.'

'That's yours, you've been sleeping on it for ages.'

'Yes, but we're changing places. It's what you agreed to. If you don't like it you don't have to come.'

Although half the furniture was still outside on the cart, her father went off in a huff, leaving them to finish on their own.

'Just before lunch too,' Beth said as she opened up the box containing the whole loaf she'd cut up into sandwiches. 'Not like Dad to go before he gets his eats.'

As they carried on afterwards, heaving on mattresses and tables, Ken said, 'I'm disappointed. Damned depressed really. I've waited and waited, held back when I didn't want to. Suddenly I saw the way we could do it. I thought I was on to a good thing.'

'It was a marvellous idea.'

'But I couldn't put your dad out of his home, could I?'

'This isn't his home.' Beth had been boiling with frustration since her father had insisted on moving to the new house with them. She didn't want him here, not now. To have just Ken and the children here would have been bliss.

'Perhaps I was trying to rush things. For you and me, I mean.'

'Ken, it can't come too soon for me. The thought of being married, I

261

was nearly in heaven. Dad's using us. He uses everybody to get what he wants.'

Ken was shaking his head, looking very down. 'But we know where we stand now, don't we?'

She tried to smile. 'We're definitely going to get married.'

'But not just yet. Not if he's coming. It's so long since I told you on the stairs how I felt about you. Remember that?'

'Of course.'

She felt Ken's arms tighten round her. 'We'll have to put it off just a little longer . . .'

To Beth, life suddenly seemed much more exciting. That Ken said he loved her and wanted to marry her made her see everything in a different light.

She liked the new house very much. Everything was so fresh and clean and convenient to town. To have a proper bed to sleep in was a huge improvement and now she could close the bedroom door when she went to bed, Dad no longer woke her up every night when he came home. He didn't seem to be settling in as well as the rest of them. His lips developed a peevish droop.

He said, 'I knew from the moment I saw this house that I wouldn't like it. It's too far from the Blood Tub.'

'There are plenty of pubs nearer here.'

'I can't find one I like.'

'You will, Dad.'

'Sleeping on that couch makes my back ache, I can hardly straighten up in the morning.'

'I didn't find it very comfortable either.'

'And I can't get at my clothes. You've taken my wardrobe into your bedroom.'

'Perhaps if you moved them to that cupboard on the landing?'

'It's too small. Too small for anything.'

It was on the tip of Beth's tongue to tell him she'd be pleased if he'd find somewhere else to live, but he went out, slamming the door behind him, before she could.

There were a lot of other changes taking place. The children started at their new schools. They had a few weeks to settle in and make new friends before the summer holidays were on them.

It gave Beth quite a pang to give in her notice at the Borough Hospital in time to start her new job. She'd been happy working there.

Best of all, Ken was home every evening and she rarely missed seeing him. They didn't often go out but tonight Ken had wanted to see Douglas Fairbanks in *The Three Musketeers*. Beth was holding on to his arm as she climbed the marble steps in front of the Scala Cinema when she saw Andrew Langford a few steps ahead of them.

'Gosh,' she gasped.

'What is it?'

'My ex-boyfriend. Haven't seen him for ages.' He was wearing a new mac, white again, with a snap brim trilby.

At the box office they caught up with him. He was alone but she wondered if he'd arranged to meet a friend. No, he was buying a single balcony seat, the most expensive. He hadn't changed, he had no friends. He turned round and recognised her.

'Hello, Andrew,' she said. A tide of crimson swept up his cheeks, he looked uncomfortable, embarrassed at their meeting. His gaze went to Ken who was buying two of the cheapest seats in the stalls. Beth made a point of introducing Ken though she could see Andrew was itching to escape. 'We're going to be married,' she said proudly. He didn't like that, she could see.

Once in their seats in the dark auditorium, Ken whispered, 'He's very posh, looks a man of importance. Very smart too. He'd have been quite a catch for you.'

Beth shook her head. 'I thought so once, but not now. I'm glad he ditched me, marrying him would have been a big mistake.'

'I can't get over it, taking to me, when you might have had him.'

'Ken, I'd much rather have you. You're twice the man he is.'

More often than not they stayed at home. Her father went out as soon as he'd eaten his tea, and often Ivor disappeared as soon as the children were in bed, leaving them alone. Beth loved those evenings.

When Ken wasn't with her she relived every precious moment of them, the tremulous joy of being alone with him, of twining their arms round each other's waists, the kisses she received and gave.

'The trouble is,' she told him, 'I want more.'

'So do I.'

'Ken, I'm coming round to the idea we should do what pleases us. For years, you've thought only of others.'

'So have you.'

'Isn't it time we thought of ourselves?'

His arms were round her, holding her close. 'Let's not wait to get married,' he whispered. 'It's what I want.'

'So do I and I don't care if it is a squash here. We'll sort something out.'

'When?'

'Let Lottie go first. What about October?' That made it seem deliciously certain.

'It's what I've always wanted, you know that, Beth. I do love you.'

Beth sighed with contentment. 'You breathe life into everything I do. You've been my mainstay and prop for years. While I was growing up you were always my friend.' It had taken her a long time to tell the difference between friendship and love.

When Beth's last afternoon at the Borough Hospital was coming to an end, she felt sorry to be leaving. Saying goodbye to people she'd worked with for so long was bringing a lump to her throat. Those she didn't know well asked where she'd be working in future, and the look of incredulous horror that came to their faces when she told them was making her uneasy. It was a big step to leave what she was used to and start afresh, particularly when there was so much controversy about the work.

The verdict had gone against Dr Stopes in her libel case, and the newspapers and magazines had a field day. The news that she intended to appeal against the verdict did not please Beth. She knew it would keep her work very much in the public eye.

'I'm sure right is on Dr Stopes's side,' Beth said to Ken. 'And I do understand that she wants justice, but if she took a lower profile, all this publicity would die down, and perhaps in time contraception would become more accepted.'

On her first morning, as she caught the ferry over to Liverpool, she had her nerves well under control. That there would be no patients for the first ten days had a calming effect. Beth knew it would give her time to learn what was expected of her.

She found Miss Wishart in the entrance hall putting up notices. She led her into the waiting area. Beth was impressed.

'What a good job you've made of this. It looks really lovely.' The walls had been distempered in white and there were blue curtains at the windows.

'This is the colour scheme Marie chose for her first clinic in Holloway and we all thought it worked very well.' It was bright and light and the wooden floor shone.

'I've found these pictures for the walls. Just large prints but they're bright and colourful.' One was a country view of fields and hills, the other of the seaside.

'We have pictures of babies at the Holloway clinic but I felt perhaps not here. Most of our clients are trying to avoid babies, it doesn't seem right to have pictures of them on the walls.'

'But you do help those who are trying to have a baby?'

'Yes indeed, we give great prominence to our fertility work, nobody can accuse us of encouraging immorality with that.'

'This will be a soothing place to wait,' Beth said.

'That's what I was aiming for. We want it to be friendly and informal, where the women won't feel intimidated. We don't want it to look too much like a hospital, but on the other hand everything must be clinical and hygienic.'

The furniture was plain and well-polished. 'When we open, I'll bring some roses from the garden at home and put a vase on that table. Dr Stopes will come up and see us when she can but it won't be just yet. I do want her to approve of what I've done.'

'I'm sure she will.'

'She's very troubled with this libel case. Her appeal is coming up and she's determined to get the verdict overturned.'

Beth said, 'It must be frightening for her. All this publicity.'

'And she's expecting a very much wanted baby.'

'So she can't come now?'

'No, she's left it all to me.'

Two middle-aged women were coming in. 'Ah, here come the others now.'

Dorinda introduced them. 'This is Nurse Carruthers, our midwife.' She was a big-boned homely woman who shook Beth's hand warmly.

'And Nurse Trowbridge, our other nurse.' Again she was older than Beth, with kindly eyes and greying hair.

'This is all of us, except for the doctor. At the Holloway clinic, we found the women were more at ease with trained nurses and midwives than with doctors. We must appear to be as much like those who come as possible, and try to meet them half way. There's often embarrassment at first, and they may well have had to walk through a jeering crowd to get in. Tomorrow we're going to announce our opening in the local papers and put posters up inviting women to come. You'll not find it so peaceful outside after that.'

'Do we give appointments?' Nurse Trowbridge wanted to know.

'No appointments. We want them to walk in and be dealt with. At least at first, until we see how it goes. We nurses will explain Marie Stopes's methods to each woman. Tell her what's available and help her make up her mind what would suit her best. Then if she decides on the diaphragm or, as it's sometimes called, the cervical cap, she goes in to be measured and fitted by the midwife. Her training makes her the expert in this sphere.'

'I've never seen a cervical cap,' Beth said.

'Our midwife is the best person to show you,' Miss Wishart said.

'Right, well, you'd better come and see them now,' Nurse Carruthers invited. They all followed her to her room, where she opened a glass cupboard and spread a row of diaphragms in a range of sizes along her desk.

'It's my job to examine the women and make sure there's no abnormality. If I suspect there is, I refer her to the clinic doctor. She will come only one or two afternoons a week.'

Dorinda added, 'All our advice is given free and the contraceptives are sold at the price the manufacturers charge us. Sometimes, for very poor women, we give a cervical cap free. The last thing Dr Stopes wants is to be accused of making a profit from the poor. All the running costs come from her own pocket.'

Beth listened to everything that was said with avid interest.

'This is the original Dutch cap which was first brought to England in the eighteen eighties.' The midwife put it in Beth's hand. 'Compare it to Marie Stopes's smaller more modern one which has to fit precisely.' She handed it to Nurse Trowbridge. 'Dr Stopes calls hers the Pro-Race cap. It's the only one we'll fit here, though the other is still used.'

Then she brought out the condoms.

'These are a new invention?' Nurse Trowbridge asked.

'Heavens, no. They date from the eighteenth century. But they've been kept a dark secret from most of the population.' Nurse Carruthers smiled. 'They used to be made of fine linen once, and had to be waxed. There were more expensive ones made from sheep's intestines. Nowadays they're all made from rubber and there's quinine pessaries to go with them.'

She brought out the douche cans to show them. 'You'll need to explain to the women exactly how these are used, but I'll go into that another day. And I'll explain about all the different spermicides which are made up into pessaries, such as quinine or quassia, which need to be used too.'

Miss Wishart said, 'We nurses will have to explain exactly how each of these things works, and that'll include a little anatomy lesson first. What we all need to remember,' she went on, 'is that these contraceptives are on sale in shops in every town, in barber's shops and chemists and often alongside Marie Stopes's books. We provide a more sheltered place for women to buy them.'

In the afternoon, a dressmaker came to measure them for their uniform.

'We'll wear loose-fitting white coats,' Miss Wishart told them. 'With a loose belt fastened with one button. The same design as worn in the Holloway clinic. I've brought one of mine to show you. They're very comfortable to wear.'

She also showed them the big muslin squares which were to be folded to make their headdress.

Over the following days, Beth heard all about the other methods of contraception that had been used since time immemorial.

'Coitus interruptus is the most frequently used method,' Nurse Carruthers told them. 'That means withdrawal before the end. It costs nothing except the husband's co-operation but it's not all that safe. Then there's the limitation of relations to the safe period, which isn't all that safe either.'

Beth marvelled at her matter-of-fact way of explaining everything. She clearly didn't feel embarrassed.

'Then there's all the homemade remedies women have used over the centuries. Half a lemon—'

'Half a lemon?' Beth couldn't suppress a giggle.

'Yes, squeezed and used as a diaphragm. There is some scientific logic to that. Lemons are acid and sperm lives in an alkaline medium. Then there's soap rubbed into a sponge; douches of soapy water or vinegar. Again, vinegar is an acid. Homemade tampons made from lint and strong thread soaked in vinegar, sour milk or rubbed with soap.'

'Do they work?'

'To some extent. Women had to hope they would, but this is the twentieth century and now the very latest things are the Pro-Race cap or the condom. They give the best available protection when used with a spermicide. I'm afraid you'll have to tell the mothers that the only guaranteed method is total abstinence from sexual relations, which takes willpower and sometimes cold baths, and is not popular with most husbands.'

'Half a lemon.' Nurse Trowbridge was still chuckling.

The midwife said. 'I believe the Egyptians used camel dung.'

Later on, the doctor came to talk to them. She said, 'Contraception has got to be made respectable and it's got to be made available for everybody. Children have to be wanted, it would reduce so much poverty and child abuse. To release women from the perennial fear of unwanted pregnancy is the greatest single service one can give.'

* * *

The schools had broken up for their summer holidays and Beth was worried about being away at the clinic all day. Jenny said Esther must bring Colin and Bobby up to her house every day to play with Noreen and Amy.

'I'll feed them at lunchtime,' she said. 'And perhaps take them out for picnics or to the beach at New Brighton. Don't you worry about them.'

Beth felt she could trust Esther, though she was only ten, and she was good with Bobby. Colin was more of a worry. He'd made friends with an equally wild lad called Dan who lived round the corner, and they evaded Beth and Jenny whenever they could.

One evening, Ivor was late coming home for his tea. Beth knew he was going out to a farm near Frankby first, to see about getting a job there. When he came home, he had a smile from ear to ear.

'I've got it!' They could see joy crackling out of him. 'I'm going to love this, Beth, I know I will. They've got a shire horse called Billy, and two ponies who pull the milk float and the trap.' The three younger ones crowded round the table, delighted to hear his news. 'I'm going to look after the horses as well as do the small milk round.'

'You'll have to get up very early.'

'I know, and help with the milking and other work when they're busy.'

'It'll be easier than humping sacks of coal round all day.'

'I never did like that much.'

'But you stuck at it, Ivor.'

'I had to, didn't I? But it takes me ages to clean off the coal dust every night. It gets in my hair and ears and everywhere. I'll not be sorry to give it up.'

For once, he was pushing the food round his plate, almost too excited to eat.

'And I'll be living in. There's two other farm boys and I'm to share a big room with them over the stables. It'll be fun, and you don't need me here, not if Ken's coming.'

Beth said, 'I was glad to have you when we first thought of moving here. Without your wages, we couldn't have done it. I hope you don't feel you're being pushed out.'

'No, I'm just so pleased to get the job. I've been trying for something better for so long.'

Beth heard the tap on the front door and rushed to open it. She knew it would be Ken. When he heard about Ivor's new job, he laughed.

'Our Pat's got a job as a nursemaid. She's going to the family that employs Maggie in Southport. Their daughter has three children now, and lives in one wing of the house. Mam's pleased she'll have Maggie there to ease her in. She was thinking of offering you the use of the room, Ivor, so she won't be lonely when we all leave.'

'Oh gosh! Tell her I'd have jumped at it if I hadn't got this job.' Ivor's eyes shone. 'With me gone, there'll be room for you here, Ken.'

'There's still your dad,' he said.

Peggy felt she'd had rather too many lectures from her younger sisters. They were always telling her where she was going wrong and she resented it.

Things were going from bad to worse between her and Sidney. When he screamed at her with vicious rage, it was second nature to retaliate and be nasty back. When he was expecting a hot meal on the table, she made sure there was nothing edible in the house. She left his clothes unwashed, and said some unforgivable things.

She'd told her sisters only part of this, but they were always advising her to make up her quarrel and get back on good terms with him. Peggy had tried, she'd been very unhappy for years and felt she couldn't go on like this. She'd tried very hard.

For a whole month, she'd been as sweet-natured as anyone could possibly be. She'd talked to Sidney, told him all that went on in her day – well, all that was good for him to know. She'd cooked the meals he liked and put them in front of him and she'd given in to sex whenever he wanted it, provided he wore those things.

She'd said to him, 'Things were wonderful when we were first married. Why can't we be like that again?'

She hadn't liked the way he looked at her. 'We were in love. That never lasts.'

'It has for Jenny and Tom.'

She knew she sounded bitter. It was hurtful to see them so friendly. Jenny was making a success where she had failed. It was seeing Jenny so happy that had made Peggy try to improve things between herself and Sidney.

But Sidney wouldn't try, he was as nasty to her as ever. Peggy came to the conclusion that when a relationship had gone as sour as theirs, it wasn't possible to turn it round.

Beth was getting on her nerves more than ever. She never stopped talking about the Marie Stopes clinic that was about to open in

Liverpool, and how pleased she was that Miss Wishart had asked her to work in it. It was a job after her own heart all right, she was more than keen. She went on about how Miss Wishart wanted her to read all Dr Stopes's books and pamphlets before she started, and was lending them to her a few at a time.

Beth also went on about wanting her to attend the clinic when it did open. Jenny was going to take her to make sure she didn't opt out. As if she would! Her biggest fear was still that she might get pregnant again.

Peggy reckoned Dorinda Wishart was training Beth to be her disciple. As always, she was more than ready to give advice though she'd no idea what marriage entailed. Beth didn't understand about Sidney, nor did Jenny. They had no idea how driven she felt about wanting to be rid of him. She was sure it was the only way she'd find any peace. She didn't want to spend the rest of her life fighting a war against him that she couldn't win.

The day the clinic opened for business, a crowd gathered outside shouting and jeering and throwing eggs, rotten apples and stones at the women who tried to walk through it to their door.

'They won't be able to keep this up for ever,' Dorinda Wishart said, tight-lipped.

Only the most determined women reached them and some of those didn't want to give their names and addresses because it provided proof they were using sinful and immoral devices to prevent pregnancy. They were afraid the jeering crowd would break into the clinic and get at the records. If their names were published in the papers, they felt they'd be not only embarrassed but in trouble.

'We've got to understand their fears. Treat them without further question,' Dorinda ordered. But it made record-keeping difficult.

In the first week, Jenny came and brought Peggy with her. Nurse Trowbridge dealt with them. Both decided on the cap and were handed over to the midwife. Lottie had wanted to come with them, her wedding was only a week or two away, but the rule was married women only. She told Beth she'd come as soon as she could afterwards.

Dr Stopes's appeal was heard. It brought another wave of publicity in the newspapers, and the jeering crowd outside the clinic which had begun to thin out now returned in force.

When the verdict was reversed and Dr Stopes was awarded peppercorn damages, Beth and her colleagues felt huge satisfaction. But they heard the following day that Sutherland was not prepared to accept defeat and was appealing for funds through Catholic newspapers to take the case to the House of Lords.

'Will it never end?' Dorinda rolled her eyes heavenwards.

Wilf had been into town to get himself a new shirt and tie to wear to Lottie's wedding. On his way home he saw Ethel and Molly waiting at the bus stop, all dressed up and obviously on their way out somewhere.

Ethel said, 'Are you doing anything on Saturday night, Wilf?'

The question surprised him, he'd thought Ethel was trying to push him away. Lottie was to be married that day, but the celebrations would be over by late afternoon.

'Come round then. I want you and me to have a quiet word.'

Their bus came at that moment and Wilf went on feeling much happier. It could only mean Ethel wanted something. Had she changed her mind and decided after all that she should marry him? The more he thought about it, the more likely it seemed. What else could she possibly want a quiet word about?

If he could move in with her, his problems would be solved. His spirits rose, he felt better all round. It could be that soon he'd have somewhere better to sleep than on that lumpy couch.

With Lottie's wedding in mind, Beth and Jenny had bought remnants of fabric in the market and had set about making new outfits for themselves and for each of the younger children. The time they spent sewing heightened their anticipation. Beth had chosen green linen for herself which matched the colour of her eyes.

It was to be a real family occasion. John would be home for it and the Clovers had offered to put him up for a couple of nights. Seppy was the only one who couldn't make it, he was in Hull with his ship.

Lottie was married on a lovely summer Saturday in the parish church of West Kirby. The clock in the massive tower had just finished chiming midday when Beth watched her sister walk down the aisle on Dad's arm, looking ethereal in an ivory satin gown with a gossamer veil which she'd managed to borrow from a friend of Mildred, the Wisharts' cook.

Lottie had whispered that she'd be the third bride to wear it, but the first came from a foremost West Kirby family. It had been a very expensive dress. Esther, Noreen and May were bridesmaids in the matching pink taffeta dresses Jenny had made for them.

It was the smartest wedding Beth had ever been to. She could see Jenny's eyes darting round, taking it all in. Peggy looked hot and bothered as she tried to keep both Rita and Eric quiet. She was wearing a hat that had belonged to their mother. It was about eight years old, but Mam had only worn it for best so it still looked new.

'A lovely wedding, isn't it?' Beth whispered.

'Much better than the one I had. Makes me think back to it though. The cause of all my problems.'

That made Beth look round for Sidney. He was in the pew behind with Frankie and Hilda.

Ken, who was beside her, nudged her and whispered that he was impressed. 'We could have something like this, if you want.'

Afterwards, they all paused outside in the sun while the church bells pealed out triumphantly from the ivy-covered tower and a photographer took pictures of the bridal party. They walked in procession then, following the groom's mother to her house.

Beth could see it was a lot bigger than the one she'd moved into, but it was terraced too, a Victorian villa with one large bay window. In the front sitting room they were offered glasses of sherry or lemonade. Beth thought the Shaw family friendly and welcoming and the groom did his best to introduce the two families to each other.

Mrs Shaw was a widow and her elderly sisters were helping her put on this reception, so Beth was doubly embarrassed to hear Dad ask if there was any beer. She was afraid he was letting the family down. His suit still smelled of mothballs although she'd hung it out in their yard yesterday.

Shortly afterwards, the door to the dining room was flung open and they were invited to help themselves. The table was groaning under a magnificent spread. Beth watched the plates of sandwiches empty instantly. The Hubbles rarely had a choice of beef, egg or tinned salmon between their bread. They did equal justice to the tinned peaches, jellies, trifles and junkets and the plates of homemade scones and slices of cake.

The iced wedding cake was cut and pieces handed round with another glass of sherry. Beth thought her father seemed full of himself as he made a long speech about his five lovely daughters. When he said Lottie was the most beautiful, she saw Peggy grimace.

In the late afternoon, the bride and groom were ready to leave for their honeymoon in Prestatyn. They planned to travel by train from Woodside Station.

It was Jenny who suggested they all travel back to Birkenhead together. It was only then that they noticed Dad and Sidney had disappeared. Even without them, the Hubble family made a large and jolly entourage on the Wirral electric train.

Peggy, now in charge of all five of her children, got off at Birkenhead North End. As Jenny's husband helped Eric and Rita out onto the platform, Peggy complained, 'Goodness knows where Sidney's got to. He should be here. I hope he remembers he has to be at work at six.'

Jenny and Tom got off at Birkenhead Park. When the rest of them came up from the underground at Hamilton Square, Beth suggested they walk down to Woodside to see the bride and groom off. They were still chattering away twenty to the dozen and wishing Lottie well when the mainline train steamed away.

'Home now?' Beth suggested, feeling the atmosphere suddenly flat. 'A cup of tea?'

'I'm hungry,' Ivor said.

'So am I,' John agreed.

Beth said, 'After that fine spread?'

'That was hours ago.'

She thought of what she might produce for their tea. 'I've got eggs and—'

'Pies,' Ken said. 'Let's get them now before we go home.'

'My treat,' John said. 'Pies all round.'

'Can we have baked potatoes too?' Colin wanted to know.

'Why not? We might as well carry on indulging ourselves. It's Lottie's wedding day, after all.'

'Smells lovely.' John sniffed appreciatively as they approached. Once inside, even Beth's mouth began to water. There were customers in the shop and two girls serving.

'Should we get a pie for Dad?' Beth pondered. 'He'll expect me to provide his tea.'

'If he wants one he can come and get his own,' John said severely. 'I saw him sneaking off with Sidney the moment the food was finished. It wouldn't have hurt them to stay and be pleasant for a bit.'

Ken said, as the young ones lined up against the counter, 'Now then, make up your minds what sort of pie you want. There's steak and kidney or—'

'I don't like kidney,' said Esther.

'Steak with mushrooms then.'

A customer was leaving with a steaming bag. One of the serving girls turned towards them. 'Yes? What can I get for you?'

Beth could see Ken staring at her, it made her take a second look. Even in the white coat and cap that covered most of her dark hair, Beth recognised her.

She laughed. 'Aren't you the singer? Veronica something?'

273

'Yes.' The girl was grinning at them. 'The one and only Veronica Eastly.'

'I knew I'd seen you somewhere before,' Ken said. 'It was here, of course.'

Beth added, 'We saw you in that show at the Floral Hall, you were wonderful. We all loved that turn where you were dressed as a bride.'

'Fame at last.' She was laughing.

'Two steak and kidney, please, Veronica.'

'It's Molly really.' She giggled. 'Veronica's my stage name.'

'What are you doing working here then?' John asked.

'My mam makes me. She owns this business.'

'Oh, and two steak and mushroom,' Beth said, 'two minced beef and onion and . . .'

A door behind the counter opened. Beth's jaw dropped as she saw her father come out with a used dinner plate in his hand.

He had shed his jacket and waistcoat, his collar and tie were gone too, the sleeves of his new shirt were rolled up and his brown braces were much in evidence.

He said, 'Which are the steak and kidney, Molly? I could manage another.'

Beth heard Ken's gasp. So did Dad. He looked up at them and the plate slid through his fingers to clatter on the floor. An instant later, he was gone.

'Oh, for goodness' sake!' Molly exclaimed. 'What's the matter with you tonight?' She scooped up the plate and followed him into the back reaches of the shop.

'Dad?' Colin was on tiptoe looking over the counter. 'Was that Dad?'

John and Ken stared at each other, mouths agape. Esther's eyes were like saucers. Beth was speechless. Lottie had been right! They hadn't believed her when she'd told them Dad had another daughter, another family. But she'd been right!

When Molly came back, an older woman followed with a tray of piping hot baked potatoes. Beth stared at her. Was this Dad's . . . ? Molly's mother?

'Shop's full,' the newcomer said. 'I'd better lend a hand.'

'Thanks, Mam.' Molly confirmed it as the trays slid onto the counter. She smiled up at John. 'D'you want anything else?'

John didn't know where to look. He fumbled for some money to pay for the pies.

'That's our dad in there,' Beth blurted out. She couldn't stop herself, she didn't care that there were new customers listening to what she was

274

saying. 'There's ten of us all told. Ask him where he's been today. Lottie, another of his daughters, was married in West Kirby Church. He gave her away.'

The woman stared back at her open-mouthed.

Molly giggled. 'Gosh!'

'I think you must be our half-sister,' Beth told her.

Chapter Twenty-Three

At the wedding reception, Wilf had seen that Sidney was bored and didn't like sherry. He'd suggested they make off to the nearest pub for a couple of beers as soon as they decently could, but time had been called before they got there and they could buy only for drinking outside. Wilf got a half-bottle of whisky and went home with Sidney to drink it there.

It was peaceful without Peggy and the kids, and when Sid had to change for the evening shift at the Blood Tub, Wilf had gone round to Ethel's, feeling he'd had a good day. He was looking forward to the evening, which he hoped was going to prove even better.

When he arrived, the shop was open and doing a good trade. He'd found Ethel alone in the living room, stitching silk flowers on a hat. He'd expected to find her cooking a chicken for his dinner, but the table wasn't set and there was no great warmth in her manner. He tried not to show his disappointment.

'Aren't we going to eat?'

She'd hesitated, looking uncomfortable. 'Are you hungry?'

'Your pies always give me an appetite.'

She'd put a plate in his hand. 'Go and get what you want then.'

'Aren't you going to eat too?' Wilf's spirits were sinking fast. It wasn't much fun eating alone. He was beginning to think he'd been mistaken about her intentions.

Her mouth was set in a hard, straight line. 'Molly and I will have a salad later. We get a bit fed up with pies all the time.'

She put out cutlery for him and there were two cups of steaming tea on the table when he returned with a heaped plate.

She watched him tuck in in silence. He'd almost cleared his plate when she said, 'You're all dressed up, Wilf. I hope you weren't expecting a night out.'

He didn't like that, but he managed to say, 'You know I'd rather stay in with you.'

Normally he told her nothing about Vi's children, it was better that she didn't know their business. But he said, 'I'm dressed up because I've been to a really posh wedding.'

'That so?' Ethel's cool eyes met his.

'Yes, one of my girls decided to get married and settle down.'

'That's what I wanted to talk to you about. Getting married and settling down.'

Wilfred perked up, he'd been right after all! He felt better immediately.

'Hang on a sec. I could do with another of your pies.'

He'd bounded into the shop and come face to face with his family spread out in a line in front of the counter. They'd all been agog at seeing him: John, Esther, Colin, Bobby and Beth, together with that Ken Clover.

It had knocked all the stuffing out of him. He'd been caught red-handed. He'd felt suddenly sick and fled back into the living room.

'As I was saying,' Ethel went on, unable to look at him now, 'I'm going to get married.'

Wilf's head was spinning, he couldn't get the look on Beth's face out of his mind.

'What?'

'What I'm trying to tell you,' he heard the impatience in her voice, 'is that I'm going to marry Harry Duncan. Do you remember him? Used to live in C Block but he's really gone up in the world. Well, once I'm married, I don't want you to come round here any more. It'll embarrass us all. Better if we draw a line under it now, Wilf.'

'What?'

'This has been dragging on between us too long. I want it to end. Molly's grown up, she doesn't need you. Not that you ever did anything for her. Well, it's over, isn't it?'

Beth was shaking as she walked home between Ken and John.

'I can't believe it! Dad has another family, a grown-up daughter.' The hot scent of pies was rising from the parcels they carried.

'How old is she?' John asked.

'What does that matter? As if there weren't enough of us.'

'But that girl's got a good voice,' Ken said.

'She didn't get it from him,' Beth retorted. 'He was doing that behind Mam's back. That really riles me.'

'Did Mam not know? She might—'

'No.' Beth was definite. 'I'm sure she didn't. I'm glad she never found out.'

'He was doing us down, not just Mam,' John pointed out, his face working furiously. 'We were so poor. I remember one winter Seppy having to go to school in boots that leaked. It was months before Mam could get him new ones.'

'Mine leaked too,' Ivor said.

'And mine!' said Esther. 'I remember a row of boots drying out in front of the range every night and our socks too.'

'And they'd be wet again the next day if it was raining.'

'Mam was driven frantic trying to make ends meet. She'd go without food herself so that we could have proper meals, and all the time some of Dad's earnings were going on *them*.'

'You don't know that,' Ken said. 'Not if they had that pie shop. According to my mother, it used to be up near Dock Cottages years ago. Your dad could have been getting your pies free from her.'

'We never saw even one pie,' Beth said bitterly. 'He never brought pies home and Mam couldn't afford them. Couldn't afford chips or any cooked food. You get more for your money if you cook at home.'

Beth was too churned up to do justice to her pie when she had it on the plate in front of her.

'Wait till our Jenny hears about this, she'll be furious. And Peggy. I'll go up straight after this to see them.'

'No, Beth,' Ken said gently. 'Better if you don't go tonight. You're tired after being out all day, they will be too. And you're angry. Leave it till tomorrow.'

'I'll be just as angry then,' she said, but she stayed at home and they spent the evening going over and over the same ground.

Beth felt far from sleep when Ken took John back to his house for the night. She went upstairs to bed and lay down beside Esther who was curled up in a ball and sleeping deeply. The more she thought about what Dad had done, the more outraged she felt.

To think she and Ken had put off their wedding to give him a home; to think of what Mam had given up for him. She was still simmering with anger and sleep seemed far away when the front door crashed shut. He'd come home! Beth was out of bed in an instant and flying downstairs. 'Dad, I couldn't believe . . .'

He slammed past her and out to the lavatory in the yard. She could hardly contain herself until he came back.

He said sullenly, 'Don't start now. I've had enough for one day. I'm too tired. I've had to walk from the Blood Tub. All the buses were heading up to the depot in Laird Street. Nothing was coming this way.'

Beth felt clear-headed and determined. After this, she was not going to consider her father's needs.

'Dad, you've got to find somewhere else to live. I'm not having you here, not after seeing you down in the pie shop.'

He was engrossed in unlacing his boots. 'Damn it, only a few weeks ago you wanted me here.'

'Never that, but I did agree you could come. You accused Ken of pushing you out of your home. He's got a soft heart.'

'Not like you.'

'Not any more, not as far as you're concerned. I know you better than he does. Ken believes in responsibility, and doing his duty to his parents and his family.'

'It's a pity you don't.'

'It was duty that made me agree to have you here. Duty that's kept me washing and cooking for you, though you stole from me. I came home when Mam died because I promised her I'd look after the little ones. That was duty too. She couldn't trust you to do it, could she? I can't forgive what you did to Mam. Where was your duty to her? To find out you had another woman and I've got a half-sister, that changes everything.'

'For God's sake I want to go to bed. Can't we talk about this in the morning?'

'I've said all I'm going to. This is the end. I'm not going to wash so much as another sock of yours. I'm not going to cut another sandwich, or cook another meal for you. It's over, and I want you out of my house.'

'You can't just put me out like that.'

'I can. If I had any sense I'd show you the door now. Tomorrow—'

'You can't! I've just given you a houseful of furniture, all I've got.'

'You can have it back, Dad. Tell me when, and I'll pile it all outside on the pavement for you. You use people, you used Mam, you aren't going to use me any more. I want you out of here tomorrow.'

'Not tomorrow! It takes time to find another place, you know that. You've got to be reasonable.'

'All right. If you've not taken your clothes and your bedding by the end of the week, I'll put them out on the pavement and bolt the doors. So help me I will. I've been far too soft with you.'

Although the next morning was Sunday, Beth was up earlier than she was on a weekday. She was still simmering. As soon as breakfast was

280

cleared away, she was off to tell Jenny what she'd seen with her own eyes.

'I want to come with you,' Esther said.

Beth knew that what she wanted to tell Jenny would be better said out of Esther's hearing, but there was no dissuading her. They towed Bobby along between them.

Jenny was cutting sandwiches in the kitchen.

'I've promised Noreen a picnic in the park,' she said. 'I know it's only at the end of the street, but it's another sunny day and it gets us all out in the fresh air. Didn't everything go well for Lottie yesterday?'

'Where's Tom?'

'He's gone down to his allotment. His father's got one there too, so they have a good old chinwag. He'll come and find us in the park afterwards.'

Beth ushered Esther and Bobby out to the back yard where Noreen was chalking on a blackboard. Then she told her sister what had happened after they'd seen the bridal couple off. Jenny's mouth dropped open.

'Isn't that what Lottie told us? That she saw Dad with that girl at a dance in West Kirby?'

'It really rankles, doesn't it?'

'Makes me feel sick that he could do that to Mam.'

'Let's go up and tell Peggy. She'll never believe this, she's always thought the world of Dad.'

'Perhaps she'll come with us to the park.'

They set off, Jenny pushing Amy in the pram, with the other children trailing behind. It was May who opened Peggy's front door. She shot back to the scullery where her mother was dishing up eggs and bacon.

'It's my aunties and Noreen and . . .'

Peggy came to the living-room door to see them but yelled at the ceiling. 'Sidney? Your breakfast's on the table. Come and get it before it goes cold.'

She pushed aside the remnants of an earlier meal to make room for the plate. While Jenny ushered all the children and the dog out into the back yard, Beth removed a pile of children's clothes from a chair so she could sit down.

Sidney came heavily downstairs. 'You lot are here early. Didn't you see enough of each other yesterday?'

He found a knife and fork in the scullery sink, wiped them on a towel and sat down to eat.

'It's Dad.' Beth couldn't hold back her indignation. She told Peggy about going to the pie shop and how they'd seen Dad there.

'He's had a lady friend for years and years. Most of his married life. He's got another grown-up daughter, can you believe that?'

'Dad?' Peggy was dumbfounded.

Sidney was tearing bread to mop up his egg yolk. 'Wilf's always been a bit of a skirt chaser.' He laughed unpleasantly. 'I'm surprised none of you knew.'

Jenny was smouldering. 'Lottie told us ages ago that she'd seen Dad with this girl Molly, and that she'd said he was her dad. We thought it must have been some sort of a joke.'

'I asked Dad to his face,' Beth fumed. 'He told me not to be daft.'

'And you believed there was nothing in it?' Sidney laughed again.

Jenny said more heatedly, 'Of course we didn't know. It's come as a right eye-opener to me.'

He pulled a face.

Beth said, 'You knew? Is that what you're saying?'

'Common knowledge in the Blood Tub. We used to tease him, tell him Ethel put aphrodisiac in her pies to bring all the men in.'

Beth could feel the gorge rising in her throat. 'That's her name? Ethel?'

'It's over her shop, Ethel Byrne.'

'Why didn't you tell me?' Peggy's face was rigid with anger. 'If you knew what Dad was up to, why didn't you tell me?'

'If I had, would you have believed me? You think the sun shines out of his backside.'

'Goddamnit, Sidney!' Peggy was absolutely livid, with both Sidney and Dad. All the men in the Blood Tub knowing that Dad had another woman and talking about it behind Mam's back to their neighbours and their wives. How could he have treated Mam like that?

She was glad when Sidney left to go to work. Moments later, all the children and the dog came bounding back inside.

Noreen pulled at her mother's skirt. 'Can we go out to play with May? She's going to take us up Biddy Hill.'

'No, we're going for a picnic in the park. I've brought everything in the pram. Daddy will come looking for us.'

Beth said, 'How about it, Peggy? Let's all go to the park. Cut some sandwiches, give your kids a picnic.'

'Oh, lovely,' they chorused. 'Can we, Mam?'

Beth helped cut a loaf into slices. Jenny spread them with marge.

'There's only plum jam,' Peggy said.

'What have you got to wrap them in?'

Peggy pushed last week's *Birkenhead News* into Beth's hand, before filling two large bottles at the scullery tap. Then she loaded it all into the pushchair and strapped Rita between the parcels. As they walked, Peggy continued to fume.

'Sidney knew all along and kept quiet. That turns my stomach. Makes me wonder what else he knows and doesn't tell me.'

'Have you told him you found his hidey-hole in the wash house?'

'No, I think of that as the bank. When I'm spent up, I take a bit more out. Not very much, but we had a shoulder of mutton last Sunday, and last month I bought a winter coat for May in the sales. He's never noticed, or if he has he's said nothing.'

As soon as the children went off to play, Beth and Jenny lay down on the grass in the shade. Peggy was still worked up. 'All men are selfish,' she said.

'Not all.' Beth was thinking of Ken. 'You aren't over the first shock of knowing we have a half-sister.'

'Molly.' Peggy's mouth twisted with bitterness. 'I could kill Dad for that. It's what he deserves.'

'I can't imagine Dad having sex.' Jenny giggled. 'Not at his age, he's too old.'

'He wasn't so old when he sired *her*.'

'Does she have any sisters or brothers?'

'We didn't ask.'

'I blame him for Mam's death.'

'I do too,' Jenny said. 'She'd be here today if only he'd been more careful.'

'To make her pregnant when he knew her heart wouldn't stand it . . .'

'I thought that was terrible at the time, but now knowing he had another woman . . . It was totally heartless. I find it unbelievable that he'd do it.'

'Unforgivable,' Beth said. 'And when I think of how he messed me up over the new house. I've told him to get out. I wish I'd never said he could come. He's made a right fool of me.'

'He's made fools of us all,' Jenny said. 'I'm having no more to do with him.'

Beth said, 'Ken and I want to get married. I'm tired of seeing you younger ones getting settled before me. We're not putting it off any longer, especially not so Dad can live with me. You'd better look out, Peg. I bet he'll want to move in with you. You were always his favourite.'

'I'm not having him. I've got the smallest house and the most children. There's no room for him. And I don't like him being in

283

cahoots with Sidney. I feel they gang up against me.'

'I'm just glad Mam never found out,' Beth said. 'This would have broken her heart.'

'I'd like to cut his goolies off,' Peggy said vehemently. 'A fitting punishment for him.'

'He's an out-and-out rotter,' Jenny said.

'What's the best way to get our revenge?' Peggy was screwing up her face in thought. 'I'd like to see him boiled in oil.'

Beth smiled. 'There isn't a pan big enough. Better if we do nothing. Better if we just forget him and get on with our own lives.'

Peggy was still hungering for revenge when Tom turned up and put an end to their discussion. Jenny opened up her picnic lunch and Peggy immediately felt shamed by the spread she produced. Jenny's sandwiches of meat paste with lettuce were packed in a tin and had greaseproof paper round them. They were moist and tasty, and there were plenty of them. She'd brought apples too and a whole sponge cake which she cut up into slices. She had lemonade for the children and two flasks of tea between the adults.

To make matters worse, when Peggy tried to push her jam butties on her own children, they hung back until Jenny offered hers. They were all eaten, however; May and Frankie ate until everything had gone.

When Beth and Jenny got up to take their families home, Peggy watched them go feeling envious. They both seemed to be getting more from life than she was.

'Come on, Mam,' May urged. 'Let's go, we've nobody to play with now.'

'I want my dinner,' Eric said.

'You've had it. The jam butties.'

'Is that all? I'm still hungry.'

'After all that food Auntie Jenny gave you?'

Reluctantly she got to her feet. It was too nice a day to go home and start cleaning. Rita refused to get in the pushchair and ran off after May. Frankie wanted to take her place, but Peggy saw no reason to push a heavy lump like him. She loaded it with empty bottles and cardigans and trailed through the park in the wake of her children.

She couldn't get what Dad had done out of her mind. She'd worshipped him when she was a girl. He'd built her up to expect so much. When she'd asked him if he thought she'd be able to be a dancer and go on the stage, he'd said, 'You'll be able to do anything you like.'

'Will you help me?'

'Course I will, but you've got it inside yourself. You'll be a star. A film star perhaps, and I'll be so proud and tell everybody you're my daughter.'

Peggy could still remember the delight she'd felt at that. 'Could I be rich?'

'One day you'll be very rich, and when you are, you'll have to look after your old dad.'

'Course I will, Daddy. I promise.'

Peggy had a bitter taste in her mouth. Not only had she failed, but she had a half-sister who was succeeding in a stage career. She wondered if Dad had said the same things to her. She wanted to see this Molly perform to find out just how good she was. She was afraid Molly had taken her place in Dad's affections, that he'd helped her instead.

Peggy had reached the duck pond. Frankie was throwing sticks into it and the ducks had departed noisily to the far side. Hilda was pulling at her skirt.

'Mam, are there any of those butties left? I want to feed the ducks.'

'No, you've eaten them all, you know that.' Peggy felt irritable and out of sorts. She wanted to wring Dad's neck with her bare hands.

The kids seemed happy to play here for a while, so she sank down on a bench. She saw the tranquillity of the lake and the sunlight dappling the ground through the leafy trees, but she was burning with vengeance. For years she'd been brooding on Sidney's wrongs and wanted to settle the score with him, but now she felt the same deadly rancour for her father. The men just didn't care how they hurt others. It was always the women who suffered.

Peggy decided she'd get her own back on both of them. Dad should be punished for what he'd done. Like Sidney, he needed to be taught a lesson. She wasn't like Beth who just wanted to get on with her own life. In this world it was an eye for an eye. She wanted to make them both squirm. But how?

The following morning Peggy saw how she could give Sidney a kick he wouldn't like. She was going shopping when she saw the rag and bone man leading his horse into their street with a swarm of children following his cart. He gave balloons or goldfish in jam jars in exchange for old clothes. He timed his visits for when the kids would be about.

'Got any old clothes?' he asked Peggy. 'Old wool coats?' Bonny was barking and leaping at May's heels.

'I've got a dog I'll sell you.' She pointed to Bonny who looked full of playful vigour. 'Here, Bonny,' she called and she came up and sniffed at the hand the rag and bone man extended to pat her. Peggy had had more than enough of the dog. She'd gone out yesterday and left her in the living room and when she'd returned she'd peed on the lino.

'What sort is she?'

'Bit of Alsatian I think, and a bit of Labrador. She's very good with children. Ten bob to you.'

'Mam!' May screamed. 'You can't sell Bonny! No!'

Peggy had pleaded with Sidney to get rid of her. The dog was a load of trouble, she was eating more than May. The rag and bone man was laughing.

'I'd be doing you a favour if I gave you a couple of bob for that.'

'She's a good guard dog. Just look at her coat, shining lovely it is. She's very healthy.'

'You can't sell her,' Hilda wailed. Frankie was trying to pull her away by the string tied to her collar.

'See how they love her?' The rag and bone man was scratching Bonny's ears and she pleased him by licking his hand.

'You got a licence to go with her?'

'No, why d'you think I want to sell her? I have to, can't afford to keep her. Frankie, bring her back.'

'Dad doesn't want you to sell her. He loves Bonny. Go down to the pub and tell him, May.'

'I'll give you half-a-crown,' the man said.

'Done, and you're getting a bargain.' She screwed the string out of Frankie's hand and handed Bonny over.

'No, Mam!' All her kids were screaming now. 'We want Bonny.'

'What about some of those balloons to keep them quiet? Come on, don't be mean.'

The rag and bone man was tying Bonny to the back of his cart. She was showing great reluctance to go, but was being pulled along.

Peggy sighed with satisfaction as she rushed to the butcher's shop on Hoylake Road. She bought mince to make a stew – even Rita would eat that. On the spur of the moment she bought a nice bit of frying steak for Sidney. She'd enjoy seeing his face when he heard where she'd got the money for it.

But May and Frankie went down to the Blood Tub to tell him, so he knew before he came home.

'Bloody hell, woman, what'd you do that for? I was right fond of that dog.' Sidney kept on and on about it between mouthfuls of the steak she'd cooked for his dinner. He hardly noticed what he was eating and leapt to his feet when he'd finished to take May out to comb the neighbourhood for the rag and bone man to try and get Bonny back. Hours later, they came back without her. May was crying and Sidney was absolutely livid.

He dragged Peggy up to the bedroom and laid into her, twisting her wrist so badly she thought he'd broken it. The next morning, she had a black eye. The sale of Bonny had driven the feud between them up another vicious notch.

He hardly spoke to her after that. Peggy was burning with hate for him and could think of nothing but how she could get even. All this was bringing out the worst in her.

Every few months, a knife sharpener with a grinding wheel fixed to the back of his bicycle worked his way along the street. Peggy begrudged the penny he asked for this service and rarely used it. Today, when he knocked on her door, it occurred to her that with a really sharp knife, she could inflict real damage on Sidney.

She lolled on her doorstep watching the old man hone her carving knife to lancet sharpness, planning how best to use it. She'd have to start while Sidney was asleep and not expecting it, because he was stronger than she was, and might wrest the knife from her. She didn't want him to turn it against her.

She'd need to stab him in his guts over and over, the soft part of the belly, or perhaps his neck, places where she could do the most damage quickly. She'd carry on plunging the knife into him until he screamed for mercy.

With the warmth of the morning sun on her face, she imagined herself creeping towards the bed to do the deed, when suddenly she saw Jenny and Beth come round the corner of the street on their way to see her again.

She felt really put out. They came into her living room and Beth put the kettle on just as though it was her own house.

Jenny said, 'Dad's been round to see me. I knew he'd come. He said Beth wasn't being fair, he'd given her all his furniture. She wanted to throw him out so she could marry Ken Clover.'

'Let me guess,' Peggy said. 'He wants to move in with you.' She couldn't look at the knife which was now on the table. The blade seemed to gleam with evil intent.

'Yes. He said I had three bedrooms and he'd be happy with the smallest. That he needed a proper bed, his back was so bad he couldn't work properly and it was getting him down.'

'When's he moving in?'

'He isn't. I told him I knew why Beth was upset with him and I wouldn't have him in my place for the same reason.'

Beth said, 'He can get lodgings, that's the best thing for him. Somewhere where they'll clean up after him and give him an evening meal.'

'I thought you said he was getting that down in the pie shop?'

'I don't know about every night. There's plenty of rooms to let. No reason why he can't get one. Then Ken and I can be married.'

Peggy felt well qualified to give advice about that. 'Make sure you know what you're doing, Beth. It can get you in more trouble than having Dad there.'

'I doubt it. I've hung on long enough. All my sisters married in their teens and here I am, twenty-six. Ken says it's high time we got on with it.'

'So when will it be?'

'October, we think.' Beth sighed. 'But Dad hasn't gone yet. All his clothes and his bedding are still in my place.'

Chapter Twenty-Four

When her sisters had gone, Peggy took the newly sharpened carving knife up to her bedroom and hid it in her dressing table drawer under some clothes. She left the drawer open far enough to get her hand inside. She mustn't risk wakening Sidney by opening drawers.

He came home after the pub closed at two o'clock. Feeling full of loathing, she watched him eat his dinner before going up for his usual nap. She hadn't forgiven him for giving her that black eye. She'd had to tell her sisters that Frankie had thrown a ball which had hit her in the face. Peggy could feel herself sweating, her skin crawled with macabre anticipation, she'd do it this afternoon.

She heard him cough, so not just yet. She imagined herself doing it; she'd grip the knife handle as though it were a dagger. She'd aim low for his belly, put all her strength behind the first thrusts.

She waited in the living room below, listening intently, willing him to drop off and start snoring. All she could hear was an occasional crackle of the newspaper he'd taken up to read. She'd shut Rita and Eric out in the yard to get them out of the way but time was going on. She was afraid the others would come home from school before she could do it.

Then came the sound of running footsteps and whoops outside in the street, followed by the thumping of small fists on the front door.

'Damn,' she said out loud. 'Damn, damn.' Impossible to do it now. She'd have to leave it until Sidney came home tonight. The kids would all be flat out in their beds then.

Peggy went through her evening routine of feeding her children and getting them into bed, feeling like a zombie. She went to bed herself at the usual time but couldn't sleep. She felt taut like a bowstring, ready for action when the moment came.

It was around midnight when she heard the front door slam shut, but there were other unusual noises downstairs. Sidney had somebody with him! Peggy pushed her feet into her shoes and ran downstairs. Her father was unrolling his eiderdown and pillows onto the bed chair.

'Who said you could come here?' Her voice was shrill.

'Sidney invited me.'

'I don't want you here, Dad. You know why.'

'Beth's been getting at you, hasn't she? Spreading lies about me.'

'Not lies.'

He was angry. 'I've got to have somewhere to put my head down, haven't I? I'll pay my whack. Here you are.' Coins rattled down on the table.

'It's not the money.'

'Not the money? That's a change.'

'Give over, Peggy, he's your pa.'

'We haven't got room.'

'I'll be all right down here.'

Peggy flounced back to her bed, furious at being thwarted. She pulled the bedclothes over her head and tried to think. She couldn't go for Sidney with the knife if Dad was downstairs. He'd be up at the first sound of trouble.

For tonight, Sidney had saved himself by bringing Dad home. But she'd get him sooner or later, and Dad was as bad as he was. She'd like to get them both.

By the next day, Wilf felt everybody had turned against him. He'd always been afraid of Vi and her girls finding out about Ethel and Molly. Now they had, he felt his life was in ruins and that he hadn't a friend anywhere.

He wasn't happy to be living in Peggy's house. She was anything but welcoming, and her manner could be quite strange. She never had meals ready on time and her place was a mess. He was worried about her as well as everything else.

He felt in need of a few beers and an hour or so in the Blood Tub with his cronies to cheer himself up. He was later than usual getting there and as he drew near he could hear the cheerful buzz of chatter and see a woman leaning head and shoulders through the shutters which opened onto the end of the public bar and served as the off-licence. He recognised the neat backside and scuffed high heels immediately.

'You've got to be sure to bring the jug back, Fanny.' It was Sidney who was serving her. 'Otherwise Mr Thomas will be on my back.' Jeffrey Thomas was the licensee and Sidney's boss.

That made Fanny Kershaw roar with laughter. 'Serve him bloody well right, won't it?'

Sidney was laughing with her. 'Bring it back, luv. All right?'

'And I'll have a tot of whisky to chase it.'

'Are you sure?'

'Course I'm sure.'

'Have an eighth on me, then.' Another guffaw of laughter. A small bottle slid across the counter, which she put in her pocket. 'See you, Fanny.'

The shutters slammed and Fanny turned round with a brimming jug of beer. She slopped some down her coat.

Wilf said, 'Hello, Fanny, not joining us inside tonight?'

Once Fanny had been an old flame of his; it hadn't lasted long, only a matter of months, and that was years ago now. He'd been able to manage three women then; he didn't think he'd be up to it now, even if he could find three.

She gave a rakish laugh. 'No, I'm not well. Just come out of hospital, I have. The Borough, d'you know it?'

'Just down the road, luv. Everybody knows the Borough.'

Even years ago she'd been a lot rougher than either Vi or Ethel, and drinking the way she did, she'd gone downhill ever since.

'Had an operation, I have. Terrible time.' She laughed again. 'I need a quiet night.'

Wilf said, 'Doesn't look as though it's been quiet up to now.'

'Are you coming up later, Wilf?'

'No thanks.' He had to laugh with her. 'You'll want to get to bed if you aren't well.'

She gave him a seductive glance from under her lashes. 'Don't I always? Bed's the best place. You know that.'

She swayed a little on her feet and slopped more of the beer over her hand. As she raised it to her mouth to lick the drops up, Wilfred saw her wristwatch flash in the gaslight. He recognised it instantly, he'd kept a similar one for himself. It was one of those he'd lifted from the *Baltimore*.

'Nice watch you've got there,' he said, holding up her wrist to make sure. 'Where'd you get it?'

'It was a present.' She snatched her hand away and more beer slopped out.

'You'd better be careful or you won't have much left in that jug. Get back home to your baby, Fanny.'

'Your baby too.'

'Get away with you, she certainly isn't.'

'And not a baby any more, she's nearly two. She'll be looking after me soon.'

'Not yet awhile, but you'll certainly need her when she can.'

Fanny shrieked with laughter again, and he laughed with her but as he watched her move off, none too steadily, Wilf wasn't pleased.

Inside the public bar, Jack O'Leary was berating Sidney. 'You shouldn't have sold her any more, that woman's had a skinful already.'

He said to Wilf, 'Mr Thomas had to put her out. She was getting disorderly.'

'Lifting her skirts,' another customer put in. 'Trying to persuade one of us to go up to her place.'

That caused another wave of laughter, and someone said, 'He was afraid she'd cause a rush and empty the bar, ruin the night's business.'

Wilf caught his son-in-law's eye and said, 'Going up later, are you, Sidney?'

The flush that ran up his cheeks surprised Wilf. 'Nah, not me.'

Someone jeered, 'She'll find someone else before he gets out of here.'

'One of your favourites, though, Sid,' Wilf said. She had to be if she was getting free whisky and free watches.

He hadn't stuck his neck out to steal those watches so Sidney could give them away to the likes of her. Fanny would never have paid for it, every penny she had went on booze. Wilf had had his suspicions of Sidney, there'd been times when he hadn't handed over as much cash as he'd expected. And hadn't he seen him ages ago going up to visit a woman and wondered who she might be? He'd told himself he'd find out, but he'd never got round to it. He found it hard to believe it could be Fanny, she must be a good bit older than Sidney. But of course he'd know her well, she'd worked here as a barmaid. Wilf wrinkled his nose. He'd met Fanny here in the bar himself, but he didn't like Sidney having anything to do with a woman like her. It was doing Peggy down.

He leaned across the bar to say to him, 'Fanny Kershaw is anybody's at any time. You shouldn't get mixed up with someone like that.'

Sidney's cheeks deepened to crimson. 'You did,' he whispered. 'Fanny told me as much, so it's no good saying you didn't. And she's not the only one. Don't get high and mighty with me. What's good for you is good for everybody else.'

Peggy was fed up to the back teeth. She was burning with resentment at the way Dad had moved in with her. What she'd planned for Sidney had to be put on hold. On Sunday, she'd roasted a rabbit and Sidney had looked for the carving knife with the cow-horn handle.

'What have you done with it?' he'd asked.

Peggy was quaking with guilt as she pretended to rummage in the kitchen drawers for it. She couldn't enjoy her dinner and anyway, with Dad here, there wasn't enough rabbit to go round.

She daren't leave the knife in the dressing table drawer for long. Sidney used the mirror and her comb on his hair every day, and if he went looking for nail scissors or handkerchiefs, he'd come across it. He'd surely be suspicious about why it was there.

As soon as she had the house to herself, Peggy brought the knife down to the living room. She didn't want to put it back in the kitchen where it would be used and its sharp edge blunted. After a moment's thought, she slid it along the back of the mantelpiece where it couldn't be seen amongst the clutter. If he found it there, she'd deny knowing how it got there. She'd say Dad must have done it.

The days ground on. One man in the house was bad enough, but two were impossible. They were always wanting meals or cups of tea or shirts ironed. Beth, on the other hand, was enjoying herself now she had so much less to do, and couldn't stop talking about Ken and their wedding plans.

When Peggy got her father by himself, she said, 'You'll have to find a place of your own, Dad. I can't be doing with you here.'

'Course I will, luv.'

'You could get lodgings, or a room somewhere.'

'I'm looking, aren't I?'

Sidney and her father chatted together the whole time, they seemed to have more in common with each other than they did with her and that riled her. Peggy felt they treated her as though she was only there to wait on them.

After a couple more weeks she could feel herself growing more edgy. Half the time she hardly knew what she was doing. Her nerves were raw, she longed to be rid of both of them so she could get some peace. She asked Jenny to take Dad in, knowing he'd move to her house to get a room to himself. Jenny refused point blank.

One Saturday morning, her father announced he was having a lie-in instead of going to the docks to try for work. Peggy found it impossible to move in the living room with him stretched out on the bed chair, and by that time all the kids were rampaging round and he expected her to keep them away from him.

'You can't lie there,' she exploded. 'Not with all the kids at home.'

He got up reluctantly and boiled a kettle so he could have a wash down in the wash house. Peggy could hear Sidney getting dressed upstairs, he'd be down in five minutes wanting his breakfast. There was no bacon left and only one egg. Sidney would bellyache if she didn't make his breakfast. She was looking for a bit of lard to fry the egg and make a bit of fried bread when her father brought in a bundle of his dirty clothes and left it beside her on the scullery draining board.

Peggy felt her control snap. 'I'm not doing your washing,' she flared.

'Just a few things to run through . . .'

'With five kids, I've got more than enough washing to see to.'

She opened the back door and tossed his things out in the yard. Then she dragged her coat from its peg and slammed out of the house, leaving the men to look after themselves and the kids. She almost ran down to Beth's house, and found her and Esther making soup for lunch in what seemed domestic bliss. The house was neat and clean.

Peggy felt in a fever of agitation. 'I've had as much as I can take. Dad's driving me mad.'

Beth said, 'I know just how you feel.'

'Sidney too, they won't lift a finger to help.' She was half crying and desperate for help. The truth came out. 'I'd like to knife both of them.'

Beth said calmly, 'I could have killed Dad many a time.'

'I'm going to leave them to it. I'm not going back, ever.'

'Sidney will be round to fetch you. He'll have no trouble finding you here.'

To Peggy, it seemed as though Beth was deliberately misunderstanding. She wasn't taking her seriously.

'I mean it, you've got to help me.'

Her sister's green eyes studied her then. 'You're too soft with him. Show him the door, Peggy.'

'Don't think I haven't tried. He says he's looking round for somewhere else.'

'Well then, get him to hurry up.'

'How?' She sank down on a chair at the table and burst into tears.

A cup of tea was pushed in front of her. Beth's voice was more sympathetic. 'It's not doing you any good having him there.'

'I know that!'

'Look, there's no shortage of lodgings.' The pages of last night's *Liverpool Echo* crackled as Beth turned to the advertisements. 'Here's one in Ilchester Road. That's within spitting distance of the Blood Tub. Own room, breakfast and evening meal, one pound two shillings and sixpence a week.'

'He only gives me fifteen shillings.'

'You're too soft with him, I insisted on seventeen and six. Show him this.'

'I've already shown him two that sounded reasonable. He always has some reason why they won't do.' Peggy felt totally helpless. 'He's got to go. I want to be rid of him.'

'All right, let's go up and see these lodgings now,' Beth said. 'If they're reasonable, we'll make him go.'

Peggy tried to pull herself together while Beth got herself and Bobby ready to go out. Esther wanted to come too. When they got to the North End, they found the lodgings were within fifty yards of the pub.

'Ideal position,' Beth said. 'Let's knock and ask if we can see the room.'

The room had been cleaned out and there was a bed with a good mattress. Mrs Craddock, the landlady, was baking bread, the smell was wonderful. She said she had two other men lodging with her.

'It's exactly what our dad needs,' Beth told her. 'We'll send him down to see for himself.'

'Come home with me to tell him,' Peggy pleaded. 'You got him out of your house, help me get him out of mine.'

When they reached Peggy's house, Frankie had spilled treacle over the table and he and Eric were licking it up. Rita was screaming because they wouldn't let her near it.

'Grandpa's gone to the Blood Tub with Daddy,' May told them. 'He said I was to look after Rita.'

'He left you alone?'

'He wouldn't care.' Peggy slumped down on the chair.

'We should have guessed he'd go to the pub.' Beth sounded exasperated.

'It's hopeless.'

'It's not hopeless,' Beth said firmly. 'We could have gone to the pub door and asked for him while we were so near.' Respectable women didn't go inside the Blood Tub. 'We could go back and do it now, then waltz him straight across the road to Mrs Craddock.'

'He'll smell of beer. Perhaps she won't want—'

'Want my dinner.' Eric was pulling at her skirt. Peggy was afraid he'd had no breakfast.

She sighed. 'I'm too tired, and anyway, what's the use?' She could see her sister looking round the living room at the mess. 'And I've got all this to clear up.'

Just as she knew she would, Beth took charge. Peggy felt herself being pushed towards the scullery sink to wash the dirty dishes. Esther was dispatched to buy half a dozen eggs and a loaf for their lunch. May and Hilda were directed to pick up the clothes that littered the living room. Beth sorted the clean ones to go upstairs and the dirty ones out to the wash house. Frankie and Eric were asked to pick up all their toys and tidy them into the cupboard.

Beth was restoring order. She wiped down the oilcloth on the table and attacked the dusty mess on the mantelpiece, bringing the litter of used envelopes and unpaid bills into the scullery and making Peggy sort through them. Most went behind the fire. Beth also brought out the carving knife, and washed and dried it.

To see Beth handling that knife made Peggy cringe. She didn't want it in the kitchen drawer but dared not say so.

'It's time I went home,' Beth said at last. She tucked the details of the lodgings behind an ornament on the mantelpiece. 'Get Dad to go down there this afternoon. Take him if you have to.'

Left on her own, Peggy boiled the eggs. There was one for each of the children and one for herself. She'd tidied everything away again when Sidney and Dad came home. They'd both got plenty of beer inside them and when Sidney found there was nothing for them to eat, he raved at her, screwing up his face and pushing it within inches of her own. Peggy felt like rushing for her knife there and then.

'I'm going for fish and chips,' he said. He took Dad, and May and Hilda followed them. Peggy collapsed on the bed chair and tried to pull herself together.

They'd eaten most of their fish and chips by the time they got back. Frankie and Eric were soon cadging the last of them.

Peggy said, as firmly as she could, 'Dad, you've got to go. I've found some lodgings for you. You'd have a room to yourself and a good bed.' She put the newspaper cutting in his hand. She could see he wasn't pleased but he studied it.

'Ilchester Road,' she told him, 'close to the Blood Tub. Handy for you.'

'I know where it is.' He screwed up the paper. 'Woman by the name of Craddock. Look what she's charging. I'm not going there. I know her, she's bossy, I couldn't get on with her.'

Peggy flared up at him. 'Dad, you're not getting on with me. You're driving me insane.'

The tears were coming again. She grabbed her coat and ran straight back to Beth's house. Beth always seemed so confident, but her plan wasn't going to work.

Her sister didn't seem pleased to see her back so soon, but Ken was with her and put on the kettle for a cup of tea.

Beth said: 'Dad's getting at you, Peg. This is his way. If he means to move, he'll look at those lodgings. He'll be going back to the Blood Tub tonight.'

'Dad'll be with me for ever,' Peggy complained.

'No, not if you're tough with him. Don't make him too comfortable.'

Ken said, 'Why don't you put your feet up here for an hour or so? You'll feel better after a rest.'

Peggy felt she needed more than a rest, but she was glad to sit down. Beth chatted on about her new job and her wedding. Ken told her they were going to the first house at the Argyle tonight, and his mother was coming to babysit. It didn't bring Peggy any comfort to see Beth so happy and pleased with her lot, quite the reverse.

It was late afternoon when May came down looking for her. She said, 'Dad sent me.' She had an unwashed Rita by the hand, they looked a scruffy pair. 'He said to tell you to come home. He's got a piece of pork in the oven for tea tonight.'

'There,' Beth said. 'At least you can't say Sidney never lifts a finger to help.'

'It's rare. Where did he get the pork, May?'

'Don't know.'

Unless Dad had pinched it, it would be belly pork which was very fatty and always upset Rita and Eric.

Beth was sponging Rita's face and handing out broken biscuits. Peggy sighed. There seemed nothing else for it but to go back home.

She fumed all the way; nobody took her seriously, nobody gave her any real help.

She found herself dishing up the meal as soon as she had her coat off. When she sat down to eat, she saw Sidney had used the cow-horn handled knife to cut up the meat. Its blade, looking wickedly sharp, dripped meat juices. She tried to ignore it, but it tantalised her, made her want to put her plan in action and drive it through Sidney's guts. She'd have to do it soon or, thanks to Beth, its edge would be blunted.

Nothing had changed; first Sidney and then Dad went down to the pub, while she had to face the mountain of dirty dishes and the clearing up. She thought of putting the knife back on the mantelpiece again, but Beth had cleaned away the clutter that had hidden it from view. Peggy pushed it to the very back of the drawer in the scullery and found she'd nicked her finger on the blade. She dripped blood on her skirt.

'Damn Beth, damn everything,' she muttered.

* * *

It was Saturday night and not far off closing time at the Blood Tub. Wilf Hubble mopped the perspiration from his face and banged on the bar with his empty glass. It was his signal to Sidney that he wanted it refilled. Wilf had hardly been civil to him since he'd discovered Sid had given a watch to Fanny Kershaw, but tonight the jollity was pushing his grievance into the background.

The wall of sound was deafening him; this had been the best evening he'd had in ages. Standing next to him was Danny Murphy, whose mouth organ was rising and falling in a plaintive Irish melody. Wilf tapped the moisture out of his own mouth organ and joined in again. Somebody clapped a hand on his shoulder.

'Long way to Tipperary, man, let's have that.'

Obligingly Wilf started playing his request, but Sidney slapped his glass of beer on the bar in front of him and he needed a gulp of that.

The merriment was alcohol enhanced and had been going full blast for some time – shouting and loud laughter, singing and playing of several different tunes at the same time. Sidney's banjo was being strummed by Alec Penn because Sidney was too busy behind the bar. Wilf caught his eye, his glass was refilled.

They were all enjoying themselves in a party atmosphere rarely equalled. Fanny Kershaw's shrill soprano led the singing, scaling loud and strong above the other noise. In mid-verse, she couldn't remember the words and ended suddenly in gales of laughter. Maudie Everett was with her, openly plying for trade.

She sashayed up to Wilf and took hold of his arm. 'How about it, mister?' She was fluttering her eyelashes at him. Wilf felt tempted, it had been a long time.

But Fanny came over like a whirlwind to hurl herself at Maudie. 'Get off, he's mine. A regular, you know that. Keep your hands off him.'

'A regular, eh?' Sidney was splitting his sides. Other customers joined in; within seconds the bar was ringing with guffaws at Wilf's expense.

Fanny's fingers were fondling his neck. She was clinging to him, trying to kiss him.

'Come on up to my place, Wilf.' She was dead drunk, all her weight was on him, he was keeping her upright. 'Come on, I'll give you a good time.'

'Lipstick all over you, Wilf,' another brayed with delight. 'Better watch out.'

'Go to it, Wilf.'

He felt disgusted, he could do better than her. Her fox fur tickled him, and it irked him that she was still wearing his watch.

'I'm not one of your regulars,' Wilf shouted in protest. 'Don't you dare say I am. You stink. I wouldn't touch a filthy whore like you.'

He heaved her off, she would have fallen if another customer hadn't caught her. Her face contorted with hate. 'You bastard, Wilf Hubble. I'll get you for this.'

He turned his back on her, buried his face in his tankard and tried to shrug it off. Fanny Kershaw was a bitch. The rowdy fun was over. Alec Penn took up Sidney's banjo again, playing a blatantly jolly, foot-tapping tune, trying to revive the party fun.

Wilf felt chilled, he wanted to be gone. Suddenly, he heard a bellow of rage and a burst of vicious swearing behind him. There was a crash as a man went down and fists began to fly. The atmosphere was suddenly tense.

'Time,' yelled the licensee. 'Everybody out. Come on, out with you all.'

As the crowd surged through the door, Wilf was drawn out with them. He knew the two antagonists well. Jack O'Leary was swearing at Danny Murphy who was being restrained by several men. Jackets were being shed in the cold night air, shirt sleeves rolled up. A circle was being formed on the cinder patch round the two men and the fight began in earnest.

Each was being cheered on by his supporters. Fanny Kershaw was in full throat again, singing the hymn 'Fight the good fight with all thy might'.

'Yahoo, Jacko,' Wilf yelled. He was preparing to enjoy this finale to a very good night's entertainment. The landlord was weaving through the spectators trying to collect empty glasses before they were tossed to the ground.

'Watch out, fellas,' someone shouted. 'The scuffers are coming.'

But the warning came too late. Wilf was aware of a policeman's helmet coming between the two sets of flying fists. The officer took a right hook to the chin and went down amidst cheers and cries of horror from the crowd. A whistle blew and Wilf saw Constable Cummins trying to push through to his colleague.

The crowd was melting away. Wilf took to his heels and ran off as fast as he could, but he was too full of beer to keep up the pace. As he slowed down on the hill leading to Peggy's house, Sidney caught him up.

'What an evening, my God!' Sidney was breathless. 'Did you see Danny Murphy sock that policeman?'

Wilf said, 'He meant to hit Jacko. What happened after that?'

'A police car came and carted them both off. The two girls too.'

'What, Fanny and Maudie?'

'They swore at Constable Cummins. A right string of oaths. They accused him of spoiling their fun. What a laugh. Spoiling their trade more like.'

That reminded Wilf of his grievance, he wasn't laughing any more. 'Like you spoil my trade. Giving away my watches to that woman. You owe me, Sid. I'm not putting any more business your way unless you cough up. What's the point? I'm taking the risks and getting damn all out of it.'

Peggy knew what had woken her up. The sound of the front door slamming beneath her was only too familiar. She turned over and forced open her eyes to check the time. The luminous blur of the alarm clock dial took a moment to clear. It was twenty to twelve.

It was her father, no mistaking that little grunt and the scratch of the bed chair against the tiles as he dragged it away from the wall. She waited for the click of the cupboard door by the fireplace as he got his eiderdown out. There it was, together with the sound of his voice and then Sid's, which he made no effort to lower. Peggy was thankful the kids were good sleepers, the men gave no thought to anybody else.

She listened for the sound of the meat safe opening. They knew there was a bit of belly pork left; she was afraid she'd lose it, as well as the dripping. Sidney wanted her to cut sandwiches for him for when he got home from work, but it was years since she'd put herself out to do that. It didn't stop him scavenging for something to eat, and now with Dad here they usually polished off what she meant to give them and the kids for breakfast.

The voices sounded less friendly. Dad sounded positively peeved.

Peggy had left the heel of one loaf down there, but she'd brought another up and hidden it in her wardrobe, together with what was left of the pound of broken biscuits she'd bought for the kids.

She realised all had gone quiet below. Surely they hadn't gone out again? She raised herself on her elbow to hear better. The back door was creaking on its hinges, they'd left it open and were out in the back yard. If they were going to the lavatory, they went one at a time.

She slid out of bed and went through to the back bedroom where the children slept. She had to squeeze her way between the double bed, the single and the cot to reach the window, where she could see the flame of a candle flickering through the wash-house window. She caught a glimpse of her father, his stance was aggressive. With a stab of alarm, she guessed what they were up to – they'd moved the mangle to count out their ill gotten gains.

Peggy shivered, suddenly scared. She'd taken a pound from the tin box only yesterday, to buy a pair of shoes she'd seen in Walsh's. Nobody could say she didn't need them. She wasn't going to Beth's wedding looking down-at-heel.

She couldn't hear anything from here, but she could guess what was happening. Her father was demanding his cut of the money and there wasn't as much in the tin as Sid had expected.

Peggy could feel the sweat breaking out on her forehead. Sidney would knock hell out of her if he thought she'd taken it. Then they came crashing out of the wash house and Peggy fled back to her bed. The back door slammed and the bolts were shot home. She could hear them clearly now they were below her.

'There was three pounds seven and six there, I know.' Sidney's voice was accusing. 'I took it all in one night.' There were some grunts from her father, then, 'I'm certain I counted it in. You must have helped yourself.'

'I haven't!' Dad was outraged. He sounded ready to thrash the table with his belt. Peggy had the willies. She heard the click as the catch on the meat safe opened, the rattle of cutlery as Sid rummaged for a knife. They were going to finish off the pork too.

'Who else is there?' Sid's voice was raised in scorn. 'Nobody knows it's there but you and me.'

'Peggy might have seen.'

When she heard her name, she fought the instinct to shrink beneath the bedclothes. Her heart was pounding with such force it was difficult to hear anything above the pumping it made. Her new shoes were still in the box in the wardrobe. What if he saw them and asked how she'd paid for them?

Her stomach turned over. She put a foot out of bed, meaning to find a safer place for them, when she stopped. The floor would creak if she stood up. They'd hear her. Tomorrow she must get rid of that box, hide the shoes, wear them, anything.

Sid's voice was raised. 'No, Peggy never sees anything. All she wants to do is to sit back with her feet up. She's got no energy. Anyway, she's not the sort to look, not curious.'

Peggy began to breathe more easily.

She only half heard her father rage, 'It's you, Sid. I've had my suspicions for a long time. You've been doing me down, not paying me my whack.'

'That's not true.'

'You're giving half the stuff away, not selling it at all. Didn't I see Fanny Kershaw wearing one of our watches? What'd you want to give one to her for?'

'Give over, Pa.'

'I don't take those risks so you can treat the likes of her. You're probably spending your share on her anyway.'

'Go to sleep. You're talking through your hat.'

She heard Sidney's step on the stairs and saw the light of the candle coming up. Peggy closed her eyes, pretending to be asleep. She had to convince him that she was, but she needn't have worried, he kept letting off little gasps of annoyance. His mind must still be on Dad, blaming him for the loss of his money.

Chapter Twenty-Five

Although still half asleep, Wilf could feel something tickling his nose. He pushed it away and was dozing off when the tickling started again and he heard a half-suppressed childish giggle.

He swore under his breath. 'Go away. Leave me alone, can't you?'

Why couldn't Peggy keep her kids under control? Vi would never have allowed him to be disturbed this early in the morning.

He felt weighed down with real problems. He had to decide where he was going to live. He couldn't stay here now Sidney was turning against him too. He could tell the Craddock woman that he'd take her lodgings and move in today, but he wasn't sure it was the best thing to do. Dock Cottages had suited him well enough and though his home in E Block had new tenants, there was another place in B. The trouble was he'd done a flit without giving notice . . .

He heard another soft giggle and lay back with his eyes closed, waiting for his tormentor to tickle him again. It didn't take long. He stood it for a few seconds then flung his arms wide and caught Hilda dangling a piece of knitting wool over his face.

'Got you, you little devil.' He brought his palm down hard, venting his frustration on her bottom. She let out a wail loud enough to wake the dead, while the other kids scattered.

'Peggy,' he yelled irritably at the ceiling. 'It's time you got up to keep these kids off me.'

'She's asleep,' May told him from the safety of the doorway.

Peggy always stayed in bed as long as she could on Sunday mornings when the children didn't have to go to school. Never got up until the kids were chasing round madly and there was no hope of any further rest for anybody.

'Go and annoy your dad,' Wilf told his grandchildren. 'Go on, upstairs with you.' None of them were yet dressed. Frankie was wearing his father's straw boater and had found his banjo.

'Sidney,' he yelled. 'Frankie's going to ruin your banjo. You shouldn't have left it on the table down here.' That should bring one of them down to rescue it.

He listened for a reply. He heard Sidney grunt from his bed overhead and Rita say clearly, 'Mam, I want my breakfast.'

Peggy's voice came then full of complaint. 'Why can't you get up and see to them for once?'

'Your job. You know how busy Saturday nights are. I was run off my feet.'

Peggy was up at last, Wilf could hear her moving about the room and shouting at the kids to get themselves dressed. She came thumping down the stairs.

'God, it smells like a brewery in here, Dad. How much did you have to drink last night?'

She was throwing up the window behind him and opening the back door. The draught gave him the shivers, she knew he couldn't stand draughts. He was near enough to ease the window down again.

'I see you finished off the pork.' There was no denying it. The empty meat plate was still on the table, together with the carving knife they'd used to cut it.

'We had a sandwich.'

'Did you go to see those lodgings last night?'

Peggy was trying to push him out and that hurt. After all he'd done for her when she was a kid. Well, he wasn't going to give her the satisfaction just yet.

'Didn't get round to it,' he grunted. 'I'll go this morning.'

Peggy clucked with impatience and deliberately pushed his packet of fags off the table before sweeping out to the scullery. She always seemed angry these days.

Wilf nudged Eric. 'Pass my Gold Flake, there's a good lad.' He lit up and lay back, pleased to hear the kettle being filled and the gas flaring under it.

'You're keeping the house much tidier,' he said. It was his way of softening Peggy up to give him a cup of tea. She'd washed up last night and was bringing the cups and plates back to the table.

May said, 'Auntie Beth's been round.'

Wilf didn't miss the look of reproach Peggy shot at her daughter. He said, 'I feel like egg and bacon this morning.'

'There's only bread and marge, and you won't be getting any of that. You haven't given me any money this week, how d'you think I can buy eggs and bacon?'

'I gave it to Sidney,' he told her. Sidney was doing him down, it was one way of getting even. He couldn't possibly pay Peggy, he'd have to keep his money for the Craddock woman if he went there. 'Get it from him.'

'I'm not having that. It's me you pay.'

Wilf sighed. 'Reach my trousers over, Eric,' he said. He found a two shilling piece in the pocket and handed it over.

'That's not enough.'

'You're telling me to leave. It'll pay for my breakfast.'

Peggy put his money in the vase on the mantelpiece without saying thank you, but she poured him a cup of tea.

'Any chance of toast?' he asked.

'Dad, you can see there isn't. I'm still waiting for Sidney to light the fire.'

Wilf sipped his tea. He'd have to go, there was no comfort here. Peggy was always in a bad mood.

May came downstairs and was jumping about on one foot.

'Dad says I've got to take him up a cup of tea and some bread. Is this for him?'

'No, tell him to come down. It's time he was up and dressed.'

'He'll be cross.'

The rapping on the front door knocker silenced them all. Wilf was near enough to flick up the torn net curtain at the window.

'Good God!' In his agitation he spilled some of his tea.

'What is it?' Peggy asked irritably.

'There's a police car at the kerb.' He glimpsed an officer just getting out from behind the wheel. 'What can they want?' There was another louder rap on the knocker.

'Who the hell's that?' Sidney called from his pillow.

Hilda opened the door and a police officer stepped inside, removing his helmet. The driver was two steps behind him and instantly the room seemed crowded with officials. Wilf swallowed hard, and felt every muscle in his body tighten.

'Good morning.' The first policeman looked him in the eye and seemed civil enough. 'Mr Sidney O'Connell, is it?'

'No, you've got the wrong man.' His first feeling was of relief. 'No.' This was nothing to do with him.

'This is my father,' Peggy said. 'Wilfred Hubble.'

The kids were silent and still, clinging to their mother, their eyes larger than usual. Their father was coming downstairs barefooted and still in his nightshirt.

'What's all this then?'

'You are Sidney O'Connell?'

He was blinking round at them, trying to look innocent.

The police officer took out his notebook. 'Last night – yes, here we are. At eleven ten precisely, an incident occurred outside the New Dock Hotel in Stewart Street. A disturbance . . .'

'A fight.' Sidney was waking up.

'Er, yes. Amongst those arrested was Miss Frances Mary Kershaw, age thirty-seven.'

Sidney chuckled. 'She told me thirty-two, the liar.'

'Charged with being drunk and disorderly and disturbing the peace.'

'I saw it all,' Sidney said with relish. 'We both saw it. A good fight and you broke it up.'

'Amongst Kershaw's possessions was a wristwatch of American manufacture, gold-plated on a moire strap, batch number . . .'

Wilf felt his gut twist. This was very different. Sidney staggered two steps to the table, looking shocked.

'A case containing watches was reported missing by Brice and Hopwood, Stevedores, on . . . let me see . . . June the fourteenth this year. They gave a list of the batch numbers and the watch found in Kershaw's possession was one of them.'

Wilf shrank back under his eiderdown, he'd kept one of those watches for himself. It was under his pillow now, they mustn't find it. He was scared stiff of what might be coming next. He'd always felt safe once he'd got the stuff away from the docks. Now, out of the blue, it seemed trouble was crashing down on his head.

'Although in a state of intoxication, Kershaw insisted she must go home, stating she'd left a two-year-old child unattended there. She was accompanied by myself and Constable Hughes who found the child to be unwell and we called an ambulance. She is presently in the Children's Hospital.'

Wilf could feel panic tearing at him. He'd really got the wind up. That stupid bitch had dropped them right into it. Sidney should have had more sense.

'. . . searched the premises and found what appeared to be evidence of stolen property . . .'

Wilf squirmed. What a stupid way to get caught! What a bloody stupid thing for Sidney to do.

'. . . together with a large number of empty spirit bottles. When asked where she'd got the goods, Kershaw stated that they'd been presents from Sidney O'Connell.'

306

'No,' Sidney said. 'No, certainly not. She was in her cups, she didn't know what she was saying. Why would I give her presents?'

'According to her statement, you are her . . . er, boy friend.'

'Fanny Kershaw?' Peggy screamed, turning on Sidney. 'You've got another woman?' An ugly laugh pealed out. 'Her? That slob?'

'No,' Sidney said. 'Of course not.'

Peggy shrieked, 'You kids, upstairs, all of you. Are you saying,' she asked the police officer, 'that Frances Kershaw and my husband are—'

'I'm not saying anything. I'm repeating what Kershaw alleges. She also stated Sidney O'Connell was the father of her child.'

'What?' Peggy turned on him, aiming a vicious fist at his shoulder. 'Another child? Don't tell me you gave her a baby?'

'No, don't be silly. Of course not. It isn't mine.' Sidney's face was grey. He was holding on to the table with both hands and looked as though he wouldn't be able to stand without it.

Peggy was hysterical with rage. She drummed her fists on Sidney's back. 'Another woman? You bastard, you've been doing me down. Spending money on that drunken floozy that should have come to me and the kids.'

One of the police officers restrained her, tried to calm her. Peggy collapsed on a chair and burst into tears.

'Mr O'Connell, I must ask you to dress and come down to the station with us. You too, Mr Hubble.'

'Why me?' Wilf demanded. 'I've done nothing.' He tucked the eiderdown close round his shoulders. He'd slept in his shirt and long johns and could feel himself shuddering. How could Sidney have been so crass?

'To help us with our inquiries.' The police officer still had his notebook open before him. 'Kershaw alleges that on several occasions you've stolen property from the docks where you work and Mr O'Connell has sold it over the bars of the New Dock Hotel.'

Wilf said, with more bravado than he felt, 'The woman is making all this up. There's no truth in it.'

The eyes of the law turned on him again. 'Her statement goes on to the effect that she saw Sidney O'Connell give you money in the yard behind the pub – where the lavatories are. She heard him say that the watches had sold well. She says she knows you, Mr Hubble, and has done for the last twelve or more years.'

Wilf was appalled. The bitch Fanny Kershaw had grassed him up as well. This was mind-blowing. His mouth was a dust bowl. He grabbed

307

his unfinished mug of tea and swilled it back but it didn't wash away the taste of terror.

'Would you get up and get dressed, Mr Hubble?'

Wilf did as he was told. The lino felt icy to his bare feet. He picked up one of his boots to put on.

Sidney said, 'Everybody knows Fanny Kershaw, you know her yourself, a drunkard, a prostitute. You can't rely on anything she says. This is nothing but a pack of lies.'

The police officer ignored him. 'Mrs O'Connell.' He turned to Peggy. 'We need to search your premises.' He was already opening the cupboard beside the grate.

Wilf felt his self-control snap. 'You bloody fool,' he screamed at Sidney. 'All this is your fault. What did you have to give her that watch for?' And before he knew what he was doing he was thumping his boot down on the table, making the crocks jump and clatter. A cup and saucer fell to the floor and shattered.

'Stop it,' Peggy shrieked at him, and he felt strong arms trying to restrain him. Wilf twisted free and drove the boot as hard as he could into the officer's face. Then in a total frenzy he grabbed the knife he saw on the meat plate and went for Sidney. He'd caused all this, he was going to give him what for.

Wilf felt he was fighting off three people. All the frustrations that had built up over the last weeks exploded inside him and he slashed out at all of them with the carving knife.

To Peggy it all seemed unreal until her father went berserk. She'd seen him thrash a table in a frenzy of temper many times before but it floored her to see him pick up the knife with the cow-horn handle and slash out at Sidney.

But Sidney was twenty years younger than her father and had more strength. It took only moments for him to wrest the knife from his hand in the way Peggy had feared he'd take it from her. Then he was slashing out wildly at Dad and at everybody else.

Both Sidney and her father were in handcuffs now. Dad was lying across the chair, moaning in agony. Sidney was leaning up against the wall taking deep breaths. He had a few nicks on his arms and one on his face, but being quick on his feet he'd got off lightly. One of the police officers had received several cuts, one deep along his jaw line. He was streaming with blood.

It was the first Peggy had heard of Fanny having a baby but she could well believe it of Sidney. If Dad could do it, so could Sidney.

They were two of a kind. And all this business of giving Fanny presents had the ring of truth about it. It was the sort of thing he did. She'd been suspicious that he was coming in at two and three o'clock in the morning on some nights, but she couldn't be sure because he turned the clock face away so she couldn't see it from the bed. He was denying everything of course, but that meant nothing.

One of the policemen was upstairs searching through her belongings. She could hear beds being moved and drawers being pulled out.

For Peggy, the urge to get her revenge was stronger than ever and she knew how to do it now. She could get even with both her father and Sidney with one stroke.

'The wash house,' she said when the policeman came down empty-handed. 'That's where you should look. Move the mangle and lift the slab beneath it. If you want proof you'll probably find what you're looking for there.'

A month later Peggy felt calmer and more rested than she had for years. She'd been able to go to bed every night at ten o'clock and get up in time to get the children off to school. There were no banging doors to wake her around midnight and, thank goodness, no Sidney demanding his marital rights. No hot meals to make at odd times of the day for him and Dad either. With only Eric and Rita not yet at school, she felt at last she had the time and energy to look after herself and the children. Both her father and Sidney were on remand awaiting trial. Peggy needed peace of mind and didn't want any further contact with either of them.

Beth and Jenny came round every day, either alone or together. They were full of sympathy. They brought cakes and vegetables to help feed her children, they suggested outings together and pressed her to visit their homes. They were trying to help and comfort her. Peggy couldn't bring herself to tell them she was delighted to see the back of Sidney, and his absence, far from saddening her, brought feelings of sheer relief.

It made her feel sick to know Sidney had been seeing another woman and had a child by her. Peggy wasn't going to forgive him for that. He was just like Dad. She couldn't forgive him either. They'd both got what they deserved.

Sidney had guaranteed himself a prison sentence by wielding the carving knife against a police officer. She was pleased about that.

Beth told her that both Dad and Sidney were shocked and upset at the thought of going to prison, but however hard they found their prison terms, Peggy felt good about it. It took them off her back.

She'd had such dark ideas about knifing Sidney, she'd hardly been in the real world, hardly sane. She didn't know whether she'd have been able to do it, but his arrest had saved her from attempting it and perhaps ending up where they were now. Peggy felt her revenge had come easily.

She'd always felt her life was following the same pattern as her mother's, but she hadn't known it was exact in so many details. She made up her mind that in future it would be very different. She was going to take charge of things. She was right off men and wasn't going to have Sidney back to live with her, not ever. Dad neither; he'd probably known all along that Sidney had another woman.

Life was more peaceful with just the kids. They were as much victims as she had been and she'd bring them up as well as she could on her own.

Peggy had had to apply for public assistance because she had no money coming in at all. She'd found being means-tested an unpleasant experience because the officials took such a high and mighty attitude. They had a reputation for being tight-fisted, but as she had five children to support they had no alternative but to give her the dole to live on. It was not all that much less than Sidney had given her and she didn't have to feed him.

Beth talked of the indignity of having to depend on the Poor Law but compared with the indignities she'd suffered at Sidney's hands, it was slight. Jenny and Tom promised a continuous supply of vegetables from their allotment and Lottie passed on clothes the Wisharts no longer wanted.

Peggy wasn't allowed to work and receive the dole but once Rita was in full-time school she'd try to go back to her old job at the tapestry works and stand on her own feet. She was going to get a life of her own. It was the best thing that had ever happened to her.

Beth had decided on a quiet wedding. She would wear the green linen dress and hat she'd had for Lottie's wedding. She and Ken intended to slip round to the registrar's office with just two witnesses, then return home to cook a good dinner for themselves and the children.

But a couple of months ago, Jenny had invited some of the family round to her house for their Sunday tea.

'It's not on, Beth,' she told her. 'You can't do us out of a good party. Didn't we all enjoy Lottie's wedding?'

'We can't afford—'

'Rubbish. Forget thrift and duty for once. We've all got our smart wedding outfits worn only once. It can still be a quiet wedding, just the family.'

Peggy said, 'The kids still have their matching pink bridesmaid's outfits. Our May would love to be a bridesmaid over again, they all would.'

'Come on upstairs, Beth,' Jenny urged. 'Try on my wedding dress, see if it fits. You and Ken have been thinking of this for so long, I think you should have a bit of a celebration. You only get married once.'

Jenny had packed her dress away in a box with dried lavender and tissue paper. She'd bought the oyster satin herself and sewn it all by hand many years ago. The dress was in a traditional style, high-necked and long-sleeved; making it had been a labour of love.

Beth stood staring at her reflection. 'It fits, doesn't it?'

'Perfectly.' Jenny unpacked her veil and headdress.

'It feels lovely on.'

'Looks lovely. Come down and show Peggy.' Beth followed her down, carefully holding the skirts up until she did a twirl on the hearth rug.

Ken said, 'You look beautiful in it, Beth. Really beautiful.'

'Something borrowed,' Jenny said, fixing the veil and headdress in position. 'It'll bring you luck. It's even brought us luck, hasn't it, Tom?'

Peggy said, 'The veil looks lovely, tones down that ginger hair of yours.'

Ken was twitching the folds into place. 'Go on, say you'll wear it. I'll have my merchant naval officer uniform dry-cleaned so as not to disgrace you.'

'Ken!' Jenny clapped her hand over her mouth. 'You aren't supposed to see the bride in her dress beforehand.'

'Well, I have now, haven't I? And I like it. Let's have a proper wedding. My mother's offered to put on a spread for us.'

So the wedding was arranged at St James's Church and because it was some distance from the new house, Dorinda Wishart asked her parents if Lottie's husband could ferry the bride, groom and guests back and forth. She was the only person invited who was not related to either the bride or the groom.

Both Beth's house and Ken's were packed to capacity as the families gathered. Maggie had saved her week's annual holiday and came home a few days before to help her mother prepare the wedding breakfast.

Beth hadn't seen her friend for a long time. Maggie's bloom of health and happiness had returned, her cheeks were rosy and her eyes bright.

'Thank you,' she whispered as she hugged Beth. 'You know what for. I'll always be grateful for what you did for me. I always knew you and Ken would get together, and I can't think of anyone I'd rather have as a sister-in-law.'

Beth's wedding day was a mellow October day of cool sunshine. Weddings near Dock Cottages always attracted a crowd outside the church and this crowd was bigger than usual as both families were well known in the area.

Beth heard the gasps of admiration as she got out of the Wisharts' car with her brother John, who was to give her away.

Ken said as they left the church, 'Doing it this way, I feel we're properly married.'

The crowd had grown. They were shouting their good wishes and congratulations. Everybody here knew what had happened to her father and Beth could feel their sympathy. The wedding party more than filled the Clover house.

'Lucky it's a fine day,' Mary Clover said as they overflowed into the back yard. Ken had whitewashed the walls, borrowed some benches and had several flower pots blooming with dahlias and chrysanthemums.

'I'm delighted,' she told Beth, 'to see you marrying Ken. You've been a good friend to us all, I know you'll make him happy.'

'He'll make me happy,' Beth said as she kissed her.

Maggie's new boyfriend had come for the wedding. Beth warmed to him when she saw he was hardly able to take his eyes away from Maggie.

'I'm hoping we'll be heading for the altar next,' he said as he shook Beth's hand. She felt Maggie had come through her trouble and would be happy with him.

Lottie had never looked so beautiful. 'Married life seems to agree with you,' Beth told her. 'You recommend it?'

'I certainly do. I'm enjoying it. It's very different nowadays.' Lottie smiled. 'When I think of what marriage meant to Mam, a baby almost every year when another mouth to feed meant increasing poverty and failing health and strength. D'you know what you and that clinic have given me?'

'And Marie Stopes?'

'Yes, of course, especially Marie Stopes. The freedom to choose whether I have a baby or not. You don't know what that means to me and Peter. We can do what we want with our lives.'

Beth said, 'I know all right. All women should have the freedom to choose whether they have children and when. Having a child changes everything in your life. Right now, I want to be married to Ken, and I also want to carry on working in that clinic. I've got Colin and Bobby to think of, but one day, Ken and I would like to have a baby of our own. We can all of us make our own choices in this day and age.'